Lost Harvest
Book One of the Harvest Trilogy

Joe Pace

Lost Harvest

Copyright © 2015 Joe Pace

All rights reserved. No part of this book may be used or reproduced by any means, graphic, electronic, or mechanical, including photocopying, recording,
taping or by any information storage retrieval system without the written permission of the publisher except in the case of brief quotations embodied in critical articles and reviews.
This is a work of fiction. All of the characters, names, incidents, organizations, and dialogue in this novel are either the products of the author's imagination or are used fictitiously. Reliquary Press books may be ordered through booksellers or by contacting:

Reliquary Press
400 Northridge Dr. Suite 300 Atlanta, GA 30350

www.reliquarypress.com

Because of the dynamic nature of the Internet, any Web addresses or links contained in this book may have changed since publication and may no longer be valid. The views expressed in this work are solely those of the author and do not necessarily reflect the views of the publisher, and the publisher hereby disclaims any responsibility for them.

ISBN: 978-1-936519-28-6
Printed in the United States of America
Reliquary Press rev. date: 7/4/2015
Cover design by Bill Coffin

Dedication

For my mother, who taught me to love books
For my father, who taught me how to tell stories

*Shed honest tears for the lost harvest,
the failed vintage.
Weep for my people's gardens and farms
that grow nothing but thistles and thornbushes.*
Isaiah 32:9-14

Officers and Crew of HMSS Harvest

Officers

William Pearce, Commander
Christine Fletcher, Lieutenant
John Pott, Lieutenant
Charles Hall, Midshipman
Hope Worth, Midshipman
Thomas Peckover, Boatswain
Yancy Waugh, Boatswain's Mate
Heywood Musgrave, Gunner
Zoltan Szakonyi, Surgeon

Orpheus Crutchfield, Sergeant of Machrines
Luther-45, Machrine
Ambrose-226, Machrine
Ogden-92, Machrine
Victor-11, Machrine

Able Starmen

Peggy Briggs
Tom Churchill
Arash el-Barzin
Taryn Hadley
Saul Lamb
Isaac Pratt
Gordan Rowland
Mathias Quintal
Xing Xiang

Civilian Passengers

Dr. Adina Reyes, Xenobiologist
Sir Eustace Green, Gardener

Prologue

Whitehall Tower
2187 AD

"Five years."

Lord John Banks stood as he spoke, his long body erect behind a chair nearly as elegant as he was. He was a handsome man, a child of generations of nobility, and as famous for that beauty and birth as he was for his role as Science Minister. His vast inherited wealth was evident in his dress, in the finery of his custom-tailored suit, and in the medically-enhanced perfection of his skin, his hair, his physique. As if enough gifts had not fallen to him, he possessed a singular penetrating intellect, an insatiable curiosity, and a talent for unpopular inquiry. The world loved John Banks, and the feeling was entirely mutual. Unfortunately, every scrap of data at his disposal, which, by virtue of his position and his brilliance, was considerable, suggested that world was about to die.

Around the long, polished table sat the other members of the Privy Council. Powerful, accomplished, wealthy men and women, advisors to the King, deeply invested in the empire they and their forebears had built, they regarded Banks with their usual respect and affection, but also with their equally usual tinge of skepticism.

"John," said Lady Patricia Howe, the thin, spidery presence at the head of the table, her voice a papery whisper and yet heavy with authority. "You can't truly expect us to believe that."

The Prime Minister of His Majesty's United Kingdom of Earth, Howe was the chief executive of this empire that spanned the globe and beyond, and her words were echoed by nods and noises of assent in the room. At the back of her mind, indeed most of the minds in the room, were the previous pronouncements of doom by John Banks, none of which had yet come to pass.

"Your Excellency, the data cannot be refuted." Banks spoke slowly and deliberately, with deference but conviction. "We are not speaking of conjecture here, or extrapolations from fragile models based on debatable assumptions. There is no question that in five years, at the latest, the food supply of the Kingdom will collapse completely and global famine will result."

This assertion was met with stony silence, and then a chuckle from the far end of the table, the locus of power opposite the Prime Minister. Short, stocky, with the mahogany features of his Indian heritage, Lord Rajek Djimonsu was officially the Chancellor of the Exchequer, though in reality he was the representative on the Privy Council of The Chamber, the voice of the Kingdom's aggregated commercial monopolies. Banks suppressed his disgust, as he so often did when Djimonsu opened his mouth. Everyone around the table was wealthy, as befit their rank, but the Chancellor was obscenely so, and his riches came not from inherited incomes, as he had little family to speak of. He was a commoner by birth, still little more than a merchant, though enormously influential. Banks disliked him, distrusted him, but knew far better than to dismiss him.

"Come, Minister, surely you joke." Djimonsu's rich, accented baritone filled the room with a voice much larger than he was. "Or else this is another of your famous flights of fancy. Why, I wonder, are they always so apocalyptic? And worse, expensive?"

There was some laughter around the table, and Banks felt his heart begin to sink. It would be difficult, so very difficult, to find help here. They tolerated him, benefited from his reflected celebrity and the love the commons bore for him, but when his brilliance threatened to interrupt the status quo, their fondness evaporated.

As though speaking to a naïve child, Djimonsu continued with an indulgent smile. "The Kingdom's granaries are full, our agrifactories are running at full capacity, and hunger has been unknown for generations. How can you project famine within five years -- indeed, at all? Our nutritional security has never been stronger."

John Banks nodded, his fine features darkening just a little. "That much is true, Chancellor. I will point out that this system you laud so grandiloquently is in large part the product of decades of research and guidance and labor from the Ministry of Science you now dismiss."

"And no small financial investment from the Chamber," Djimonsu retorted smoothly. Banks inclined his head, ever so slightly, conceding the point, though his eyes narrowed.

"Yes," Banks said. "I agree that both Science and Commerce are to be thanked...and blamed, in equal measure. So why not work together to repair this crisis we have together wrought? The facts remain. The very success of our food programs will prove our undoing. As has been discussed before in this room, the vast majority of His Majesty's subjects rely on grains for sustenance. The consumer products made from them are myriad, but all derive from the same three grains: wheat, corn, and rice. Over the centuries, we have so perfected the replication of these grains that energy investment in other, less efficient foodstuffs has been all but replaced by grain-based facsimiles, augmented by the yeast and algae yields. Actual meat proteins, organic fruits and vegetables, are now luxuries."

"Yes, yes." This growl came from Lady Rebecca Cornwall, the fleshy, florid Minister of Defense. "We know all of this, Banks. The commons eat. Come to the point."

"I will, milady. You see, we have so refined our three master grains that each is reliant on a single variant. There is no genetic diversity to them, which was necessary for successful mass replication, and yet that very characteristic has left them vulnerable to the coming calamity. You see, those master grains are dying. Without an infusion of new genetic variation within five years, they will all be dead. Not long afterwards, so will all of us."

One

The Star Lord

There was something comforting about Trafalgar Square.

It was open, for one thing, and you could see the sky as more than a narrow blue strip high above, squeezed between thousand-meter buildings. Here you could almost imagine the world as it was when the square was first built, when the British Crown reached out across the living seas, extending its sway with wooden ships and intrepid captains. John Banks was a romantic; his education in the sciences had not interfered with his learning of languages, architecture and history. He admired the aesthetic of the place, and fiercely loved this small bastion of London, here at the very heart of a globe-encompassing empire, one which still remembered its roots as an island that conquered the world.

Having come from his offices in the Royal Academy at Piccadilly Circus, he entered the Square from the northwest, down Whitcomb Street, the looming presence of the massive and handsome National Gallery to his left. Banks did not stride swiftly across the flat stones of the square, as so many others did, but lingered, strolling, feeling the pull of the past. One of the things he loved about being a Briton was the sense of continuity, of connection to antiquity. Most of all he enjoyed the statuary, even though they were a bit martial for his taste. Napier subduing India, Jellicoe defeating the Germans, Cornwallis returning those pesky American colonials to the fold. Kings, generals, admirals. The grandest of all, of course, was Nelson's column, reaching up in vertical salute to the great man himself. His favorite, which he visited now, was smaller, nestled in the southwest corner, of a man in repose, a robe draped around his frail frame, left hand against his chin in a thoughtful moment. This was a thinker, a scientist: Edward Jenner.

"Don't think, try," murmured Banks, repeating the father of immunology's mantra as he gazed up into the bronze eyes. "We shall certainly aim to do both." Jenner's defeat of smallpox centuries before had been a signal triumph of the human mind over an illness that had preyed on humanity for millennia. *Now it's my turn*, Banks thought. Perhaps, if he was successful, there might be a statue of him in Trafalgar in years to come. If he failed...if he failed, there wouldn't be anyone left to notice.

Banks sighed and turned away from Jenner's unmoving gaze. He had an appointment, and it did not do to keep the Star Lord waiting. He walked across the Square to Whitehall, and felt the sudden encroachment of the buildings on either side, cutting off the sun. The streets of London, and of most cities, were lit at street level day and night by the glowing of lamp-panels set into the buildings themselves. The vehicular traffic was constant, even in midmorning, with the workday some hours old. Even with the bulk of the public using the rapid-transit underground tube network, the sidewalks were choked with pedestrians. Swarms of humanity engulfed him, and as always, the battle between encroachment and belonging raged within him. *You are never alone in London*, Banks thought with a tight smile, remembering the trite tourism logo from some years past. Most people were seldom alone at all; born, living, dying in the ever-buzzing honeycomb, the ever-milling anthill that Earth had become. The Minister was one of those rare few with the wealth and prestige to enjoy a home with even the scarcest concept of personal space, one that did not abut others on six sides.

And yet, he thought, even as he enjoyed his isolated residence, there was something comforting about the press of the crowd all around. Famous as he was, his face known to billions, not one other stopped, or even gawked at him as he joined the throng. It would be the height of impoliteness to invade his privacy. *The intimate solitude*, a prominent sociologist had called it in a popular book a decade or so earlier, this collective urge to be alone together. The walls around the individual were reinforced by personal entertainment devices carried by virtually all those around Banks, plugged in to their own worlds.

Before long, he arrived at the row of centuries-old arches that lined the front of Admiralty House. The Minister passed through the central and largest of these, and traversed the small courtyard to the main door. Four tall marble columns stood sentinel there, and alongside these stood two ramrod-straight Royal Marines at attention in full scarlet dress, antique decorative rifles at their shoulders. Neither spared Banks a glance as he pushed through the replica-wood double doors.

He was on time, not an altogether common occurrence for him, and he was rewarded for his punctuality by being shown directly into a large office lined with dark windows and boasting a tasteful collection of nautical effects. Two works always captured his attention on his visits to the Admiralty. First was a massive oil painting of the HMS *Resolution*, from some four hundred years before, under the command of the near-mythical Captain James Cook. The second was of a similar size, and was a starkly beautiful digital rendition of the HMSS *Drake*, the ship Captain Jane Baker had taken to the edge of the galaxy and back. Banks was always reassured by these images, reminded that whatever else the man might have become during his tenure, the Star Lord remained, at heart, more explorer than warrior.

"You still miss her?"

There was warmth in the question, and in the man himself as he entered through a paneled door. The former Timothy MacKinnon, now Duke of Exeter, First Lord of the Admiralty, often called the Star Lord, was smaller than his titles, short and squat with a full black-and-gray beard, eyes lidded yet still afire with curiosity and intellect under a prominent brow. Exeter sat heavily in an antique wooden rocking chair, exquisitely carved, and indicated a nearby couch. Banks sat as well, with a small sigh.

"I always will, I'm afraid. Both Jane and the *Drake*."

"She was a singular woman," Exeter said, with a small shake of his shaggy head. "Twelve years this spring, since we lost her."

Banks nodded, his gaze returning to the image of the *Drake*. At least once a day he thought of that first great voyage, now nearly twenty years past. He had been so much younger then, the universe a new and vast playground for his mind and ambitions. As a civilian scientist, he had joined then-Lieutenant Jane Baker on her journeys to uncharted sectors of space, forging an unbreakable bond of respect and affection despite their vastly different backgrounds.

"I would to heaven I had gone with her again on that third voyage."

"Then I might be mourning the loss of you both, my friend." Exeter's sharp eyes narrowed slightly. "I have always meant to ask you, John, about the rumors..."

Laughing with genuine mirth, Banks waved a hand in the air. "Oh, I have heard them, of course, but they are empty chatter. No, Jane was only my friend, never my lover. Truth be told, I don't know if she ever had a love other than the *Drake*."

Banks understood the whispers, naturally. They had both been heroes, and made for a juicily odd coupling – the elegant, aristocratic Banks, academic giant, and the unattractive commoner Baker, intrepid starfaring explorer. Neither he nor Baker had ever married, and the tabloid journals did their very best to establish a fictional romance between the two in the popular imagination, if nowhere else. But of course, it had never been, could never have been. Banks turned in his seat, and faced Exeter again.

"I come here to talk not about the past, but the future. And whether we are to have one."

"I know," the Duke replied, pulling at the bottom of his beard. "I was at Whitehall, remember? I was there in Whitehall, remember? You are arguing with facts, and facts are insufficient to carry your cause, Minister. What you need are favors. Alliances. Friends."

"I have few enough of those in that room, and I had thought to count you among them. You could have spoken up." Banks' tone became frosty, and Exeter raised an eyebrow, head cocked.

"Don't play the victim with me, John. Any enemies you have at Privy you've made for yourself. You'll forgive me if I'm not eager to assume those animosities for myself. I have the Fleet to look after, and some of your enemies are people I need."

"Is that the kind of courage you showed at Pegasus, Timothy? Is that how you won your flag?"

The Star Lord stared, his jaw working side to side as he ground his teeth at the casual use of his given name, the cheap insult to his service record. A dangerous flush had begun under his collar, creeping up into his bristles. He seemed on the verge of standing, or shouting, or both, but instead he settled back in the chair, rocking slowly.

"I will let that pass, because I know you do not mean it. But do not presume too much of our friendship, Minister." His tone was gentle, but Banks knew he had touched a nerve unnecessarily, and regretted it. Exeter was an ally, if not an outspoken one, and Banks knew he was vitally important to what he hoped to accomplish. That, and the Pegasus jibe had been both unworthy and inaccurate. Exeter had always been a bold starship captain, and his climb from the upper deck to the Privy Council was entirely meritorious.

"My apologies, my Lord." The Duke inclined his head, as if to dismiss the matter. "But your voice and aid would have mattered a great deal at Privy."

"You will have to settle for my aid out here, where it can do you some good. First, though, you should know that none of what I might do would be as a favor to you. I happen to agree with your position. My analysts report that your science bears out." Banks found himself full of surging gratitude, and felt even more sheepish about his outburst. He even laughed ruefully.

"My analysts, and yours, can see the truth of it. What of Djimonsu? Surely the Chamber has access to whatever experts it chooses, and can independently verify our findings."

"You hit close to the mark," muttered Exeter, scowling. "The Chamber has nothing to gain from changes in the status quo, John. The data you report, and their terrifying import, threaten their bottom line. And so they choose experts who do their damndest to refute your findings."

"They would," said Banks, aghast, "intentionally falsify information? Put everyone at risk to preserve their own wealth?"

"You cannot possibly be this naïve. You are one of the best minds on the planet, Minister, would you please try to act like it? In any event, it is not a matter of falsification. It is a simple matter of selecting different sets of facts. Challenging your underlying assumptions. They do not wish to believe the truth you present, and so they craft a different, more pleasing one. You are a brilliant scientist, Minister, but a truly lousy politician."

"I take that as a compliment," Banks sniffed.

"You shouldn't, not if you're going to play at this level. It is that shortcoming that dooms your agenda, however righteous." The Star Lord grimaced. "It is an omnipresent political truism, my friend. For those with the most, change brings the most risk. And to preserve their wealth and power, they will redefine reality itself."

Banks knew he spoke the truth. He pictured Rajek Djimonsu, nestled comfortably at the Privy table, deftly guiding the affairs of the Empire in the directions most profitable to the Chamber. For years he had jousted with the Chancellor, at times on this very subject, and always come off the worse for it, regardless of the force of his arguments. Even the current crisis might have been averted, had his ministry's research on hybrid vigor not been shorn of funding by a nervous Treasury.

"All that aside for the moment," Exeter continued as Banks grit his teeth, "this is your audience, John. You told me last night that you have need of a ship. Ships I have, of course. I assume you have identified some remedy to the calamity you described to the Council?"

"I have." Banks leaned forward in his chair, thrusting one hand out, jabbing at the space between himself and Exeter. "I believe that our master grains can be revived." The Star Lord's chin moved forward, just slightly, but Banks knew the man well enough to know it was an encouragement to continue. "What we need are DNA samples from fresh strains of each."

"But there are only the single strains," Exeter said.

"Yes…here on Earth. In our headlong rush to perfect their DNA, we shortsightedly failed to retain genetic samples of earlier strains. We've done all we can in the decades since, exhausting the traditional – and some very innovative – means of replenishing them. We've introduced mutations, bred selective viruses, all the tricks. What we need now can only be found off-planet."

"And you believe it can be found?"

"Not 'can be found', my Lord. *Has* been found. Let me show you what I would have shown the Council, had they allowed me to make my full presentation." Banks slipped a data chip from a pocket inside his jacket and, with nodded encouragement from Exeter, inserted it into an aperture just below the surface of the beautiful teakwood table between them. A holo-monitor sprouted from the tabletop, and displayed the ghostly three-dimensional image of a slowly rotating sphere, variegated green and blue and white.

"You found it," Exeter whispered. Banks shook his head.

"No, not I. Jane Baker, on her final voyage." Banks reached one hand into the display, his thumb and forefinger apart, and deftly squeezed them together. The planet shrank, becoming a bright red dot against a galactic star-chart.

"Cygnus." The Duke's hand rubbed at his beard again.

"Yes," Banks replied. "Kepler-22B, or as it's more commonly known, Cygnus. Jane's final discovery, as it turned out. Before...before the nasty business there, she unearthed how incredibly compatible the Cygni and human genetic structures are. More specifically, and more pertinent to our immediate needs, the xenobotanist on her crew, Dr. Tyson, made some startling observations about the nature of the flora there. Most notably, the rather remarkable congruence of nucleotide sequences between their staple grains and ours. It made some sense, of course, that with our similar digestive systems we would consume similar foodstuffs."

"Similar," said Exeter. "Not identical."

"And that will be our salvation." Banks manipulated the display again, and charts of data appeared, followed by two virtual double-helix DNA models. "Captain Baker ate their wheat, as did her crew, Admiral. Their corn. We can eat their grains, digest them, draw sustenance from them. But it is more than that. Dr. Tyson's analyses survived the escape from Cygnus twelve years ago." He indicated the helixes as they twisted in tandem above the table, the various nucleotides glowing with their assigned colors. "One of these is our master rice grain. The other is just one of many Cygnus equivalents. The genetic variations are still robust there, and haven't yet been standardized. Watch." With a swipe of his hand, Banks pushed the images into overlap. They did not match up exactly, but almost, enough. "Genetic compatibility. The grains can hybridize. These Cygni DNA strains can restore diversity to our stock, and avert this looming famine."

The holo folded in on itself and vanished. Banks forced himself to be silent in the next few moments, warring against his own tendency to keep chattering past need, burying his point in extraneous words. He watched as Exeter considered, stroking that beard, knitting that thick brow in concentration. Finally, the Duke spoke.

"You really think it can be done."

"I do, my Lord. What's more, it may be our only chance. The leading xenobotanists in the Empire tell me that we will need seed samples, and preferably living plants, in no more than a year's time if they are to successfully engineer new, stable hybrid strains in time to avert the collapse of the food stocks. Cygnus is perhaps two months distant for our deep-space vessels. Factor in lead time prior to initial departure, plus several weeks of work by our scientists while on site, and the margins for error begin to grow uncomfortably slim."

"Cygnus." Exeter blew out a ponderous sigh, like a great mythic whale. "We haven't been there in all the years since Baker's death. No contact at all. And when we left, it was with our tail between our legs; the greatest empire in the known galaxy fleeing a backwater planet not even capable of interstellar travel."

"From the reports of the *Drake*'s crew, it is a complicated planet, my Lord. Rival factions of intellectuals, military, and their clergy alternate control, and there is no way of knowing what the last dozen years have wrought in their internal politics. We have no time to reconnoiter for more intelligence. And, frankly, I see no other option."

The Star Lord rose with a grunt, not in a way that signaled an end to the meeting, but rather the restless movement of a man who spent most of his prime years on the command deck of a starship. Clapping both hands behind his broad back, he stood, silently gazing out one of the tall windows of his office. He then walked to the ornate sideboard and poured an amber liquid into two glasses. Exeter offered one to Banks, who tried to refuse.

"Take it," snapped the Star Lord, and Banks did. He brought it to his nose, and the Scotch had a wonderful, sharp aroma. Knowing Exeter, it was likely real, imported from the last true distillery in the Edinburgh District, rather than the synthetic liquor the commoners endured. Sipping, he allowed himself a moment to savor the drink before returning his attention to the Duke, who spoke in a low voice as he stared at his own glass. "You know, matters of the Fleet are my bailiwick, but I cannot act with impunity here. With the unknown conditions on Cygnus, the violent end to our last visit, and the urgency of our errand, I would sooner send an armada, but the forces against you at Privy are considerable. We must act swiftly, you say, and quietly, too, I think, to avoid bureaucratic entanglements. I can send a ship, but it will not be a ship of the line, perhaps not even a frigate. And her complement," he raised an eyebrow, "will be modest at best. I have no post-captains at hand, and I will only be able to send a minimal squad of machrines."

"I doubt a frigate would be the best option at any rate," Banks said. "The amount of tonnage we're talking about, with the irrigation and support systems needed for seedlings, would be far more readily accommodated by a cargo vessel."

Exeter nodded, and ran a weary hand through one of his graying temples with a sigh, looking up at the image of the *Drake*.

"A shame, really, that we don't have her to send. I would have greater confidence in your plan."

"As would I," replied Banks, swirling his glass. "But I may have the next best option, to the extent that such a thing exists."

"One of her officers?" the Duke frowned at this, thinking. "Clark is commandant at Greenwich, and I can't move him without attracting notice. Zhu is dead. Martinez and the Agincourt are out past Nelson Station, and won't be back for a year or more. Who else is there?"

"Pearce."

"Pearce? William Pearce?" The Duke's brow furrowed as he tried to dredge up what he knew of the man. "A Lieutenant, wasn't he? Commoner? Never made commander, if I recall. Last I heard, he had left the service to become a commercial cargo-runner."

"He's an experienced navigator, my lord," Banks said smoothly. "He's been in space these last few years, not ashore growing fat and lazy on the captains' list. Sailed with Jane on her last voyage, so he's already been where we need him to go. He speaks some Cygni, and there are few enough in the service who can boast that claim. Besides," he added, "who better than a cargo-runner to run some very precious cargo?"

Exeter slumped back into his rocking chair. "So you propose we send a merchantman, commanded by a failed naval officer, with only a handful of machrines, to a planet that killed our greatest explorer and routed her crew."

"You sum it up aptly, sir. And yet it would seem to be our only hope."

Two

Pearce

The *Britannia* was an old ship, and as she settled into her berth at Spithead Orbital Station, her ancient titanium-steel hull shuddered. All the same, Captain William Pearce wore a seldom-seen smile as he gave the orders from the command deck to reef home all gravity sails and make the ship fast to her moorings. Pearce's starmanship was second to none, and he expected his crew to follow every order with precision and alacrity. Now, though, his commands were a little less brusque, his tone a little less grating than usual. Their just-completed run to the New Indies system had been his third in the last two years and by far the most profitable. The *Britannia* might be a relic, but she had a big belly, and her holds were stuffed with the rare liquors and exotic delicacies the New Indies were known for. Opal rum, greatfruits, actual meat -- the sort of food and drink only the very wealthy could afford, the very symbols of aristocratic status. The take from this voyage would vault Pearce and his family out of a working-class life and into the lowest tier of affluence.

Born into the laboring world, without the benefit of exalted family name or inherited wealth or property, his prospects on Earth had been limited. Gone to space as a young man of eighteen, educated but not a gentleman, Pearce had learned the Royal Navy's trade before the mast as an able-bodied starman. By virtue of his talents as a navigator and his own constant effort, he was soon rated a midshipman and eventually Lieutenant, but there his career had stalled. Without name or sponsor, with little all-important "interest" at the Admiralty, let alone having been present for one of the worst disasters the Fleet had ever known, he stood scant chance of advancing to post-captain rank. So he had made the move to the merchant marine, and improved his financial prospects. He had begun to make peace with his lot, though he would still dream at times of the second epaulette, of making the post-list, of someday raising a flag of his own as an Admiral.

Dreams are for children, he thought, trying not to think about what post-rank could mean for his family. A weary thirty-five, he was no longer a child, and dreamed even less than he smiled.

Pearce came from an earlier generation of star-mariner, before the Navy had begun to filter artificial sunlight into His Majesty's ships to regulate body chemistry, and he was pale, almost chalky. When he had joined the Royal Navy years before, Pearce had expected to endure aheliopathy, the malady that for more than a century had afflicted half or more of the crews on the years-long voyages of deep-space discovery. Star-mariners called it space scurvy, as a nod to the malady of their seagoing forebears, though lack of vitamin C, or any nutritional deficiency, could never be isolated as the cause. A solution eluded researchers for decades, but Pearce was lucky to sail under the legendary and visionary Captain Jane Baker. Baker had no medical or scientific background; indeed, she was a commoner, born to mineral-diggers on Io, but she had a rare instinct for psychology, and part of her genius was to pinpoint the effects of aheliopathy as related to emotional, rather than physical health. Among her many innovations was a photocell that captured stellar light and amplified it to ward off the effects of the disorder on her crew. On her three legendary voyages, Captain Baker lost men and women to accidents and ill luck and, most famously and tragically, native insurgency, but never a one to space scurvy. It had been from her that Pearce learned stellar navigation, crew management, enlightened interaction with the indigenous peoples of other planets, and avoided illness.

Still, Pearce was pale, as were many of those under his command. Not so Christine Fletcher, his ship's master and second in command. This was no surprise; in most respects Fletcher was unlike her captain. She was jovial where he was taciturn, dark and attractive where he was not, and beloved rather than merely respected by the crew belowdecks, with an easy charisma that beguiled most everyone. Perhaps most importantly, she came from less common stock than did Pearce. Fletcher was an Ochoa on her mother's side, an old family that held a baronetcy in St. Kitts, with, the rumor went, an entire quarter-acre of their own land. Pearce had never visited, but Fletcher had told him there was actual soil there, and grass. Like most those of his social class, Pearce had never trod on Earthly grass. Her family's house, on Brimstone Hill at the knees of Mt. Liamulga, even had a view of unreclaimed patches of the Caribbean, black-green and lifeless, but still, water under sky.

Despite their differences, Fletcher's association with Pearce had been profitable for them both. She was an excellent first officer, a talented pilot, a virtual genius at systems repair, and though he would never admit to anyone, Pearce had privately vowed never to go to space without her. He watched her in silence as the last groans and clicks of the Britannia died away, admiring her flawless management of the exercise. She was efficient and competent, and if she were friendlier with the crew than he, so much the better. As the commander of the vessel he was a god among the stars, necessarily apart from and above the women and men under his authority. Despite her gentile birth, Fletcher had a common touch that Pearce, a commoner himself, lacked. If she gave the crew someone on the upper deck to trust, the ship could only benefit. As he watched, he was also reminded how beautiful she was, how broad-shouldered and strong and yet undeniably feminine. Still, nothing stirred in him except deep professional regard and camaraderie. For this he was exquisitely thankful. If there had been anything more, if he had desired her, it could have threatened their lucrative association. And he would never hurt Mary, not for all the Opal rum he had ever carried.

"Christine," Pearce said once she had finished seeing his orders carried out. She turned to him and smiled, her teeth a perfect blinding white, her lips black against her mahogany skin.

"Bill." He nearly flinched at the casual address, but then remembered they were at anchor now, and she was, after all, his social superior. Back ashore, he wasn't Captain Pearce. *Just Bill*, he thought.

"If you will be so good as to coordinate the unloading with the terminal officer, I will proceed straight to the surface to make the advance arrangements with our import agent." Fletcher nodded.

"The usual for *Brit*?" She patted one of the walls of the vessel. "Inspection and recondition?"

"Yes. She'll be a few weeks in the yards, at least. Please ask Garwood to pay particular attention to her anterior mainmast; I think the last fluxstorm might have shifted her hips a fraction. Nothing else out of the ordinary. I suspect you and the rest of the crew should be ashore by tomorrow."

"Sounds good. Well done, Bill, as always." She turned to leave the command deck, then stopped when Pearce coughed quietly.

"Mary and I...we would be delighted to have you to dinner tomorrow night. Should your schedule permit, of course. James does so love to see his Aunt Christine." That blinding smile again.

"Oh Bill, that is sweet, but I'm skiffing over to the island to see my grandfather."

"Ah. Yes, of course. Of course. Another time, then." She must have detected the disappointment in his voice, because she hesitated. Into the intervening silence came a loud bang from outside the ship, and angry voices. Pearce waved a hand.

"Best lend a hand," he said. "Or the stevedores will play harry with our cargo." In another moment, without a backward glance, she was gone.

Social superior, Pearce thought, but only for an instant. His mind shifted swiftly to thoughts of home, of Mary, of his son. He had not seen them in months, and yet he still lingered. By skill and temperament he was a creature of the stars, confident with a full spread of sail and star-room to navigate. Planetside, he stumbled and diminished. When he finally disembarked from the *Britannia*, he wondered how long it would be before he would feel the completeness of space again. Competition was fierce for merchant commissions, and there was no guarantee when the next would come his way.

While his mind ruminated, Pearce's feet moved of their own volition, carrying him down the well-known corridors of Spithead. There were other orbital stations, of course, dozens of them, and he knew many of them, but he considered this his home port. He used a wall comm console to send word ahead to Mary at their apartment on the Isle of Man. The name was a historical curiosity, as no open water remained between Cumbria and Ireland; the entirety of the British Isles had long since become a single teeming mass. Still, he was a Briton, and Britons clung to their traditions and their artifacts. Spotting a transparent section of station wall, he paused to gaze down at the rotating orb below. *Home.* Not just to him, but to thirty billion people, all of them technically Britons, subjects of His Royal Highness, King Charles V. But the Pearces were ethnically Britons, counting as ancestors those who had lived under a King whose reign was limited to the islands, at a time when they were islands in truth and not just convention. *Commoners we may be,* he thought, *but British commoners, at least.*

The ferries left for the surface every hour, so there was only a short wait once Pearce arrived at the personnel terminal, duty bag over his shoulder. Four or five others sat in the rounded metal chairs, each plugged into his device, filament-thin cords trailing from their ears to their laps. One was familiar to Pearce, a young merchant officer he had seen at Spithead before, but he knew better than to nod, or wave, or make any sign of recognition. It would have been useless, not to mention rude. The man's eyes were closed, his brain pleasantly swamped by his specific neuro-customized mix of words and music. Pearce had never quite gotten the hang of them, though many of his fellow-officers swore by the things. *Maybe I just don't know how to relax,* he thought. *Or maybe I simply haven't hit on the right formula yet.* The shuttle came then, a portly, doddering oil-eater. Filing in with the others, Pearce closed his own eyes and let his mind drift to thoughts of home.

About an hour later, the shuttle touched down at the Douglas Bay modal hub, and Pearce felt Earth beneath his feet for the first time in four months. Some star-mariners swore they could feel the world spinning underneath them when they weren't in space, but he thought that was mostly just talk. On-board artificial gravity and environmental systems were so advanced now that they simulated not merely diurnal patterns but seasonal rhythms, and unless you looked out a port glass, you would never have known you were in space. *But you do know. You never really forget that the void is inches away.* He felt heavier ashore, and, strangely, trapped. They were above him, below him, his neighbors and fellow subjects of the King, in teeming numbers. Here, he was one of tens of billions, and he felt a momentary pang of longing for the sense of freedom and elbow-room of a cramped starship parsecs away, for the intimacy of a crew at work, for the elation he felt while doing what he knew he was made to do.

Mary understood that about him, God bless her, and he loved her as much for that as for anything else. She knew he was drawn to that void, and that he was more at home among the stars than with her. He had never been unfaithful to her, at least, not with another woman. Sometimes he wondered if that would be worse or better for her than sharing his heart with the stars. It was not an experiment he ever intended to carry out.

He was in the Gray Apartments then, the vast cluster of fifty-story buildings that housed millions. They were comfortable places, and not cheap. As he walked down the forty-fifth corridor of building twelve, he noted with pleasure the clean, well-lit floor and walls. He had grown up in far less affluence. His own parents had shared their rooms with two other families, rooms that smelled unremittingly of the agrifactories where his father worked. Pearce had gone into the Navy as soon as he was old enough, to get away from that odor as much as the overcrowding. *There are no smells in space*, he thought, and then he was at his own door. He keyed in his access code, the door slid open, and he stepped inside.

"Dad!"

James was taller than Pearce remembered, but not much. At thirteen, the boy still only stood a little taller than a meter and half. And he moved stiffly, with none of the kinetic restlessness a child his age should have. His eyes were prominent in his pale face, so much like his own, and they were intelligent eyes, curious eyes, that right now reflected only joy at his father's homecoming. Pearce dropped his bag and crossed the room to embrace his son, unable to ignore how thin he was. After a moment, he broke and held James at arms' length, hands on both his shoulders.

"Looking good, son," he lied. "Before I know it you'll be ready for a ship of your own." It was what he always said when he first came home, and it never failed to light the boy up from inside. Until now. This time James merely smiled, just a little, and that joy in his eyes dimmed.

"Sure, Dad. Why not." There was a heaviness in his son's voice that had not been there before, and it chilled Pearce's heart. The boy had always been cheerful, even through all the procedures and surgeries and tests that he had undergone. Each year he grew slower and weaker and smaller than other boys his age, yet there was a durable optimism, a seeming imperviousness to his own progressive erosion, that gave James a fierce, infectious charisma. Pearce looked for some hint of that now, some echo of the boy who always joked with his doctors and thought the full-body scanners were an adventure. But he looked without success.

Tell me he hasn't given up on himself, Pearce thought. *Tell me we have more time than that.*

"Billy."

Mary Pearce stood in the doorway to the kitchen, hugging herself with white arms. Her long red hair was up, not quite as fiery as it once was, and there were lines creeping across her sharp features, but Pearce loved her, and went to her. She smelled of synthed olives, and something flowery, and nothing the least bit like the agrifactories. He kissed her, as long and deeply as he dared in front of James, and brutally shoved aside his concerns. His arm still around her waist, holding her against his hip, he turned to face their son.

"When did he grow up, Mary?"

"Dad, come on." James smiled, that small, sad smile again, and reddened the way his mom did when she was embarrassed. *He has her Irish blood.*

"I have something for you," Pearce said, remembering. "In my bag."

With a touch on the panel latch, the boy opened the long, cylindrical case. Carefully tucked in amongst the rolled clothes and toiletries was a wad of red cloth no larger than his fist. Pearce watched, looking forward to an excited gasp that never came. Instead, once he unrolled the cloth and saw the miniature starship fall into the palm of his delicate hand, James merely stared at it.

"It's a toy," he said dully.

"It's a Greyhound-class sloop," Pearce said. "The ships the Navy used to break the heliosheath at the edge of the solar system for the first time, back in '97." When James failed to react to this, Pearce frowned and glanced at his wife, but she looked down and did not meet his gaze. "We've been trying to find one for years, remember? It completes our collection of the pre-2100 models."

"Your collection."

James carefully set the exquisitely detailed miniature on the table. It was beautiful, sleek and needle-shaped, slate-gray, with a sweeping fin that ran underneath its entire length. Pearce had paid three times what it was worth when he found it in a New Indies trading shop, reveling in the anticipation of bringing it home. For the better part of a decade he had been seeking out the little ships, sharing them with his son, telling him stories of humanity's earliest forays into the stars. There were hundreds of models in the series, and at least half were now lining the shelves in James' bedroom, from the frail Lunar module that first reached the moon more than two centuries before, to the gargantuan modern frigates, the fortresses of His Majesty's Royal Navy. With as much as Pearce had been away from home, this had been his one unbreakable link with James, their great shared passion.

And now his son walked away from it, without a word, into his room, and closed the door.

****

After dinner, after James went to bed, they made love, not without passion, and it had that special urgency that came when he was newly home. Afterwards, as he lay in the tangled sheets, she rose and swiftly pulled on a robe. *I wish she wouldn't do that.* He thought she was beautiful, despite their passage beyond youth into the sagging solidity of early middle age. Mary had always been modest, to the point of shyness, even when they had been younger. She was a Kirkpatrick, a Catholic, and had been taught shame from the cradle. Their physical intimacy was always in the dark, and that had ever been a source of equal mild frustration and erotic mystery for Pearce. He somehow doubted that Christine Fletcher ever hurried to get dressed after her sexual encounters.

That's damned odd, he thought, and wondered what on Earth had made him think of her that way now, when he never did during all their time together in space.

"I love you, Mary." He said it because he knew it would please her, but also because it was true. He also wanted to shake the stray thought of Christine from his mind. She glanced back over her shoulder, her hair unbound and wild, still more red than gray, and smiled at him. In the dimness of their bedroom, in the fading glow of the sex, he could swear she was twenty again, the fierce and desirable girl who had approached the young midshipman on the street and complimented him on his new uniform. *I must have been a fine figure of a man,* thought Pearce, *when I had a future.* Mary sat, pulling her legs up under her, and took his hand. She held it, gently, as if not quite believing he was there.

"When will you be going out again, Billy?" She said it lightly, as if she were just making conversation, but he sensed the tightness in her, and knew this to be the opening salvo in a more complicated discussion, one they'd had before.

"I don't know," he replied honestly. "As soon as I can." He knew it wasn't what she wanted to hear, felt the grip on his hand tighten, but he never lied to her. He knew she both loved and hated him for that.

"I'd thought…" she began, "I'd thought maybe you could stay for a while this time. For James…"

"I'm doing this for James." His voice grew stern, just a hint of his quarterdeck bark. "Do you think I enjoy being out there so much, away from the both of you?"

"Yes," she replied, quietly, her eyes beginning to brighten, as if she might cry. "I know you do, and so do you, William Pearce, so let's not fool ourselves on that score." He spread his hands, pulling the one from her grasp.

"Guilty, Mary. I do love what I do, and I'm damn good at it, and I won't be made to feel ashamed of that. I'm not the Catholic here." It was an unnecessary taunt, and beneath him, but they had been down this path before, always ending in tears, and a small, unworthy part of him resented the damned robe. She chose to ignore the remark, and persisted.

"James needs you here, Billy, not out there. You can't help him out there."

"Yes, I can. Damn it all, I can. This was a profitable trip, and a few more like this…"

"There could be ten more like it and it still wouldn't make a bit of difference!" She interrupted him, taking his hand back in both of hers. "You've made enough money to make us comfortable, and to buy all the Common 2 meds in the world, but he doesn't need any more bloody Common 2 meds!" She was crying now, the tears bursting free from her eyes and streaming down her freckled face. Pearce always looked away when she cried, hating to see it, but this time he couldn't. Mary never cursed. Something had changed.

"What is it, love?" he asked, quietly. She fell into him, and he wrapped her in his arms and waited a moment, and then asked again. "What happened while I was gone?" He could feel her shaking against him, sobbing, and he stroked one hand against her back, cold terror creeping into his chest.

"The last round of tests," she said wetly, muffled against him, still crumpled in his embrace. "Dr. Mendoza said the meds are having diminishing effectiveness." She looked up, her damp face inches from his, her eyes shining with grief and impotent rage. "That's what he said, 'diminishing effectiveness'. Billy, he said that if James doesn't have the procedure in the next two years, he'll be…" Mary put a hand to her mouth and drew a shuddering breath in through her nose. "He'll be dead in three years. He needs his father, not more money for meds."

Pearce stared at her, trying not to process what she had said. He knew James was sick, of course, they had known that virtually his entire life. And he knew what the doctors had told them, that McNally-Fink killed before adulthood. But he had put that information somewhere else, somewhere he didn't have to deal with it, and told himself that there were years and years before James became a teenager and approached that fatal threshold. With medication, the disease could be managed, the doctors had said. With medications, expensive medications, the boy could have a decent quality of life in the years that remained. What he couldn't do was have access to the gene replacement therapy that could counter the syndrome and give him a future. It was massively expensive, and not available to commoners. *Mary's right*, he thought, as his wife dissolved against him in another paroxysm of weeping. I could have twenty trips like this last one and never make enough to afford it. He thought then of the Greyhound model, still sitting abandoned on the table by the door.

"He knows." It was a statement, not a question, and Mary's head nodded silently against him. James had always been brave in the face of this disease. He had always spoken of how he would defeat it, how he would beat it back and grow up strong and tall and travel the stars like his father. All those illusions were gone now. His son knew there were only so many tomorrows now, that each day would be worse than the one before. *My sweet boy*. His mind flooded with vivid memories, of the day James was born, of carrying the infant boy on board the Drake, where he was blessed by Jane Baker herself on her last day orbiting Earth. By the time the ship returned home a year later, Baker was dead and James had been diagnosed. Pearce had been gone more than he had been home these last ten years, and now his son, his doomed son, was thirteen, and he had missed most of it. He wouldn't miss any more.

"I'll stay," he whispered to Mary, burying his nose in her unkempt curls.

Three

Dreams

The summons had come via messenger, on actual notepaper, in a sealed envelope. When the brown-jacketed girl handed it to him at the door, he had known at once it had been sent by someone of great importance. Who else had access to such luxury? It felt like real paper, too, not the synthetics that some upper-class climbers used as a status symbol. In the service, it was tradition for captains to receive their sailing instructions from the Admiralty on paper, and he still remembered the packet that had come with orders for his final naval assignment, more than ten years before. That had been the last time he had seen – or touched – genuine paper.

For a moment his heart had quickened, as he thought this message might be along those lines, something unlooked-for from the Star Lord, some miraculous resuscitation of his career, but the girl had been a private courier, not a uniformed yeoman. On the front of the small envelope – too small to be an official communiqué anyway, he noted – his name appeared in flowing script, with his address. The reverse bore merely a simple, embossed red B superimposed over the sealed flap. He thought to ask the messenger girl who had sent it, but she was gone.

"Bill?" It was Mary, calling him from inside their small apartments. "Bill, who was that?"

"A courier, dear," he replied, stepping back across the threshold. He broke the seal, splitting the B into two equal halves, and drew out the card within. The inscription, in the same flowing hand that had addressed the envelope, read:

Dear Lt. Pearce,

Please do me the favor of joining me at my Spring Grove home for supper on Saturday next. Shall we say eight in the evening? A private compartment will await your convenience at the Douglas Bay tube station at twenty minutes before eight. Please do bring your lovely wife.

Yours cordially,

Lord John Banks
Fifteenth Earl of Northumberland
Science Minister to His Royal Majesty

"Well?" asked Mary. "What does it say? Who is it from?" She saw the look on her husband's face, and her heart skipped a beat. "Not the Admiralty." It was a question, a statement, and a prayer. She knew it was unworthy of her, and that she should feel differently, but she dreaded the unlikely day when the Navy called her husband back to service.

"No." Pearce closed the door, still staring at the paper, a deep crease in his brow. "No, it's from Lord John Banks."

"The Earl?" Mary knew who he was, of course, everyone did; the man was a celebrity, as much for being the handsomest bachelor in the Empire as for being perhaps the smartest man. "What does he want?" Pearce handed the paper to his wife, who read it rapidly, and then again as if she were dissecting each sentence into its elemental parts.

"He calls me lovely," she said, a wry smile on her lips, "as though we'd ever met."

"And me Lieutenant, a rank I haven't held for years. You know these aristocrats, Mary. They learn their courtesies like we commoners learn to read." He took back the paper, folded it into its envelope, and tucked it into his jacket.

"I'm going to need a new dress," Mary said.

"You'll go?" Pearce asked, a little surprised. His wife had been social enough when they were first together, Pearce a young Navy lieutenant. During his time ashore, they had enjoyed many dinners and parties with other young officers and their wives or husbands, but after James' diagnosis, Mary had retreated. Now she made a sour face at Pearce's question.

"This can hardly be an idle invitation, love. Something's afoot. And regardless, when a member of the Privy Council says come, you come. I'll arrange for Edith to check in on James during the night, and we'll go."

****

Saturday next came, and William and Mary Pearce were at the Douglas Bay tube station at twenty minutes before eight, he in a muted black suit and she in her new dress, indigo with white trim. Pearce tried vainly to recall the last time the two of them had ventured out into society. He dimly remembered a dinner in Old Soho with Colin Wilcox and his wife, right after both men had become Lieutenants. *Fifteen years ago? Maybe more.* They had all gotten drunk on an imported Centauri vintage, more than they could afford, but back then even a junior

Lieutenant's pay had seemed like all the money in the world. Pearce could still recall how good the stripes had felt on his sleeve, and how much he loved to look at the golden anchor embroidered on his hat. Mary had stitched it on herself, in an outdated display of pride and tradition. They had been impossibly young then, naïve and hopeful about the world. Pearce posted to the *Wyvern*, a science vessel mapping the Leitzel cluster under her taciturn old Commander Jemadari Okoye. Wilcox drew service on the *Furious*, a battleship engaged in the Altair suppression. Pearce had come home. Wilcox never did. *I haven't thought about Colin in years.* He wondered whatever happened to his young wife, though he couldn't picture her face no matter how hard he tried.

"It's here, Billy."

The hiss of brakes and a brief gust of wind in his face jerked Pearce from his reminiscence. Sitting on a cushion of air alongside the platform, fitted neatly within the curvature of the tube tunnel, was a round little compartment. Accustomed to the kilometer-long mass transit trams, Pearce hesitated, but after a moment, a seam in the car split, widening into a door. A man stepped out, dressed in deep-blue dripping with lace, stylized in a modern reinvention of old-fashioned livery, with a cap that he removed as he bowed to them in silence. Mary took the hand he offered, and allowed herself to be escorted into the compartment. Pearce followed. The interior was plush and comfortable, evidently one of Banks' own private cars.

"Make yourselves comfortable, please," said the driver, and the Pearces sat on one of the two soft couches inside. The door closed soundlessly, and with no prelude the car was moving down the tunnel, though far more smoothly than any public tram Pearce had ever ridden. *Faster, too,* he suspected. A shimmering, translucent screen had dropped between the passenger section of the compartment and the driver's cab, and Pearce assumed this indicated privacy. He took Mary's hand and smiled at her.

"I have no idea what the Minister wants, but this can't possibly be a purely social call."

"Social?" Mary laughed, and it was her old laugh, the one Pearce remembered from the years before James was diagnosed. *She's enjoying this,* he thought. *And why not?* There had surely been little enough joy in her life lately. "That would imply we belong in society, love."

"True enough. I suppose it is possible that he has need of a merchant captain, but it seems a lot of trouble to go to simply to arrange a commission."

"Perhaps he just likes to evaluate his potential employees in person," Mary offered thoughtfully. "Or he could be bored."

"Nothing like commoners to liven up an evening," Pearce replied. With a sudden chirp, the screen faded out, and the driver turned to face them.

"We've arrived," he declared. In another moment he had debarked, to open their door from the outside.

"Six minutes from Douglas Bay to Isleworth Station?" Pearce asked, glancing at his wrist chronometer. It would have been at least a twenty minute trip on commercial tram. The driver assisted Mary out of the car, and then stood aside to allow Pearce to exit.

"Not Isleworth Station, sir," responded the driver as he bowed. "This is the Minister's private tube stop at Spring Grove. The public trams do not come here."

Pearce stood alongside his wife and stared. A massive, imposing red-brick mansion filled his view, ancient Victorian in style and sprawling. At least thirty of his own apartment could easily fit into the house. *All this for a single man's use!*

"So this is how the other half lives," he murmured as they moved down the stone walkway, flanked on either side by low hedges and modest, but deeply green, swaths of grass. Pearce had never seen grass on Earth, and here was nearly a full quarter-acre, seeming all the space in the world. There was untrammeled sky above, rimmed on all sides by the glow of the city, but at the center, a patch of indigo, pricked by a single star. It was breathtaking. His life had always been bounded by cramped quarters on board ship, or cramped rooms here on Earth. This was unapologetic opulence.

"Not the other half, Bill," said Mary. "The other one tenth of one percent."

They arrived at the front door, and it opened before they could press the bell. Inside was a tall, spare man, well past middle age, dressed similarly to the driver, though his uniform was all black, and on his head was a powdered white wig. Pearce glanced at Mary, who arched an eyebrow in return. Lord John Banks had a reputation for eccentric devotion to anachronism, and Pearce was seeing it was well-earned.

"Mr. Pearce. Ma'am." The servant nodded at each in turn, then gestured that they should enter. "Lord Banks awaits you in the parlor. Please follow me."

Pearce did so, Mary alongside, trying not to goggle at the sumptuous luxury all around them. He had never in his life seen such riches on display, from the priceless oil paintings on the walls to the statuary in every corner. The floor was uncarpeted, a rarity. Instead they walked along on dark wood, true wood, he knew, hundreds of years old. Mary's hold on his hand tightened, and he suspected she was not enjoying herself nearly as much as before. It was one thing to contemplate an invitation to dinner by one of the Kingdom's leading citizens. It was quite another to find oneself in his home, surrounded by such obvious wealth.

"Down the rabbit hole," whispered Mary in his ear.

Pearce had expected that everything inside the mansion would be huge, but in a moment the hallway opened into a room that was almost cozy. A fireplace burned in one wall – on closer inspection, he noticed it was an actual fire, not a holographic depiction – and this room was covered with a rug, of a design that he knew was Centari. He had imported them himself, more than once, and they were exceedingly precious. Several people were in the room, some standing and some sitting, but Pearce's gaze was drawn to a long, low couch before a wall lined with books, hundreds of them, where the great man himself perched. As they entered, Lord John Banks, Earl of Northumberland, rose with fluid grace and crossed the room to greet them, taking Pearce's hand with one of his own and grasping his elbow with the other.

"Ah, Lieutenant Pearce! So kind of you to join us this evening." Even as he bowed his head, Pearce found the use of his old naval rank discordant.

"Simply Mr. Pearce now, my Lord. I have not been in the service for some years now." Banks nodded and raised a hand in acquiescence.

"As you wish, my friend." He turned his attention to Mary. "This, of course, is your ravishing wife."

"Yes. Minister, may I present Mary Pearce." *Ravishing*? He loved his wife dearly, but ravishing was not a verb he had ever thought to apply to her. More highborn courtesies, he supposed. Mary curtsied properly, and Banks released his grip on Pearce's hand and deftly seized one of hers.

"You may. In fact, you must. How splendid. Your servant, mum." He bent over her hand, brushing his lips against her fingers, and for the first time Pearce understood, in part, why the man was so universally revered. He was certainly overly formal, a bit antiquated in his habits, but it took one sideways glance at the rising red bloom in Mary's cheeks to know that the touch of gentility was not wasted on her. *Probably not on most women*, he thought. He knew that Banks was not married, never had been. *If I had that effect on women, I'd probably never marry either. That, and if I were worth half the Crown Jewels of the King. And the hundred other ifs that apply to John Banks but few other men.*

"Mrs. and Mr. Pearce," Banks went on, and Pearce thought he detected the smallest hint of amusement at his use of the common title. "May I present you to the rest of our company this evening? First, the

First Lord of the Admiralty, the Duke of Exeter, and the Duchess." Pearce's eyes widened as the stocky nobleman and his handsome wife came forward. The Star Lord was the supreme ruler of the entire Fleet, and to low-ranking officers like Pearce had been, he might as well have been God. Moreover, of course Pearce had heard of Admiral McKinnon, a legend in the service even before his elevation to the peerage. He stammered out his greeting and introduction of Mary, who was surely as struck as he was. Neither of them had ever met so much as a Count before, let alone so exalted a personage as a Duke, a mere step below the Royal Family. The Duchess Exeter was older, as her husband was, and portly as well, but she had a broad, pleasant face, and her eyes twinkled with charm and kindness as she kissed Mary on both cheeks.

"Such a relief that John invited another lady," she said welcomingly. A necklace of blue gemstones, each twice as large as Pearce's thumbnail, glittered in silver netting draped around her thick throat. "I was half afraid the entire evening would be spoiled by unremitting man-talk."

"Oh, your – my – I'm no lady," Mary said haltingly, her face now fully given over to crimson, up to the red roots of her hair. The Duchess waved a dismissive hand.

"Ladies are as they behave, child, not as they are born, and I am more than happy to extend the courtesy until you disprove it." Banks, smiling, all culture and urbanity, was introducing the other two guests.

"The fellow over by the window is my particular friend, Sir Eustace Green, Knight of the Bath, and Royal Gardener at the King's Botanic Gardens at Kew." The man was round-shouldered and stooped, graying, but nodded cheerfully at them. "And skulking there by the fireplace is Doctor Adina Reyes, the Kingdom's foremost xenobiologist, and a fellow Member of the Royal Society." Youngish, olive-skinned and rather haughtily beautiful, Dr. Reyes arched one eyebrow by way of marginal greeting. "An eclectic bunch we are, but that always makes for the best conviviality, I find."

"I thought you said…" Pearce heard Mary whispering to the Duchess, who chuckled heartily in response.

"Oh, now, Dr. Reyes – she truly is no lady. Never fear, my dear, if she hears us say so, she will only take it as a compliment. She is a scientist, and brilliant, of course, but carved from ice, I think." Pearce forced his attention back to the Duke, who was speaking to him directly.

"You sailed with Baker," he was saying, steel eyes fixed on Pearce, who nodded. "The Fleet has never seen her like, I'm afraid," Exeter grunted, and Banks sighed nearby.

"You will have to sit with us at dinner, Mr. Pearce, and we can entertain his Lordship as we swap tall tales of our old shipmate."

For the first time, Pearce began to understand why they had been invited. He had been obtuse not to think of it before. Banks had sailed with Baker on her first voyage, Pearce on her third. *He merely wants to reminisce,* Pearce thought, and his breathing grew easier. So far, they had navigated the introductions to Banks and his eminent guests moderately well, and now he knew what was expected of him. It was, after all, a purely social call. And who knew? Perhaps the way might be paved for some future lucrative shipping commissions. He had quite forgotten, for the moment, his promise to Mary to remain on Earth.

"To table, then," Banks announced, ushering them through a door into the most ornate dining room, featuring the finest laid table, Pearce had ever seen. Quite suddenly, his anxieties diminished; he realized he was famished.

****

Pearce took the glass of port that Banks offered him, and the seat as well. The men of the company, and Dr. Reyes, had retired to the parlor, while the Duchess escorted Mary on a tour of the house and grounds. Pearce had never known his stomach to be more full; he was replete with roast fowl and various imported greens, all real and not grain-synthetics, and warm, crusty rolls, followed by several bottles of exquisite wines. Importing his share of liquors in the past decade, he had become, if not expert, then certainly conversant, and the vintages were of staggering quality. He wondered if this was a typical dinner party for Banks, or a special effort, and he rather suspected the former. The end result was that he was not merely stuffed but warmly, pleasantly drunk as well, and when a cigar was pressed into his hands, already lit and smoking, he accepted that, too.

A man could get used to this, thought Pearce, even as he did his best not to be seduced by the unattainable opulence. He knew Mary's head had been turned by the food as well, but also by the antique china place settings, the sterling silver flatware, and the crystal goblets, not to mention the flurry of servants clearing each course before the next was set. For dessert there had been actual ice cream in chocolate sauce, and with the first spoonful he thought his wife's face would shatter with delight. He had watched her, through a haze of spirits, caught up in the absurdity of their actually being at such a dinner, and saw her as he had when they were younger, when they had fallen in love. *Ravishing indeed,* he had thought, as a curled lock of scarlet hair fell to dangle alongside her white cheek.

Banks now sat alongside him on the couch, all grace and easy nobility. Exeter was in a rocking chair, head back and eyes half-closed, puffing contentedly on a cigar. Sir Green had found the sofa as well, on the other side of Banks, and Dr. Reyes was back at the fireplace, leaning against the mantel, holding neither cigar nor glass. Green had become more jovial as the night wore on, but Reyes had neither drunk nor spoken throughout dinner, and eaten only sparingly. She was staring into the fire, and it played sinister tricks on her sharp face, carving deep and flickering lines around the edges of her nose, her eyes, her thin lips.

Pearce found his own gaze drawn inexorably to the fire as well. He had never seen real fire before, except in vids. As a source for human light and heat it had been long since abandoned, though he knew that the very wealthiest still used true fire as a decoration. Imagine burning authentic wood! The stuff was so scarce, so protected, so expensive, that the idea of turning it into smoke and ash for a transitory visual effect was the height of vanity. *Which was, of course, the purpose*, thought Pearce. *Money enough to literally burn.* It was one of the great horrors of the starman, a fire in space, where oxygen was scarce and explosions were death, and yet, he could not deny the beauty of the flames. There was a kind of music to them, a soft staccato crackle with popping grace notes, and they moved as though alive, writhing in the black-lined stone hearth, casting as much shadow as light. It was hypnotic. He remembered reading as a student that the ancients had worshipped fire, and he could, for the first time, sense why.

"Thank you for indulging us at table," Banks was saying, drawing Pearce from his drunken musings. "I fear we may have bored the others with our talk of times gone by."

"Never in life," Green interjected. His round face had gone from gray to very pink, especially in his cheeks and over much of his nose. "To hear from two men who knew our late Captain Baker so well was most edifying and enjoyable." Exeter grunted his assent. Reyes, alone at the mantel, said nothing.

"I wish I could have been with you on Cygnus," the Minister said, and it seemed to Pearce that even though he spoke to him, he exchanged a look with the Star Lord as he said it. A sudden chill descended upon him at the mention of the word, and he shuddered despite the warmth of the cigar in his hand and the radiating heat of the hearth.

"I am glad you were not, my Lord," he said in a low voice, not lifting his eyes from his glass. "Would that we had never gone at all."

"You think so?" Exeter was speaking now, gruffly, though his eyes opened no wider. "Tragic losses, of course, but such is the way of exploration."

"We did learn a great deal," said Green, leaning forward animatedly, nearly falling into Banks' lap in his excitement. "Our knowledge of the flora and fauna of Kepler-22 revealed some exciting parallels to our own earthly life forms." Now it seemed that Banks and Exeter shared a long glance. *Something is happening*, Pearce thought, and he wished all at once that he had not drunk quite so much. He set his glass on the table nearby, placed his cigar gently into the tray there, and folded his hands together in his lap.

"Far be it for me to argue with such men," he said, choosing his words carefully, "but the price, my Lords, was too high. For Captain Baker…for many of us that were there. It was…" he paused, gathering himself. As much as he had thought of Cygnus over the years, fought nightmares, he had never spoken of it aloud, not to Christine Fletcher, not even to Mary, not until now. "It was utterly horrific."

It was silent for long minutes, until Banks placed a familiar hand on his shoulder and squeezed.

"We need you to go back." He said it quietly, but to Pearce it was as if a thunderclap had sounded in the middle of the parlor. Pearce tried to reply, tried to make his throat loosen enough to make meaningful sound, but all he could manage was a weak shake of his head. "I quite understand your reluctance," Banks continued gently. "But Mr. Pearce, this is no idle cruise we propose. Our entire existence may depend on it." Then, much as he had some days earlier at the Admiralty for the Star Lord, Banks presented his plan for rescuing the food stock of Earth by introducing fresh genetic material from Cygnus. Pearce watched the holographic presentation, comprehending only a few of the more technical scientific points. All the while, he found his mind, abruptly sobering, fighting back against a cascade of memories from that deadly voyage years before.

"I am sorry, Minister," he muttered when Banks concluded. "But there is no way I am suitable. I am no longer a commissioned naval officer, and have been out of the service these dozen years."

"A small matter," dismissed Exeter. "You think I cannot make and unmake officers at my pleasure? I am prepared to reinstate you, Pearce, at the rank of Commander for the purposes of this mission. With…" his voice rose to drown out Pearce's attempted protests, "…with promotion to Post-Captain upon your successful return." Pearce blinked. It was tortuous, having the stuff of his dreams dangled before him, blockaded by the stuff of his nightmares.

"No," he managed, somehow. "Please, there must be someone else."

"There is not," Exeter barked, his lidded eyes now bearing a tinge of disappointment. "And I was made to believe you were a sterner creature."

"We were not there, my friend," murmured Banks, placating, his arm sliding protectively around Pearce's shoulder. "William," he said, and Pearce looked up, surprised by the use of his first name, as though he were the social equal of this noble giant seated next to him. "We do not ask this lightly. But if the future of humanity cannot move you, will you consider a more…personal motivation?" He touched the pad he held, which he had used for his presentation moments before, and it illuminated again. A picture came into focus, of James.

The bastards, Pearce thought.

"His illness can be cured," Banks said soothingly, as if he were not engaged in overt emotional blackmail. "A grateful Empire can arrange just about anything."

****

"Lieutenant."

The whisper in his ear was urgent, the gravelly voice familiar. His eyes opened at once, with a star-mariner's penchant for coming swiftly from deep sleep to instant wakefulness. It was just before dawn, a time he had never truly experienced before coming to Cygnus. He had developed affection for it in the weeks since their arrival. It was quiet, among other things, and he had never known quiet, either on Earth or on board ship. The grayness that lingered ahead of the rising sun had a texture to it, a near-tangibility that did not exist in the artificial light of apartments or corridors or city streets at home, where it was either bright or dark, with no in-between.

Formlessness faded, and from the gloom came features that Pearce knew, and from them a whisper.

"Quickly. Quietly." It was Venn Arkadas. Pearce began to ask a question, but stopped when Arkadas placed a hand over his own mouth and shook his head. He swiftly pulled on his uniform shirt and pants. Whatever was afoot, it must be grave. Arkadas wore the usual brown jacket and trousers of the intellectual caste, but beneath a voluminous black cape, and his always impeccably coiffed white hair was hanging loose about his shoulders.

Pearce found his boots, shoved his feet into them, and stared intently at him while strapping his standard-issue hand laser to his hip.

This was Arkadas' house, here on the edge of town, not too far from the promontory where the *Drake* encampment was. Arkadas had been Pearce's host, and had become his friend, teaching him the tongue and folkways of the local Cygni. It was Arkadas who had explained, at length, the ongoing feuds between the intellectual, military, and religious castes that made Cygni politics unstable and volatile. I can trust him, Pearce thought.

It was then that Pearce heard the first screams.

He was on his feet, heading for the main room of the house and the front door there, when Arkadas grabbed his arm, shaking his head again, furiously. No, he mouthed, and moved instead to the rear of the room, where there was a door leading into the back alley. Pearce followed, hearing again the sound of screaming, only it was different now, no longer human. It was the sound of the *karabin*, the strange Cygni weapon Pearce had seen at a staged demonstration weeks before. There was no crack like the ancient guns of Earth, nor the smooth whine of the pulse rifles the Royal Machrines used. Instead, there was a hiss followed by a terrifying sound, like the cry of a bird of prey, as the firearm expelled not a projectile but a column of rushing air that struck with murderous force. The technology involved was simple, barely industrial, and deadly.

Pearce hurried along the alley with Arkadas until they reached a small plaza that looked out and up at the *Drake*'s base. Point Friendship, they had called it, and the name had been fitting for the month that the explorers from the United Kingdom of Earth had been ashore. Captain Baker had conducted yet another successful first contact, establishing the beginnings of a relationship, with a world rich in natural resources that had long since become scare on Earth. Wood, water, foodstuffs, minerals; Cygnus appeared abundant in all of these, and a prime prospect for a long-lasting and mutually beneficial trade partnership.

Now, less than a kilometer from the *Drake*'s shuttle, Pearce saw open conflict. The telltale white arcs of pulse fire lit the gray stillness of the predawn sky, and from the sounds that carried with eerie clarity, found their marks. Much nearer, the sound of booted feet striking the flat-stoned streets approached, and Pearce flattened himself against the wall of Arakadas' house, pinning the Cygni scholar behind him in the shadows. A column of blue-jacketed Cygni soldiers ran past the mouth of the alley, curved wood-and-iron *karabins* on their shoulders. Pearce held his breath, counting at least twenty of them before they were gone, headed toward whatever was happening at Point Friendship. Seizing his friend by the collar, Pearce leaned in so that his mouth was scant centimeters from his ear, and hissed his question.

"What the hell is happening?"

"The clergy," whispered Arkadas, and Pearce could see the tears that were spilling from his eyes, eyes that were the crystalline blue of so many Cygni males. "Since you arrived, their leadership has been claiming that you are only here to plunder us, that you are conquerors from the stars, and we must repel you now if we are to survive." Pearce did not even bother to argue the inherent foolishness of the assertion. He and Arkadas had spoken too many times of the clergy's distrust of Captain Baker. Only the military's coalition with the intellectuals had secured the government's welcoming attitude toward the Earthers.

"Have they seized control?" Pearce asked, urgently, and Arkadas nodded.

"The military have gone over to their side."

Then it was no good, Pearce knew. The light garrison at the encampment would have been taken totally by surprise, and despite their technological advantage, they would be hard pressed. That, and Pearce knew he was not the only officer of the *Drake* ashore in town, staying with a generous host.

Captain Baker, he thought.

Pearce released Arkadas and reached for his sidearm, turning it on. He felt the warm cycling of the laser spool inside the grip, and tried to think back to his training. He had never fired it at a live soul before.

"Will you be all right?" he asked.

"Maybe." Arkadas shrugged. "When the coalitions shift, anything is possible. Who knows what the day may bring. But I am in no immediate danger."

"That makes one of us. Goodbye, my friend. I do not think we will meet again."

Pearce left the alley, darting from shadow to shadow across the plaza, wishing his footsteps could be quieter. He expected each moment to be his last, to hear that awful hiss before the karabin struck, but his luck held. At one point, he turned back to catch one last glimpse of Arkadas, but the Cygni was gone. A moment later, Pearce reached the last small building at the edge of the plaza. Perhaps a hundred yards of open ground lay between him and the shuttle, and the slowly rising sun cast its new rays on a scene that would chill him forever. The shuttle sat, as it always did, in front of a small clutch of outbuildings the *Drake*'s crew had erected as part of the camp. A crowd of blue jackets surrounded the small ship, forming a swarming mass held at bay, as far as he could tell, by ten Machrines and a handful of able starmen.

Thank God the *karabins* take so long to reload their air chambers, Pearce thought, or they'd all be dead already. Arkadas had once told him that Cygni soldiers were trained to fire their *karabin*, taking advantage of the fear-inspiring sound as well as the deadly force, and then to engage in close combat with the short, iron-clad clubs they carried as well.

Pearce saw a smaller cluster, a bit farther away. A tall figure was standing erect, firing with a hand laser like his own, while two Machrines methodically cleared a path ahead of them, trying to gain the encampment. It was Captain Baker, fighting her way back to her ship. Gritting his teeth, Pearce bolted toward them, and in moments was at her side.

"Good to see you, Lieutenant," she greeted, and Pearce was struck by her casual tone, as if they had met up on a hillside picking berries. Did nothing ever faze this woman? Coolly, she sighted her weapon and fired over his shoulder. A cry told Pearce she had hit her target, and he whirled around to find that more Cygni soldiers were still coming. Without thinking, he fired as well, and at that moment the sunrise began to blaze in full, and he saw clearly as his beam caught one of the blue-jackets squarely in the chest. It was the first time he had killed anyone, but there was no time to dwell on that.

"Come on," Baker was saying, and she pulled on Pearce's arm. "I think we're the last two stragglers. When we get to the shuttle we can get back to the ship, and maybe I can figure out how to negotiate a ceasefire." She met his gaze, and for the first time, Pearce saw sadness there, and weakness. "I don't want to kill any more of these people than we have to, Lieutenant."

Despite her statement she fired again, killing another onrushing Cygni soldier. Together, with the two robot Machrines before them, Baker and Pearce pushed forward. Somehow, they managed to find a seam in the crowd surrounding the shuttle, and Pearce was suddenly among the ables. One of them, Arash el-Barzin, grinned at him and fired into the blue crowd.

"Welcome back, sir." Pearce never forgot the way that smile melted off el-Barzin's face like hot wax, becoming, in an instant, a mask of utter horror. Turning, he saw what his shipmate had seen. Captain Baker had been struck in the back by a *karabin*, and stumbled to one knee. One of the Machrines, Pearce thought it was one of the Alexander models, was by her side, trying to shield her from the blows that were raining down upon her, with limited success. He began to race back toward her, but el-Barzin seized his shoulder, holding him back. One of the clubs had struck her in the back of the head, and she was sprawled on the ground, unmoving. A cry ripped from his throat, but Pearce was being dragged backward, into the shuttle's open cargo door, by el-Barzin and another crewman.

"Fall back!" el-Barzin was shouting, though he was not in command. Somewhere in his mind, Pearce realized that *he* was the ranking officer on the ground, but his mind was frozen, watching as the Cygni left off their clubbing of the broken and lifeless Captain Baker. Their attention had turned to the unfortunate Machrine that had tried so valiantly to rescue the captain. Pearce could see the designation-badge, dented and scraped. Alexander-457. Its arms hung loose from its shoulders, connected by sparking cables, light flickering in those white, inhuman eye slots, as the sound of metal on metal rang with each strike. In the instant before the shuttle doors closed, those eyes and that plasticene face locked onto Pearce, and he swore that he saw in them agony, pleading, and even fear.

"Bill!"

It took long minutes for Pearce to realize that he was on Earth, in his own bed, and his wife was gripping both shoulders, shaking him awake. He looked at her and tried to focus on her face as the nightmarish images of Cygnus slowly receded.

"I'm all right," he croaked, finally. "Just a bad dream."

"A bad dream," Mary repeated. "About that planet."

Pearce thought about lying to her, if only to make her feel better, but knew he couldn't fool her. He nodded. She released her hold on him and crossed her arms over her chest.

"Mary, it was a just a dream."

"A nightmare."

"Fine." He closed his eyes, exhausted. "Have it your way. A nightmare."

"And that's where the Minister wants you to go. Back to the place that's given you nightmares for more than ten years. You're soaked through with sweat, Billy."

"They've been getting better." It was the truth, sort of. Pearce didn't have the heart to tell her that he only had the dreams when he was home, when he slept here. Somehow, illogically, the nightmares never seemed to find him on board ship, and he'd been there a lot lately.

"I'm going to take a shower."

He left her there, next to the swamp his sweat had made, and shuffled into the bathroom. As the hot water cycled in the shower stall, he rubbed his hands over his face. It had been so vivid, so real, especially the part about the Machrine. Usually he woke filled with renewed grief about Baker's death, guilt over his inability to save her, but this time it was the destruction of the robot he couldn't shake. It didn't make any sense. Machrines were programmed to serve, to fight, and if necessary, be destroyed. They had no concept of their own disposability and possessed no sense of self or identity beyond what was needed to function as part of their unit. Their programming allowed them to display what appeared to be courage, but how could there be true bravery if there was not also fear? The shower had reached the ideal temperature, and he stepped in. He knew he would be limited to the allotted five minutes, and that this meant he would get no shower in the morning, but it was worth it as the sweat and salt sluiced from his skin.

Pearce knew better than to succumb to maudlin anthropomorphizing of the robots. They were machines, not men. The roboticists of the Bailey Institute kept improving their designs, giving their creations personality, humor, and other traits that made for collegial deep-space companions, but they had not yet given them humanity. And they never could. Robotics operated under the well-known axiom of Positronic Horizon Theory, which stipulated that artificial intelligence, however sophisticated, could mimic sentience but could never truly achieve it. The Theory was well-known because it was well-publicized, in an effort to minimize any resentment or fear people might feel toward the mechanical men. Robots could never be self-aware, could never exceed their programming, and so could never be a threat to humans.

Even their usefulness was limited. They were, and could only be, Machrines. Pearce had heard once that a clever marketing consultant had suggested that name, since the robots were designed to replace human Marines as the Admiralty's fighting corps. Machines + Marines = Machrines. They were useless as starmen, unable to reef, nor hand, nor steer. They lacked, by design and by nature, the instinct or creativity to work a ship.

Pearce knew all of that, and had served alongside Machrines with little or no reflection on the matter. They were tools, like a hydraulic jack or a sonic wrench, to be activated at need and then put away when finished. Still, the dying light in Alexander-457's optics haunted him. His thoughts turned to Venn Arkadas. Had the scholar survived the military junta of twelve years before? How many political upheavals had there been since? Most importantly, who held power there now?

With a quiet hiss, the stream of water died away, and Pearce took a towel from the stack nearby. He had to go back. How could he not? Banks and Exeter hadn't really given him the option to turn the job down. Tossing the now-damp towel into a basket, he pulled on a pair of shorts and turned off the bathroom light. A faint glow came from the bedroom, and he could see the outline of his wife sitting up in the bed, her knees drawn up to her chest, where she hugged them like a child.

"Mary, go back to sleep," he said, with no real conviction.

"You're going to go." It wasn't a question, not really. Pearce sighed and sat at her feet, finding her eyes with his own.

"What would you have me do? Yes, I promised you I would stay. I think you can admit things have changed a bit since then."

"I'm not angry," she said softly, with the ghost of a smile on her lips. "And how could I ever hold you to a promise at such a cost?" She reached for his hand and took it, staring at their intertwining white fingers, gray in the shadows cast from the small bedside lamp.

"They could find someone else," Pearce offered. "There are other star-mariners." She shook her head.

"No. They want you because you're their best choice, and by no small margin. You speak the language, you've been there before, you have all that deep-space experience." A laugh burst from Pearce's throat.

"You seem to know a lot about it."

"Well," she replied, with a slight blush on her cheeks, "did you think all the Duchess did was show me the house?"

"Hmph," snorted Pearce in mock indignation. "They're using you to get to me, too, it seems."

"Yes. And James."

"And James."

"That's why it has to be you, Bill." Mary's eyes shone from the dark of her face in the half-light. "Not only are you the best choice for them, you're the only chance for James."

Save the world, and your son with it.

"Talk to him," she continued. "He's not a little boy anymore. And...and it might be your last chance."

Pearce stood, squeezed Mary's hand, and let it fall. Wordlessly, he walked down the hall to James' room, where he paused, his hand poised over the access button next to the closed door. *When did this door start being shut?* He couldn't remember. It had always been open at first, when James was an infant, and then after the diagnosis. Pearce loved his son, but realized all of a sudden that he did not really know him. He tried to convince himself that his love was real and tangible, not an abstract thing, but it was harder than he liked. When he thought of James, and he did often, he thought of him as a newborn, asleep in his crib, all promise and potential and as-yet undiagnosed with a fatal disease. Or he thought of him as a toddler, still healthy-seeming, still round-cheeked, before they grew gaunt and hollow. He never really thought, it occurred to him, of his son as a person in his own right, with thoughts and feelings and brutally truncated dreams.

What would it be like to know the limit of your years? Now James knew the truth of his condition; medicines and doctors and unremitting discomfort were not inconveniences, but his own death, steadily stalking him since before his own birth. Pearce had faced death before, on Cygnus, during stellar storms, and once during a cargo dispute that got nasty at The Exchange. He had been aware every time that he might die, but it was always only one possible outcome, and he had always known that it could be avoided if he were tough enough, smart enough, lucky enough. He had never regarded death as a certainty.

It was, now, for his only son.

The thought made him ache. For himself, for James, but for Mary, too. She had never been happier, he knew, than when she was pregnant and when James was tiny. Pearce knew why. The child was with her, always, the constant companion that the father so rarely was, with his frequent and long absences. When James was born, his mother's affections centered on him totally, completely, unabashedly, to the point that Pearce himself found it hard to build a relationship with his son, or maintain one with Mary.

Do all men lose their wives to their children?

He touched the panel, and the door slid open. It was black inside, and Pearce's long shadow stretched out into the shaft of light that stabbed into the room. Finding the interior light control, he inched it up just a couple of centimeters, and the resulting dusk was gauzy and unreal. James was asleep in his bed, a tangle of arms and sheets and legs. The room itself could have been that of a teen boy anywhere, anywhen, clothes strewn across the floor, vidreaders, controllers for a variety of computer-interaction consoles, moving digital pictures of cricketers, and the few toys that had survived the transition from boy to pre-man. Pearce's eyes went to the shelves on the long opposite wall, shelves he had built himself, loaded with more than a hundred of the small collectible model ships. They were indistinct in the gloom, colors flat and muted, mostly indistinguishable from one another, but Pearce knew by heart where and when he had found most of them. He moved to the shelf and picked up one of the largest, a Raleigh-class methane tanker from the previous century.

"Dad."

Softly murmured though it was, the word startled Pearce. James was still lying down, but his eyes were open, and they were looking at his father. Pearce smiled, a sad little half smile, and put the miniature tanker back on the shelf.

"You know the truth," Pearce said without preamble.

"Yeah." The boy's eyes began to brim with tears, but Pearce thought they looked more angry than sad. He sat next to his son on the bed. *So big*, he thought, small as James was for his age. He still imagined him sleeping in that crib, the way he had last seen him before leaving for Cygnus with Jane Baker.

"I've been asked to go to space again," Pearce began, haltingly.

"Mom said."

"Did she tell you that there is a chance if I – if the trip goes well, that – that there's an operation, Jimmy. A procedure that isn't an option for us now, but might be if I succeed." *Was this a mistake? Was the boy still too young for this kind of discussion?*

"I might be cured?"

Pearce nodded. "There is that chance. The…the only chance, James. But I won't lie to you, it's a dangerous trip. I might not return. Even if I do, the results might not be good enough to earn your surgery. It's a slim chance…"

"But still a chance." James sat upright. The tears were gone now, replaced with a steely look in his son's eyes, a man's glare that Pearce had never seen there before.

"Yes," he replied softly. "A chance. The other option is that I could stay. We can manage your pain, we can still have some good years together. We can get to know each other…"

"Why?" asked James. He stood now, kicking free of his blankets. "What good is that to me? I'm sorry, Dad, but I want to live. I know you've been gone so much because you think it might help me, but you've still been gone, and Mom and I have done fine by ourselves. What's the point of a year with you now? So you can feel better after I'm dead?"

"Jimmy…" Pearce wanted to reach out, to touch his son, but James was out of arm's reach, standing with his small fists balled, staring at his father with that same fierce, flaring look in his eyes. *His mother's look*, Pearce realized.

"I want to live," James repeated, his voice rising. "If there's a chance, I want to take it. If you don't, I…I'll never forgive you. And you'll never be my father, not really."

There was a stony silence in the room then, James' words hanging in the air like the haze after a storm. Finally, Pearce rose. He placed a hand on the boy's shoulder and looked down at him. So small, so frail, and yet so filled with determination to carry on, to survive, to endure. Through his own pain and shame, Pearce felt the licking flames of intense pride.

"James," he said, and his son met his gaze. "I'll go. And though Hell itself might bar the way, I will come back and we will make you whole." A lump filled his throat, and he was barely able to whisper the next words. "I promise."

Days later, when he unpacked his gear on board the *Harvest*, Pearce found, wrapped in his socks, the very first model he had ever brought home for his son. It was a tiny, perfect replica of Jane Baker's *Drake*, blue-gray and dignified and perfect, the ideal starship, just as he remembered it the day he had joined her crew. Fingers trembling, Pearce set it on a shelf in his cramped quarters. Each night, as he fell asleep, he would stare at it, and he would promise to bring it back to James, along with all the rest of the days of his life.

Four

Space

The island was crowded, like everywhere else on the planet, but here, at least, you could see sky, a sky that was still mostly blue by day. It was night now, and that sky was black as Christine Fletcher stood on the veranda of her grandfather's bungalow on the once-island of St. Kitts. Looking up, through the spreading glow of the city of Basseterre, a handful of stars were visible. She didn't know how Bill could stand it in the heart of the teeming megalopolis of old Britain, with all those people and buildings on every side. *How does a star-mariner live where he cannot see the stars?* She took a swallow from the glass of newly-imported opal rum in her hand, and savored the pleasant tingle that filled her body. It was a cool night, and the liquor was a welcome fire in her belly. *One of the benefits of a career in the merchant marine,* she thought.

The warmth of the rum and the familiarity of the place induced a wave of nostalgia. Fletcher had grown up here, a child of the islands, a concept that was far more cultural than geographic. Humanity's hunger for housing, and the vast agrifactory complexes that nourished them, had swallowed up most of what had once been the Caribbean Sea. The great reclamation projects of the early 22nd century had transformed the face of the Earth and now, instead of a string of islands, the Lesser Antilles were merely the eastern edge of the massive single continent that dominated the western hemisphere from pole to pole. Patches of water remained, ponds, really, black and lifeless, little more than detention tanks for industrial effluvia. Perhaps a mile distant, Fletcher could see one now, from the veranda, a flat dark hole in the otherwise unrelenting lights.

She had seen the holovids, of course, with footage from long before her birth, showing St. Kitts as a true island, along with the others – Nevis, Monserrat, St. Martin, Barbados, and many more – that were now neighboring land-locked cities in the Caribbean district of the United Kingdom of Earth. As a young girl she had been endlessly fascinated by the green, forested hills that her native land had once been, surrounded by an endless rippling turquoise, teeming with life. *Fish,* she thought, remembering the word from old lessons as she pictured the odd looking creatures she had only seen on vid.

Still, to the extent she had one on Earth, this was home. This was where she had played as a child, climbing Mt. Liamulga, dodging the ancient combustion automobiles that still ran in the back alleys of the city, writing her daydreaming poetry. This was where she had gone to school, first kissed a boy, and first broke a boy's heart. She had been happy here, mostly, but had left when the first chance came. She was back now, and still mostly happy, but knew she would leave again soon. *And where will you go then, Christine?*

A sound came from behind her, a glass door sliding open, disturbing her reverie. Her grandfather closed the door and walked out to stand beside her at the railing. He was older, she noticed, but still a robust, arresting man, straight and erect, with silvery hair and coppery skin. His loose-sleeved white shirt was unbuttoned halfway down his chest, a white-black thicket bristling into the gap. In one hand was a glass much like hers, in the other, the bottle of opal rum, orange-yellow in the half-light. He refilled her glass and then his own, and held his out in salute.

"Good romo, girl." His voice had the old, lilting accents so many islanders clung to, a rare mark of identity in a homogenizing global Kingdom where everyone watched the same vids, ate the same foods, spoke the same language. At least they could make that language their own. And if their islands were no longer truly islands, all the more important to sound like true islanders. Miguel Diego Ochoa held the drink under his nose for a moment, his eyes closed, then slowly took a sip. The delight was evident on his face, and it made Fletcher smile.

"Anything for my Papi." She took another drink herself. A quiet voice from within told her to take it easy, but a louder voice laughed at the caution. This was hardly her first drink. She was an officer on a commercial cargo ship, after all, and often had a tot or two with the crew. Besides, she was home, and there was hardly a safer place for her in all the galaxy than in this house. Her mother's father was the only parent she had ever known, and along with her sister, the only person in the world she truly loved. He leaned against the railing, looking at her from underneath bushy eyebrows, studying her, and in that moment Fletcher felt that she might be twelve years old again.

"You're unhappy," he said, and she laughed.

"Of course not, Papi."

"Girl, please." His rich baritone was kind and loving, but firm. He took another swallow of the rum. "You can lie to whomever you want, your sister later tonight, yourself even, but don't try it with me. I raised you from a baby, and I know your lying face."

"I'm not unhappy," said Fletcher, and she meant it. "I'm just... just...restless, maybe?"

"That, too." Ochoa smiled, and his teeth were as white as hers. "You always were a *spranskious* thing, Christie. I can still remember that boy you brought around when you were what, sixteen? Nice boy, good family, but he never stood a chance. He might as well have tried to wrap his arms around a hurricane. Do you remember him?"

"John Crawford," she muttered with a sheepish smile.

"Yes, that was it. He knocks on my door one night, this John, and he says, 'Mr. Ochoa,' – polite boy, this John – he says, 'Christie's not like other girls.' Polite boy, but maybe not that bright, I remember thinking. I told him, 'No, there's none other like her on this spinning Earth.' He replies, 'I know, sir.' Then – and this is the part I'll never forget – he says, 'Do you think she'll ever settle down for me?'"

"He said that?" Fletcher asked, horrified.

"He did. He did. And I said to him, 'No, son, she won't. But don't feel bad. She won't settle down for me, either." They both laughed then, and drank their rum, and looked at the stars they could see.

"Poor Johnny," murmured Fletcher after a while. *I haven't thought about him in years.* She wondered, idly, what might have become of him. *Married, most likely, with children of his own by some nice, proper girl.* "He was very sweet, but oh-so-dull." She noticed that her grandfather was looking at her with that same penetrating, denuding stare.

"And have you yet found anything, Christie, in this wide galaxy, that isn't?"

The silence that followed was thick, as she digested his words. Her Papi had always understood her, always. When her schoolteachers found it impossible to control her, and asked Ochoa why Christine Fletcher couldn't be more like her well-behaved older sister, Isabelle, he understood, and asked them why the sun couldn't be more like the moon. When she refused to take the muscle drugs that would have elevated her from Caribbean champion sprinter to the All-Kingdom Games, he understood. When she wanted to go to the stars, and the very thought of it broke his heart, still he understood. He was, to her mind, the very definition of noble, not just by birth and title, holding the familial Ochoa baronetcy in the Antilles, but with his strength, his warmth, his compassion.

"Christie, you never knew your mum and dad."

"No," she whispered. "No, I was a baby when they left."

"Well," he continued, "I've told you before that you're a lot like your mum. So is Isabelle." Fletcher snorted at that.

"Isabelle and I are nothing alike."

"And?" Ochoa shrugged. "None of us is just one thing. Your mother was your wildness, Isabelle's maturity, and more. She was my daughter. Anyway, this Sam Fletcher…he was a hell of a man, your father. Nothing less could have won your mum. And the two of them, together..." he paused, gazing out over the lights of the city, and in that moment Fletcher saw him as an old man, nearly ninety, despite the youth in his eyes and voice. He had spoken of her mother before, but rarely of her father. She waited, and after a moment he continued. "Well, together they were magic. I never saw your mother more alive than when they were together. I wish you could have known them, Christie." He sighed, deep and shuddering, the sigh of a man who had lost the best part of himself. "They could have had whatever they wanted on this world, for themselves and their two perfect little girls, but it turned out what they wanted wasn't on this world. When the chance came to join the colony project on Jactura, off they went, with instructions to send the two of you along once they were settled." He smiled at her, but his eyes were moist. "But they never made it, did they? Perils of space travel, we were told."

"Papi..." she reached out a hand and took hold of his arm. *That's why it hurt him so much when I left Earth.* She had been blind not to see it before.

Voices came then, from inside the house. It was Isabelle, with her family. She hadn't seen her sister, or her brother-in-law and niece, in months. Still, she hesitated. Her grandfather had never been this candid with her before, and a large part of her wished that they had more time alone. But whatever it was, the rum or the stars, the rare wistful mood of Miguel Diego Ochoa had passed, and he was again, suddenly, the strong and impenetrable man who had raised the both of them. The moment was gone.

****

It had been years since St. James Park had been a park in anything more than name. Once, it had been a spreading green expanse of more than fifty acres, frequented by the residents of London, with a long pond, frequented by ducks. At one end of the pond there had even been a spit of land called Ducks Island. The entire swath of openness had stretched from Buckingham Palace, the residence of the King, in the west, to Whitehall in the east. It was an arrangement, the ancient saying went, that allowed the Royal Family and Parliament to keep an eye on one another.

Lord Rajek Djimonsu stood on the wide balcony on the western face of His Majesty's Treasury building, ten stories from the street below. His offices comprised the entire tenth floor, the top of this august and imposing white-brick structure, and this balcony was his alone. Sometimes he would stand here, as he did now, as the day was waning, and try to imagine his predecessors from long ago, standing in the same spot, peering across the greensward at the Palace. It seemed undignified, somehow, unseemly, as if the thought of so much grass and water and sky were not already enough to make him shudder. There was still a St. James Park, but it was so much more efficiently used now. Not for the first time, the Lord Chancellor of the Exchequer lauded the wisdom of those planners who converted all that useless space into retail stores and commercial offices and housing for the ever-teeming Londoners. The buildings rose high overhead, nearly touching at their apex, a tiny square of darkening blue at the top. It was progress and commerce and rents, and Lord Djimonsu loved it.

Eventually, he retreated through massive glass doors to the interior. If he was not the most powerful subject of the King in the whole of the Empire, he was in the conversation, and there was always more work to be done. *One does not control the world by daydreaming on balconies.* The doors shut behind him with an audible click. They were old doors, and he liked the way they made that sound of finality as they closed, proof positive that a barrier existed between him and the outside. The gentle hiss of automatic sliders was so much less satisfying.

Djimonsu moved to his desk, a silvery metallic island in a sea of sharp edges, reflective glass and white furniture. When he first ascended to this post, he had found his immediate predecessor had left behind an office weighed down by the traditional wood-paneling and leather-upholstery that was so favored by the upper officers of Government and the old moneyed class. He had ordered it all torn out at once. He had seen enough of that staid taste as a young man in the India Department, where all the bureaucrats tried so hard to out-British the British. It was always the nineteenth century somewhere in New Delhi, always the past. Here, in the beating commercial heart of the United Kingdom of Earth, the future was what mattered.

The Lord Chancellor stood, as he always did while working. He did not like the feeling of being motionless. His dark eyes tracked the twenty monitors arrayed around the walls of the long, narrow, gleaming office. Each display was tuned to constant analysis of the most important markets across the Empire, both here on Earth and across the known galaxy. Graphs flashed past, highlighting textile production in the East Asia Department, mineral commodities in Africa, luxury pharmaceutical imports from Sirius, worldwide agrifactory output. Djimonsu touched the panels on his desk, moving the Crown's resources into one sector and out of another, manipulating a price here and dumping a rotten stock there. This was his primary element, the high purpose to which he was eminently suited. If he had been forced to develop a certain political aptitude to enhance and enable his economic genius, so be it.

His attention moved back to the screen showing the price trendlines for grain. Yet again, he wondered if John Banks might somehow be right. The Minister of Science was undeniably brilliant, though with an irksome tendency to assume disasters always lurked just over the horizon. He didn't want Banks to be right. The nutrition industry was a uniquely mature and lucrative enterprise, and had been for many years. It was a key profit center for many of the companies that made up the Chamber, one that required limited investments in research, maintenance, or marketing. The collapse of the sector would be highly inconvenient, perhaps even ruinous, for some extremely powerful people. Dramatic change to accommodate the new realities Banks foretold would be expensive.

Still, his own inclination to disbelieve the Minister of Science did not stop Djimonsu from conducting his own inquiries into the matter. If anything, it made him more diligent. He had earned his station in life as a pragmatist, not an ideologue, and he carefully considered all the aspects of the decisions he made each day. After all, trillions of pounds flowed in and out of the Kingdom's treasury depending on his choices. He consulted with Chamber-funded scientists as well as independent research labs, and the results were mixed. Either way, there was a gamble to be made. He could accept Banks' scenario, and recommend that the entire agrifactory system make wholesale and ludicrously expensive changes in anticipation of a crisis that might never materialize. And if that crisis never came, the waste would range into the untold billions. Surely not the ringing crescendo he sought for his career!

And if I reject his findings? If we do nothing? Things would most likely remain the same, and investors did love stability. The likeliest threat to that stability was not that the dire predictions would come to pass, but rather that Banks would attempt some heroic gesture that would result in disruption to the markets. The Privy Council had taken his presentation under advisement. That is to say, they had ignored it. Banks, however, was not a man to go quietly if he felt the danger was real. *He's going to try something.* Djimonsu needed to know what that was, and stop it. Fortunately, he had the resources necessary to do just that.

Sliding aside one of the panels on his desk, the Lord Chancellor revealed a second, smaller set of smooth buttons. He touched several in sequence, and then waited a few moments. Before long, a voice answered through the speakers recessed in the surface of the desk, unrecognizable, modulated by computer scrambler.

"This is Henry."

Djimonsu smiled. He had many operatives throughout the Kingdom, embedded close to the various centers of influence in the military, the bureaucracy, the political parties, the palace, the board rooms. Information was power, and he went to great lengths to be the most-informed man on – or off – Earth. Each of his agents bore the name of one of the monarchs in the long British line: Edward, Victoria, William, Katherine. Henry was among his most reliable, and valuable.

"Henry, report."

"It is as you suspected, my Lord. The Minister closeted this afternoon with the Star Lord."

So, thought Djimonsu, *whatever he wants is off-planet.*

"He needs a ship," he said.

"And he has found one," replied the metallic voice. "From his current fleet. The crew is being assembled even now. As I understand it, their plan is to procure some new extraterrestrial food supply and bring it back here. Departure is estimated at within two weeks."

From his current fleet. Damn. If Lord Exeter came to the Privy Council to commission a new vessel, or to expend extra-budgetary funds, Djimonsu could stop him. By using the Admiralty's existing resources, however modest, Exeter skirted that potential roadblock. *No one ever said the man was a fool.*

Djimonsu sighed, looking back toward the towering wall of glass that looked out over St. James Park. As before, he could not see the Palace, but he knew it was there, beyond the forest of skyscraping buildings. *I am a Privy Councilor*, he thought, *a Peer of the Realm*. It was his duty to his King and His Subjects to ensure that the great British companies continued to thrive, to produce and procure the goods and services needed by the burgeoning Kingdom. From humble island origins centuries before, the British people had forged and sustained an empire that first spanned the globe, then burst free of those terrestrial boundaries to reach out into the stars. And it was the companies of the Chamber that made it all possible; in particular, the Big Five, the corporations that enjoyed the broad, centuries-old monopolies the Crown had granted them in various sectors: the venerable Galactic East India Company, importing exotic foodstuffs and luxury consumer goods from the corners of known space. The Royal Bank of Britain, financier to the royal family and almost everyone else. The Universal Lever Company, supplier of consumer goods to the King's subjects, from clothes to furniture. Reis Inc., the galaxy-spanning telecommunications empire. And the vast FoodCo agrifactory conglomerate, feeding the tens of billions of Britons on Earth and across the galaxy.

Like generations of investors before him, the Lord Chancellor was a gambling man at heart. A cautious gambler, certainly, who liked to know as much as he could about the stakes and the wager before the throw, but a gambler just the same. And when pressed, he would always bet on the system that had been in place for decades and worked so well. The stakes were too high to simply let the Science Minister and the Star Lord pursue this folly. If word leaked about Banks' claims, there could be a dangerous and destructive panic. Worse, if by some chance their mad mission succeeded, they might establish competition for the monopolies enjoyed by the Chamber's agrifactory interests. That, he could not permit.

"Very well," he said, leaning over his desk as he spoke. "Arrange for one of our people to be on that ship, Henry. It is our duty to protect the Kingdom from this fool's errand." Djimonsu shut off the channel. *The best gamblers play with loaded dice.*

****

The shuttle docked at the Port Zante terminal, in the heart of Basseterre. Once, decades before, this had been a deep-water port of call for ferries, cruise liners and cargo ships. Even further back, it had served as an anchorage for the great sailing ships of the 18th century; frigates, barques and merchantmen stopping over between Europe and Spanish Main, or plying the Caribbean trade in sugar, gold, or slaves. Now it was like any other station in the Kingdom, a shiny steel riot of landing strips and control towers.

William Pearce had never been to St. Kitts. Fletcher had invited him, of course, but it had never really been convenient. During his stays on Earth, Pearce had been content to spend his time in London with Mary and James. For a man who had traveled farther into the unknown than almost anyone on Earth, he had seen precious little of his own home planet. Part of the reason for that, he told himself, was that there was not much that could truly be considered exotic about other corners of the globe. The homogenization of human culture that began in the late twentieth century had only accelerated during the twenty-first, and now London food, language, and music were indistinguishable from those in Kyoto, or Johannesburg, or Riyadh. As for natural wonders, most of those were long gone as well. All but the deepest oceans had been reclaimed for more living space, and from the poles to the equator, the world had become a fairly uniform quilt of steel, plastic and glass. Here and there a bit of the jungles and deserts and a mountain or two had been preserved as curiosities, but these were tourist destinations where people on vacation could visit a few square miles of managed wilderness. Open space had become a luxury humanity could no longer afford.

The main thoroughfare in Basseterre was Bay Road, so named because it once ran alongside the blue waters of Basseterre Bay, the narrow bite the Caribbean Sea used to make into the island of St. Kitts from the Fisherman's Wharf to the long-defunct oil refineries. Now, buildings towered over both sides of the road, with a wide gap to the south where the sky peeked in above the Zante Terminal. It was almost noon, and the day was hot. The Kingdom's engineers had succeeded in moderating the climate of Earth over the previous century, making hurricanes, tsunami, blizzards, and other disastrous natural phenomena all but unknown. Still, the mercury rose higher here in the tropics than in London, and even though Pearce had eschewed the heavy blue jacket and cockaded hat as both too warm and too formal, he found himself sweating in his white uniform shirtsleeves and trousers.

And the people. He knew that St. Kitts had a fraction of the population that London did, but there were never crowds like this, even on the streets of England's busiest cities. There, the swift and efficient tube system siphoned off at least some of the human foot traffic. Here, there were no tubes, the roads were still choked with antique combustion cars, and the sidewalks between roadway and buildings were sometimes thronged so thickly with people that Pearce had to shoulder his way past.

He had traded messages with Fletcher early that morning, asking to see her, and she had invited him to come to dinner that night at her grandfather's house. The appointment was still several hours off, and Pearce's stomach was making its midday rumble, so he decided to find lunch. Running a sleeve across his brow, Pearce ducked through the front door into a nearby Greenstalls. The controlled temperature of the cafeteria was a relief after his brief warm walk from the shuttle, though there were still more people inside than he thought possible. There were five queues, and each moved slowly, but that wasn't uncommon. Greenstalls was the mid-range brand of the FoodCo restaurant spectrum, and popular around the world. At the low end was Ploughman's, a favorite of the commons with a well-earned reputation for middling quality delivered swiftly, while the upper classes generally chose Roast, which was excellent, expensive, and exclusive. Pearce was a Greenstalls man, though he knew his way around a Ploughman's, too. He had never seen the inside of a Roast.

Maybe once all this is done, he thought. *I'll take Mary to the Roast in Piccadilly, and James, too, once he's well.* It was a fortifying thought, and cheered him as he inched his way forward to the vending counter. Once there, he was about to punch in the code for one of his usual selections, a simple pork pie and onion (number 22F36, which he knew by heart), when he hesitated. He usually just entered this code, or one of a handful of others he preferred, and like all the other patrons, he would collect his meal through the adjacent delivery window after a few moments. It had been a long time since he scrolled through the screen's catalog, with small images of all the different choices available. Greenstalls had perhaps seventy main lunch options, with a host of possible side dishes. The beverage station was nearby, with a similar interface. Pearce ignored the grumbling of the customer behind him and tapped his finger against the corner of the display screen, flipping the virtual page. Bacon sandwich, fish and chips, black pudding, even cucumber sandwiches. Each was presented appetizingly in its respective picture, and his stomach growled.

It's all the same. He had always known that, of course, in the parts of his mind that were well cordoned-off from his empty belly, but after Banks' discourse on the nature of human nutrition, the reality of it came crashing down on him. The meals would taste as they were supposed to, depending somewhat on the quality of the restaurant, but it was all the same. Three grains. *Three dying grains.* It had never bothered him before that the variety in his diet was utterly illusory, that everything he ate was virtually identical genetically. And why should it matter? It was nutritious, and it kept him, and billions upon billions of his fellow humans, on his feet. *What does it matter?* He couldn't say why, but it did. The curtain had been pulled back, and as much as he wanted to forget what Banks had said the night before, he couldn't. You could not uneat the apple of the tree of knowledge, no matter how much you craved a return to ignorance.

"Hey." Behind him in line, a tall, lithe man, so black he was nearly purple, was holding up both hands in a gesture of impatience. "Some of us want to eat today, brother," he said in the affected singsong lilt of the native islander. *Not me,* Pearce thought. He knew his hunger would eventually get the better of his uneasiness, and he would eat again, but not now. And he would never look at food the same way again.

"Sorry," muttered Pearce as he shouldered his way out of the Greenstalls and back into the sweltering crowds of Bay Road. His experience in the eatery had unsettled him, and he did not like the sensation. He was a career star-mariner, used to eating the same things at the same time each day, and this disruption in his equilibrium was unwelcome in the extreme. *I'm nervous,* he thought, as he stepped onto a nearby group-tram whose signage declared it was headed west toward the Brimstone Hill section of Basseterre. From there, Fletcher's directions told him he could easily walk to her grandfather's house, where she had grown up and was staying.

There were plenty of good reasons for his anxiety. He was going back to Cygnus, where God only knew what he might find, on a mission to prevent the starvation of Earth. As if that weren't enough, they had thrown his son's life into the bargain, as well. *No wonder I lost my appetite.* He needed Christine Fletcher with him for this. She had never been a naval officer, serving her whole career in the merchant marine, and yet she was still the best star-mariner he knew. She was deeply competent, running a ship's crew with effortless precision, but it was more than that. She was good at the things he was not, at things that mattered during a deep-space voyage. She inspired loyalty and had an easy charisma that he envied, a magnetism that buoyed the morale of everyone on board, including him. If they were to succeed in this task that could not fail, he needed Christine Fletcher.

Pearce had said as much to the Star Lord when he had agreed to the task. His reinstatement in the Navy had been immediate, with promotion to commander, as promised. They had discussed timetables, potential ships, and when the conversation turned to crew, Pearce had insisted on Christine Fletcher as his executive. Lord Exeter had balked at first, insisting that the first officer of a navy ship had to be a naval officer. It had been Banks, in his usual inimitable style, who had deftly severed the knot by suggesting that Fletcher be made a Lieutenant in the Royal Navy. Exeter had grudgingly acquiesced, and the envelope bearing her commission was in Pearce's bag even now.

And how she'll hate that, he thought.

He had promised a gift to Mary as partial apology for dashing off across the Atlantic to recruit Fletcher, perhaps a dress dyed in the distinctive *batik* style for which St. Kitts was famous, but Pearce had lost all interest in exploring the shops of Basseterre. It was still entirely too early to call on Fletcher, but he resolved to go anyway. He knew that as soon as he convinced her to sign on, the tight ache in his chest would loosen, if only a little.

The tram ride did nothing to put him at ease. It was a rickety, antique model that still made use of cable-cushion technology that had been cutting edge eighty years before, and it wheezed and grunted along Canyon Street only marginally faster than he could have walked. The long, thin carriage was constantly full, regardless of how many passengers boarded or disembarked at each stop, and despite the heat of the day, Pearce was thankful for the open windows on each side.

Eventually they arrived at the Brimstone Hill station, where he fought his way to the crowded exit, squeezing out just before the automatic doors snapped shut with an authoritative clang.

Here in the western part of the city, the skyscrapers of Basseterre had thinned out and smaller buildings had gradually taken over. There was more sky here than Pearce had ever seen, and the sun, usually seen in London as a yellow sliver peeking through the cracks in the steel canopy overhead, was full and round and painfully bright. Shading his eyes with a hand, Pearce could see that the road here was lined with what appeared to be single-family homes, a sign that here there lived gentry, perhaps even nobility. The houses were still crowded close together, often touching, but few were more than two or three stories tall, and all had some kind of open area in front of the door. A yard, he seemed to remember Fletcher calling it. And these yards had grass, and flowers, a personal splash of color and life for each family. Once, Pearce would have been agape, but the memory of Banks' garden at Spring Grove was still fresh.

Fletcher's instructions directed him to turn down Charles Street, which he did, and as he walked, the homes grew larger and more opulent. There was a singular effort to keep alive the architectural conceit of island culture here, with an abundance of pink brick, yellow trim, and white crushed-stone walkways. It was all very alien to Pearce, in many ways as alien as any far-flung planet he had visited.

Perhaps I was wrong, he thought, *not to explore my own world more.* Certainly the cities were similar to the point of being identical, sprawling metal siblings. But here, at the fringes of the unrelenting urban sameness, people were making an effort to preserve some sense of cultural self. He wondered if the same was true elsewhere, if the outskirts of Moscow or Lima retained some vestiges of Russian or Peruvian ethnic traditions. It was an article of faith in the King's schools that the strength of humanity came from their shared global culture, which had over the centuries come to reflect a decided British quality. No surprise there; the United Kingdom, even before it had come to hold global political power, had always been the worldwide leader in entertainment, producing the bulk of the Earth's popular music, holovids, and literature. There were vestiges of other influences, but these became increasingly hard to trace as the whole melted together over the decades. Standing in front of Fletcher's grandfather's house, Pearce wondered if too much had been sacrificed to achieve global unity. *How much of ourselves have we lost?* He was an ethnic Briton, and proud of it, but what of a native of the African Department, or Cathay? Could they be a good subject of the King and still proud of their ethnicity as well?

The house of Baronet Miguel Diego Ochoa was handsome, as all the houses were, tall and stately, yet not forbidding. Pearce tried to imagine Fletcher growing up here, seeing the full sun and touching dirt and grass every day. Small wonder she exuded such charm and magnetic energy. Covering the pathway from road to front porch in a few quick steps, Pearce touched the bell panel on the door. A few moments later, the bright blue door opened inward on old-style hinges to reveal an older gentleman, white-haired and dignified. *Ochoa*, assumed Pearce. *Fletcher's grandfather.*

"Yes?" There was that inflection again, that islander's cadence, though with a deeper timbre coming from Ochoa.

"Sir? I am Commander William Pearce, of His Majesty's Navy, here to see Fletcher. I mean, Christine. Your granddaughter," he finished, feeling a bit foolish.

"I know who all of those people are," replied the baronet, his eyes twinkling. "They are all here, and are expecting you, though perhaps not at this hour. Please come in, Commander." He stepped aside, and spread a hand toward the interior of the house by way of invitation. Pearce followed into a hallway that was shady and cool, with a breath of a breeze. Windows, or another door, must be open somewhere in the house. That was a novel concept to Pearce. Why not merely close up and activate the climate management system for ideal temperature and humidity? He noticed then that Ochoa was holding his right palm out in greeting, so he thrust out his own and they shook hands.

"Welcome, Commander."

"Please, sir, call me William, or Bill."

"Then you must call me Miguel. Christine has spoken of you often. She respects you, Bill." Pearce found himself absurdly grateful for the secondhand compliment, though it was most likely a routine courtesy.

"She is too kind, I'm afraid. Your granddaughter is an exceptional star-mariner." Miguel nodded, though he did not smile. *He is being polite*, Pearce thought, *but he is not pleased to see me.*

"She is on the porch, with a friend." Ochoa pointed, and Pearce thanked him as he headed down the hallway in that direction. Something had changed during his brief conversation with Fletcher's grandfather, but for the life of him he could not figure out what it was. It had begun amicably enough, even with a shared laugh, but in scarcely more than a heartbeat, the old man had cooled considerably. It made Pearce uncomfortable, but he had no time to consider it at the moment. A square of blue-white sky beckoned, and, assuming that was the door to the porch, he moved toward it.

The door was another antique model, a sliding glass door that was operated manually. It was already open a crack, creating the source of the wind in the hallway. Sounds were coming in as well -- a low, repetitive beat that Pearce recognized as the Latin music Fletcher would play sometimes on board ship, and the giggling conversation of two young women. Through the clear glass, Pearce could see them, sitting with their backs to him in low, brightly colored chairs. Heads topped by long, dark hair poked above each chair, and beyond them was the low wall of the veranda with nothing but sky beyond. It was breathtaking. Pearce had seen so much openness before, but always on other planets. Here, it almost made him dizzy, as though he might fly off the face of the Earth itself and be lost forever. Gathering himself, Pearce pushed open the slider and stepped onto the porch.

"Papi?" asked the woman on the left, with a voice that he recognized as Fletcher's.

"Sorry, no," Pearce replied. "Try again."

Fletcher got up from her seat, and right away Pearce saw that she was mostly naked. She had on a very small orange bathing suit bottom, held together by silver hoops at each hip, but that was it. A scant meter away she stood, her brown skin glistening with what Pearce assumed to be some sort of lotion or oil to protect her from the sun, her breasts young and round and tipped with dark brown, almost black nipples. Pearce forced himself to think of Mary, of her milky white skin, but all he could picture were her sagging mother's breasts and puffy pink nipples. *Turn away!* He wrenched his gaze to the side, staring out into that endless blue. He had noticed, to his Anglican dismay, that the other young woman was equally topless, equally young, and equally perfect.

"Christine," he managed to blurt out, "do...do you mind?" She had told him of this strange, archaic habit once before. *Sun-bathing*, she called it, sitting outdoors and warming your body in the sun. It seemed a peculiar pastime, and he had never imagined it was the sort of thing you would do undressed, certainly not undressed and with a friend.

"What? Oh." Fletcher lazily picked up a nearby towel and wrapped it around her chest, and her companion did the same, laughing. "Honestly, Bill. It's as if you've never seen tits before. You're on the island, sweetie. Relax." She put a hand on his arm, below the elbow, where his long sleeves covered his own pasty flesh. She kissed him lightly, on the cheek. "I am happy to see you, though. Early, aren't you?"

"Yes." Bill exhaled, recovering his equilibrium, chastising himself for his vague disappointment that she had covered up. "My shuttle got in early, and as we say in the service, there's not a moment to be lost."

"In the…" Fletcher drew back for a minute, and a smile began to dawn on her face. "Bill? Is that a Navy uniform you're wearing?" She looked down to where her hand was touching his arm, and her fingertips brushed the three gold bands embroidered above the cuff. "Commander? Bill, congratulations!" She hugged him, something she had not ever done before, and Pearce, momentarily at a loss for how to respond, finally gave her a small pat on the back, located strategically on the wrapped towel.

"Thank you," he said huskily as she disengaged.

"But I've been rude!" she cried. "Jacinta, this is my friend, Bill Pearce. He's a Commander in His Majesty's Royal Navy!" The other young woman stood up, thankfully clutching a towel of her own over her breasts. She was pretty, in truth prettier than Fletcher, but she regarded him with a cool, jaded eye and shook his hand diffidently. *He's so old*, she mouthed to Fletcher before sitting back down in her chair. Fletcher laughed.

"Don't mind Jacinta. She's in the market for a man, and I think I got her excited when I mentioned your rank." She kicked at the chair playfully. "He's married anyway."

Bill had to smile himself. In the past few days he had almost forgotten Fletcher's talent for lighting up a room, her infectious spirit, her laughter. And her reaction warmed him. He had told her more than once of his ambitions to return to the Navy, on their long journeys as shipmates. He had not, however, expected her to react with such joy at his news.

"So that's why you made the jump over here," she was saying. "All these years I've been inviting you to visit, and now you come so we can drool over your stripes? I thought you had another cargo commission for us already."

"I do," he said, without hesitation. He had thought of how best to broach this ever since he had secured Exeter's agreement the night before, and he had finally settled on the direct approach. Reaching into his pocket, Pearce withdrew the small white envelope with her name written in neat script on the front. He handed it to her, and waited.

Fletcher held the envelope in her hands for a moment, and he knew she was wondering at the use of paper. Merchant charters always came electronically. Only one entity still relied on paper for formal communications. Soon enough she tore the seal open and unfolded the sheet within. Pearce watched, holding his breath.

"The Navy." It was a statement, not a question. Her tone was flat, and betrayed no hint of what was going on in her mind. Pearce could not afford to let her decline.

"I need you for this, Christine…Lieutenant Fletcher."

****

"I've followed Bill's orders in space before, Papi. This wouldn't be any different."

Fletcher stacked the plates and took them into the kitchen, placing them into the machine to be sterilized. Coming back into the spacious dining room where they had eaten, she picked up fistfuls of silverware. It was late; it had been a long afternoon and evening, and she was tired. Pearce clearly was as well, having already retired to one of the guest bedrooms. Ochoa sat in a rocking chair near the wide bay windows that overlooked the front garden. They were cracked open, and the smoke from Ochoa's pipe drifted out through the gap into the purple night air.

"That is where you're mistaken, child. It would be completely different. Listen to yourself. *Bill*, you say. He comes to your home, you embrace him as a friend." Ochoa raised a hand, deflecting her interruption unspoken. "I do not say any of this is wrong of you. But it would no longer be like this. You will call him Commander, and Sir. His orders will carry the weight of the Crown. If you accept this commission, you must know that your relationship will change. What is more, you will change. You will have to."

"You are so melodramatic," she said. "I haven't told Bill whether I intend to accept or not. In any case, from what he tells me, this is a science mission on behalf of the King and Minister Banks. You always say how much you like him."

"Everyone likes Banks," grunted Ochoa. He took his pipe from his mouth and pointed the stem at her. "That is not the point. The point, I think, is that you are restless again. Not that you ever stopped being restless, so perhaps it is better to say you are restless still. The stars call to you, as they did to your mother. And along comes a man, a good man, an honest one, and says to follow him out there, and just like your mother, you do." He paused, looking out the window. Lights glowed from every house on the street, pushing back against the dark of night and obscuring any stars that might be overhead. Still, Ochoa stared into the heavens, and Fletcher knew that he was thinking about his daughter, who had gone out there and never come back to him or her children.

"Please, Papi. It's nothing like that. Mama was in love with Daddy." She set down the forks and spoons and knelt on the floor by her grandfather's feet. "I'm not in love with Bill. Far from it."

"You don't want to sleep with him, you mean," Ochoa said, replacing his pipe between his teeth. "That doesn't mean you don't love him. There is love, and then there is love. You've been with him more than any other man in your life, except me. But this Pearce, he does not truly concern me. You seek to roam, and he is merely a convenient excuse." He stroked her dark hair, then lifted her chin with one of his gnarled fingers. "What has he told you about where you are going, girl? What do you know of Cygnus?"

"A little," Fletcher replied. "It's far. About as far as anyone has gone. I suppose I'd be lying if I said that didn't intrigue me. He said the natives there are fascinating, at least some of them. And he mentioned that Captain Baker died there." Ochoa took his hand from her chin and rubbed his eyes.

"You are too young to remember," he said. "Captain Jane Baker is a name in a history book to you, a story from a vid, but she was more than that. She was a folk hero, a legend. And she was killed by these Cygni your Bill Pearce finds so fascinating. No matter. I have long ago learned that trying to give you advice doesn't work." Fletcher could almost hear her grandfather creak as he rose from the chair, slowly unfolding to his full height. "And I am tired now, but I will just say that this is not something you can do on one whim, and then simply undo on another. The Royal Navy takes things very seriously." He fixed her with his steeliest gaze, beneath those bushy eyebrows. "Far more so than you ever have, girl."

Ochoa turned, and shuffled toward the stairs. Watching him go, Fletcher was filled with the sudden premonition that she might never see him again, and that her last memory of him would be a rambling, disappointed lecture. It was more than she could bear.

"Papi," she called, and he hesitated on the bottom stair. "I love you."

"There is love and there is love," he said again. He then turned, just enough to look over his shoulder at her. "Someday, I hope you find anything, on this Earth or off, to love as much as I have loved you and your sister." His eyes were wet and ancient as he smiled. "Good night, Christine."

Five

In His Majesty's Royal Navy

The orbital dockyards at Spithead were a busy place, with the loading and unloading of merchant craft, the human flow of passenger traffic, and naval vessels in refit. From the viewing platform she watched them all, rapt, her nose all but pressed against the floor-to-ceiling window like a schoolgirl less than half her age. She had never been off-planet before, never even to these orbital yards a scant thousand kilometers above the surface of the Earth, but she had always loved starships. The very idea of penetrating the black veil of space and groping into the unexplored corners of the galaxy both terrified and thrilled her.

Only twenty-two, Hope Worth was the daughter of an officer in His Majesty's Royal Navy, and just that morning had put on her midshipman's dress uniform for the first time, for her commissioning. She had modeled it for her parents, the crisp white pants, the trim blue jacket, even the ceremonial cocked hat resting atop her close-cropped brown hair. Her father, retired Captain Samuel Worth, towering over her by nearly a third of a meter, had smoothed the white turnbacks on her jacket collar, briefly polishing the gold buttons there with his sleeve. He had removed her hat then, handing it to her and saying, his voice little more than a raspy whisper, that she should never wear it indoors.

He's proud of me, she had thought. *My father's proud of me.*

She thought it again now as she watched the ships, marveling at the size of them, as a massive Navy cruiser slipped its moorings and began to drift past. The HMSS *Cromwell*, as the proud markings along the shimmering silver-blue hull proclaimed, took nearly half an hour to ease its bulk out of the yards. If anything dimmed Worth's excitement, it was her near certainty that she wasn't posting to a battleship. HMSS *Harvest*, her orders had read, and that was no name for a cruiser. More likely a service tender, or a science vessel. In the end, it hardly mattered. She was going to space, as her father had thirty years before.

"That's a big ship."

Worth was momentarily startled to find she wasn't alone on the platform, and then a little embarrassed she hadn't even noticed the man at her elbow until he had spoken. Now that she turned from the window and looked at him, she realized the descriptor "man" was somewhat generous. Young as she was, he seemed younger still, little more than a boy, and yet he was dressed exactly the same as she was, even clutching his hat with the same awkward grip, careful not to ruin the brushed felt. He was short, though not as short as she was, thin and gangly, and pale, with splotchy patches of red creeping up from his collar into his cheeks. His eyes were an unremarkable muddy hazel, but sharp, focused intently on the stern of the *Cromwell* as she got under way. And he was vaguely familiar, though she couldn't place him.

"Yes, she is," Worth replied politely. It was only then that she realized she wasn't only excited, she was lonely, too. She had gone from her family's house in Boston to the Royal Naval College at Greenwich, where her days and nights had been filled with the noise and presence of instructors and fellow cadets. She had never really been alone before, and feeling suddenly and absurdly grateful for the company, she sighed. "I wish I were posted to her." She smiled at him. No one had ever called Hope Worth beautiful. Instead, she suffered under the perpetual labels of cute, or perky, or something equally nauseating. *Starship captains aren't perky, or cute*, she thought. But she had been told, and truthfully, that her smile was her best feature, and she used it now on her fellow midshipman. "Hope Worth," she said, adding "midshipman," unnecessarily.

The boy swallowed, and ventured a smile himself, which fell well short of hers. His teeth were crooked, the mark of common roots, but it was an honest smile that lit up his entire face. Her own family was no less common, of course, but her father's rank had entitled her to advanced medical services, including dental work.

"Charles Hall," he replied, and after a small pause, he, too, added, "midshipman," holding out his hat as if it were some kind of evidence. They both laughed, a little, and nervously, at their own awkwardness. Into the silence, Hall ventured, "I know who you are, though. We were at Greenwich together."

So that's where I've seen you, she thought, though even with the context she couldn't cull a single specific memory of him from the last three years.

"I'm posted to the *Harvest*," he said, filling what was fast becoming an awkward silence.

"Then we'll be shipmates," Worth said, her smile returning, and even broader than before. It made sense, of course. There couldn't be that many Navy ships filling their crews at the moment, certainly only one that was ordering its midshipmen to report to Pier 12B on the evening of the seventeenth, no later than 1900 hours. Whoever the commander of this *Harvest* was, he clearly wasn't afraid to go to space with junior officers right out of Greenwich. *Either that*, thought Worth with a twinge of unease, *or we're all he can get*. As if by some unspoken mutual consent,

Hall and Worth turned back to face the now much emptier spacedock, and it was then that they saw the HMSS *Harvest* for the first time.

After the elegant expanse of the *Cromwell*, even with her modest expectations, it was a disappointment. Certainly it was not the kind of ship Worth had dreamed of as a child, when she went to sleep picturing her father on the command deck. Far from the majesty of a star-cruiser, she was a dark, unlovely gray from stern to stem, her hull pockmarked by thousands of tiny encounters with countless meteorites and the galactic detritus of deep space. She was squat, her lines awkward and ungainly, little more than a bulbous cargo hold.

"A merchant ship," muttered Hall, his voice as full of disappointment and disapproval as her heart. "Barely even refit."

"And your home for as long as you last," growled a low voice from behind them, "so you'd best learn to speak of her with some respect." Turning around, the first thing both midshipmen noticed was the double yellow stripe on each dark blue sleeve of the man who had spoken. Worth quickly touched her forehead with a knuckle.

"Yes, sir," she said.

"Y-yes, sir," stammered Hall, following suit with a shaky salute of his own. The lieutenant was standing at ramrod attention, his feet shoulder-width apart, hands clasped behind his back, gripping his own ceremonial hat. His broad accent marked him as a native of the Australian District, or perhaps New Zealand. He was unremarkable in height and build, nearly bald but for a graying fringe of stubble, with a square jaw that at the moment was set into a stern scowl as he surveyed both junior officers with narrow, ice-blue eyes. Worth felt a tingle of terror until the expression softened, slowly becoming a wry smile.

"She is a right old dog of a barge at that, but I'm sure we'll come to love her anyway. At ease, gentlemen." Worth and Hall relaxed, if only a little. "You must be our new middies, right out of the womb. Lieutenant John Pott." He held out a hand, and for a moment, Worth thought he meant to shake hands, before realizing he wanted their orders. She handed hers over, and Hall followed suit. Pott gave them a cursory glance, nodded, and beckoned to them with his other hand. "Grab your bags and follow me." Without another word, he turned and left the observation deck, the midshipmen hurrying to trail behind.

Pott led them along the labyrinthine corridors of Spithead with the casual ease of a frequent visitor. It was evening, and fairly quiet, especially with the Cromwell gone, and they encountered few other personnel until they arrived at a cramped warehouse that was buzzing with activity. Men and women in the light gray worksuits of able starmen emerged in a steady stream from the mouth of a round hallway, seized large plastic containers, and carried them back where they had come from. One of them, a strikingly handsome Latino who was even shorter than Worth, noticed Pott and stopped to touch his forehead.

"No worries, Quintal," Pott said, returning the salute. "Back to work with you." The crewman nodded, and with the most fleeting of glances at Worth, returned to his labors. "That's Matias Quintal," explained Pott to the midshipmen. "One of our newly-assigned ables." He leaned in a bit closer, and whispered roughly, "thinks he's a bit much, hey? They're good lads, most of them, right plodders, even the sheilas, but you've got to stay on them." He winked at them. "Come on, then." And he headed for the round doorway, dodging the crewmen, and once again Worth and Hall followed in his wake, lugging their heavy duffels.

As soon as Worth set foot into the tubular corridor, she felt the floor sag ever so slightly beneath her. She lost her balance just a bit, and with her free hand grabbed Hall's elbow. She steadied immediately, and let go just as quickly.

"Sorry," she mumbled, a trifle embarrassed. Hall said nothing, and looked a bit uncomfortable himself. Lieutenant Pott was grinning at them over his shoulder.

"This is the gangway to the *Harvest*," he called. "Flexible polymer tubing. Takes a bit of getting used to, but strong as anything." He rapped the waxy yellow wall, and it gave a healthy thrum. Then something barreled into Worth's back, and sent her sprawling. She gave small yelp, more of surprise than pain.

"Out of the way," snapped a voice above her. It was one of the ables, this one tall and well-muscled, sweating from his work, a dark green container in his arms.

"Oi!" barked Pott in return. "That's an officer you just bowled, Lamb. Watch your step and your tone!" Hall was helping her back onto her feet, and Worth knew she was blushing fiercely, which she hated.

"It's nothing, really," she said, straightening her jacket and trying to preserve what little remained of her dignity.

"Like hell," Pott growled. "This is His Majesty's Navy and we do things properly. Right, Lamb? Apologize to the midshipman." Worth wanted nothing more than for the whole thing to be over, but she knew that Pott was right. If the crew knew her for a pushover, they would never respect her, and she could never be an effective officer. She tried to stand a little taller, lift her chin ever so slightly, and look the able in the face.

"Sorry," he said, almost spitting the word. "*Sir*. May I go back to work now?"

"Off with you." Pott gestured, and the man disappeared down the gangway toward the ship, with his burden. The lieutenant shook his head. "A nasty piece of work, Saul Lamb. You'll never love him, nor he you, but he's a rip-snorting starman. Tough but fair, that's the ticket with these fellows." He crouched, picking up Worth's hat from the floor of the tube. One corner was bent and the felt crushed, and Pott smoothed it as best he could before handing it back to her. She stared at it, wondering if all her excitement and anticipation from earlier that day would be as trampled, too.

Worth followed Pott in silence as they trudged down the remainder of the long gangway, Hall alongside, staring down, clearly lost in some thoughts of his own. At regular intervals crewmen passed them, and Worth made it a point to avoid their hustling bodies and their eyes. In a few moments, they arrived at the main hatch of the *Harvest*, and Pott stopped them with a raised arm.

"Left step, now."

"What?" asked Hall.

"Your first step on your new ship," Worth answered him, "should never be with your right foot. Bad luck."

Pott smiled at her. "Your father tell you that?"

"Yes." She blushed again. Stop that!

"I served under Captain Worth some years ago, as a middie myself," Pott said. "Only a short local cruise, the Jupiter run, but long enough to know he was a top-notch officer." He stared at her. "I look forward to seeing if you measure up."

Worth loved her father, worshiped him, but found herself feeling the tiniest hint of resentment toward her accomplished name, and for the first time, the expectation that had always been more of a challenge now felt like a burden to bear. Clenching her jaw tight, she stepped across the threshold onto the *Harvest*, left foot first. Hall did the same, somewhat more diffidently, and Pott beckoned for them to continue to follow him. They did so, down a close, cramped hallway lit only by the orange emergency tracking lights along the seams where the floor met the walls.

"Something else my father told me," Worth ventured, "is that Navy crewmen meet a certain standard. If Lamb and some of these others are so...nasty, as you put it, why are we taking them into space with us?" The look he returned was not unkindly, though there was the hint of amusement at her innocence.

"Not the ship you wanted, and now not the crew? No disrespect to your father, of course, but while Captain Worth could handpick his jacks, this ship and this commander weren't exactly at the top of the list come assignment time."

"For them," muttered Hall darkly, jerking a thumb back toward where the crewmen were working, "or for us?" Worth remembered Hall's deflated comments at the viewing platform. *He's as disappointed as I am,* she realized.

"Funny thing about ladders," Pott said icily, all trace of good humor gone, "so many of them seem to start at the bottom rung." He tapped the breast pocket of his jacket, where he had placed their orders. "You're in the King's Navy now, lad. Best leave that petulant attitude ashore, both of you. This is a rowdy lot, to be sure, but they work hard, and it's tough enough to maintain discipline without spoiled, sulking officers. Understand me?"

"Yes, sir," they both replied, stung by the rebuke.

From there, the remainder of the evening was given over to their initial orientation on the *Harvest*. In the weeks ahead they would come to know her intimately, her every rivet and electrical subsystem, but now they were strangers, and Pott began by escorting them through each section of the ship in turn. They visited the cavernous main cargo bay, where able starmen were hurriedly erecting the strange constructs that Pott revealed to be hydroponic vats, but did not elaborate further. The galley and the officers' mess were next, where Pott explained that the midshipmen would take their meals in the common mess belowdecks, with the crew.

"Another reason to get along with them," the lieutenant said. "Otherwise they can make your life fairly miserable. Remember, there are nine of them and only two of you, and some of them have been in the service since before you were born. They'll salute you, but if you come over as if you know a damned thing, they'll laugh at you in their cups. Better to listen, to learn, and to earn their respect through work and not rank."

In the Surgery, they met the ship's surgeon, the elderly, white-bearded Zoltan Szakonyi, who chased them out so he could continue his own preparations. They passed then through the cramped engine room amidships, the domain of the boatswain, Thomas Peckover. Responsible for the massive gravity sails that powered the deep-space drives of the *Harvest*, Peckover was thoroughly professional in his description of how the sails functioned – and utterly devoid of personal warmth or charm. During the entire hour he spent showing his guests the sail housings, and the complicated rigging used to manage the massive but delicate crystalline sails, he never smiled once.

"Humor can be overrated," Pott observed as they clambered up the long, narrow companionway leading from the engine room to the command deck. This was the interior of the slender fin that rose up from the hull, midway between the Harvest's broad shoulders. It was just cold enough that Worth could see her breath. "Even if human warmth is wasted on him, Peckover is extremely competent. Don't sweat the climb, by the by. The tower lift should be functional again soon. Something about power conduits. Just one more item on the punchlist for our lovely old girl." The ladder ended in a hatch that Pott slid aside, and beyond was a snug, poorly-lit, circular room. "This," Pott said, "is the conn, the command center. We just call her the Quarterdeck."

It was smaller than Worth had expected, but if she had learned anything in the last couple of hours, it was that her expectations were all but worthless. It seemed like every story her father had ever told her involved the sprawling, shining bridges of sleek battle cruisers, where the lifts were never off-line and the crewmen were never rude pricks. *Why would he tell me stories like that?* she thought. *He had been a midshipman once too, right?* Surely Captain Worth had served on boring science vessels, or grimy cargo carriers. What was it Pott had said? *Funny thing about ladders...*

She tried to look at it dispassionately. Everything was the same ugly gray-black she had seen throughout the ship – *had they never heard of paint?* – with a wide viewscreen that dominated the forward wall. There was one chair in the middle, slightly raised -- the command chair -- with others arrayed nearby.

"You're the Navigator, Hall. This is your pilot's station." Pott patted the back of one of the chairs near the screen, directly in front of and below the command chair. The captain's knees would all but brush his back. Hall sat, ran a palm across the top of the instrument panel, its displays all dark, then took the manual nav-stick almost lovingly in his hand.

"Can't imagine you'll need that much," laughed Pott, clapping a friendly hand on the midshipman's shoulder. "Even an old girl like the *Harvest* flies mostly by instrument panel. And you, Worth – you're over there, at Operations." He pointed to the front left corner. She sat, too, though not quite with the same reverence Hall had shown. She knew from the Royal College that navigators were a breed apart, talented and high-strung, with a sort of manic reverence for their equipment. Operations officers were more pragmatic. Instruments were tools, no more. *And that's why command officers come out of Ops and not Nav*, she thought. Her father, of course, had been Ops.

It was after eleven by the time the two tired midshipmen made it back to their berths belowdecks. *2300*, Worth corrected herself. *Navy time.* The *Harvest* was not a big ship, and most of her tonnage was taken up by her spacious cargo holds. The captain and the other senior officers, "including me," Pott had explained, had slightly roomier quarters on the main deck, nearer to the command center. Down here, in the section of the Harvest's belly nearest her fat bow, was where the midshipmen would bunk, sharing a corridor with the able starmen and other lower-ranking crew members such as Yancy Waugh, the boatswain's mate, and Orpheus Crutchfield, the sergeant in charge of the Machrine detail, among others. Worth mumbled an exhausted good night to Hall before slipping into her quarters. She knew they would be tiny, and for the first time that night, her expectations were met. The lights came on automatically as she entered, illuminating a small bunk with drawers underneath, and a narrow closet. There was a multi-use panel on the wall, currently dark, and Worth activated it with a touch, dropping her bag on the bed. It chirped to life, displaying its various functions.

Standard fare, she thought as she cycled through the options. She could communicate with other crew members, watch vids, study ship specs, or choose from a variety of static images to bring some personalized décor to the room. With another touch she selected the mirror function, and watched as her own face leapt into view. She knew she was exhausted, that she must look awful, but the girl in the screen looked so sad, so deflated, in such stark contrast to her buoyant excitement earlier that day, that she nearly burst into tears. Purple lines sagged under her eyes, her skin waxen and gray in the dim light, her hair an unkempt, mousy brown, but the worst was the disappointment in her rounded shoulders, her drooping chin, her flat gaze.

You're on a starship! she cried silently, forcing herself to push her shoulders back, thinking of her father. This was what she had dreamed of since childhood, what she had always wanted and worked for. Seizing her hat from the wall hook where she'd left it, with every intention of putting it on and trying to recapture the magic from her family's living room, all she could see was the corner where the hat had been crushed during her encounter with Lamb. It was too much to bear. She threw down the hat, turned off the screen, and sat on the bed, ready to give in and weep.

No.

Her small mouth screwed up in a defiant scowl, her smooth brow knitted with anger, mostly at herself. At her sides her hands clenched fistfuls of thick gray blanket.

No.

She was a Worth, a daughter of the Royal Navy, a commissioned officer of the King, and she would damn well not crawl under the covers and cry over a damaged hat. With a sudden fervor, she opened her bag and searched through the contents until she found what she was looking for. *Didn't think I'd need this on the first night.* Opening the small black folding case, she set about working to repair the hat. The kit included a card-sized instruction pad, and she consulted it carefully, mimicking the movements shown, fighting through the clumsiness of fingers new to the task and the fog of fatigue. *If I can just make this right…*

The morning came early, and yet the chime of her alarm found Worth already awake. She had slept without dreams, at least none she could recall, and despite the short hours, felt rested. Her eyes were drawn to that cockaded hat, hanging on its hook. Perhaps not as crisp as it had been once, but it was more than serviceable. Like the *Harvest* herself…not perfect, but a start.

It was not long before she was up and dressed, in the snug gray pants, white shirt, and blue jacket that was the midshipman's working uniform. In the closet of her quarters hung the dress blues from the night before, and Worth vowed to store her disappointments there as well. *The bottom rung is just the first one*, she thought as she made her way down the short corridor to the common mess. It was a narrow room, with polymer aluminum tables, benches that folded down from the walls attached. At the far end was the dispenser array, fully automated. Once, she knew, there had been cooking staffs on board ships, working around the clock to prepare meals for their crew. In antiquity, in the era of sailing ships on the open ocean, there had been actual fires in the galley, which made her shudder. What it must have been like, surrounded by dry wood and pitch and canvas, knowing that the slightest inattention or mishap could lead to an all-consuming inferno.

There were no fires on the *Harvest*, just the usual range of selections that the nutri-computer would process and deliver, currently set to the breakfast assortment. Worth punched in the code for toast and coffee. She had never been much of a morning eater, and wasn't sure her stomach could handle anything heavier on this particular morning. Despite her newfound resolve from the night before, she remained nervous, with a persistent fluttering just behind her navel. In less than two minutes a slot opened and a tray emerged with her toast, just the right amount of black, and a steaming mug of coffee. She cupped a hand on the drink and felt its warmth. It was chilly on the ship.

"Cold?" The voice startled her, but she managed not to spill her coffee. It was Saul Lamb, the able-bodied starman who had bumped into her the day before. He was in a plain white short-sleeved shirt, tight across his chest, and brown working-pants. He wasn't smiling, but neither did he seem unfriendly. His black hair was clean and neatly combed, though his cheeks were dark with new growth.

"A bit," Worth replied. "They warn you at Greenwich about the temperature on board, but I never really thought about it until now."

"Colder on the other side of the hull," he grunted. "Excuse me, sir." He had moved to within a foot of her, and Worth realized she was blocking his access to the dispenser.

"Oh. Sorry." She scooted out of the way, and Lamb spent the next few moments silently obtaining his breakfast, which turned out to be a single banana. He peeled it deftly, looking vaguely simian with his long arms and unshaven jaw. He took a big bite, and scowled.

"I had a real one once," he said thickly, his mouth full of the yellow fruit. "They still grow them on Ganymede, in them big greenhouses. Fruit for the nobles, you know. Like as can't get them here on Earth." He shoved the rest of the banana in his mouth, as if he couldn't finish it fast enough. "Anyway, that was with Strickland, a right old bastard but a good captain, merchant service and all." He finally swallowed, sparing Worth the ongoing spectacle of him talking while he chewed, his mouth wide open. "Made some money with him, we did. And he gave us bananas at Ganymede, for work done right." His laugh was a bark, moist and mirthless. "Thought he was doing us a favor, old Strickland. All he done was ruin bananas for us. After the real thing, these synthetics are like insulator caulking."

"Then why do you eat them?" Worth had no idea why he was telling her this story. For some reason, this familiarity was more unsettling than his surliness the night before.

"To remind me who and what I am." He shrugged, and stared at her in a way that chilled her to the core. It was a look that saw not her rank but her body, stripped of its clothes, suddenly naked before the appraising gaze of a man who generally took the things he wanted. "And in case I ever get my hands on another real banana, I'll be able to appreciate it proper." He leaned in close to her, and she shied away, keeping her tray between them, but he just dropped the empty peel in the recycler behind her. Saying no more, Lamb turned and walked toward the exit, stretching his hands high above his head, the bones in his back and arms cracking with the morning. When he reached the door, the crewman turned around briefly.

"By the way, since it was late last night when you and the other lady came on board…"

"Hall," she blurted. "Midshipman *Charles* Hall." She tried to put an emphasis on his rank and his first name, but her voice cracked midway through.

"Hmph. Could have sworn you was both girls. My mistake. At any rate, it was late, so we put off the wetting 'til Friday night."

"Wetting?"

"Seems there's some other things they left out at Greenwich. If it's a surprise, well, then I won't spoil it. Friday night. Sir." And he was gone.

What was that about? Worth had lost her appetite for toast, for anything, but she ate it anyway, mechanically, dutifully. Others had begun to trickle into the galley, singly or in pairs, touching their foreheads with a knuckle in casual salute to the low-ranking officer in their mess. She recognized Quintal from the night before, and a few of the others Pott had pointed out during the orientation. Before long the room was almost full, with ten or so men and women sitting at the tables, eating oatmeal or sausage and eggs or simply having their coffee. None of them spoke to her, absorbed in their morning routines or speaking together in low voices. It was as though she did not exist at all, and it was the loneliest moment she had ever known.

"Hey."

She hadn't seen Charles Hall come in with the others, but there he was, next to her. Again, as on the viewing platform the night before, he had materialized seemingly out of nowhere, without so much as a sound. *How does he do that?* He was wearing the same duty uniform she was, though it seemed overlarge on his thin frame, as though he wore his older brother's castoffs. In one hand he held an egg sandwich, and in the other a cup of what seemed to be –

"Milk," he said, when he saw her looking at it. He took a sip, and shrugged. "What can I say, I like it. I know they'll make fun of me for it. They sure did at Greenwich."

"How is it I didn't know you there?" she asked. Hall laughed, just a little.

"Don't feel bad, Hope. Nobody did, not really. I sort of…kept to myself, is all. Not everybody can be Sam Worth's daughter." She felt the tips of her ears start to burn, and her face must have given away her annoyance, because Hall held up his milk defensively in front of him. "Come on, you can't say you didn't know you were sort of famous. Your father wasn't just a starship captain, he was one of *those* captains. The ones we all read about, the ones who made us want to go to space ourselves. Baker, Li Ying, Ingram, Worth."

"Maybe that's why I was so popular," she said, her voice dripping with sarcasm. *Was he crazy?* She had barely had any friends at all during her time at Greenwich, not quite fitting in anywhere. Her grades were fine, but not strong enough to be one of the academic elite. She certainly was never one of the social butterflies, and could count her dates on one hand.

"We were intimidated." Hall nibbled at his sandwich. "You never talked to anyone, so I think everyone just figured you were full of yourself because of your father."

"Great." *Great.* "So all that time I was being shy, everyone thought I was stuck up." She sighed. Eager to change the subject, she said, "You know so much, what's a wetting? That crewman, Lamb, was talking about it."

"A wedding? Like with a bride and groom?"

"No, dummy. A wet-ting. TT, not DD."

"I know, dummy, I was making fun of you." He smiled, that same crooked-tooth smile from when they had first met. "From what I understand, it's a kind of party, celebrating newly commissioned officers. I guess they can get pretty wild."

A chime rang, signaling the start of the first watch and the onset of the *Harvest*'s dockyard workday. Worth reported to Lieutenant Pott on the quarterdeck along with Hall, and was given her work schedule. It was daunting, even for graduates of Greenwich, with its famously rigorous standards. For ten hours a day they would supervise crews of starmen inspecting, repairing, cleaning, and upgrading the *Harvest*. Supervising, she swiftly discovered, was an extremely fluid term. By dinnertime each night her hands were black with grime, her clothes saturated with sweat, and her muscles sore with exertion.

"It's not just the refit work," Pott told them. "It's the intimate knowledge you have to have of every task on board this vessel. You can't order a jack to reef if you don't know how to do it yourself. More importantly, they have to know you have some idea what the hell you're talking about, or they'll never respect you." Worth was no stranger to labor. *Hard work will never betray you* had always been another of Captain Worth's favorite little sayings, and even without that prod she would still have been industrious at Greenwich. She had needed to be, to keep up with the coursework, and there had been little enough in the way of social distraction to fill up her scant free time. Of course, the day's efforts were only part of what Pott had in store. Each morning, after breakfast, he confronted the midshipmen with a battery of questions, an hour-long in-depth oral examination on some aspect of the ship's functioning covering anything from the stress tolerances on the deep-space drives to the interstellar communication system to the sewage disposal process. Worth found herself immersed each night in technical manuals, sitting in the mess with Hall for hours at a time, a pot of coffee steaming between them, as they quizzed one another on topics Pott had hinted he might cover the next morning.

She spent so much time with Hall, seizing mealtimes and after hours to study, that it was widely assumed among the crew that they were a romantic item, though described in far less polite terms. The ables had taken to calling them Rita and Nex, after a popular kidvid. It wasn't endearing, or a compliment. In the series, Rita was a young, vaguely feline, overtly sexual space explorer and Nex was the idiotic sidekick who drooled after her throughout the galaxy. Worth tried to ignore the jibes, pretending not to hear them. *Keep your head down, keep working*, she told herself. If they see that it doesn't bother you, they'll stop.

The regimen, and the juvenile taunts, were exhausting, especially in those first days on board, and Worth all but forgot about Friday night until Friday night came.

****

It would be good to be back in space.

Commander William Pearce sat in the center chair on the quarterdeck, imagining the day soon to come, when distant stars would slip past on the viewscreen, a concert of white waves. He had sat in the chair many times on duty in the *Drake*, but that had been Baker's ship. Even limping home from Cygnus, under the command of a stunned Jasper Clark, it had been Baker's ship, her ghost looming everywhere, especially the quarterdeck. Now, the *Harvest* was his ship.

Britannia had been his, too, but there was a parsec of difference between a private commercial ship and one flying the colors of His Majesty's Royal Navy. Ugly and unlovable as she may be, the *Harvest* was his ship, and not only by virtue of his commission. In the month following the dinner at Lord Banks' house, Pearce had virtually lived on board, only leaving for brief, infrequent visits home. There had been more refit work to do than time to do it in. *Harvest* came to him with a long history as a tender vessel, supplying materiel to the Kingdom's military exploits in the Parnham cluster, and she showed both her age and hard use. She really could benefit from a complete overhaul, but there wasn't that kind of time. So they had done the best they could do, and he had ordered the Royal Navy's motto displayed prominently on the quarterdeck: *Per Ardua Ad Astra* – Through Adversity to the Stars. More than once he had thought the motto of the King's Own Tactical Wing, the personal pilots to the Royal Family, might be more appropriate: *Per Diem, Per Noctum* – By Day and By Night. Pearce had scarcely slept in weeks.

He had not been alone, at least. Upon assuming command of the *Harvest*, Pearce had met Lieutenant John Pott, the man assigned by the

Admiralty to serve as his third-in command. He had not known him then, except by vague reputation, but in the days since, he had gotten to know the garrulous officer better, and to like him better. Pott proved competent and experienced, seeming to share many of Pearce's opinions about the management of a starship, and he steadily became the captain's strong right hand in the long struggle to get the *Harvest* ready for the stars. He was a Navy lifer, one who had spent a long time as a midshipman before advancing to Lieutenant, and who had been a Lieutenant now for almost as long. The service was full of these sorts of officers, men and women without powerful friends or family name, who would never advance to that first epaulette and were destined to eventually serve under commanding officers younger than they were. Pearce was not without sympathy. It was what his career would have resembled, had he stayed in the service. It was only this one purest chance that catapulted him into the center chair.

It was a chance he did not intend to squander.

So, they had worked through the weeks, bullying the tired old ship into a semblance of health. The gravity sails had to be completely replaced, tattered and useless as they were. When fully deployed, the sails covered more than 250,000 square kilometers, more than the entire surface area of the old British Isles, and yet none of it was more than ten centimeters thick. A polymer of crystalline aluminum, it contained over five hundred trillion microscopic absorbent particles that soaked up gravitic energy and conducted it along a network of slender conduits to the masts, and thence to the main drives. It had been a triumphant technology when first unveiled decades before, reliable for deep-space travel, able to manipulate the gravity fields between star systems to propel the craft faster than light. The problem with the sails was their complexity and internal systemic reliance. If one segment failed or sustained damage, the entire network could break down. And with the size of the sails, it was not unlikely for them to frequently encounter debris in space – asteroids, small comets – that could cause damage. Consequently, a great deal of time was spent on maintenance and repairs during long voyages.   That, and gravity, posed some of the greatest challenges.

While everywhere in the cosmos, gravity was not everywhere in equal strength. Pockets existed of near-zero-grav, whole empty parsecs all but devoid of the pull of faraway stars, where a ship reliant on gravity drives could be becalmed. Many of these were marked on the star-charts, especially on the more travelled tracks Pearce intended to use, but the galaxy had a way of changing, of making fools of even the most painstaking star-mariners.

In the case of the sails, Lord Exeter was as good as his word, and somehow the Admiralty found new sheets for the *Harvest*, as well as top-line conversion engines to replace the aging ones already on board. The gathering of a crew was less simple. Pott was a godsend, and Peckover, the boatswain, came highly recommended. Pearce also managed to recruit Arash el-Barzin, the crewman who had saved his life on Cygnus all those years before, as well as another seasoned jack, Gordan Rowland. The midshipmen, Worth and Hall, straight out of Greenwich, were young and untried, but willing. Beyond that, the ranks of petty officers and able starmen were filled from the shore roster, and though most seemed competent enough, too many were discipline cases left behind by captains with the time and seniority to be more selective.

We're saving the world, Pearce thought as he repeatedly exercised a crew of grumpy starmen too slow in setting and furling the shrouds. *And we're doing it with the dregs of the service.* "Again," he shouted, ignoring the dark looks from the sweaty ables. "Faster!"

"Come on, lads," cried el-Barzin. "Captain wants it under five minutes, he gets it under five minutes!"

"The sheets deploy automatic-like," growled Isaac Pratt, monstrous in both size and temperament, leaning on the long steel-shafted mast. "Why break us on it when they can do it just as easy with a button, from up top?"

"Shut your mouth, Pratt," yelled Rowland from a few feet away.

"You going to shut it for me?" Pratt asked. "Not alone, you ain't."

"You think I'm the only one here wants it shut?" Rowland retorted, and several of the other ables laughed, though not the ones nearest Pratt. Rowland was funny, and the others liked him, but most of them were less amused by him than afraid of Pratt.

"Enough," bellowed Pearce. "You think this is mindless exercise? You think I would do this for no reason?" The captain moved closer to Pratt. He was easily a third of a meter shorter than the crewman, but he walked straight at him, his jaw working side to side in a building rage. Pearce was no stranger to the sometime brutality of the belowdecks. As a young midshipman, he had messed with the ables, and knew that there were fine men and women among them in mixture with thugs and bullies. Pearce himself was not gently born, but there were degrees of common, and Pratt was the commonest creature he had yet encountered. Savage, cruel, brimming with some rage that he nursed with twisted pride.

"Yes, the sails deploy automatically," he went on. "Unless the systems fail. Unless something breaks or jams or catches. And if, during this voyage, our lives ever depend on getting those sails in or out fast, without the help of the computer, I'll be damned if I die out there because your lazy ass isn't up to it!" He was yelling now, scant inches away from Pratt, his nose below the able's chin, but the larger man still shrank back a bit from his commander. There was a pounding in Pearce's head, a red throb between his temples. It was utterly quiet in the sailroom, every eye locked on the captain and Pratt.

They don't know the stakes, Pearce thought. *And most of them are too dumb to understand even if they did know.* He knew he had been right to dress down Pratt, but now he needed to reel it back in. *Chastisement and praise, a captain's tools for a working ship.*

"Come on, then," he said, in as close to a normal voice as he could manage. "Strong lad like you, afraid of a little sweat? Show these boys how you heave. Get it under five minutes twice in a row and there're extra drink rations in the galley tonight. Again!" A cheer went up from the crew, even Pratt, and Pearce silently hoped that he was effectively walking that thin line between martinet and patsy. A captain had to be strong and respected, even feared a little, but not hated. Nor could he be a friend and confidant. That was why he had recruited Christine Fletcher, with her magic touch. Not only was she a hell of a pilot and a resourceful flight engineer, she was to be his go-between, his conduit to the hearts and minds of the crew. But where the hell was she? The *Harvest* was due to sail in less than a week, and she hadn't yet reported. *She will*, he thought. *She has to.*

****

She had ridden these ferries countless times, and never thought much of it. A quick adjustment to her neuro-mix, and she would barely notice the long minutes slipping past. This time, the mélange of images and sounds tailored to the unique pleasure centers in her brain failed to entertain, sedate, or even distract her. For the first time she could recall in her young life, Christine Fletcher was nervous. Even in her days as a sprinter, the jitters at the starting line had been thrilling, not frightening.

Not nervous, excited, she tried to convince herself, without much success. Face against the thick viewplate in the elderly shuttle's hull, she tried to catch a glimpse of the docked *Harvest*, but the angle of approach was wrong, and all she could see through the tiny rectangular window was the bulky infrastructure of the Spithead yards, and stars beyond. It hardly mattered that she couldn't see the ship. Bill had told her it was very like their old *Britannia*, so she could readily imagine it, fat and jolly and comfortable.

Not Bill, she chided herself. *Captain Pearce*. Though she had called him that for years during their commercial voyages, there was something different and peculiar in the word now. It wasn't even his formal title; he was a commander, a step below a full post-captain, but while in command of one of His Majesty's ships, he warranted the honorific of Captain. The uniform she wore, seemingly designed for maximum discomfort, was strange, too. The white shirt was crisp and stiff and itched, and the blue jacket hung heavy and hot, with a collar so high it scratched her neck. The yellow Lieutenant's stripes on the sleeves stared at her, reminding her of the choice she'd made, and even now, after weeks of indecision, she couldn't say whether she had made it out of loyalty, friendship, curiosity, or boredom.

After an interminable wait, the ferry finally docked at the orbital station, and Fletcher gathered up her shoulder duffel and officer's hat. Naval tradition had long ago settled that starships were indoors and hats were not to be worn, and orbital platforms and dockyards were likewise to be considered indoors for protocol purposes. Fletcher was grateful. When she wore it, she felt like nothing so much as a little girl playing at dress-up, or a partygoer at a masquerade.

This was a side of Spithead Fletcher didn't know. Merchant traffic came and went on the other side of the dockyards, Piers 21 through 40. The corridors followed the same rough layout over here, though it was hard not to notice that some doors were closed and obviously secured, emblazoned with red security warnings. As men and women in gray worksuits passed by, they touched their foreheads in a deferential salute.

I outrank them, she realized. Half their lives in the Royal Navy, some of them, and she was their superior officer even as she took her first steps into their world. It wasn't that she was unaccustomed to superiority; she had grown up as a child of nobility. A lower rung of nobility, to be sure, her grandfather's baronetcy a far cry from an earl like Banks or a duke, yet even a middling aristocrat might as well be a god to any commoner. But she had been raised to treat everyone, if not as equals, at least as human beings. She knew plenty of others who didn't share that sentiment, neighbors and relatives and friends of the family who regarded the teeming commons as either unthinking and unfeeling automata to be ignored, or else wild, unrestrained animals to be avoided.

Her grandfather would have none of it. "Girls," he would tell Fletcher and her sister, "the day you think a shred of land and an old piece of paper from a long-dead king make you a better person than this man or that woman, you make sure to tell me so I can knock that fool idea out of your head." *Papi doesn't act noble,* thought Fletcher, *he is noble,* and there was a difference.

When she arrived at Pier 12B, it was quieter than she expected. In her years working with Bill – Captain Pearce – the week before launch was always a riot of activity and bustle, last-minute loading and repairs. But now, only five days before launch, in the heart of the afternoon watch, the warehouse adjacent to the *Harvest* gangway was virtually empty, with neither hurrying crew nor gear awaiting their hands. One solitary figure, eyes closed, sat on an overturned storage bin and leaned against the wall. He wore one of those worksuits identifying him as an able starman, the gray sleeves rolled up over thickly-muscled arms, the top partially unzipped, exposing a white shirt beneath. There were dark smudges on both the uniform and the face, signs of a morning's labor. He was handsome, in a rough and common sort of way.

Fletcher hesitated, staring for a moment. The *Harvest's* complement was so modest that shore watch was shared out between officers and crew. This was clearly the sentry, and just as clearly, he was asleep. Should she scold him? On a merchant ship, as long as the duty didn't involve guarding some precious cargo, she would have nudged him awake, made a joke of it and warned the crewman how lucky it was she and not the captain had found him. But she was now second in command of one of His Majesty's royal vessels, and she had thoroughly read the King's Regulations and Admiralty Instructions that Pearce had sent her. Sleeping on duty was a significant offense in the Navy.

"Well?" The voice was a low rasp, drifting quietly and low from the motionless starman. His dark eyes were open, little more than a sliver, but he was watching her with them. "You gonna stand there all day, or yell at me proper?" He raised a slow, lazy arm and touched a knuckle to his black hair. "Sir."

Saul Lamb, thought Fletcher. She had read the manifest, knew the likeness and reputation and personal history of each of the crew. Born into near-abject poverty in the Scots District, Lamb had been to space often enough, on merchant ships when he could, on Navy ships when pressed. His disciplinary file was long and varied, but somehow he had always managed to avoid real trouble, and stay employed because he was a skilled jack. She knew the type. *Fancies himself a wit, but will throw hands as readily as words.* Best to dose him with his own medicine.

"Yell?" she raised an eyebrow and frowned. "You going to give me a reason to yell, Lamb? Is being ugly against the King's Regs now?" Lamb's laugh was a coarse bark, and it erupted from him in a short burst, almost as if it surprised him. He stood up, smiled crookedly, and bowed slightly from the waist, touching his hairline again, with greater ceremony.

"Able Starman Saul Lamb," he said.

"Lieutenant Christine Fletcher," she replied, nodding at the salute, and she smiled back, just a little, just enough. "Sleep on your own time, Lamb. Next time it could be Captain Pearce who finds you, or me in a less forgiving mood."

"Weren't sleepin'," he said, sitting back down and putting his hands behind his head. "Though I could use it. We all could, the way we been workin'." He leaned back again, closing his eyes. "Welcome to the *Harvest*, Lieutenant. Pearce been waitin' on you."

"That's Captain Pearce," she said, adjusting the strap of her bag on her shoulder. She was getting anxious to be aboard, but she knew from his file that Lamb was the kind of jack likely to have influence among the rest of the crew, and it was important to build a rapport with him from the beginning. "And I'm glad to hear you've been hard at it. A ship runs best when we all work. I'll see you aboard." Turning on her heel, she walked to the circular mouth of the round polymer gangway, sensing his eyes watching her go. He'd hardly be the first to desire her, she knew, and hardly the first to underestimate her for it.

Fletcher navigated the gangway with practiced ease, and when she stepped onto the dull-gray plate of the *Harvest*'s floor, it felt a little like coming home. *He'll be on the quarterdeck*, she thought, and wound her way through the dark, quiet guts of the ship, so similar to the *Britannia*, up the command fin to the bridge. The doors of the lift opened with a smooth hiss, smelling of benzene. *Newly repaired*, she figured. God only knew how much work Bill had done getting the old bird ready to fly. Stepping out into the snug quarterdeck, she saw a man and woman she did not know leaning against the center console, and under that, a pair of short legs in working-officer trousers.

"Try her again," came a muffled, yet familiar voice from beneath the station. The woman, a young redhead, a girl really, tapped a sequence on the board, which chirped merrily for a moment before breaking into a sustained wail. "Stop! Stop!" cried the voice, and Fletcher laughed out loud as the girl scrambled to shut down the malfunctioning system.

"You never could fix a balky nav relay," Fletcher said into the subsequent silence. Two heads swiveled to look her way, and a sudden loud bang came from below.

"Damn!" Captain Pearce roared, emerging from the access port, rubbing his reddening forehead where he had struck it sitting up in surprise. He stared a moment, as if disbelieving. "Good of you to come,

Lieutenant." Fletcher could hear the word *finally*, unsaid but only just. Pointing to the other officers, he made swift introductions. "Lieutenant John Pott, Midshipman Hope Worth, this is Lieutenant Christine Fletcher, second in command of the *Harvest*. If we ever get the bloody beast out of spacedock." Fletcher smiled at her shipmates by way of greeting, and Pott nodded in return, while Worth snapped a swift salute. It was all Fletcher could do not to giggle, the poor girl was so painfully earnest. Instead, she returned the gesture and turned her attention to Pearce.

"Reporting for duty, sir." Before he could respond, she glanced over his shoulder, dropping her bag to the deck and removing her jacket, which she tossed onto the command chair. "Permission to come aboard. Nav console giving you grief?"

Now Pearce was the one to grin. "Granted! Nobody knows their way around these relays like Fletcher," he said, leaning toward Pott. "Once, she won a bet in the New Indies by disconnecting and reconnecting all eleven in sixty seconds."

"Fifty-four," she said. "And after drinking seven Spinning Nebulas, too. Lightened that poor blighter's wallet a fair piece that night." She could see Pott's eyebrows raise, but the story was true. *Mostly true*. She did shave a second off the time every year.

Pearce indicated the console. "She's all yours. Mister Worth, please convey Lieutenant Fletcher's baggage to her quarters." Placing a hand on her shoulder, he leaned in close. "It is good to have you aboard," he murmured. "Thank you." Then he was gone, the young midshipman trailing behind with Fletcher's things.

"Go back a bit with the captain, do you," asked Pott, after the doors slid shut, in an unmistakable Australian twang. Fletcher glanced at him sidelong as she began examining the faulty panel. He was scruffy, with salt-and-pepper bristles around his jaw. Not unhandsome, he projected a kind of rough competence, and was probably fifteen years her elder. And after weeks during which he'd been second only to Pearce, she was now his senior officer.

"A bit," she replied carefully, sitting on the floor and shining a handlight into the dangling electronic guts under the unit. "We made a few trading runs together these past few years."

"Merchant marine," he said flatly. "And this is your first cruise in one of His Majesty's ships?" She set down the handlight with a sharp clang.

"Look, Pott, is it? I'm new to your Navy. We both know that. But I'm here because the captain wants me here, which means the Admiralty wants me here, which means the King wants me here. Otherwise I wouldn't have the damn commission in my pocket or the damn stripes on my sleeve. If that bothers you, I'm happy to hear all about it over a drink in the mess later, my treat. But right now, I'm going to fix these relays. You can help me, or I can kick your ass and then you'll help me. Up to you." She finished and there was a long pause, during which she wondered if he would challenge her, walk away, or stand there like an idiot.

"Sixty seconds?" he finally asked.

"Fifty-four."

"Seven Spinners?"

"Maybe eight. Didn't want the old man thinking I'm a drunk."

Finally, Pott laughed, a rolling, thundering laugh.

"You might be all right, Fletcher. And if you can fix this console, those drinks will be on me."

Six

Ignition

"No books tonight."

Taryn Hadley sat down across from Worth in the mess, nudging Hall down the bench with her hip and shoulder. Worth sort of liked Hadley. She was one of the two female ables, and you could talk to her, which was more than could be said of Peggy Briggs. Briggs, eating her dinner at another table with Saul Lamb and some of the rougher crewmen, was big and scary and almost never spoke. Hadley wasn't big, wasn't scary, and never shut up. Worth knew the men found her sexy; she had even noticed Hall looking at her. She understood why. The woman was built like a holovid model, fleshy or flat in all the right spots. It was a fact she clearly relished, wearing working-uniforms at least two sizes too small. Hadley was always friendly, but now she was even more so, and Worth noticed the cup in her hand and smelled what was in it. *The wetting*, she remembered.

She knew that most ables liked their liquor. It was an ancient naval tradition, dating back centuries to a time when ship's crews had been half-drunk more often than not, and regarded their rum rations as a God-given right. More than one commander had cut those rations or eliminated them altogether, to his eventual regret. Some things had changed in His Majesty's Royal Navy in the long years since Nelson or Anson strode their wooden decks, and some had not. There were still rum rations, though not nearly as stupefyingly generous as before, and never served to sailors then expected to work the ship. The crew still jealously guarded their drink, a welcome source of good cheer on long star voyages.

Glancing about, Worth noticed that the mess was mostly full. The chiseled, terrifying Briggs had left, nor did she see the quiet Xi Xiang; they must have been on duty. But Isaac Pratt was there, huge and brooding, manfully ignoring whatever it was Tom Churchill was blathering at him. Cheeks already ruddy with drink, Churchill was universally disdained by the others, though seemingly ignorant of it. He worked less and less competently, and talked more and more stupidly than any of them, and at the moment, he was waving his cup in broad arcs to punctuate some story, blissfully unaware that Pratt was edging closer to annoyance. *I would never want to annoy that man*, she thought of Pratt.

The short, swarthy Latino, Mathias Quintal, was there, too, chatting amiably with Saul Lamb by the beverage dispenser. Lamb had shaved, she noticed, and was wearing a clean shirt. There was something bizarrely magnetic about Lamb, though whether it was despite his air of barely controlled violence or because of it, she couldn't say. He must have felt her stare, because he turned his head and smiled at her, a tooth-filled smile, and she looked hurriedly away, reddening. She forced herself to look at another table, where the two older ables were seated, cups at their elbows, playing a game of hologram chess. The board and pieces, fragments of blue and red light, hovered over the table between Arash el-Barzin and Gordan Rowland. Rowland was almost fatherly, his face lined and kind, graying at the temples and with a slight paunch around his midsection. He was married with a little girl, Worth knew from her review of the manifest, and had always been unfailingly pleasant to her when they shared duty. El-Barzin was even older than Rowland, who was at least forty, but he didn't look it. Taut and slender, a coiled spring of muscle and endless deep-space experience, he was the captain of the jacks, their clear leader, though he rarely made a point of it. Other than Lieutenant Pott, it was el-Barzin who had taught Worth and Hall the most, over the course of their pre-launch work and training. The man seemed to know every seam and bolt of the *Harvest* intimately, almost effortlessly. Once, Worth had remarked something to that effect, and el-Barzin had laughed. "When you've had as many years in space as I have, sir, you'll know just as much."

"Hey," Hadley was saying, "are you here to stare at the old men, or to have some fun? Lamb!" she called. "Quintal! We need some refreshment for our officers here." The two ables looked over from their conversation, and both grinned. Lamb's smile was still wolfish, unsettling, but Quintal's was more of a smirk, a slanted line across his inscrutable face.

"Of course," Quintal said, and he deftly extracted two rations from the dispenser. The cups were clear, hard plasteen, tinted vaguely blue, and the brownish hue of the drink showed through muddy and dark. When Worth took hers, it was warm to the touch. Quintal's face was close to hers, and she could smell that he had begun some time earlier. "Grog," he said, "is best served hot." He clinked her cup with his own, and watched expectantly.

Worth stared at it for a moment. She knew about liquor, of course. She was young, but not a child. Her father had been no stranger to alcohol, frequently hosting gatherings while ashore, the apartment full of fellow-officers and other luminaries, the rum, wine and other spirits always integral guests. She had seen Captain Worth with glass in hand many times, but she had never seen him approach the level of drunkenness his friends often achieved.

"Control, Hope," he would tell her when she was old enough to make an appearance at the levees. "It is sociable to be convivial, but always stay in control. Look." He would point at some old shipmate, in advanced lubrication, inevitably slouched in a chair, or storytelling in a too-loud, too-slurred voice, or tottering about, in danger of crashing into other guests, or the furniture, or the floor. "You're a fool if you let the booze master you. Don't be a fool, Hope."

This advice, as had so much of her father's, stayed with Worth when she went to Greenwich, and she made it a point never to drink more than a single cup at any time. It contributed to her reputation as a standoffish prude, and after a few months she would be invited to only the most inclusive parties, which reduced her need to exercise control.

Just the one, then, she thought, and sipped, somewhat more daintily than she intended, at the cup. It was indeed grog, descended from the ancestral Navy drink, hot rum mixed with water and lemon.

"It's Her Majesty the Queen!" mocked Quintal, with that lopsided smirk, and they laughed at her. Her first instinct was to blush and withdraw, but she forced herself not to. Instead she inclined her head, raised her free hand in a regally dismissive wave, and the laughter swelled. Something relaxed within her chest. *They're just people,* she thought. Not so different from her, even with their rougher talk and manners. They liked to laugh, to eat and drink and love, and she resolved then to give them no reason to hate her.

The evening progressed, drink and music flowing together with talk of old cruises and shipmates.

"I shipped with your father," Rowland told her, "twice. A great captain, your old man. There's those of us who would have reefed for him into the heart of a star if he'd ordered. Had a way with a ship and a crew, like…like a musician, I suppose. Couldn't never put your finger on it, but you knew everything would be all right with Captain Worth on deck. Wasn't no gladhander, a tight ship and all, but always fair to the jacks."

"Where's he, then?" asked Pratt in a growl. "Who's this Pearce, anyway? A right tin tyrant, ain't he?"

"You're as stupid as you are ugly," called el-Barzin from the next table, where he and Lamb were at cards. From the darkening look on Lamb's face, the older crewman was having the better luck. El-Barzin fixed his eyes on his huge crewmate. "Stow your salt-talk, Pratt, I won't have it."

"Oh, he won't have it," put in Lamb, voice thick with drink, flinging his cards on the table. "You an officer, then, Arash? You want to lord it about over the commons like Pearce?"

"I said stow it." El-Barzin's voice grew low and dangerous. "First, that's Captain Pearce, you bloody fool. There's officers on deck. Young, aye, but officers still. Second, the man's a right cracking officer, I should know. And third, he's no more lordly than any of us. From common stock, he is. Born as low as you or me, but he worked with his mind as much as his back, and up he climbed. I don't begrudge the man his success."

"You'd never know he was common," Lamb spat while Pratt scowled in silence, trembling slightly as though in barely restrained violence. *There's no way he's afraid of el-Barzin*, Worth thought. Something, though, was holding all that rage back, if only just. Afraid of punishment? *Or afraid of what he might do?* "Not like Fletcher. Damn." Lamb shook his head. "She's noble-born, but don't act like it, and he ain't but acts like he is. The way he barks at us ables. Busts us proper, don't he?"

"You talk like you ain't never shipped before," Rowland said. "Like this is some joy cruise to Io. That woman come on just yesterday, and already you're talking like you know her. Just 'cause she's pretty and smiles at you don't mean she ain't an officer. Watch your step, boy." He'd had his share of grog, as had el-Barzin and the others, but while the edges of the room had taken on a rosy glow for Worth, and her belly was warm and her head fuzzy, the two older starmen seemed no different than when the night had begun. *Old hands*, she thought, *with old bellies*, and for some reason that made her giggle, the sound bubbling out of her before she could stop it.

Lamb stared at her, and she could feel Hadley's gaze as well, though Pratt's eyes were still fixed on his drink. Quintal lurked in his own thoughts as always, while Churchill sat, glassy-eyed and slack-jawed, drunk.

"Think that's funny, yeah?" Lamb asked. "Him calling me boy? You got a low opinion of the jacks, just like Pearce and your pop, too, I'll bet, no matter what this old man says. Just another too-good, too-high, too-mighty damned officer, looking down her nose at the dumb brutes below."

"N-no," she stammered, cheeks burning, horrified and humiliated. "I just…"

"Oh, leave her be," Hadley said, resting a hand on Lamb's burly arm. "Girls giggle, man, I should know. Especially when the drink is in. Leave it." Worth could have hugged her, but Lamb still glowered. Like the seasoned sailor she was, Hadley changed her tack. "Dance with me," she chirped, taking Lamb by the hand and tugging him away. "Music!" she cried, and Quintal obliged, tapping at the vidpanel until a popular song drifted from the speakers set in the wall. Hadley pulled Lamb close, framing her hips against his, guiding his hands lower and lower down her gently curving back.

"Are you all right?" Hall was beside her, a cup of his own in his hand, though his clear eyes said he'd had less than the others. Worth nodded, almost absently, glad he was there but still unable to ignore the weight and heat of Lamb's stare, a brutal beam that wouldn't release her even as his hands roamed Hadley's lush, ever-willing body.

"You be careful, sir." It was Rowland, still seated next to her, his voice breaking the spell of Lamb's eyes. Rowland pointed at Pratt. "He's a rugged one, there, strong like a Machrine, but hot and cold, and I think there's even a conscience in there sometimes, struggling to stay on top. But that one," he nodded at Lamb, "that's a right vicious bugger, that is. You be strong and you be smart, and don't you ever be afraid, or he'll smell it on you, like a reek."

Worth felt herself lifted from her seat, forcibly, yanked to her feet like a child. Lamb had dumped Hadley in Pratt's broad lap, with rough unceremony, and now he was enveloping Worth with those strong, hairy arms.

"Come on, give us a dance, *sir*," he hissed mockingly, his breath hot and moist in her ear. "Not a bad little piece, are you? Probably never had a man in you, either. At least," his eyes flicked toward Hall, "not a real one, at any rate." He held her by the waist with one arm, his free hand on her breasts, groping, pinching, and whether it was the grog, or the giving way of some wall of patience and fear within her, Worth punched him. Hard, in the face, not a girlish slap but a closed-fist blow with all the might her small frame could put behind it. Lamb released her, staggering back a pace, momentary shock yielding to a slow-burning wrath, one cheek bearing a red welt. The room was suddenly and deathly quiet, except for the strains of Quintal's music, still streaming from the wall in misplaced merriment.

"You little bitch," Lamb snarled, and raised a hand to swat her down. Somehow, Charles Hall was between them first, and Lamb's heavy fist connected with him instead of her, knocking the midshipman heavily to the deck. Worth screamed despite herself, while Rowland and el-Barzin seized Lamb by the arms, dragging him bodily against the wall and holding him there, against his enraged struggles. *They're stronger than they look*, she thought vaguely, but so was Lamb, who looked strong enough to begin with, and threatened to break free from their grip. She wanted nothing more than to kneel, to check on Hall, lying and groaning on the floor, but she couldn't. Not yet. She glanced over her shoulder at Pratt, at Churchill, at Hadley, and at Quintal, standing at the dispensers, calmly refilling his drink, that self-satisfied little grin still on his face. *What would they do?* Would they come to Lamb's aid, or Rowland and el-Barzin's? Or would they stand fast?

"Knock it off, Lamb," demanded el-Barzin, straining to keep his hold on the man. "Striking an officer? You want the lash?" Lamb continued his struggles, bidding to break free of his smaller restrainers, and Rowland called out.

"You men, there!" he shouted. "Pratt, Quintal, you, too, Hadley. Churchill, you useless sot! Lend a hand, here, calm your mate before he hurts himself."

Pratt stood, slowly, and all the eyes in the galley, except Hall's, focused on him. His face no longer looked angry, but had become instead an impassive, unreadable mask.

"We'll have no talk of punishment," he said, and it wasn't a request, or a demand, but a simple statement of fact. Worth could see a glance pass between el-Barzin and Rowland, a glance that clearly said *I don't think we can hold this crazy bastard much longer.* El-Barzin, the eldest, most seasoned able, the one who, in a more perfect world, the others would all defer to and respect, nodded. Worth could tell that it galled him, ran counter to everything he believed, but clearly he had done some quick math and decided against escalation, against summoning the Captain or Pott or Crutchfield and his Machrines. Maybe it was a small measure of solidarity belowdecks, or perhaps the prospect of a long space voyage with a crew that distrusted and hated each other. Maybe it was pure expedience.

Pratt came and took up a fistful of Lamb's shirt. Both were tall, both strong, but Pratt was far more of both.

"That's enough, Saul," he said, and it would have been difficult for Lamb, infuriated as he was, to ignore the command. If he was afraid of anyone, it was Pratt. Finally, he sagged, and Worth turned her attention to Hall. He was barely conscious, though not by much, a purpling mark above his right eye and a stupid, absent smile on his face, revealing those crooked teeth.

"Some hero," he muttered, groggily, and his eyes rolled back in his head as he fainted.

"Mister Worth."

She looked up, still cradling Hall's head. El-Barzin still had his hands on Lamb, but now he was propping him up more than holding him back. All the fight seemed to have gone out of the crewman with Pratt's looming presence.

"I suggest you and Hadley take Mister Hall up to Surgery," El-Barzin continued, quietly, urgently. "That was some spill he took, hitting his head on the table like that. We'll get this one to his bunk, and back to work tomorrow for us all."

Worth realized with cold suddenness that she was the senior officer, indeed the only conscious officer, present. El-Barzin was making it look like she was in charge, though his experience and calm authority were clearly in control. *Preserving the flimsy fiction of chain of command*, she thought. She knew she should report it all -- the drunkenness, the violence, the insubordination -- but some instinct told her to follow el-Barzin's lead, to cede some ground now in exchange for the trust of the crewmen. She nodded, and stood.

"Very good," she said, and somehow her voice didn't crack. There was no more joy left from the grog, no more pleasant buzzing, just a throb at her temples and an all-encompassing leaden fatigue. She wanted to go to bed, she wanted her father, she wanted some magic button that could reset the entire night. Instead, somehow, she faced it.

"Quintal, get Churchill to help you clean the galley. Pratt, help Lamb find his bunk with these men. Hadley, with me." As she said each name, she forced herself to look each starman in the face. Churchill was vacant, Quintal amused, Hadley a little sad. El-Barzin and Rowland both showed relief and approval. Pratt revealed nothing, his face an utter blank. It was Lamb's eyes that were the worst, but she steeled herself and burrowed into those brown holes, hating him, and with every last ounce of herself she willed the message, *you will never touch me again, you filthy animal*. There was no response, no answer, just the slow smoldering burn of anger deferred but not dead. She continued to see those eyes, feral and repulsively magnetic, long after Lamb was gone.

We haven't even left Earth yet, she thought later, *and it's already been a long cruise.*

****

Kew was a marvel, but for Banks it held little novelty. He had affection for the sprawling gardens, for the unique treasures it held – a handsome little rowan, for instance, and a crimson-leafed maple, both the last known of their kind – and could never be truly indifferent to the collection as a scientist, but there was no wonder left in it for him. In part, his apathy stemmed from over-familiarity. His late father, the Fourteenth Earl of Northumberland, had been an old friend of the King, and together, along with Sir Eustace, they had shared an enthusiasm for botany. Banks respected botany, but it was merely one among the constellation of his academic interests. For him, this was a place of business, not unlike an office or a coffee-house. Other men, other women, could be slack-jawed in awe of the open air and rambling verdure, but not him. Likewise, and for the same reasons, the Royal Presence had long since lost any spellbinding majesty it might once have had.

The Royal Family were no longer the absolute monarchs they had once been, but neither were they the mere puppets or ceremonial figureheads that the populist democratic crusaders of the eighteenth and nineteenth centuries would have made of them. To be sure, the American agitations of the latter half of the 1700s had been inconvenient, and had required political as well as military remedies. Fortunately, Prime Ministers from Pitt to Churchill to Thatcher came to realize that the loyalty of would-be rebels was rather easily purchased with seats in Parliament. In the end, those movements had been only modestly successful, effectively co-opted by the King's royalist allies. There were concessions, greater influence for the House of Lords, even some window dressing for the Commons in Parliament, but the monarchy endured.

The current King, Charles V, was a largely useless creature; feckless, simple, barely literate, and yet by virtue of bloodline and a talented, discreet Privy Council, he had sat the throne for nearly forty years, and was, from all accounts, widely esteemed by his subjects. He loved his gardens, his birds and butterflies, and being outdoors. Even now, well past seventy, he was quite spry on his walks, and capable of astonishment at the smallest surprises or pleasures. He was an elderly child.

Queen Katherine was an entirely different matter.

The King's second wife, Katherine had been procured for the thorny, and as yet unsuccessful, proposition of producing a male heir (the deceased Queen Patricia, the King's first wife, had generated three quarrelsome, tedious, political daughters – it remained a palace joke of some durability as to exactly how Queen Pat had lured King Charles to bed enough times for that happen). Not yet thirty, slightly thickset, aristocratic, and in possession of a keen mind and ready wit, Queen Katherine had very quickly assumed the royal role in the affairs of the Kingdom that her husband happily left vacant. The Privy Council had initially reacted to her activity with dismissive scorn, which swiftly evaporated as the Queen demonstrated her precocious grasp of the art of governing.

It was a damp morning, with a light drizzle, when Banks was asked to stroll at Kew with their Majesties, and the gardens were a different kind of beautiful in the gray mist. Leaves and needles were a deeper green, the muted colors of flowers and berries an impressionistic canvas. The Queen wore a stylish lavender cloak with a hood to keep off the weather, but the King was bareheaded, his long wisps of silver hair plastered across his face.

"Isn't the rain wonderful?" asked King Charles of no one in particular. "I do love when they let it rain. I should instruct them to do it more often. What do you think, Banks? Hm?"

"Sire," Banks dipped his head, "it should rain or snow or hail at your pleasure."

"I think, my love," interrupted Queen Katherine, "that what your science minister would say in a less guarded moment is that your weather-tamers know their craft and you should leave it to them." The King frowned, then brightened.

"Worms!" he exclaimed. "There are sure to be worms!"

"Yes, dear. Why don't you take your little pail and collect some? You can feed them to your birds later." He dashed off, leaving Banks alone with Her Majesty. She almost sighed, but did not. Banks admired her restraint, and her decorum. She was a fierce defender of the King, a jealous guardian of his reign, and by extension, her own.

"I understand," she said, turning to him, the motherly tone she adopted with her husband gone, replaced by her matter-of-fact business voice. Banks knew well that there was a coquettish, flirting voice, too, unleashed at need, as well as various other personas. The Queen was a deft political animal. "I understand you have sent a ship to the far reaches of the galaxy, to procure more exotic specimens for the King's gardens."

"The Star Lord sends ships, Highness, not me."

"Don't be coy," she snapped. "I dislike coy. It is so very British."

"Guilty." Banks spread his hands and hitched his most charming smile to his handsome face. It worked better in the sunshine, he knew. "I am, after all, British, as are we all." It was the slightest feint, intended to do no real harm, but perhaps to unnerve her a tiny amount. The Queen was, after all, a native of America, and it was well-rumored that her ancestors some four hundred years before had participated in those abortive rebellions against the then-English throne. In any event, she was too well-bred and too shrewd to show any disquiet.

"Your...particular friend, Sir Eustace, was here some days ago." She emphasized the word *particular*, and Banks knew his ever-so-gentle sally had not gone unnoticed. If she was trying to upset him with inferences about his relationship with Eustace, it was a weak riposte. Their relationship was one of London's worst-kept secrets.

"I would imagine, Majesty, that the Royal Gardener might spend some time at the Royal Gardens now and again."

She actually giggled then, and whether it was in earnest or for show he could not tell, but it certainly sounded authentic. She really was not beautiful, though there was a certain animation, a kind of electricity, that she created around herself, and it was hard to look away when she smiled or laughed. She was an Adams, a child of privilege and pedigree, her father the seventh Duke of Boston. She had married the King when she was only twenty-two. Despite her youth, Banks knew ministers who had ignored or underestimated her to their own peril.

"Wit is so much better than coy," she said. "Let us be candid with one another, Banks."

He waited in silence, not sure where this was headed. A lifetime around politicians had taught him the virtue of patience.

"Tell me more about this most recent calamitous prediction of yours, if you please."

The Queen, thought Banks, was a well-informed woman.

"It was discussed at Privy, Highness."

"Coy again." She rolled her eyes, and somehow the affectation had charm.

"I would not want to speak out of turn."

"When the Queen asks, it becomes your turn. I know what was said at Privy. Lord Djimonsu was most expansive with his thoughts on the matter."

"The Chancellor is my honored colleague," said Banks, carefully. And then, less so, "Begging your royal pardon, Majesty, he is also an enormous ass." The giggle rose again, throaty and young.

"Yes, yes, he is, but he is also my ass, and as all women always have, I use my ass to my own advantage. Now I would use you, Minister. I have his thoughts. Will you give me yours, or am I left to surmise his are thorough and accurate?"

Banks had been very cleverly trapped, and he knew it. He took a moment to gather himself, unused to being cornered this way. A butterfly landed on a nearby hawthorn, and he made a show of studying its orange and yellow wings. The rain had all but stopped, and a few white shafts of sun penetrated the gray above. Banks looked to the sky, thinking about Pearce and the *Harvest*, due to launch in only a few hours. And there was Eustace, poor old Eustace, already aboard, excited and anxious and determined to succeed. Could he trust the Queen? What were her motives? If she was an ally of Djimonsu, the ship and its mission could be compromised. That he could not allow, whatever the risk.

"Your Majesty, I stand by what I told my fellow Privy Councilors. It is…unfortunate in the extreme that they did not see clear to pursue a remedy." He sighed. "I will simply have to try again another time to convince them." With a silent whisper of color, the butterfly disappeared.

"And this botanical adventure of which Eustace spoke?"

"Just that." Banks looked the young Queen squarely in the eye and grinned. The gaze that returned was icy and impossible to interpret. Banks kept his face pleasantly neutral, but inside he churned. Every one of his eggs was in that steel and plastic basket in orbit at Spithead. He knew he was running a dangerous game, lying to the Queen, but he could see no other choice. If the journey of the *Harvest* succeeded, he would happily forfeit his titles and incomes in exchange for humanity's future. And if it failed…if it failed, what did the rest matter? Banks had no wife, no children. He would be the last Earl of Northumberland, at least, the last Banks to hold the title. He had no shortage of nephews and cousins who would no doubt angle and compete for the honor, but he scarcely cared about that. The legacy that concerned him was not Spring Grove, much as he loved it, or his ancestral, and concluding, bloodline, but rather the continuation of his species. With luck, he would be the savior of humanity, and all of mankind would be his true heirs.

At that moment King Charles returned, somewhat crestfallen, soaking wet, with mud and blades of grass stuck to his knees and fingers.

"Only one worm," he declared plaintively.

"Yes, love," said Queen Katherine, still holding Banks with her stare. "Only one worm indeed."

****

Pearce stared out the tiny window of his cabin as the massive presence of Jupiter loomed against a static backdrop of stars. The launch had gone smoothly, despite all the repairs the *Harvest* had needed while in spacedock, and the old girl was as healthy as she would ever be. Now, with Spithead behind and the infinite universe ahead, he was almost excited. This was where he belonged, where he could be of use.

"Enter," he said when the chime of his door sounded. Fletcher strode in, in the Navy uniform that still looked so strange and formal on her lithe frame. Pearce stood and handed her a flute of champagne.

"To the *Harvest*," she said, raising it.

"And her crew," he replied, and then added the traditional Navy blessing, "Good fortune to her and all who sail with her." They touched glasses, and each took a sip. Pearce looked out the window again. "They that go down to the sea in ships, that do business in great waters, these see the works of the Lord, and His wonders in the deep."

"That's pretty, Bill," Fletcher said, and then caught herself with the slightest giggle. "Sorry. *Sir*. That's taking some getting used to, but I'm working on it." She sat, still holding her flute, one finger rubbing idly along the lip. "I never had you as a religious man, sir."

"The 107th Psalm," Pearce murmured. "Captain Baker had it on the wall of her star-cabin on the *Drake*. I've never forgotten it." He was silent a moment, thinking of Jane Baker and all the other star-mariners who had left Earth uttering the same blessings, but never made it back. He coughed and set down his glass, the champagne inside almost untouched.

"In another 24 hours we'll clear Pluto and the gravity converters should be fully enriched, so we'll take in the sails and engage the interstellar drives. Then I'll need you and Mister Hall to plot a course for Kepler. The King wants his new plants, and he wants them before the year is out."

"Seems a long way to go for flowers," Fletcher said.

Pearce suppressed a flicker of annoyance. He knew Fletcher was irreverent, and had to remind himself that nobles had a different tolerance for the King's whims.

"It's a long way to go for anything. Make sure the route passes through Lyra, Christine. That system is a wealth of gravity currents, and a brief diversion there will save us two weeks of travel."

"I know that, sir. And so do the Procyeans. It's a favorite ambush spot of theirs. It's a risk."

They stared at one another across the desk for a moment while Fletcher tried to suppress a smile and failed.

"What?" demanded Pearce.

"You. Us. How often have we had conversations like these? Only now you're the one wanting to take risks, and I'm arguing for caution."

"Only warranted risks. Listen, Pott seems good, but I don't know him or trust him – yet, anyway – the way I do you. The midshipmen are impossibly young, and the crew is less than I'd hoped. As my emissary to them all, you are vital. We must succeed. The stakes…" he trailed off. He wanted to tell her the true purpose of their mission, to take her fully into his confidence, but Banks and Exeter had counseled against it. In a small drawer near his left hand, a drawer encrypted to open only at the voice prompt of the commanding officer of the Harvest, was a datachip that outlined his orders in their entirety, a safeguard in the event something happened to him. Unless he was incapacitated, killed, or otherwise removed from command, he would be the only one on board, with the exceptions of Reyes and Green, who knew their true objective at Cygnus.

"I know," Fletcher said softly, with that warm, slow-burning smile. She reached out and put a hand on Pearce's, and only then did the captain realize his were clenched into fists. "I know how much this means to you. A promotion for you would mean a lot for James, wouldn't it?" She looked at him, round eyes full of concern and affection. "I promise, I will do everything I can to make this voyage a success for you."

"Thank you," he said after a long pause. "You have no idea how much that means."

Seven

Gravity

"Captain, perimeter scans show something astern, and closing."

Pearce had been reviewing duty roster reports, and looked up from the tablet in his hand.

"More precise, please, Mister Worth."

"An energy signature, sir." Hope Worth was young, but competent, and Pearce waited as long as he could for the midshipman to relay useful information. No use berating the girl. Seconds ticked past, and Pearce's patience waned. He was about to repeat his request for more data when Worth shook her head and turned from her scanning console. "Unfamiliar, sir. The computers classify it as ion combustion, but it's nothing I've ever seen before."

Of course not, thought Pearce. *You've been in space for about ten minutes.* Fletcher moved quickly to Worth's side and looked over her shoulder at her screen.

"I have," she growled. "Raiders, Captain."

Damn. Ion combustion was an antiquated technology, compared to gravity sails. It was reliant on unstable and dangerous ignition engines, and had long since been abandoned by the Royal Navy. The age of ion travel had been a short and brutal one for vessels and their crews, with a loss rate of forty percent on deep space missions. It did make for faster ships, though. *And some nasty weaponry.* Which, in addition to its cheap availability, made it the power source of choice for extralegal pirates.

"How far away?"

"Five hundred thousand kilometers and closing, Captain."

"Beat to quarters," Pearce ordered, and Fletcher repeated the command over the shipwide comm system. As a low, steady, artificial drumbeat filled the air, men and women tensed at their stations. Pearce could feel his own body begin to respond, from the sharpening of his focus to the tightening of his bowels. He gripped the arms of his command chair once, then forced himself to relax his fingers and breathe out slowly. Fletcher was at his side, and her green-gold eyes fixed on his.

"The price for the Lyran shortcut," she murmured, so quiet only he could hear. Pearce narrowed his gaze, still looking straight ahead at the main viewscreen, wondering if she were about to resume their argument, but she simply shrugged and sighed. "Sometimes you gamble and lose."

"We haven't lost yet." He gritted his teeth and rattled off a series of commands in clipped barks. "Reef the gravity sails! No sense in having one of them carried away by an early shot from those thugs. Helm! Hard to starboard, if you please, and commence evasive protocols. They'll not have this ship, by God."

The moments that followed were full of crew executing their orders, perhaps not as fluidly as Pearce might have liked, but they were hardly a seasoned group. He doubted that any of them had ever taken hostile fire. *That's about to change.* He did notice that Thomas Peckover, the boatswain, had briskly abandoned his remote engineering station on the Quarterdeck before Pearce was halfway through his order, headed for his main post in the engine room. *There's a start.* An alarm sounded -- a tinny, electronic noise meant to replicate an ancient ship's bell -- and the entire world turned on its axis. The command deck tilted hard to the right, and to their credit, none of the crew went sprawling. A moment later the *Harvest* shook, her interior lights dimming for a moment. Charlie Hall, at navigation, turned and looked at Pearce, his face bloodless.

"Ion cannon, son," Pearce said, and the officer nodded, licking his white lips.

"Just missed us, sir. If we'd stayed our course…"

"That's why we didn't." Pearce would have been pleased, except this was just the beginning. "Procyean raiders like to fire early, Mister Hall, to disable their prey from a distance. They'll fire again, but we may have bought ourselves a few minutes while they shift into a new attack pattern." He knew more, of course, from tales told by fellow merchant star-mariners, but he wasn't going to tell this frightened young man about those stories, about how, once their victims couldn't fight back, Procyeans would board the targeted vessel, strip her of her cargo and any technology of value, and then sell her crew at the galactic slave markets thousands of parsecs from home. You could resist, of course, but you wouldn't die fighting. They would simply cripple you until you were no longer a threat, and then sell you at a reduced price.

"Lieutenant Fletcher, if I recall correctly, we are not far from the Hitzelberg proto-star."

Fletcher consulted the NavWork system, and nodded. "Yes, sir. Less than two hundred AUs. With gravity converters, we could be there in under two minutes."

Cutting it fine, Pearce thought. He checked the gravity store monitor at his fingertips, confirming that the converters were fully fueled.

"Very well. Mister Hall, lay in a course for Hitzelberg, please, and engage the converters." Hall's hands played across his helm console, and in a heartbeat they accelerated smoothly.

The *Harvest* wasn't nearly fast enough to outrun a ship using ion combustion, and it certainly couldn't outfight her. Pearce thought of the electron carronades he had on board. He glanced across the Quarterdeck at the gunnery station and Heywood Musgrave, his gunner, idle through no fault of his own. He would have laughed if it weren't so damned pathetic. Navy regs called for a gunner on every armed vessel, regardless of whether or not those armaments amounted to anything. Electron carronades! *Might as well be water pistols in any kind of close engagement.* He tried to convince himself that Banks and the Star Lord had done the best they could, secretly and swiftly outfitting a voyage no one else wanted, but he wished, again, that more of his suggestions had been heeded. *Like more advanced weaponry.* Gravity-conversion was ideal for deep-space travel, reaching speeds in excess of a parsec a day, but was next to useless in close-ship action. The *Harvest* rattled again, harder, and the shipboard illumination actually blinked out for a long second before relighting. *They couldn't have found us a damn cruiser for this mission?*

"Another miss, sir. Closer this time."

"Thank you, Mister Worth." Pearce tried to remember what the re-energizing lags were for ion cannons. *Sixty seconds? Thirty?* He forced himself not to ask how much longer it would be before they reached Hitzelberg. It would either be in time, or it wouldn't.

A reddish brightness emerged from the pinpricked black of the viewscreen, and began to swell in size. *The Hitzelberg proto-star*, Pearce thought grimly, silently urging it to grow faster. "Mister Hall, the instant we arrive at the edge of the accretion disk, disengage the converters, and deploy the sails." Hall's mouth hung open, and he began to blink furiously.

"Captain, within the edge of the event horizon..." His voice trailed off as Pearce stared at him. "Yes, sir. Disk edge in three...two... one..."

A familiar whine filled the deck as the gravity conversion engines shut down, and the *Harvest* plunged into the rust-colored haze that surrounded Hitzelberg. The fetal star had been in the process of being born for millions of years, gathering dust and gases and other loose material into its orbit, material that would, in the distant future, become planets, moons, asteroids -- the stuff of a star system. The pulsing center of the cloud, where hydrogen and helium piled in upon one another in the ever-denser hydrostatic core, would someday be the newest star in the galaxy. But not yet. Until then, within the accretion disk there would be swirling matter, wildly fluctuating gravity, and unpredictable plasma eruptions.

Pearce was thrown from his chair as the Harvest suddenly tilted ninety degrees to port. Bodies tumbled about the command deck amid shouts of surprise, and he felt Hall thud into him. He seized the young navigator by the upper arm, and with his free hand seized a railing. Pulling himself to the helm, he thrust Hall into his seat. Worth, he noticed, had managed to keep her station. *Good girl.* "Strap in!" he bellowed. Then louder, "all of you!"

"Did they fire again?" Pearce shook his head. He didn't know who had asked the question, but it had not been another attack from the pirates.

"No. Until our gravity sails fully deploy, we are at the mercy of the turbulence inside the disk." He did not spare a glance to the rest of the crew on duty, but instead focused on Hall. He was young, his face unlined and inexperienced, but his duty profile reported a marked aptitude for manual navigation. *On simulators,* thought Pearce. He lowered his mouth to within inches of Hall's ear, and hissed softly through clenched teeth. "Son, the instant those sails deploy, assume manual control. The computers are useless in here. You have to feel the eddies and the currents, respond to them instantly, even anticipate them, you understand?" The helmsman nodded, once, almost imperceptibly. A small change came over his face, the jaw no longer slack, the eyes no longer wide with fear or astonishment, but almost serene as he wrapped his right hand around the manual stick. "The Star Lord himself told me you're the best young navigator in the Navy," Pearce lied. "Prove it now or we're all dead."

The ship righted itself, and Pearce could feel more than hear the taut thrum that told him the sails were deployed and locked, and the *Harvest* was now under steerage way. He tore his attention away from Hall, and looked around the deck. Everyone seemed intact for the moment. His gaze found Worth, and she answered his unasked question.

"The scanners are having some trouble with the interference here, Captain, but as far as I can tell, the raiders haven't followed us in."

"Is that what you wanted?" Fletcher asked, suddenly at his side, frowning. "We can't hide in here forever, and they're likely to wait for a bit."

"No," replied Pearce. "No, I want those greedy bastards to give chase. I want to see if they can last as long in here as we can." He glanced sidelong at her. "Another gamble, Lieutenant." Before she could respond, he turned back to Worth. "Send a distress message, Mister Worth. Merchant channel, not Navy, you understand? Say that our cargo of precious metals and rare liquors is about to be seized by Procyean raiders. And Mister Worth, don't encode it."

"Sir?"

"I want this message to be intercepted. Send it!" The ship heaved, pitched, and then settled back into its course. This time, Pearce noticed, everyone stayed strapped in their seats.

"Sorry, sir," said Hall, not taking his eyes off the viewscreen or his hand off the stick. "These currents are damned tricky." He realized his language. "Sorry, sir." Pearce actually smiled.

"Never mind, Mister Hall. You're doing splendidly. Keep her nose into the wind as best you can." *Perhaps there's some steel to the lad after all.*

"Captain!" Worth's voice rose with excitement. "Scans show the Procyean vessel has passed through the edge of the Hitzelberg accretion disk!"

"Greed, Mister Worth, is a universal constant." He never thought he would be pleased to hear that he had pirates on his tail. "Mister Hall, can you ease off the controls a bit? Give the impression that the *Harvest* is struggling."

"The impression?" Hall laughed, a thin, high-pitched sound. Sweat beaded on his white forehead. "Of course, sir." An instant later, the ship was weaving from side to side in a wild dance, with no rhythm and no pattern. Pearce wondered if the midshipman was doing a masterful job of mimicking a ship out of control, or if he were only just keeping it from actually becoming so.

"Raiders closing, sir," Worth reported. "A hundred thousand kilometers to stern."

Come on, you bastards. Fire! Much closer, and he couldn't be sure his own ship would survive. "Abaft view on screen."

The Procyean vessel appeared before them, surrounded by the swirling red and black detritus of the Hitzelberg disk, the picture imperfect and grainy through the sludge. It was an inelegant thing, thick and menacing, without sails or ornament to interrupt the dull, scarred gray of its hull. Pearce could see the ion cannon, mounted below the main body, and he could see the ominous orange glow that was building in the maw of that huge cylinder. Pearce activated the comm unit by his arm. "Sternshields, Mister Peckover."

"But Captain, they'll never hold against that thing!" came the crackling reply. "And if we divert power..."

"Now!" barked Pearce. If his theory held, he wasn't concerned about the raiders' weapon, and if he was wrong, it hardly mattered, but he was not in the mood to argue with the boatswain. For a heartbeat, he wondered what the hell was the matter with this younger generation of officers. It would never have occurred to him to debate an order from Jane Baker, least of all during a close-ship action when seconds could mean the difference between survival and a fiery death.

A moment later, nothing but a brilliant white bloom filled the viewscreen, and the *Harvest* lurched forward. Peckover must have obeyed the order despite his misgivings, or else the ship would have been consumed in the explosion. The radiance swiftly faded, and when it did, the other ship was gone.

"Captain, I show no sign of the Procyeans."

"Let that be a lesson to you, Mister Worth. Never try to activate an unstable ion combustion reaction in the midst of a dynamic gravity field." Pearce favored her with the faintest smile.

"And if that hadn't worked?" Fletcher asked. He couldn't fathom the look on her face. *Was it relief? Or surprise that old Bill Pearce was proving to be a bit tougher and more resilient than she'd thought?*

"We'd be ashes. Or, if we weren't, we'd try something else. He punched the comm again. "Good work, Mister Peckover. Well done. Now reef those sails, mister, and..."

Before Pearce could complete his sentence, the command deck darkened again, and with a stomach-churning swoon, the *Harvest* plummeted into a spiral. Even strapped in, Pearce fought the sudden and intense vertigo. It was nearly a full minute before the battered vessel regained some kind of normal attitude, and even then it shuddered, like a living thing in shock.

"What the hell was that?"

"Gravity plume, Captain." Somehow, Worth's voice was level. "And we're still in it."

"Tiller control nominal," Hall reported. "I can keep her mostly steady, but our trajectory is toward the heart of Hitzelberg, sir. Into the hydrostatic core."

"Mister Peckover," Pearce shouted into the comm, "reef the sails, activate the converters, and let's get out of here. There's so much gravimetric current, we should be able to break free fairly easily."

"Sir, I've been trying. The sails won't respond."

"What do you mean, won't respond?" Pearce bellowed.

"Just that, sir. I get nothing from the automatic sheet controls. Something in the system isn't functioning."

Pearce rubbed his hand along his jaw. *The kids have shown their mettle*, he thought. *If we get out of this, they might make decent officers. If we get out of this...* "I see. Stand by. Mister Worth, how long before we're dragged into the core? I know the pull isn't constant, but assume an average rate of speed." She did some quick calculations at her console.

"Twenty minutes, Captain."

Christ.

"All right. Christine, we'll have to horse the sheets home manually. Get down there and assist Peckover."

"Aye, sir."

As his first officer left the Quarterdeck, he wished he could be the one hurrying down that lift; that he could be the one organizing the starmen into the teams of two that would go outside the hull and furl the sails by hand. Hell, he wished he could be the one pulling on a pressure suit and risking his own life to save the ship. But he knew better. Not only was he needed here, but his days of climbing the shrouds in the vacuum of space were well behind him. All he could do was sit and wait, and pray that his ables could do their jobs. Unlike the green officers he'd been given, Exeter had been able to procure him some seasoned jacks. It might make the difference of a few minutes. At the moment, a few minutes would be all the difference in the world.

A welcome crackle came over the comm channel. "Sails coming home now, Captain."

"Thank you, Mister Peckover. Mister Hall, stand ready to engage conversion on my order."

"Yes, sir."

"Mister Worth?"

"Eleven minutes, sir."

Christ. Eleven minutes to the hottest fire there is. He tried to find reassurance in the fact that they wouldn't actually burn, that the Harvest would crumple from the sudden increase in gravitic pressures as they approached the core, long before they reached the actual inferno of the unborn star. Death should be fairly instantaneous for all of them.

What was taking so damn long?

"Sails almost home, sir." Hall frowned. Perspiration dripped from his eyebrows and the tip of his long nose as he struggled to maintain manual control of the helm while still monitoring the disposition of the gravity sails. "There seems to be some problem with the starboard sheet."

"Problem? What kind of problem?"

The comm chirped to life on his armrest. "Fletcher here, sir! The bloody tackles are fouled on the last starboard courses. The team's working on it now." Pearce tried not to think that it was substandard materials, tried not to think that this never happened on cruisers or frigates, tried not to think that his entire ship was in jeopardy because the Star Lord claimed limits to his own influence.

"Understood, Lieutenant Fletcher. We have precisely six minutes."

He left the channel open, listening to the chatter down in the belly of the Harvest. One minute went by, then two, then three. Pearce waited. Looming in the center of the viewscreen, blindingly white, was the furious hydrogen-helium orgy at the core of Hitzelberg. Unless they could get those sheets in, it was the last thing he would ever see. A snippet of an old song danced through his mind in those terrifying moments. *We are stardust...billion year old carbon...we are golden...caught in the Devil's bargain...*

"One minute, Captain." Worth's lower lip trembled, just a little, and her eyes were bright. She was, after all, not so much older than his own James. Pearce wanted to say something to comfort or reassure her, but his mouth was dry and his heart heavy. He wondered if Banks would try to send another ship on the same mission, perhaps one with a better commander.

"Captain, the sheets are home!" Hall's cry was exultant as he reached for the conversion control.

"Sir!" It was Fletcher over the comm. "Sir, wait! Rowland and el-Barzin are still out there! Their harness split! Sir! Bill! They're floating away, Captain! I need to send the other team to retrieve them – two minutes, that's all we need!" In agony, Pearce looked to Worth, who shook her head, seeming close to tears.

"Thirty s-seconds, sir."

"Request denied, Lieutenant. Secure the mast doors. Mister Hall, engage conversion."

The midshipman executed the order, and the main engines of the *Harvest* roared to life, the ship careening out of the disk, leaving behind fiery gases, swirling currents, and two members of his crew. *The best two.* All was quiet as Pearce unstrapped himself and stood. He let his vision float unfocused around the command deck, trying in vain to swallow the growing lump in his throat. Finally, into that awful silence, he spoke, surprised to find his voice steady.

"Well done, all of you." He placed a light hand on Hall's shoulder, finding it slumped and drenched in sweat. "You are relieved, Mister Hall. Get some rest."

"Yes, sir."

The young midshipman rose from his station, and Pearce noticed that he shared a brief look with Worth before walking shakily to the exit hatch. *Something there more than camaraderie?* In any other circumstances, he would have made a mental note to consider it later; commanders should be aware of the relationships between officers. Now, it was forgotten as his mind was drowned by thoughts of the men he had left behind to die in the Hitzelberg proto-star, and of the eyes of the upper deck on him now. *I saved them*, he thought, *and they know it*. They also knew the price. He wondered if they would consider it a fair trade. He wondered if he ever would. Ordering the relief officer at the helm to resume their original course, he left the Quarterdeck without another word.

****

Pearce watched through the viewport as the not-yet-star retreated from view. His son, James, often watched holovids for school, and there had been one on ancient biology that he had seen with the boy, and never quite forgotten. Before the Great Extinction on Earth, a century and a half ago, there had been bewildering biodiversity on the planet. Plants, animals, and bacteria, in almost limitless variation. Apparently there had been bizarre creatures, tiny eight-legged beasts known as spiders, which subsisted by trapping luckless insects. The holovid he so vividly recalled was very old footage of a spider that had captured a winged bug, and was dragging it down into its lair to consume at leisure. That was what had almost happened to them in Hitzelberg. They had escaped, at the cost of two lives. *And the Procyeans dead as well*, he thought, trying to evoke some sympathy for them in his heart. After all, it wasn't their fault that the United Kingdom had appropriated their homeworld a hundred years before and damned too many Procyeans to a life of interstellar piracy.

Then he thought of Arash el-Barzin and Gordan Rowland, abandoned to the crushing pressures of the hydrostatic core, and all the pity drained out of him.

A faint chime told him that he had a visitor. He sighed, not wanting to see anyone just then, wanting only to compose messages of condolence to the families of his lost crewmen. A glance out the small viewport in his star cabin showed the blur of stars, and he knew that they were improbably back on their way toward Cygnus, back on the errand of mercy that the best mind on Earth had told him was vital to the very survival of humanity. To that end, he supposed, all of them were expendable. The chime sounded again.

"Yes, enter," he acknowledged, grudgingly dismissing the luxury of solitary grief he could not afford to indulge.

It was Christine Fletcher. Pearce ground a knuckle into his eye. All he wanted to do was sleep. She was angry, he could tell, full of sorrow and rage and fatigue, just as he was.

"Tell me Bill...Captain. Are men really dying for a garden?"

"What?" He had expected her to rail at him for his order to leave Rowland and el-Barzin behind, in that passionate way of hers, but this was cold fury.

"Tell me we're not dying out here so the King can add another exotic topiary to his gardens. Tell me Arash and Gordan's lives meant more than that."

"Christine, there wasn't time..."

"I know." She stared at him. "I know you made the only decision you could. If we had lingered, the whole crew would be dead. But I have to tell you, Captain, those men were leaders belowdecks, especially Arash. And he was our best foremost jack. I don't think anyone else could have gotten those sheets in. When that last course fouled, I thought we were all dead, but Arash and Gordan just went to work, swift and sure, like we were in spacedock." Now the tears came, spilling one at a time and then in torrents, down her cheeks. "And they did it. Then, as we were pulling them in, their harness gave way." She threw something onto the floor at his feet. It was a length of woven fiber-plastic harness, and one end was shredded and split where it had torn asunder.

"If this bloody shrub run is so important, they could at least have given us some good goddamned equipment. Why are we here?"

Pearce bristled. Part of him longed to tell her, and part of him was out of patience with her. He had known Arash longer than she had, after all. *He saved my life on Cygnus*, he wanted to shout. *He was worth ten of the rest of the jacks*. Instead, he forced himself to swallow his anger, his sorrow, and answer Fletcher in a cool, even voice.

"We are here because our King desires us to be here."

"If we die for his passing pleasures, he's not much of a King, is he?"

There was stony silence then, the words of treason hanging in the air between them. Pearce coughed, stood as straight as he could manage, and clasped his hands behind his back.

"You're exhausted, Miss Fletcher, and grieving, as am I. We'll say no more of this." Slowly, Fletcher nodded, though whether in agreement or for lack of anything else to do, Pearce could not tell.

"Dismissed, then."

Fletcher left, saying no more. Pearce picked up the truncated strap and fingered the end of it. It was impossible, of course, but part of him felt the frigid cold of the void in those splayed fibers, the icy death that had claimed his two best starmen.

Dr. Reyes strode unannounced through the door that had remained open after Fletcher's departure, without prelude or chime, poised and calm as ever. She sat, folding one slender leg over the other, and smiled. On her, a smile was a rare and remarkably predatory expression.

"I wanted to congratulate you, Pearce, on your skillful management of that encounter." Pearce stared at the harness, and felt no pride at all. He had outsmarted an itinerant people, homeless because of the avarice of his world, and it had cost him two of the finest men in his command.

"A shame about the crewmen, but you shouldn't work yourself up over that. There are, after all, thirty billion more humans to worry about."

"Not on this ship." It was all he could do not to scream in her face. How could she be so cold and unfeeling? How could anyone, gently born or not, be so callously indifferent to death? *Rowland and el-Barzin.* He forced himself to remember their faces as he remembered their names. Rowland he had only just begun to know, but el-Barzin... the man had saved his life, all those years ago on Cygnus. Now he had repaid that with cold death. He stared at the ragged end of the harness: a corner cut, a shilling saved, two lives lost.

"Secondary-market fiber, Doctor. Does the Minister even want this voyage to succeed? Does the Star Lord?" He paused. "El-Barzin spoke fluent Cygni. Do you?" Pearce was on brittle ground, and he knew it. Reyes was not his friend, and she was certainly not his social peer, but he was too tired and too stricken to be more politic. "Five of us became familiar with the tongue twelve years ago. The *Harvest* left Spithead with two of us on board. Now there's just one. Me. More can learn with the linguistic programs before we arrive, but not to the relative fluency of someone who has been ashore there." She shrugged, and then her face shifted from indifference to haughty conviction.

"You will overcome these obstacles, Pearce. You have no choice." She leaned forward. "And if every man and woman aboard this ship dies to accomplish our task, the price remains nothing compared to what we are trying to save."

Pearce rose, his rage burning inside him, hot as any proto-star.

"Dr. Reyes, you are the leading mind in your field, a member of the Royal Society, a colleague of Lord Banks, and above all, a gentlewoman. But you are still a civilian, and on this ship, I speak for the

King himself. You will call me *Captain* Pearce, and you will obey any order I might give you."

Reyes recoiled, as though he had slapped her in the face. She clearly wasn't used to being spoken to that way, and for a heartbeat her mouth hung slightly open. Before she could respond, Pearce moved around his desk, and bent close.

"And right now I order you to get the hell out of my cabin."

Their eyes locked together for more than a moment. Pearce could feel the animosity radiating from her, but he did not care. *Gordan Rowland. Arash el-Barzin.* Eventually, Reyes broke away, rising out of the chair, moving stiffly, with far less than her usual grace. She walked to the door, and left without looking back.

You've made your point, he thought, leaning heavily on his desk. *And, it seems, an enemy.*

Eight

Command Decisions

    Christine Fletcher liked it here, down in the fat belly of the ungainly *Harvest*. She knew why Pearce had chosen it, and she had to agree. Certainly there were practical and logistical reasons that this kind of vessel was so well suited for a deep-space commercial voyage, matters of propulsion and vacuum-displacement and freight capacity, but there were intangibles as well. Like the captain, she felt at home on a cargo ship. The *Harvest* simply felt right. Her hull design, her navigation, her schematics: all were similar to the *Britannia*, that dear old tub. Fletcher tried to imagine herself at the helm of a shiny new naval cruiser, and the thought both amused and terrified her.

    The *Harvest*'s hold was not fitted out with the stacking storage units she was accustomed to. Instead, she walked along row after row of empty, dry hydroponic planters, vats that once filled with nutrient-rich solutions would house the array of new flora they were to acquire at Cygnus. All was gray and sterile now, but Fletcher could imagine how it would look when the vats were full of green, flowering life, and how the air in here would smell of growing things.

    She thought, too, of Cygnus, and of Bill Pearce. In all the years she had worked with him in the close quarters of space, she had never seen him so tense, so quick to anger. He had always been brusque, but now he was driving the crew hard, jumping on the smallest mistakes with disproportionate punishments. Was it simply a matter of being back in the Navy? Or was it this return to Cygnus? She knew, everyone knew, that the famous Captain Baker had died there, when the natives attacked the crew of the *Drake*. There had been a holovid made six or seven years before dramatizing the event, and like everyone else in the Kingdom, Fletcher had seen it more than once. She knew that Pearce had sailed with Baker, but had been surprised to learn that he had been right there with Baker when it happened. That hadn't been in the vid. Arash el-Barzin had told her about it. And now he was gone.

    And we're going back there for plants? It didn't add up. For most of the crew, their thinking was classic starman stoicism. Questioning your orders just didn't happen in the King's Navy. You did your job, and let the officers worry about where the ship went and why. There was a certain fatalistic logic in it, she supposed. *Why be concerned with what you can't control*? But Fletcher wasn't steeped in the Navy tradition of blind obedience. She was a product of the more egalitarian merchant marine, and used to knowing the score. *It doesn't make any damn sense*, she thought for the hundredth time, gripping the edge of one of the planters. Going back to a world that was known to be dangerous, because the King wanted some flowers? Had the Kingdom become that decadent, that willing to put lives at risk on a royal whim? There had to be more to it than that, but Pearce refused to take her into his confidence. That was what confused, and angered, her the most.

A sound came from beyond a nearby set of doors, from one of the secondary bays. It had been a kind of thumping and a cry, all muffled and faint. Frowning, she pressed the access panel and the door slid open. Inside, she saw able starman Isaac Pratt sitting on the floor, long yellow hair unbound, rubbing the back of his shaggy head. It was hot in the small, box-shaped bay, and all the hydroponic equipment stored there had been stacked against one wall. One of the robot Machrines, Luther-45, stood over Pratt, as impassive as ever. A handful of other crewmen lounged on boxes or leaned against the walls.

"All right, Pratt?" she asked, and noticed the sheepish grins and stifled laughter of the others as Pratt hurriedly clambered to his feet. He was a big brute of a man, but surprisingly graceful.

"Just a knock to the nugget, sir. No worries."

"You were wrestling with Luther." She looked at the Machrine, who still had not moved.

"Yes, sir. We're allowed. It's part of our rec time allowance."

Fletcher nodded. That was true, but something nibbled at the edge of her memory, something she had read in the endless datastreamed regulations the Admiralty had sent upon her commissioning.

"All safety protocols observed, I assume?" This was greeted with silence, and furtive looks, which were all the answers Fletcher needed.

"Robot roulette, then." Again, there was no response, and she knew she was right. They had been caught at their illicit little game, and now it was up to her to decide how to handle it. It was specifically against shipboard regs, and she should report it directly to the captain. It would be the proper thing to do, and maybe that was partly why she didn't do it. Another reason was that she knew the crew got bored on long star voyages, that they needed outlets for aggression and boredom. It was something that Pearce also knew, but he had never developed an instinctive feel for where the line was between recreation and mischief. Fletcher was very aware that one of the reasons he had brought her along was that she did have an instinct for that line.

"How does it work?" she asked. "You, Pratt, explain it to me." She moved to a stack of crates and sat lightly on top, crossing her legs.

"And does it have to be so damned hot in here while you do it?" One of the crewmen laughed and much of the tension went out of the room. It was another of the able starmen: the short, handsome Latino, Matias Quintal. Fletcher undid the buttons at the cuffs of her duty shirt and rolled her sleeves up above her elbows. Pratt, his hand still rubbing the back of his head, performed a sort of half-shrug.

"Not much to it, really. If you come up through the Navy down here belowdecks, sir, you learn it pretty early on."

"You are stalling," she said. "I'm not going to report you, Pratt, unless you disobey me. Now, how does it work?"

"It's simple." Quintal stepped forward, grinning. "Sir." Fletcher watched him. There was something of the islands in his movement, something fluid and seductive. *Careful*, she thought. *This one is a charmer and he knows it.* Fortunately, she had long experience with the type, and was far more amused than aroused. "You know the Machrines are programmed to train with human sparring partners in a variety of modes – boxing, wrestling, judo, even some alien forms of martial arts. And, as you mentioned earlier, there are safety protocols. Among these are the basic codes that prevent our metal friends from seriously injuring one of us. Isn't that right, Luther?" For the first time, the robot spoke.

"Yes, Matias." He turned to face Fletcher, his rectangular optic apertures flashing. Fletcher had not spent years in space with these machines the way Pratt, or Quintal, or so many of the others had, and she was still unused to the perfectly human voice coming from Luther-45's flat plastic faceplate. It was a pleasant voice, with the accent of London itself, not even the hint of static or electronic origin, and it was unnerving. "All Machrines are programmed not to harm our crewmates."

"True enough." Quintal patted Luther on the metal shoulder, the way one might a friendly dog. "What he's not telling you is that those codes are designed to be overridden."

"They are?" Fletcher asked. "Why? Isn't that dangerous?"

"Makes sense," replied Pratt, with a grunt. "Have to be able to instruct them who their hostile targets are. Each member of the crew is digitally topo-mapped and input into each Machrine's database as friendly, and then they can evaluate potential targets from any distance, instantly. We call it painting. You were painted like that when you came on board, sir; we all were. It's routine."

"And what is painted can be unpainted." Quintal had not stopped moving, and he was at her side, now. "So when we play robot roulette, we introduce the element of true risk to the game. We take turns engaging the machrine in whatever type of hand-to-hand combat we choose. In the first round, we alter his programming so that there is a five to ten percent chance that his safety protocols disengage."

"Meaning there is a chance he will try to kill you."

"Yes. And in each subsequent round, that chance increases by ten percent. So, the second round is a fifteen to twenty percent chance, the third round twenty-five to thirty, and so on."

"And when does the game end?" The room was still overly warm, the way a gymnasium might be. Without really thinking, Fletcher loosened the neck of her shirt. She did not fail to notice Quintal's eyes drinking in her cleavage before flitting back to meet her eyes.

"It ends when someone gets hurt, or when no one will dare to fight."

"And what round are you boys on now?"

"Five," said Pratt. Fletcher did the math quickly.

"So there's an even chance that whoever goes next is risking their life."

"Yes, sir." Quintal's dark eyes glittered as he smiled. "And there's the fun."

"Who's next?" she asked, intrigued despite the shouting of her conscience that the line had long ago been crossed. This risk to crew members was why regs prohibited the sport. That, and those accustomed to withholding one secret from their commanding officer often found it habit-forming to do so.

"I am."

Fletcher had thought there were only male starmen in the bay, but it was a woman who stepped forward now. Her mistake was understandable, as Peggy Briggs was at least as much man as woman. She was as tall as Pratt, and damn near as strong. She was wearing a sleeveless white shirt, tight across a flat and masculine chest, the arms it bared corded with muscle. Her eyes were a striking gray-green, and she might have been pretty once, but she had gone out of her way to change that, with close-cropped spiky blond hair, black anchors tattooed on either side of her thick neck, and a perpetual scowl. Pratt and Quintal were leaders belowdecks, but nobody messed around with Peggy Briggs.

She stepped forward, lean body tensed for combat, those eyes fixed on Luther.

"Peggy, I strongly recommend against this. There is now a significant chance you may be injured or killed." The robot's voice was as mellifluous as ever, but Briggs said nothing, merely beckoning with what must have been a pre-arranged signal, because in a heartbeat, Luther was on her. Fletcher had never seen anything, man or machine, move so fast. Somehow, Briggs was just as quick, and dodged, turning aside the swift strike that Luther had aimed at her face. She drove her shoulder into its midsection. Even though it had no human organs, no vulnerable soft belly, Luther was programmed, as all Machrines were, to mimic reactions within human tolerances. So Briggs drove it back, momentarily, before the robot's hands smashed down in a single combined blow to her back. Falling to the floor, she rolled, avoiding the groping steel fingers that sought to entrap her, then sprang to her feet a meter or so away. Slowly, the combatants circled one another. There was no way to tell whether the crewman was merely fighting, or fighting for her life.

Fletcher was so absorbed by the spectacle that she didn't notice when William Pearce walked in.

****

Bill Pearce certainly noticed his first officer.

A few minutes earlier, he had been in the star cabin, his tiny office adjacent to the command room they called the Quarterdeck. As the stars zoomed past the windows behind his cramped desk, he tried again to record a vid-message to Gordan Rowland's widow.

"Mrs. Rowland, your husband died to save his ship."

For the fifth time, Pearce deleted the message. It was such a trite, empty sentiment. He tried to imagine Mary receiving a message like that from some commanding officer of his, and knew that she wouldn't give a damn how heroic his death had been. All she would know, all Elaine Rowland would know, is that her husband, the father of her child, was never coming back. Pearce forced himself to look again at the screen of his monitor, where Rowland's file was on display. One of the embedded images, in sharp clarity, showed Rowland and his wife, smiling, their three-year old daughter, Rimi, laughing in their arms.

Damn, he thought. *That little girl is never going to know her father.* El-Barzin's message had been easier. The man had left no close relatives behind, so it had been a simple matter of entering the details of his death into the log, along with recommendations to the Admiralty for posthumous decoration. This was different. *There's not a thing I can say.* But it was his duty, and he did it. Once it was finished, necessary and hollow, he placed it in the transmission queue.

They were sailing under restricted deep-space communications protocols, which meant all ship-to-shore correspondence was reviewed by Pearce prior to the weekly message he would send back to the Admiralty with all approved content. For newcomers to the Navy it was a bit of a hassle, but the career hands were used to it. It would take several days for the signal to reach Earth anyway, a lag that would only increase as they traveled farther from home. After recording and sending a status report to Banks, Pearce was finishing his review of the handful of vid-letters that had been submitted – fairly standard "hi mum" stuff, or bland sexual innuendo for a distant partner, a stray reference or two to Hitzelberg he had to redact – when his door chime range.

"Enter," he said, and the door slid open to reveal Charlie Hall, more white-faced than usual. "Come in, Mister Hall."

"Sorry to bother you, sir."

"No bother. What can I do for you?"

"It's…well, it's some of the crew, sir." The midshipman was looking at the floor, scuffling one foot, and his voice was a barely audible stutter.

"What about them?" demanded Pearce with mounting impatience. "Look at me, for heaven's sake. You're an officer." Hall's eyes jerked up, and were so filled with discomfort and indecision that the captain felt a brief pang of pity. He softened his tone. "What is it, son?"

"Sergeant Crutchfield brought it to my attention, sir. Some of the machrines are showing signs of unusual wear. Scratches, and the like."

"Unusual, as in more than would be expected from normal training use?"

"Y-yes, sir. So I poked around a little, asked a few questions, and…"

"Robot roulette," spat Pearce, his thick brows knitting together.

"I think so, Captain."

"Lead the way, then." Pearce rose from his chair, feeling his anger begin to rise within him. He did his best to control it, to master it rather than submit to it, but he could feel the tightening knot in his belly, the involuntary clenching of his hands into fists, and the grinding of his teeth just the same. *Robot roulette*, he thought as he followed Hall through the Quarterdeck and into the lift that took them down the command tower, past the engine room and toward the cargo bays. A practice as old as the machrines themselves, dangerous to real and artificial crewmen alike, and long since specifically prohibited by Navy regulations. With the losses of Rowland and el-Barzin so fresh, he had no intention of recording any more condolence messages, particularly for stupid and unnecessary self-inflicted casualties.

Pearce strode through the cavernous main bay, past the empty vats, toward the door Hall indicated with his hand. With a touch of the panel it opened, revealing a tableau not unlike the one that Fletcher had seen not long before, with the exception that his first officer was among those watching the forbidden sport, with all appearance of benign interest. Something burst inside Pearce. He had been as forbearing of Christine Fletcher, as tolerant of her diffidence toward rank and procedure, as he could possibly manage, and she repaid him not with loyalty, but by allowing insubordinate behavior right under her nose; indeed, even participating in it.

"What the devil's all this about?" he shouted, though of course he knew, and five pairs of eyes all oriented on him at once, their owners paralyzed with shock and dismay. Luther-45 stood stock-still, arms at his sides, though his chin dropped just a little toward the floor, as though he, too, were embarrassed to be caught in wrongdoing. "This isn't the damned merchant marine! You, there," he barked at Pratt as his rage began to boil over. "What do you mean by this?"

"Beg your pardon sir, but there's been robot roulette on His Majesty's ships as long as there's been robots."

Not on Captain Baker's ships! thought Pearce, but what he roared instead was "Not on mine!"

Pearce felt a hand on his elbow, and he rotated his neck slowly to see Christine Fletcher, the ship's master and his first mate, looking at him calmly, with the hint of a smile. Her hair was unbound, and she wore no duty coat over her uniform shirt, which had the top three buttons undone. The swell of her cleavage was clearly visible, and images, unbidden, of her nude breasts in St. Kitts flashed in his mind, adding fuel to his wrath.

"Unhand me, Lieutenant Fletcher," he snarled. "You forget yourself." She moved her hand as though she had touched a live fusion engine, all traces of amicability swiftly gone.

"Bill, there's no harm done here. Some of the crew were simply having a bit of fun."

"A bit of fun?" He rounded on her now, his chastisement of Pratt forgotten. "No harm? This is a blasted King's ship and we'll have some damned discipline. We will be starmanlike!" He made a show of looking her up and down, and his lips curled into a sneer. "Though who can blame them if they lack discipline? Look at you, woman. Out of uniform. Cavorting with the crew belowdecks. And you an officer and a noblewoman."

All color drained from Fletcher's face, and she backed away, expressionless. Later, Pearce would wonder if that moment, that exact moment, had been the one from which all the others followed, if events had inexorably been set in motion. But in that instant, the hot pressure throbbed in his temples, and the betrayal and isolation crushed down on him, leaving no room for nuance or consideration.

"Mister Hall, summon Sergeant Crutchfield, if you would. Please instruct him to bring the other three machrines here with him."

Midshipman Hall had been lurking unobtrusively in the open doorway, and now the human heads in the small secondary bay swiveled, fixing on him. Pearce was not so enraged that he could not see the hatred and contempt radiating from those faces, and when Pratt took a single step in the direction of the junior officer, he wasted no time in reacting.

"Stand fast, Pratt. You're in enough trouble as it is. Luther," he added, and the robot, animated by the use of his designation in a command tone, stirred.

"Yes, Captain?"

"Take Crewman Pratt into physical custody, if you please."

"Yes, sir." Luther-45 moved nimbly behind Pratt and took hold of the starman's wrists. Pratt began to struggle, but winced as the machrine applied greater pressure, irresistibly moving his hands behind his back.

"Give it up, Isaac," muttered Briggs. "You're only going to get hurt." It always startled Pearce that such a soft, gentle voice could come from such a physically imposing woman. *Probably why she never talks.*

There was silence for long minutes, as they waited. They stared at one another, not moving, not speaking, scarcely sharing the same space at all. Pearce could all but feel the distance yawning between him and the crewmen, growing larger with each passing moment. Isaac Pratt, held firm in the grasp of the robot, no longer resisting, sullen. Mathias Quintal, inscrutable, smirking. Peggy Briggs, carved from unfeeling rock. Tom Churchill, near to tears with fear. He could not bring himself to look at Christine Fletcher.

What could have been two lifetimes later, Sergeant Orpheus Crutchfield blotted out the doorway like an eclipse, his looming, ebony form casting a shadow that filled the small hold. Behind him were three machrines, duplicates of Luther except for the nameplate designations on their chests. Ogden-92. Victor-11. Ambrose-226.

"Captain?" Crutchfield betrayed nothing more than a slight perplexity.

"Take these jacks into custody, if you please," Pearce ordered evenly. "You may detain them in one of the other adjunct bays until the crew has been mustered for punishment." Never taking his eyes off his offending crewmen, Pearce addressed Hall. "Assemble the crew, Mister Hall. A taste of the Cat for these four, I think." With no questions and no wasted motion, the sergeant directed his synthetic squad to escort the four crewmen into an adjoining chamber, and Hall scurried off to carry out his commander's orders. The door closed behind them, leaving Pearce alone with Lieutenant Christine Fletcher.

"Captain..." she said, not looking him in the eye, her voice soft. "You can't mean to flog them."

Pearce glared at her. The initial heat of his wrath had ebbed, but now her arrogance brought it rushing back. With difficulty, he swallowed his first, caustic response. Instead, through grinding teeth, he said, "I can and I do. And if not for regs concerning penalties for officers, I would lump you in with them. Damn, Christine! What can you have been thinking?"

She paused a moment before answering, and Pearce wondered if she were pondering her response, or if she was, like him, laboring to manage her temper.

"As I said, Captain, I thought it a largely harmless pastime. The crew needs distractions on a long voyage like this."

"Harmless? It would seem you and I have different ideas about what a crew needs!"

"Yes!" Fletcher was flaring now, her resentment spilling over, shouting across the chasm between them. "That's why you brought me, remember?"

Pearce knew there was some truth in that. Wrong as she was about the particulars, wrong as she was to flaunt Navy traditions and to treat his authority lightly, she was right that he had brought her specifically to bridge that gulf between himself and the crew. The realization only made him angrier. At her, at himself, at the situation, at the fraying thread that held their shared enterprise together, the fraying thread connecting his son to a future.

"Enough," he said. "The men will be flogged. As for you, Lieutenant Fletcher, you are relieved of your duties as executive officer of this ship. You will now report to Lieutenant Pott, who will assume those duties. Is that clear?"

Fletcher did not speak. She looked at him, her mouth hanging open for a long heartbeat before she snapped her jaw shut and thrust it forward.

"Yes...sir."

"Good. Muster in the main bay with the rest of the crew for punishment. Dismissed."

She stalked past him without another glance, without another word. In the empty room, Pearce finally faltered, leaning heavily against the stack of crates. It was only then he noticed the gouges his fingernails had dug into his palms, and the sheen of sweat on his face. He had always known that commanding officers were isolated, but for the first time, the stark truth of it came crashing down on him. *I am alone out here,* he realized. And it terrified him.

****

As he had ordered, the entire crew was assembled in the spacious cargo bay for the administration of punishment. The *Harvest* herself was in an autonomous high-altitude orbit around the gaseous sixth planet of the Korin system, helium and hydrogen dancing orange and red across the massive, arcing surface below. Officers and ables alike stood at attention in their dress uniforms while the machrines, under the supervision of Sergeant Crutchfield, brought out the offenders. Mathias Quintal, Isaac Pratt, and Tom Churchill were all naked to the waist, as was Peggy Briggs, though she wore a bandeau of thin black cloth where breasts would be on other women. Each of the four was attended by one of the robots, who lined the starmen up in the center of the bay, with a space of a little over a meter between them. The guilty wrists were bound with plexisteel manacles, and a cable dangled from each, reaching to the floor. Swiftly, with ruthless and programmed efficiency, the machrines affixed the other end of each cable to an eyebolt in the floor. Briggs had no expression on her broad face, staring straight ahead past her crewmates. Pearce wondered if she had been flogged before. Pratt certainly had, telltale hairline scars crisscrossed the man's massive, muscle-knotted back, and his face bore a look of hardened defiance. *Yes, he's felt it before, and more than once.* Churchill was the only one of the four who betrayed any fright; his beady little eyes darted about from one side of the bay to the other, as though he were seeking out a friendly face among the rest of the crew. Finding none, he eventually fixed his gaze on the floor, though he continued to tremble, and Pearce thought he saw sweat on his shoulders and back. Was Quintal smiling? *No,* Pearce thought. Quintal was an experienced enough starman to know what was in store. That was just his damned smirk, the one he always wore, as if he was the only one in on a joke. *We'll see if that's still there when this is over.*

The offenders secured, the machrines retreated, with the exception of Ogden-92, who remained nearby. Pearce stepped forward, a bound, old-paper copy of the King's Regulations and Instructions of the Admiralty under his arm. It was traditional for each ship of His Majesty's Royal Navy to carry one of these archaic books, even though the long list of regulations was more readily accessed via computer or vidscreen. Observing the requisite theater, the captain opened the book and read aloud from the centuries-old text, much of it still couched in traditional language. "Article Twenty-Three of the King's Regulations and Instructions of the Admiralty," Pearce began, his voice thick but clear. "If any person in the fleet shall quarrel or fight with any other person in the fleet, or use reproachful or provoking speeches or gestures, tending to make any quarrel or disturbance, he shall, upon being convicted thereof, suffer such punishment as the offence shall deserve, in keeping with the customs of the service."

"They ain't persons though, are they?" grumbled Pratt.

"Be silent." One eye twitched, but Pearce retained control of his temper and the dignity of his rank. Pratt scowled, but held his tongue. "As captain of this vessel, I find these men in violation of this regulation. Machrine Ogden-92, do your duty."

Sergeant Crutchfield handed the robot a thick brown bag. Reaching inside it, Ogden withdrew a short metallic cylinder. At the press of a button, nine long, thin filaments sprouted and grew to about two meters in length. Already quiet, the crew somehow managed to become more silent still.

The Cat O'Nine Tails. Pearce hated it. It was an ugly spectacle to watch, unpleasant in the extreme. Still, some discipline was needed, and even though it inflicted significant anguish, the Cat did no real structural damage to the body of those punished, unlike the far more barbaric floggings of centuries past that crippled or even killed. Even so, it was a brutal, inhumane instrument, one of the few vestiges of the old Navy that had endured into the modern, presumably more enlightened, age. The Cat was not used, as the lash had once been, for minor offenses; more lenient sanctions, such as confinement to quarters or docking of pay, sufficed for these. It was reserved, instead, for those crimes the Navy had once considered capital offenses. In deep space, crew were too valuable, too difficult to replace to simply shoot or even hang, as once would have been the case. So, they tasted the Cat instead.

There was only one Cat on board, and with multiple wrongdoers to reprimand, Ogden-92 would apply each of the lashes to each crewman, in turn. Each of the nine filaments was preprogrammed to release a timed electrostatic charge directly into the nervous system, causing a set amount of pain for a set duration. Ogden began with Pratt, moving to Quintal, then Churchill, and finally to Briggs. The robot wielded the Cat with inhuman precision, striking all four within five seconds. The first lash discharged sufficient energy to cause slight discomfort, essentially a tingling sensation, lasting only a single second. During that time, none of the assembled crew moved, or spoke. Only

Ogden knew when the second lash would fall, the silent alert of a random internal chronometer instructing him when to proceed, sometime between one and sixty seconds later. That second lash was somewhat more unpleasant, though still not truly painful, and lasted just two seconds. The punishment continued with rigorous, almost ritualistic precision through the third (three seconds) and fourth lashes (four seconds), each with a corresponding increase in the charge.

When the fifth lash touched Churchill's back, barely two minutes into the exercise, he cried out. *The gut-punch lash*, Pearce thought, recalling how he had heard it described by others who had felt it. The fourth lash was the first that really hurt, it was said, and the fifth could take your breath away. And it lasted for a full five seconds. The others under punishment remained impassive, though Pearce imagined he detected a note of disdain for his weaker crewmate in Pratt's glower.

Ogden went on to apply the sixth lash like the machine he was, impervious to the suffering of those he chastised, impervious to any pleas for clemency they might attempt. Churchill did not cry out this time, despite the increased intensity and longer duration of the charge, though a trickle of blood at the corner of his mouth told Pearce the man had bitten his tongue. At the seventh lash, midway through the seven-second duration, Quintal betrayed his agony with a sharp intake of breath through his nose, while Churchill, by far the softest creature involved, had begun to weep, tears streaming down his face, body shaking with sobs. Pratt remained silent, though his entire torso was glistening with sweat, and the veins in his neck and arms stood out like thick red rope. Pearce looked at Briggs. Her demeanor had not changed once during the entire punishment. No grimaces, no grunts, not even the barest flicker in her impassivity. The captain marveled at her strength of will, even as he wondered at her humanity.

The eighth lash, delivering eight long seconds of soul-crushing pain, finally drew a groan from Mathias Quintal, a low, guttural sound emitting from his closed mouth as his dark eyes rolled up into his head, becoming blank white orbs. He had tried to keep up with Pratt and Briggs, but they outmassed him by no small margin, and many their size and bigger had broken by number eight. Churchill, the poor weak fool, had urinated on himself and dropped to his knees. Ambrose-226 and Victor-11 swiftly drew him back up to his feet, though when they released him he promptly fell again. Crutchfield barked an order, and the machrines propped Churchill up again, between them, and held him fast.

One more and this ugliness is over, Pearce thought.

A full minute passed before Ogden-92 let fly the ninth and final touch of the Cat, and with it nine seconds of the kind of pain only encountered in the worst kind of nightmares. Two seconds into the discharge, Churchill's body writhed in grotesque spasm, his screams giving way to a high-pitched, animalistic keening, and he vomited something brown. Quintal fell to the deck, twitching and moaning. Only Briggs and Pratt kept their feet, though at long last Pratt made a sound, a roaring bellow that echoed through the bay, throughout the entire *Harvest*. *If not for the vacuum beyond the hull*, Pearce thought, *they'd hear him back in London.* Briggs remained silent, her teeth now bared in a feral grimace, blood and saliva bubbling pink down her chin. Then the nine seconds were over, and the punishment with it.

The entire exercise had lasted no more than ten minutes.

"Dismissed," Pearce said softly, and the machrines undid the restraints. It was an ancient naval tradition that once the penalty had been paid, wrongdoers were restored to status, the slate clean.

Dr. Szakonyi came forward to check on the offenders, though their injuries were, by design, entirely psychological. Pearce watched as some of the other starmen went to their crewmates to offer assistance and commiseration. Saul Lamb gave Briggs an approving look as he and Xiang helped Quintal to his unsteady feet. She ignored him, ignored everyone, as she stalked from the bay, erect and unbowed, the only evidence of her ordeal the slightest red glow on her back, even now fading. Taryn Hadley brought Pratt into a less than motherly hug, pressing his sweat-soaked head against her pillowy chest. The task of tending to Churchill fell to Waugh, who looked none too thrilled with the detail. Churchill was held in fairly low regard by most belowdecks, largely (and correctly) seen as an insipid flunky.

Pearce turned aside. There would be resentment for a time among the crew, but there was nothing that could be done about that. *Put it out of your mind. You did what was necessary, nothing more.* Then he made eye contact with Fletcher. There, he found reproach. Not for his demotion of her, but for his punishment of the ables. Grinding his jaw, he brushed past her, past his other officers, and out of the bay.

****

"A glass of wine with you, Sir Green."

The aged knight held his glass aloft and toasted "to the King" before downing most of the contents in one prolonged swallow. Pearce returned the gesture, with a somewhat smaller sip.

"To our success," he addressed the table, "and to a speedy return home." This drew echoes and a thump on the table from Lieutenant Pott. Pearce did not truly enjoy hosting dinner for the officers and his civilian guests, but it was part of his duty, and whatever else his faults, inattention to duty was not one of them. Green, he saw, was perturbed.

"I found the entire exhibition utterly barbaric."

The white flesh of Sir Green's scalp glowed a mottled scarlet beneath his wispy gray flyaway hair as he visibly trembled, one hand clutching at the other. The steaming plate of ham cutlets and whipped squash on the table before him lay untouched, though Pearce noticed the man's wine glass had been emptied.

"I cannot disagree." Pearce cut his synthetic meat with exaggerated deliberation and chewed mechanically at the piece he put in his mouth. He looked around the table in the officers' mess. Fletcher stared at her plate, hands on her lap, unmoving. Pott ate with his usual enthusiasm, the indelible habit of a life in the service. Peckover was absent, on duty, and Szakoyni watched with mild interest. Green was nearly apoplectic, but Dr. Reyes was the soul of composure next to him, even as she arched an eyebrow.

"You agree, Captain?"

"Naturally," Pearce replied. "Any sane creature would find the Cat a hellish device."

"And yet you ordered it used! You ordered it used and ordered every man and woman on the ship to observe the nasty business!" Green shouted, half standing.

"Yes, and I will again, if required. In the meantime, Sir Eustace, please keep your seat and keep your voice down. I do not mind your questioning my authority here in private. Your status, of course, permits such...discourse. However, the *Harvest* has thin interior walls, and I would not appreciate any of the crew overhearing your kindly-intentioned sentiments."

"My...my what? And who bloody well cares if they do overhear?"

"I do," Pearce answered curtly, the slightest tinge of irritation creeping into his voice. "And for the same reason I ordered everyone to be present, in keeping with Navy regulations. There will be discipline on this ship, sir, and I will enforce it as needed." He laid his knife and fork on his plate with a clatter. "We are a small community here, very far from home. And to succeed in our mission, indeed to survive at all, especially with such crewmen as the Admiralty has seen fit to give us, there must be discipline. And it begins with me. Here on this ship, I speak with the King's own voice."

"The King!" Green choked. "What arrogance!"

"Not at all," interjected Reyes smoothly. "I think you will find that commanders of naval vessels enjoy precisely that station. I, for one, found the sanctions entirely appropriate. I had no idea you were such a humanist, Eustace. Not one of those punished was gently born, after all." She turned to face Pearce, almost as an afterthought. "No offense, of course, Captain."

Pearce merely smiled thinly in response and chewed his ham, fairly certain offense had been intended. Her endorsement of his position was neither encouraging nor comfortable. He did not like her, nor trust her. *What game is that woman playing?* Reyes was aloof, cold, and thoroughly charmless. She was undeniably brilliant, of course – Pearce had sat in on a few sessions between her and Sir Green, and had swiftly given up on trying to understand their conversations about progeny tests, bare-root seedlings, and hydroponic reagent purity. He thought of the words they had exchanged after the encounter with the pirates. *Maybe*, he thought, *she's just a bitch*.

"Humanism hardly equates to egalitarianism, Dr. Reyes," spluttered the Royal Gardener. "Believing in the inherent dignity of all people hardly qualifies as a call to end the monarchy. I merely abhor violence. Surely there must be some gentler way to enforce discipline? Some withholding of privilege, some reduction in rank?"

"Captain," mumbled Fletcher, standing abruptly. "May I be excused? I am not feeling well."

"No, you may not," snapped Pearce. "Keep your seat, Lieutenant Fletcher."

"Sir," she said quietly, her eyes downcast, "haven't you embarrassed me enough tonight?"

"If you are embarrassed, it is your own doing, not mine. Sit."

Fletcher sat down, heavily. Pott had the good grace to appear not to notice, and the rest of the table was well-bred enough to ignore the outburst.

"You may have the King's voice, Pearce, but I have his ear," said Green smugly. *At least he's not shouting anymore*, Pearce thought. *I should be grateful for that, anyway.* "And you can be sure that I will be complaining most strenuously upon our return about these infamous practices."

"Sir Eustace," said Pearce, and he actually found himself smiling, "I would like nothing more. All else aside, it would mean that we had gotten home safe."

****

The servants were gone, and the sun had long since set. All the lights were out in the parlor where John Banks sat alone, his aquiline face lit only by the gentle, flickering glow from the fireplace. A solitary red light on the knee-high table in front of him blinked politely but insistently, announcing (as it had for the last half-hour) a new encoded message from Pearce. Banks took one more slow and fortifying sip of Chianti, set the glass down with a sigh, and activated the viewsceen. It flared to life, and with it the face of William Pearce.

He seems so tired, thought Banks. Pearce's face was drawn and even paler than usual.

"My Lords," he began. "The *Harvest* continues en route to Cygnus. We did experience a setback in the Lyra system and some subsequent crew discipline issues." He proceeded, grimfaced and pale, to describe the encounter with the Procyean pirates, as well as the robot roulette incident, including his demotion of Christine Fletcher. "Despite these obstacles, I remain convinced we will arrive as scheduled at Cygnus, and accomplish our objectives. I will continue to update you as long as I can. Pearce out." The screen went blank.

Banks sat back in his sofa as the screen sank seamlessly into the tabletop. Given the communications restrictions that the Harvest was traveling under, all messages, including this one, came first to the Admiralty. *That means Exeter has already seen this.* He knew the Star Lord would be fuming. Pearce had been insistent on having Fletcher, and Banks had been insistent on having Pearce. So Banks had argued for her inclusion on the voyage over Exeter's misgivings. And now she was giving Pearce trouble. *Perhaps the Star Lord had been right*, he thought. With no formal training and no psychological screening, they had made her a Lieutenant in His Majesty's Royal Navy, and second in command of a starship? It had all seemed so clear, so simple, in the cozy confines of Exeter's offices.

For the very first time, Banks began to worry in earnest about the success of the mission. About the people they had chosen to lead it. About his friend, Eustace. Sir Green had thought this his last chance for a grand adventure, to wander outside his well-ordered gardens and into the wilds of space. *He's not young*, Banks thought tenderly. *Neither of us are.* He felt the old gardener's absence keenly, missing his kind smiles, his erudite wit, his loving touch. Trying to imagine Eustace all alone out there, across billions of miles of frigid vacuum, made him shiver despite the well-regulated warmth in the room. The thought of Eustace never coming home, of a world without him...

Old fool, he called himself. If Green never came back, if the *Harvest* failed, there would be no more world for anyone. Banks retrieved his wineglass, felt the warmth of the Chianti through the curve of the crystal, and tried to ignore the crushing weight in his heart. The uncertain future of all humanity hung from the slender thread he and Exeter had managed to spin. Staring at the blackness beyond the parlor's authentic glass windows, he felt small. The universe, all of it, was out there. And the vast bulk of it was unexplored. Admiralty star charts resembled the world maps from the previous millennia, tiny regions of familiarity surrounded by a fringe drawn from rumor and scattered reports, and beyond that, the vast unknown. Banks had an ancient map like that in his Ministry office, and where the unknown or uncharted persisted, there were fanciful illustrations of undulating serpents or beckoning mermaids or other mythological beasts, and in one place the scrawled warning, *here there be dragons*. It was all so much more romantic, and terrifying, than the Admiralty's stark, sterile charts of empty quadrants, filled with untracked blackness.

In the brief decades since human science had begun outwitting the paradoxes of mass and time and distance, the King's ships had penetrated only a small corner of just one of the infinite galaxies known to exist, all spinning away from one another and from whatever shared birthplace they might have known. Even within the infinitesimal shard of space which humanity had managed to grope through, there was bewildering diversity. Among those planets considered Earth-like, enjoying sufficiently similar tolerances of temperature, atmosphere, and orbital distance, the native flora and fauna and other forms of life occupied every notch on the continuum of human imagination and beyond, in a stunning panoply of variety.

Amongst all of this, there were even sentient creatures; some bipedal, some verbally communicative, some bearing vague physical resemblance to humans. Among the scientists in Banks' ministry were xenobiogenesis theorists who spent their careers in the grasping study of the origins of life in the cosmos. Their work included Ingram's Taxonomy, the herculean and virtually impossible effort to slot every form of life encountered into meaningful categories based on shared characteristics. The people of Kepler-22B bore the designation Homo cygnusi, so close were they physiologically and even genetically to Homo sapiens. Speculation existed that that the two peoples, of Earth and Cygnus, descended from some common ancestry, a theory dismissed in serious academic circles but persistent on the scientific fringe. There had been a mildly sensational paper presented some years earlier, hypothesizing that when a massive prehistoric asteroid collided with

Earth, dooming the dinosaurs, it had struck with force enough to launch terran matter into space with speed and trajectory sufficient to escape the solar system. According to the paper, that matter was laden with DNA that could have endured the long trek to another world.

Banks himself was an agnostic on the question of panspermia, the theory of galactic origins for humanity which might well have seeded similar planets with similar genetic raw material. He was not an evolutionary biologist, nor an astronomer, and stepped only gingerly into the debate when it emerged from time to time to trouble the deliberations of the Royal Society. At the moment, he did not care why Kepler-22B shared such close kinship with Earth. He did not care why, except with some vague scientific curiosity, the Cygni should be so human-like. He only cared that they were, and that in that similarity, the deliverance of all humanity might reside. And now that he had done all he could to bring that deliverance to pass, he could only wait.

He not only felt small, he felt powerless.

****

Lord Rajek Djimonsu felt powerful.

He stood, alone as always, in his brightly lit office. It was past midnight, but the sun never set on the markets of the United Kingdom. The Tokyo Exchange would be closing soon, and a late run on desalinization technology bore watching. In just three or four hours, the Colonial Crown Index would be opening in New York, and the Chancellor had carefully orchestrated a quiet deal that would prop up algae prices long enough to wriggle free of some poorly-performing royal investments in that sector. He was a fiscal Cromwell, the Lord Protector of the Kingdom's economic health, the threats to which were potentially legion. The pound sterling never slept, and Djimonsu rarely did either, perhaps three or four hours out of twenty-four.

He was married, of course. That had been arranged by his father, when Djimonsu had been all of eight. His wife was neither attractive nor intelligent, but she had come from a family redolent with wealth and name, and that had been more than enough for the late Bijali Djimonsu. There was no hint of the woman in the Lord Chancellor's office, no handsome framed portrait of the Privy Councilor with his doting spouse and three children. His daughters and their mother were safely distant in Mumbai, where their bumbling provincialism could do his career no harm. There were other female companions as needed, appropriate to his station. One had visited him earlier that evening, discreetly of course, a yellow-haired native Briton. *Yet another delectable daughter of Albion*, he thought. They were always pale Britons – the vendors knew his tastes. He had entertained her in his sprawling apartments a floor below this office – exquisite wines, imported foods, professional sex. Through the complicity and generosity of grateful patrons, it was a scene he repeated there often.

There. Never here. Here, between the gleaming walls of the Treasury, he had only one true love, and that was Britannia herself, the United Kingdom of Earth. And there was nothing he would not do for her.

A shrill chirping interrupted his thoughts. Djimonsu had twelve different sounds assigned to varying categories of incoming message, and he knew them all intimately, the better to know whether any given call or alert was worth his time at that moment. This sound he would never ignore. *Henry*. With a touch, he accessed the text of the message. It had come from halfway across the galaxy, and it was utterly innocuous. *Be a good girl. Listen to your mother.* Blah, blah, blah. Djimonsu smirked, an expression he had perfected over the years. Banal trivialities, designed to slip, scarcely noticed, through the perfunctory review of the commander of the *Harvest*, across the vast emptiness of the galaxy, past the somewhat more advanced scrutiny of the Admiralty, to one of his agents here on Earth, to him. It took less than a minute for the translator program to de-encrypt the language and rearrange the letters into meaningful intelligence. As he read, the Chancellor's smirk became a broad smile.

It begins, he thought. Pearce was exhibiting signs of strain. Discipline problems with the crew. Discord among the officers. Pirate attacks. And all of this before the expedition had even reached Cygnus. *You've done well, Henry.* Satisfied for the moment, Djimonsu encoded and archived the message. He tried to return his gaze to the monitors, but suddenly realized how tired he was. There was nothing there that wouldn't keep until morning, and he had done his service for King and country that night. *Lord, I hope I'm right*, he thought, before recalling his own maxim: a strong man may have doubts before a decision, but never after. It was time to sleep, if only for a while, and to dream of satisfied clients and an orderly world.

Nine

Landfall

"It's so…green."

Pearce knew what Musgrave meant. The orb that filled the viewscreen was a pastel smudge against the blackness beyond, like a child's marble from antiquity. Earth, viewed from orbit, was a bruise of mottled black and indigo, all sprawled cities and lifeless oceans. The lights kept virtually every mile of the globe glowing unnaturally, illuminating a ball of hard edges and unremitting progress. This was none of those things. This blue-green jewel was the planet known to His Majesty's Royal Navy as Kepler-22B, charted by Captain Jane Baker on her third, and fatal, voyage. The indigenous people there were the only sentient race thus far found in the old-style constellation of Cygnus. They had their own name for themselves, something difficult enough to properly pronounce that they were usually referred to simply as the Cygni.

"Are those…" Hall asked, his mouth slightly open in wonder. Pearce nodded.

"Icecaps." Their orbital attitude was almost precisely equatorial, giving them a clear view of both polar regions. Massive bursts of white spread out from both top and bottom, a spectacle of frozen water.

"Right on the surface like that." Hall's whistle was low and impressed, and not a little astonished. Earth had not seen icecaps in living memory. For a man like Hall, who, like so many of the working-class, had lived his life amongst steel and concrete and then the vacuum of space, he might as well have been looking out at Eden before the fall.

"Prepare the cutter," Pearce ordered. "Pott, you have the *Harvest* until I return. Worth, please extend my courtesies and request that Sir Green and Dr. Reyes join us on board. Lieutenant Fletcher, with me." She followed him off the Quarterdeck to his star-cabin. Once they were inside, he asked her to close the door and sit down.

"You've studied the language?" he asked.

"Yes, sir." She stood at artificially rigid attention, looking over his shoulder.

"Damn you, Lieutenant. Christine!" Her gaze shifted to his eyes. "I regret this…this coolness between us. I may be partially at fault, but now is not the time. I need your support and cooperation if we are to be successful. And we must be successful. Now, you have studied the language?" Fletcher didn't relax her posture, but he thought her tone was slightly less brisk, and she continued to meet his eyes. *It will have to do*, he thought.

"Yes, Captain."

"Good. Thank you. Now, I am not certain what we will encounter when we land. These Cygni have a volatile society. They may welcome us with open arms, or they may meet us with violence. It has been twelve years since an Englishman has set foot on their planet, and we were not...on the best of terms at the conclusion of that visit. Regardless, we must have their cooperation, so I am empowered to treat them with great generosity and patience. Christine, the men will do as you and I do. Our conduct will inform theirs. Do you understand me?"

"Yes, sir." The ghost of a smile drifted across her lips. "Best behavior, sir."

"It is more than that. We will be here for three weeks, maybe four. Dr. Reyes tells me it may take that long for her to complete her work. In that time, should we be so fortunate to restore friendship with the Cygni, there will be great opportunity for...cultural exchange."

"The language program included instruction on what we know of their xenopology, Captain. I believe I understand you."

"Very good." He stood, leaning forward with his hands on his desk. "Lieutenant Fletcher, I want you to coordinate our operations on the planet below. Make sure the scientists have what they need, but also oversee the crew. Schedule their shore leave rotations, if we get that far. Manage their contact and relations with the Cygni. I am sure to be occupied with the rigors of formal diplomacy, so I need you to manage the informal." He rose. In their years in space together, his trust in her had never wavered until now, and it had never been more vital. Sighing, he spread his hands in a gesture that was equal parts exasperation and supplication.

"I have always relied upon your judgment and loyalty, Christine. I know we have had our troubles on the voyage here. We must set those aside, if we are to accomplish our goals. You are to be my representative ashore. There is no one I would rather rely on. I must know that I can trust you completely."

He came out from behind the desk, and he touched her arm. Could they bridge the crevasse, and recapture the luck and accord they had shared before? She had been such a vital part of his lucrative merchant career. Now, when he most needed her, it wasn't the same. Something was different. Was it the rigors of Navy structure? Was it her? *Or is it me?* he thought. *Am I pressing too hard, with all that's on the line?* It didn't matter. There was no changing what had gone before. The future was all that mattered now.

****

The *Harvest*'s two launches were small, and there was barely room in this one for the eight bodies now strapped into their seats. Fletcher slipped into the pilot's chair, while Worth sat alongside at the support station, with Pearce in his slightly elevated command perch just behind them. In the passenger section rode the scientists. Dr. Reyes looked icy and reserved as usual, while Sir Green's expression betrayed his anxious enthusiasm. Pearce understood that this was the man's maiden voyage to an alien planet. He found it hard to understand how someone could live their whole life, especially one as privileged as his, and not even visit the Mars cities or the terrafarmed nurseries of Io or Europa. Excitement showed on Worth's face as well, but the young midshipman did her best to appear calm. In the rear, at their posts by the cutter's entrance, were the Royal Machrines. Sergeant Crutchfield had insisted on coming himself, along with two of the robots, Luther-45 and Victor-11. Crutchfield wore his scarlet field uniform, with crossed white bandolier and pulse rifle, and the plastisteel skin of the Machrines echoed the aesthetics. In his heart, Pearce wished for one of Captain Baker's large landing shuttles, and twelve Machrines, rather than just two and their human officer. *Even that hadn't been enough for her*, he thought. With no idea what they would find on the surface, this would have to be enough.

He also wished that he could have left Reyes and Green aboard the *Harvest*, but neither would hear of it. Had this been an initial contact with an unknown civilization, Admiralty protocols would have prohibited civilians from joining the first landing, but since there had been contact with the Cygni before, those protocols did not strictly apply. That was a point Reyes in particular had made, rather heatedly, when Pearce had tried to convince them to wait until he had reconnoitered the situation below.

"Captain, I believe it is written in your orders that Sir Green and I are to be consulted on all matters in this expedition once we arrive at Kepler-22B," she had said in his cabin, as Green sat nearby, his hands folded over his belly, smiling benignly. "I suggest you read them again if you have forgotten. I am certain Lord Exeter was quite specific."

Pearce had his doubts whether Exeter had written that portion of his orders, yet the language was there. It was highly irregular, but then, everything about this voyage was highly irregular. So the scientists were part of this motley eight-member team, in whose collective hands somehow rested mankind's future. *And my son's*, thought Pearce briefly, before dismissing that thought to the nether regions of his own brain. He would have no time or energy for distractions in the hours ahead.

Fletcher navigated the launch expertly through the upper stratosphere, while the massive emerald-and-sapphire orb, four times the size of Earth, swelled steadily beneath them. She was following the approach trajectory that Pearce had outlined for her, heading inexorably toward the same landfall that Baker's crew had made a dozen years before. During the several planning sessions preceding departure, there had been much debate about the relative dangers and benefits of such an approach. Lord Banks had been insistent that it was the only logical choice, despite the violent circumstances of the *Drake*'s expulsion. Kepler-22B was a vast planet, and one with a level of political development roughly equivalent to Earth's late 18th century. There was no known world government, and a strong likelihood that the language Pearce knew as Cygni was a regional dialect. Setting down elsewhere would probably result in linguistic barriers that would slow progress. Even more importantly, these Cygni, on the northeast corner of the second-largest landmass, had met Earthers before. The relations with the natives had been mixed, varying among the different castes, and there was the potential that the factions that had befriended Baker were once more in power. If so, renewal of those old ties was one of the primary reasons Pearce had been chosen to command this mission.

*And if not…*well, if not, Pearce had his orders. If they couldn't obtain what they needed through peaceful cooperation, he was empowered to seize it by force. *With what force, exactly?* he wondered, with a glance at his three soldiers.

As a final consideration, their understanding of Cygnusian ecology was woefully incomplete, and there was the possibility that the grains they sought were peculiar to that region. And so they were headed back to the scene of their dramatic exit. Pearce could picture the spit of land as though he had been there yesterday, hear the shouts of his crewmates and the eerie sounds of those alien weapons, screaming in the predawn. Alexander-457's eyes flickering, beseeching.

"Captain, ten kilometers of altitude and well into the troposphere. Approaching cloud layer now." Fletcher turned to look at him, nothing in her eyes but confidence. *She's only been on commercial runs*, he thought, *following established trade routes*. He nodded at her.

"Proceed, Lieutenant." Then, louder, he addressed the entire party. "We believe the Cygni have only been visited by guests from another world once in their entire history, and everything we know about this world suggests that they are largely preindustrial, with no electronic detection devices monitoring their atmosphere. However, once we penetrate the cloud layer, we will be visible to the naked eye. Worth, estimate on arrival?"

"Eight minutes, Captain."

"Very good. You have all been briefed, but I will remind you that no one is to speak or act unless expressly ordered to do so by me. Is that understood?" There was a murmur of assent.

"And if something happens to you?" Pearce wasn't looking at her, but he could hear the smirk in Reyes' voice. He wished, for the hundredth time, that John Banks had known a more companionable xenobotanist.

"Nothing will," growled Crutchfield, and Pearce felt a surge of gratitude toward the bearlike soldier.

"Thank you, sergeant. Still, in the event I am detained or... incapacitated, you will immediately return to the launch under Fletcher's command and retreat to the *Harvest*. I want no harm done to these people, if we can help it."

The clouds parted then, and they emerged into the lower atmosphere of Cygnus. They were some six or seven kilometers above the surface, most of which was open ocean, a shade of blue which none of them, except Pearce, had ever seen before. The cabin grew still.

"My grandfather tells stories of when there was an expanse of water like this between the Caribbean and England." Fletcher never took her attention off her controls, but there was a hollowness and wonder in her voice that made Pearce frown.

"You've seen ocean before," he said. "Two of the New Indies worlds have living seas."

"Not like this." Fletcher's voice was husky, and Pearce could only categorize her expression as one of longing. He noted, with approval, that her fascination wasn't interfering with her piloting. "And we never get this close."

That was true. The commerce at New Indies was almost entirely conducted at The Exchange, the enormous trading station in orbit around the fourth world of that system.

"Well," he said, with a wry smile, "you'll certainly get a closer look at these waters. Proceed to Point Friendship, Lieutenant."

It was morning on Cygnus, during their long summer, and the first rays of the alien sun reflected in dappled glory off the waking blue of the trackless ocean below. Fletcher banked the cutter, dropping lower and turning the equivalent of east, and the far horizon grew thicker, then corrugated, as the interior peaks swelled purple in the distance. As they came closer still, the sun struck the lands between sea and mountains in a riot of green.

"Are those..." Worth asked, staring.

"Trees," answered Green, breathlessly. "Or their native counterparts, at any rate. The reports tell of low, leafy specimens near the water that resemble our own elms."

"*Pilapus*," murmured Pearce, the word coming back to him all at once.

"And," continued Green, aglow with scholarly excitement, "as you travel inland, there are species that tower a hundred feet in the air or more, like the forests primeval!"

"*Tamms*," said Pearce, with a faraway look on his face. "*Jalakas, Mands, Stamas.*"

"Impressive, Captain," said Reyes, with an inscrutable grin. "You could have been a fair xenobotanist in another life."

"Captain Baker encouraged us to learn the language," he offered with a shrug. "I was young enough and naïve enough to take the suggestion seriously." He leaned forward to gaze out the front viewport, and put a hand on Fletcher's shoulder, as he had done on dozens of trading runs before. It was an unthinking reflex, a conditioned habit, but he became aware of it when she flinched at his touch. Immediately, he withdrew his hand, as if he had touched something hot, and clasped them both behind his back.

"Point Friendship ahead, Captain," Fletcher announced awkwardly into the silence. Pearce put the uncomfortable moment out of his mind, focusing on the thick spit of land thrusting out into the water. *Point Friendship.* Where Pearce had last set foot on Cygnus, and where Jane Baker had last drawn breath. It was broad, flat, and green, covered by a sward of grasslike meadow. There was no indication that the *Drake*'s shuttle had ever been there a decade before, no sign of the temporary encampment that had once been established there, save the thin dark line of road leading from the peninsula to the sprawling native settlement nearby.

"Horfa," he announced to the others. The largest town in the region, it was mostly as he remembered it, though not exactly. There were differences – buildings here and there that he did not recall from his previous stay, and it certainly seemed to spread across more of the countryside and thrust further skyward than before. *Naturally there would be changes after ten years,* he thought, *and your memories might be clouded by the intervening time.* A crowd of people had gathered in a tight cluster near the westward-facing gate. The cutter wasn't yet close enough to make out any individuals, but the assembly seemed collectively expectant.

"It would appear we've been noticed," Fletcher observed. "A welcoming committee?"

"Let's hope," Pearce replied. He left his sudden misgivings unsaid, and tried to ignore the clenching knot in his belly. *There had been a crowd that predawn morning, too.* Were there Cygni in that group below who had been there a decade before? Who had lost a loved one there? He found it strange he had never thought about that before. The Machrines and crew of the Drake had injured or killed several native Cygni while fighting their way free of the peninsula to which he was about to return. Pearce recalled vividly his own part in that skirmish. Would those scars have even begun to heal in the last ten years? *Would they heal in a hundred?*

"Take us down, Lieutenant," he ordered. Fletcher's skill was on display yet again, as she smoothly guided the small vessel, on full manual, into an approach path. Everyone on board seemed to hold their breath, not through any concern over her ability, but in tense anticipation of what was about to happen. Of them all, only Pearce, Fletcher, and Crutchfield had been out of Earth's home system, and only the Captain had set foot on alien soil. A soft bump, and the cutter landed. "Skillfully done," he said to Fletcher, and he meant it, considering she had previously only piloted through atmosphere to a terrestrial landing in simulations. Pearce then forced himself to smile, to channel his jangling nerves into something closer to enthusiasm for the venture, and picked up his cockaded hat, placing it under his arm. "Not a moment to lose," he joked, echoing the oft-repeated motto of one of the Navy's ancient literary heroes. No one laughed, and no one moved. Pearce made a gesture toward Crutchfield. "After you, Sergeant."

The side of the cutter split neatly open with a hiss, dropping to become the gangway. Brilliant, pale blue spilled in. Orpheus Crutchfield put one hand at his forehead to shade his eyes, while the other dropped, as if in need of reassurance, to the laser sidearm at his hip. Tall as he was, the sergeant had to bend over to step through the opening. Luther-45 followed, silent and obedient and erect, pulse rifle strapped to his broad metal back. Then William Pearce stepped into the breach, placing his hat on his head, looking out onto the jade world of Kepler-22B.

The air was as thick as he remembered, as rich in oxygen, as pungent with the tang of the sea all around. It filled his lungs, while his nose bathed in the scent of living things. The years since his last visit melted away with the powerful memory of the senses, and he felt at once a young man, on his first voyage, full of hope and nerves and expectation. He forced himself to inhale deeply and calm down. *They will look to you*, he thought. *You set the example now.* Crutchfield and Luther had taken up their positions where the gangway met the brown-green of the peninsular meadow. Pearce walked down, doing his best to appear nonchalant, as if he set foot on alien worlds every day, including those he had once fled in mortal terror. High overhead, puffy white clouds drifted past, and the entire scene took on a dreamlike, unreal quality, even when Pearce's boots made contact with the spongy turf.

He nodded at Crutchfield, unspoken recognition of the man's courage in being first ashore. He knew the sergeant had been in the service for years, under the command of better captains than he, and on more reputable ships. Briefly, and without purpose, he wondered what the man had done to earn such dubious duty. It hardly mattered now. By the sound behind him, he could tell that the others were disembarking as well. A quick glance over his shoulder, and he saw Reyes and Green, followed by Worth and Fletcher. A bitch, an old academic, a tyro and a malcontent. *With this, we save the world.*

Friendship Point was not large; the finger of land measured no more than fifty meters across at its widest, and perhaps a hundred meters from stem to stern. Pearce took a few steps from the cutter and stood still, listening to the waves lapping against the shore, to the buzzing of insects…or, at least, their ecological equivalents. He swept his gaze around, trying to remember exactly where Jane Baker fell, and his eyes found a gray, weather-stained plinth not far away. His brow furrowed in curiosity, he strode to it. It was not tall, just over a meter or so high, and smooth on the sides, with a stone sculpture on top in the shape of an open book. The pages were inscribed, and Pearce leaned over it to read. His spoken Cygni was excellent, but their written language was a blend of pictographs and an utterly alien alphabet, and he had never mastered it. Still, he was able to discern most of the meaning.

"What is it?" Disturbed from his translation, Pearce glanced back. It was Fletcher.

"It's a monument," he replied, softly, as though he were in a cemetery. Lightly, almost reverently, he ran a finger across the hard surface of the carving. "This is where Captain Baker died." He swallowed the unexpected lump in his throat and continued, almost in a whisper. "This marks where they buried her. It reads, 'Our friend and benefactor from afar.'"

"Friend?" Reyes stepped alongside Pearce, glaring at the inscription as if it would make sense to her. "Benefactor? I thought they killed her."

"They did," Pearce said, frowning. "I was there. I watched as they beat her to death. I could be reading it improperly, of course. *Judar*, the word-symbol for friend, is quite clear. But the Cygni symbols for 'benefactor' and 'visitor' are nearly identical, and like so much of this blasted language, rely on spoken inflection." He fixed Reyes with a withering glare. "El-Barzin would have known. He came as close to mastering the language as anyone other than Baker herself." Sorely tempted to more pointedly remind Reyes of how disposable she had found el-Barzin after his death at Hitzelberg, Pearce bit his tongue. It was petty, and there was no use in it. Instead, he lifted his gaze from the monument, following the rough road that led to Horfa. They would find out soon enough.

"Let's go."

Luther-45 and Sergeant Crutchfield went first, again, scanning the brightening dawn for any threat. Pearce followed, Fletcher falling in alongside. There was an eagerness about her that almost made him smile. She had always been intrepid in their merchant days, curious about systems she hadn't seen, keen to explore the lesser-traveled pathways of interstellar commerce. *Perhaps this is just the tonic*, Pearce thought hopefully, *for whatever distemper has been making her so erratic and unhappy ever since Spithead*. The scientists both trailed behind, Sir Eustace distracted by every alien flora and Reyes all but dragging him along to keep up. Hope Worth returned to join Victor-11 in the cutter.

It wasn't a long walk, and for that Pearce was thankful. The slightly stronger gravity and thicker air were already beginning to tell, and with the exception of the robot, they were all a little out of breath when the foliage ahead cleared to reveal the western gate of Horfa. It was little more than a stone archway set into a low wooden palisade, one Pearce knew well from the many times he had passed beneath it before. But he had no attention to spare for architectural reminiscences now. Beneath the arch was the Cygni greeting party. There were perhaps thirty of them, and as they drew closer, Pearce could begin to distinguish the distinct styles of dress that differentiated the castes. He could see the soft browns of the intellectuals and the sharper blue jackets of the military. That, at least, appeared to be unchanged. Missing only were the black and red robes of the clergy, but that was unsurprising. The religious caste numbered very few, and were almost never seen away from their *takats*, their holy sanctuaries. Pearce had never met one himself. There seemed to be a lot more blue than brown, and all of the soldiers appeared armed. Most were wielding the forced-air *karabins*, but a few, those with the white-blaze chest decorations worn by officers, carried smaller sidearms that were unfamiliar to Pearce.

When the *Harvest* party closed to within fifty meters, Pearce saw something he did find familiar. There were two figures at the forefront of the Cygni group, one from each caste present. The soldier was a stranger to him, but the intellectual was not. He knew that long, glossy white hair, so carefully arranged, those fathomless blue eyes, and that friendly face, a bit more lined, but unmistakable. *Venn Arkadas*. Unable to help himself, Pearce broke into a wide grin at the sight of his old friend.

"*Judar*," he said, and he grasped one hand in the other, holding them out in front of his waist in the Cygni gesture of greeting. And then he held his breath.

He did not have to do so for very long. Arkadas strode forward, closing the gap between them swiftly, and taking Pearce's hands in his own.

"*Judar*," he replied in kind. His skin was warm, almost hot to the touch, and Pearce remembered that Cygni natives had higher body temperatures than did Englishmen. "Welcome back, Lieutenant."

"Commander, now," Pearce gently corrected his old friend, with pride and affection in his voice, the Cygni language rusty on his tongue. He recalled a day, early in his first visit, when he had sat in Arkadas' house, drinking *edan* and explaining in his embryonic grasp of the Cygni language that *Lieutenant* was not his name but his rank. Arkadas made a pleased sound in his throat, and leaned in close.

"You are not the only one. I am now first among the intellectuals, a member of the Council, and partially responsible for Horfa and our outlying districts."

Pearce felt his heart leap at the news. Not only had his friend survived the tumults of ten years before, but he had achieved a leadership role that could only help the desperate mission of the *Harvest*. Then he thought of that word, *partial*, hoping he had understood it properly.

"I am pleased for you," he said, and meant it. Arkadas had been a generous host during his previous stay, and Pearce would always believe the man had saved his life that final morning. "I was worried about what might happen to you when the coalitions shifted." Arkadas waved his hand, a universal gesture of dismissal.

"Not long after your departure, all three factions found common ground, a rare concordance in our history, and a happy condition that endures even now."

"That is good news," Pearce said. He glanced at the clutch of soldiers, who were still at rigid attention some meters away. "To be honest, I wasn't sure whether to expect a warm welcome, a bristling resistance, or something in between." He broke off as the blue-clad man who had been standing alongside Arkadas moved to join them. He was handsome, as all Cygni men seemed to be, with a lean, slender form and jet-black hair that was common to the military caste. He also had blue eyes, but where Arkadas' were clear and bright, his were stormy, almost gray, and a light scar ran down underneath one to the corner of his mouth, which smiled with tight lips.

"This," introduced Arkadas, "is my counterpart, and fellow Councilor, General Zuru Leyndar." To him, Arkadas said, "my friend, Commander William Pearce." Leyndar folded his hands briskly, and nodded.

"It is good to meet you," Pearce said, feeling stiffly formal, wishing he had more mastery of subtlety in the tongue. "And good to be back during such peaceful days."

"You will find that not all is as you left it," Leyndar said, and he stared at Pearce with those slate eyes.

"General Leyndar was at the Point that day," Arkadas said, softly.

"You would not remember me," Leyndar said. "I was only one soldier among many."

"As was I," Pearce replied, his own voice brusque. He had thought it might come to this. How many friends had the man lost that morning? Part of him wanted to tell Leyndar that his people had started it, and part of him wanted to demand why, but he knew this was neither the time nor the place. *Later, perhaps*. Now, he needed their cooperation.

"I am...sorry for the misunderstanding between us," he said, casting about for the words, wondering if he was getting the tone right. This was what he had practiced over and over in his head on the long journey from Earth, the essential moment that could decide all. "We were friends once, and our King wishes that we should be so again." He took off his hat and bowed, clearly deferential. *Diplomacy first*, his instructions had explicitly read. *If that should fail, resort to other means*. Here, then, was his best diplomacy. To his surprise, Leyndar's smile widened.

"Welcome back to Cygnus, Commander Pearce," he said.

"It is our great hope," Arkadas said earnestly, seeming to sag with some relief, "that there is much we can learn from one another." His eyes flickered over Pearce's shoulder. Turning, Pearce saw that Christine Fletcher had moved up into their little group. *How long has she been there?* He wondered, too, how conscientiously she had studied the language, and how much of the exchange she had understood.

"Gentlemen, this is Lieutenant Christine Fletcher, one of my officers." Both Cygni men greeted her with smiles, and with a different kind of charm than that they had exhibited with Pearce. He had seen this before. The intellectual caste was dominated by males, and he had never seen a female member of the military at all. Women Cygni were relegated to supporting roles as wives, mothers, and domestic laborers, with two exceptions. There were a few female intellectuals, and he understood this to be a fairly recent phenomenon. The other major exception was the clergy, which, as far as he understood, was entirely comprised of women. He didn't pretend to understand all of the sexual politics of Cygnus, but he knew that beautiful women were highly prized. And among her other qualities, Christine Fletcher was beautiful.

While Arkadas and Leyndar tried to charm his officer, Pearce beckoned the rest of his crew to join them. He made introductions, navigating from English to Cygni and back, and he noticed Arkadas' eyes narrow with curiosity as he explained the credentials of Green and Reyes. *He misses nothing.* Pearce also noticed the General's prolonged stare at Luther-11, and was thinking of what strong, unpleasant memories the robot must be evoking, when he saw that a third Cygni had joined them. He was dressed similarly to Arkadas -- another intellectual -- but where his friend was solidly middle aged, this was a young man, and breathtakingly handsome, even by Cygni standards. His white hair was short, almost shaved, his skin a lustrous bronze, and his eyes were the pale blue of a cloudless noon sky.

"This," Arkadas was saying, "is Fol Jairo, my protégé."

Pearce had heard once, he did not remember where, that there had been a time before science had tamed the Terran skies, when lightning could strike Earth without warning. *It is striking now*, he thought, and it was striking Christine Fletcher. Her eyes were locked onto Jairo, and she adjusted her cocked hat in a girlishly self-conscious way he never thought he would see from her. She was, to all appearances, smitten. Meanwhile, Jairo whispered something in Arkadas' ear, and the older man nodded vigorously.

"Yes, yes. No need to stand about outdoors. Please, join us for some refreshment inside. We can talk in more comfort." He spread a hand in the direction of the gate and indicated that Pearce and his crew should follow him. The soldiers parted before him, and Arkadas led the way under the stone gate and into Horfa.

Ten

Bloom

Outside the walls, Pearce had been able to glimpse the largely agrarian countryside he remembered, the farms dotting the horizon and the sounds and smells of herd animals in the distant pastures. Once inside, the buildings were mostly timber and stone in the distinctive layered Cygni style. That was comfortingly familiar, as were many of the structures themselves. Still...something was different, though he was unable to pinpoint what. He looked at Arkadas, walking just ahead of him. It was a stroke of luck that his old friend was in a position to be so helpful. As an old star-mariner, he was disinclined to trust good fortune. *You're paranoid and anxious*, he chided himself. They had experienced nothing but ill luck so far. The odds had been bound to tilt in their favor eventually.

The main thoroughfare of Horfa was crowded, though the denizens were not engaged in their usual morning labors. They were as vividly dressed as ever, in an array of orange and yellow, green and white, every shade but those three reserved for the castes. Most stood in doorways, watching the alien procession in groups of three or four, clutching their children protectively. Captain Baker had worked so hard, so patiently, to earn the trust of the Cygni during the first visit by Englishmen to this planet. Was it all lost, now? He thought then of the memorial at Friendship Point. *No*, he thought. *Some remnant of goodwill remains*. It fell to him to nurture that ember into a flame strong enough to sustain the work they needed to do there.

They came to a three-story building that Pearce recalled vividly, with a face of mortared stone flanked by two large gray statues. One held a book and pointed up, face skyward, while the other grasped a bladed weapon with both hands. Above the wide doorway was an inscription, in stylized Cygni symbols, translating to *Mind and Heart*. This was the Law-House, the town hall, the center of political life in Horfa. They were escorted through the door and down a wood-floored hallway into a spacious library with a wide table and several chairs. A servant scurried to stoke the fire in the hearth, and Arkadas closed the door behind them. Everyone sat except for Crutchfield and Luther-45, who kept their vigil on either side of the door.

"It is good to see you again," Arkadas said, shooing away the servant, his tasks complete. "But it has been some time, Commander.

Our people will be curious why you are here, and the sooner we can give them truth rather than rumor, the safer we all will be."

Pearce glanced around the table. Green was almost explosively excited, while Reyes was the opposite in her customary glacial cool. Worth was striving to find that midshipman's balance between attentive and unobtrusive, while Fletcher, he was pleased to see, appeared focused. Of the Cygni, Arkadas was all genial welcome, Leyndar a wall of martial reserve, and Jairo a cipher. Withholding a sigh, Pearce hitched what he hoped was a casual smile to his face. He was about to weave threads of truth with deception, and that was not something with which he had much skill or comfort.

"We've wanted to return for some time now." *Lie.* "It was hard to know, though, just what happened after we left ten years ago. You could have been engaged in a civil war, or harboring resentment against us." *Truth.* He spread his hands and shrugged. "As in so many other things, it is the desires of the King that set events in motion." *Truth.* "You've met, briefly, Sir Green and Dr. Reyes. They are here because our King is a botanical enthusiast, and wishes to expand his gardens to include several of the species he has read about in the scientific reports of our previous visit." *Half-truth.* "In particular, he desires some of your food crops, to diversify and enrich his table." Even Pearce couldn't say how much of that was truth and how much falsehood.

"So you're looking for..." Arkadas prompted.

"Seeds," Pearce said. "Young plants. Some time to study them here, and then some samples to bring back with us when we leave."

"And in return?" General Leyndar asked from his end of the table, in front of the fire.

"A fair exchange," Pearce replied. "Technology."

"What kind of technology?" There were windows in one wall, between the bookcases -- high, narrow windows, casting the room into alternating bands of light and dark. It was mostly dim where Leyndar sat, and the orange flames behind him lit only his thin silhouette. Pearce hesitated a moment before replying. This was the question he and Banks had discussed at some length. Guidelines existed for the provision of technology to developing worlds, designed by the Royal Society to allow cultures to advance at a natural and proper rate. It had been a great deal of work to identify what could appropriately be shared with the Cygni, and they were about to run within a breath of crossing the line. But Lord Banks had been convinced that the Kingdom's need was too great to risk failure. *Some lines mattered more than others.* Pearce nodded at Sir Green.

"Agricultural techniques," the gardener said, with his usual rapid enthusiasm. "In the course of studying your crops, we can provide you with some advanced techniques and practices that will reduce your labor and increase your yield." He glanced at Pearce and continued. "I also understand your people have been experimenting with steam and water power for textile manufacturing and steel production for some decades now. We can offer some guidance that will...accelerate that process." There was silence around the table. Pearce could not make out Leyndar's eyes, but he could feel the soldier's gaze on him. Finally, Arkadas spoke.

"It is a start." He smiled. "You will find us very apt pupils, my friend."

"Excellent," Pearce said. "Lieutenant Fletcher will handle the details."

"Jairo is our lead scholar on the matters of green and growing things," Arkadas indicated the younger Cygni. "She can coordinate directly with him."

An electric look passed between the two subordinates. Pearce was on the verge of asking for another Cygni, or withdrawing Fletcher from the assignment, but he saw no way to do so without insulting Arkadas or shattering what brittle trust might still remain between himself and his lieutenant. *It will just be a few weeks*, he thought as he rose from his seat. Arkadas was on his feet as well.

"Our hospitality is yours during your visit," he was saying. "I hope that you and your crew will enjoy your stay, and that this business will be a profitable one for us all."

****

As it turned out, they could not have hoped for a better local contact than Jairo. He listened carefully to Sir Green and Dr. Reyes and quickly brought them to where they needed to go, brokering introductions to the wealthiest landowners of the Horfan countryside and helping to establish three harvesting and testing sites: one in the wheat plains, one in the cornfields, and one in the lowland rice patties farther distant. Christine Fletcher roamed with him on these rounds and beyond, riding on the broad backs of *zaldi*, shaggy horse-like creatures that had been domesticated by the Cygni centuries before as beasts of burden, transport, and warfare. After a lifetime of traveling in enclosed metal boxes, this was a wholly new and seductive experience for her. She was used to her mode of transport smelling of metallic benzene, not living equine lather.

Jairo was a scholar of the discipline he called *acik havada*. Translated roughly, the closest approximation was "outdoors". His expertise was broad and deep, surprisingly so given his age. Fletcher had little idea how analogous Cygni life cycles were with humans', but if she had to approximate, she would have put Jairo at no more than forty, not all that much older than she was herself. As they rode, he pointed out the different plants and animals they encountered in the forests and fields. His descriptions of each were almost poetic. The yellow star known as Kepler-22 to the Admiralty, known as *Muo* (roughly, "sky mother" in the Cygni language) here, was a little smaller than Earth's Sol, burned a little less brightly, but still bathed the planet in enough of the right kind of heat and radiation to support life. Cygnus rotated slowly and tilted at just the right angle to ensure very little extreme weather and long, warm growing seasons. When it did rain, Jairo showed Fletcher trees that spread wide, hungry leaves, drinking in the water as it fell, and streams that swelled in their courses, and the music of raindrops on sheltered ponds.

One early morning, perhaps a week after the arrival of the *Harvest*, they traveled to the cliffs south of Horfa, overlooking the sea. There, feathered creatures of every color of vivid brilliance rooked by the thousands, and she watched as the *ptica* flocks rose into the sky as one, their haunting cry filling the dawn sky. But even inundated by that impossibly beautiful sight and sound, it was the rising sun on the flowers that took her breath away.

Fletcher was accustomed to the hues and shades of home. When the sun rose over Earth, it could be beautiful, an orange heartbeat between black and gray. But the light caressed nothing but steel, concretia, and glass. Even the cultivated gardens of the wealthy existed mostly in protected domes, hermetic oases from the unremitting artificiality of the world. She thought of Brimstone Hill, against the rust-colored shoulders of Mt. Liamulga. She climbed there often as a child, to the ancient fort that still perched at the summit, a crumbling relic from centuries past. The sky spread out overhead there, as it still did over parts of her island home. Once, when she was eleven, she had found a flower growing in a crack in one of the redoubts. It had been a stunted, almost-yellow thing, but it was the first time she had seen one in the wild, uncultivated. It had been her secret, and she had smuggled enriched soil from her grandfather's garden to share with it. In her youthful naivety, she had not known how wildly expensive such soil was, or how closely her grandfather monitored its use. She was caught, and when she confessed about the flower, her grandfather made her bring him to the fort. When they arrived, the flower was withered and brown, and Fletcher had been punished for wasting the soil. She never saw another wildflower, but she never forgot the one she did see.

That morning, they were all around her.

Fletcher sat down near the edge of the cliffs, feeling the soft, moss-like vegetation with her bare feet. Wildflowers surrounded her, in vivid carpets of red and yellow. She had learned the names of some of them from Jairo - dainty paintcups, and many-armed thalias – but a lifetime would never be enough to learn them all. A breeze, warm and loving, drifted in from the sea and toyed with the strands of her hair. It was warm, and she undid her braids and took off her jacket. The warmth of the small sun as it climbed was an embrace against her dark skin as she lay down amid the flowers.

That morning Jairo touched her bare shoulder, and she shuddered with the warmth of it. Fletcher had been touched by men, of course, but this was different. Intellectually, she understood that Cygni had somewhat higher body temperatures than Earthers, but the feel of him against her skin was living flame.

That was the first time they made love, there on the cliffs, surrounded by wildflowers, *ptica* overhead, screaming and wheeling.

The second time was at sea.

The oceans on Cygnus were immense, deep, and teeming with life. The boat Jairo had brought her aboard was tiny, a bare speck against the vast blue-green with an unbroken line of water and sky all around. Some kind of animals trailed the craft, leaping out into the air, their silvery skin iridescent in the foam. Their wind-caught spray soaked Christine Fletcher to the skin.

It was magnificent.

"You like it?" Jairo asked, in English. He had insisted that she teach him, even as he tutored her in his native tongue, adding idiom and patois to the sterility of her computer learning.

"I've never known anything like it," she replied.

Was this what true islanders felt? she wondered, leaning against the wooden railing and breathing the sharp tang of the air. *Is this what it had been like to sail?* This was life, freedom, and fertility, not the antiseptic vacuum and confinement of starships. It spoke to something in her soul, something ancient and resonant. She had flown over the remnants of the Atlantic many times, shuttling from St. Kitts to London, and in her mind she knew it had once been like this – bursting with life in endless diversity and numbers – but now it was an empty, dead sewer of brackish water, hot and silent. Her heart had never reacted to the tragedy of the long-extinguished romance and danger and liberty of the seas her ancestors had wandered, explored, loved.

She lay down on the deck of the boat and Jairo was above her. All around him was endless, cloudless sky, the identical shade of blue as his eyes. Fletcher could feel the heat of him, radiating through his skin everywhere they touched – his hands, his thighs, the heat of the smooth, sun-drenched deck beneath her, on her bare back, her bare legs. Her awareness was overwhelmed with sensations more forcibly present and real than any she had ever known. She had known rapture before, but not like this. This was fire.

That was the second time, and it was not the last.

I never knew, Fletcher thought, with explosive realization. She had never known what she was looking for. In truth, she hadn't known that she was looking at all. But now, she knew that she had found it. She was in love, with a man and a place and a time, and she never wanted to leave any of them.

****

Hope Worth didn't quite know what to do with herself.

For the first time she could remember, there wasn't any work to do. She wasn't part of the team collecting plant specimens with the natives and her only other responsibilities were minimal. Like the rest of the crew, officers and jacks alike, she had a healthy amount of shore leave, alternating with shipboard duties on the *Harvest*. No studying, no classes, just unstructured free time on the surface. So, at the urging of Captain Pearce, she explored the city of Horfa, its outlying settlements, the farms, even the edge of the wilderness, usually alongside Charlie Hall.

Worth didn't quite know what to do with him, either. She had never really known anyone like him before. Beginning with her own father, then including her classmates and even her instructors at Greenwich, the men in her life had almost universally been ambitious, confident, even arrogant. But Hall wasn't any of these. He was quiet and withdrawn, an almost timid starship pilot. And clearly a talented one, as smart and instinctive as any of the strutting peacocks at the Naval College. It was endearing, in its way. *He doesn't believe in himself,* Worth thought. *Maybe he just needs someone to do it for him.*

She laughed out loud at the thought, at the possibility that she might be falling in love with anyone, let alone someone like Charlie.

"What?" he asked. They were wandering through one of the sprawling hedge mazes the Cygni of this region seemed so fond of. *Drysfa,* they called them, and they were everywhere. The wealthier intellectuals had large private ones on the grounds of their vast estates, and the worker castes visited the immense public ones during their leisure time. They were a blatant consumption of space, an overt demonstration that here on Cygnus there was more land than could ever be used.

"Nothing," she replied, smiling at him. "Just amazed by all the sky. Still." He nodded, and they kept walking, though her eyes were on him as much as the winding green walls and high blue welkin above. She had known more plenty in her childhood than he had. The daughter of a successful naval officer, she and her family had enjoyed their share of conveniences and privileges - good schooling, some variety of diet, and even occasional access to the gardens. She knew Hall's experience had been less comfortable, and while this expanse of green foliage and endless sky dazzled her, it must have been even more overwhelming to him.

The hedges towered over them both, well over four meters high on either side of the path. Hall stepped into the cool of shadow, and it occurred to her that she had never seen the sun on his face before they came to Cygnus. As he moved into the dimmer light, the pale pallor returned to his skin, and she thought he seemed smaller and younger somehow.

"What are you doing?" she asked.

"Taking a break." He wiped a hand across his forehead, and rested his hands on his hips. "I'm not used to so much walking. Or that sun beating down. I'm actually sweating."

"Just think – it's cooler than our own sun." She held out a hand. "Come on. I want to see if we can find our way through." Hall hesitated, then reached out took her hand.

As it turned out, they couldn't.

"How big is this thing?" Hall asked, more in wonder than frustration.

"I think we've been down this part twice. Maybe three times. See? That fountain has that same three fish-things."

"Great. We're lost."

"Lost?" Worth laughed. "Aren't you a navigator, Charlie?" He plucked a handful of leaves from the hedge nearby and threw them at her playfully.

"Space is one thing. This maze…" he shook his head.

"We're alone," Worth said, standing close to him. There was a tiny yellow leaf in his sandy-brown hair, and she reached up and brushed it away, letting the tips of her fingers trail gently against his ear.

"I know," he said, his face pointed toward the sky, eyes closed, the sun dappling his sharp features. He was almost handsome. "It's so quiet. I never had any quiet growing up, there were always so many…

people…" He trailed off as she laid one finger over his lips, moving closer still, leaning into him.

"That's not what I meant, Charlie." It was unlike her to be so forward, but she knew if she waited for him she would be waiting forever, he was so shy. She didn't know if she loved him or not, like the way her mom and dad felt about each other, but they were young and they were alone and she liked him a lot. They'd spent so much time together, on duty and in their books, and she had come to feel so natural, so comfortable with him. *And he took Lamb's punch for me*, she thought, remembering that awful night in the galley. *That has to count for something.*

She looked in his eyes, those muddy-hazel eyes, curious what he was thinking and feeling. At least he was looking back at her, not at his feet. That was a start. *He has to know what I'm doing.* Her hand moved from his hair to the back of his neck.

"Oh," he said.

"Charlie," Worth murmured, moving even closer, so close she knew he could count the freckles on her nose.

"Yeah?"

"When we argue about this later, just remember that I kissed you first." And she did, closing her eyes, pressing her lips against his, wrapping her arms around him. His mouth was slightly open, and she was pleasantly surprised to find that his kiss was just the right mix of wet and soft, pliable and firm. After a heartbeat of stunned hesitation, she felt him respond, felt the pressure of his arms on her back, felt the transition from a kiss to kissing.

Then they were falling.

Hall had leaned back, taking her with him in their embrace, against a nearby privet wall, and it gave way with minimal resistance. The both of them crashed through leaves and branches, coming to rest in the grass beneath the broken hedge.

"Someone's going to be upset that we ruined their *drysfa*," Worth said, lying on top of Hall, his arms still holding her.

"I have to admit that I don't care," he replied, and he pulled her back down to him with both hands.

****

Green watched Dr. Reyes as she reviewed the final numbers of their latest analysis. She was sitting, impossibly erect, at one of the portable workstations they'd cobbled together in a vacant barn. The look on her face suggested a foul odor under her nose.

Probably true, thought Sir Eustace Green. After all, this structure had housed herd animals until fairly recently, and evidence of their prior residency could be readily seen – and smelled – in heaps of aging dung piled near the walls. There were other scents, too, less unpleasant, of leather and dry grasses and other things that Green could only guess at. Even the dung-smell itself was mild, mellowing as time passed without fresh deposits, a source more of amusement and intrigue than disgust. Green was fascinated; here was a window into the past of his own species – a people who still engaged in animal husbandry, maintaining flocks and herds of creatures that would be milked, slaughtered, eaten. *How scandalously, wonderfully inefficient*, he thought. Green was wealthy and noble enough, of course, to have eaten actual flesh-meat before, though the event was scarcely commonplace. Here, these people ate meat almost every day.

What a planet, he thought.

Green was in heaven, or close enough. This was a world alive, in its youth, not seized by a rotting dotage and choked by an overpopulated humanity. Leaves and flowers encroached on pathways, and green things burst from every surface: dirt and wood and even stone; life defiant, life perpetual. There were a thousand specimens he could harvest and return to Kew, a million, a billion. But time pressed. They had already been on-planet for two weeks, and in that time had conducted innumerable tests on the specimens collected with the help of that excellent and adventurous local lad, Jairo. Their suspicions had been borne out, suspicions rooted in Tyson's rudimentary work from a decade before. This was no simple dash-and-grab job. Cygnus had grains compatible at the genetic level to those back on Earth, compatibility that would allow for replenishment of the stocks the Kingdom relied upon to feed its teeming mouths. But there were differences in cellular replication and germination cycles, differences that required precise chromosomal combinations during hybridization. They had yet to hit on the proper sequencing, though they drew closer with each subsequent experiment.

"Still 15% dark with the nanopore sequencer," Reyes said, her voice as flat and toneless as ever.

"More molecular adaptors?" asked Green, unsurprised, and she nodded grimly. The Cygni grains were proving stubborn in yielding up the details of their genetic code to the spectral analyses designed for terrestrial flora. It was puzzling, since the basic chemistry of Cygnus so closely mirrored Earth's that genetic analysis should have been much simpler. Green had already had to recalibrate one of the three mobile spectrometers with a nanopore mixture even richer in proteins, in order to slow the DNA strands during reading. *Nature, as ever, so loathe to give up her secrets even to the most persistent prying*, thought Green with gleeful frustration. As Reyes assisted him to load and program the cumbersome machine with fresh samples of Cygni wheat cells, the elderly gardener marveled at her ability to labor in such close proximity, day after day, and yet develop no discernable camaraderie. Green had worked for more than half a century in botany, that most sociable of natural sciences, and had collaborated with dozens of talented men and women from across the Kingdom. Some of them had been distant and difficult, of course, but none ever so aloof as Dr. Adina Reyes. Since before their departure from Spithead, Green had done his best to apply his personal charm and his professional enthusiasm, but had failed to ignite even the slightest warmth. It made the long hours and isolated location a challenge to bear. He had hoped for one last great collaboration, a partnership that would change his field of botany and her sub-field of xenobotany forever. He had dreamed of it. *Linneaus, Fuchs, Mendel, Esau…Green.*

The old knight sighed and sagged back into a canvas chair as the spectrometer quietly whirred to life, probing deeper into the obstinate gene sequences within. Reyes sat, too, in another chair across the broad wooden floor. *Fatigue!* Green thought idly. *She's human!* A cloud of insects drifted close to his head, high-pitched, irritating. He brushed them aside with a splutter, and a corner of Reyes' mouth twitched ever so slightly in amusement.

"Still enamored of this primitive world?" she asked.

"At this moment?" Green took out a pocket handkerchief and wiped his face and neck. The midmorning was warm, and the interior of the ancient barn was stuffy, humid and plagued by too many of these tiny flying bugs. Even so, he had rarely been happier, and he said so.

"You're a pathetic old romantic," said Reyes.

"Indeed I am," he replied, "and proud of it." He rose, went to the cool-storage unit they'd installed on their first day, and procured two plastic canteens of water, offering one to Reyes. She took it, and Green returned to his seat. They both drank in silence for a moment, watching as the spectrometer did its work.

"No romance for you, then, Reyes?"

His question was greeted stonily at first, and frankly Green had expected no better. But he found he was tired of her implacable, icy façade, tired of working so closely in this magical verdant wonderland and yet not being able to talk about its enchantments with the one person who ought to appreciate them better than anyone. After a moment, to his immense surprise, she replied.

"I don't believe in romance."

"Don't believe in it?" Green grinned. "Residue of a broken heart, my dear?" This earned a snort of derision and a scowl.

"You misunderstand me. I don't mean that all this soft romanticism in the face of so-called natural beauty is a distraction or a nuisance. When I say I don't believe in it, I mean I am skeptical it exists."

"But of course it exists!" protested Green, leaning forward animatedly. "You can't tell me there isn't beauty in the infinite diversity of life in the universe. The Fisher-Dunn Theorem..."

"Solipsistic nonsense." Reyes took a small sip from her canteen that would have been dainty had she been even slightly feminine.

"Dunn and Fisher mathematically proved that beauty and love exist," persevered Green doggedly. "The universe is infinite, and therefore home to infinite forms. If any and all forms exist, then perfect beauty exists, even allowing for observer bias."

"Self-serving naïveté," Reyes replied evenly. "Delusional idealism."

"You'll excuse me for asking, then," said Green, "but if those who love the universe so much engender such hostility in you, if the very universe itself offends you, what the devil are you doing out here on this mission? Why save humanity if you don't believe in what makes us human?"

"We disagree on what makes us human, Eustace. You say beauty and romance, I say intellect and reason."

"The two need not be mutually exclusive," he protested.

"We disagree again. But it makes no matter. You are welcome to your philosophy, as childish and outdated as it may be. I don't believe in romanticism, but what I truly loathe is chaos."

"You're one of those order fetishists, then," Green said. "An artificialist." She nodded slightly in acknowledgment.

"Humanity has struggled, from our earliest moments, to control our environment, not to coddle and sentimentalize it. Nature, uncontrolled, is chaos. A threat, not an idol."

"Foolish girl." Green was more sad than angry. "It's those like you, worshipers of progress at any cost, who have gotten us into this mess to begin with."

"Please. You blame man's ingenuity, but I would blame his lack of control. No breeding policies, no controls on population, have given us more mouths than we can feed. You worship life and its abundance, and yet it is that overabundance that threatens all of us. You asked me why I came out here, why I agreed to help you and Lord Banks. The answer is that I seek to restore equilibrium, to restore order. Chaos breeds chaos. Only from order can we rationally seek to extend our control over the universe we inhabit. Control and order are the keys to human destiny."

Green was speechless. Reyes was still looking at him, seeming to wait for some response she could eviscerate, but he wasn't interested in debating her any longer. She was a zealot, an ideologue, and he might as well argue with his shoe.

Into the uncomfortable silence came the chime of the spectrometer, announcing the completion of the analysis. Green lurched from his chair and accessed the initial results at the workstation. His eyes scanned the first screen, then the second, seeking out the familiar red numbers, but the display was an ocean of green. He turned to face Reyes.

"It's beautiful," he said.

****

Pearce disembarked from the cutter alongside a handful of other personnel coming back to the *Harvest* for duty shifts. It had been a quiet ride, each star-mariner lost in his own contemplations. He was thankful for Pott, his thoroughly competent, seemingly indefatigable Australian Lieutenant, but the man deserved some shore leave, too, and with Fletcher consumed by her work on the surface, they were the only two remaining senior officers to share shipboard duty, so they rotated every couple of days. To be honest, the captain didn't mind. *I might be the only one happy to be coming aboard*, he thought. He liked being on his ship. It had an orderly familiarity that gave him a sense of control, of order. It wasn't that matters ashore were problematic; to the contrary, since their arrival everything had fallen into quiet routine rather swiftly. Regular reports from Sir Green were optimistic about the progress of their gathering and testing of the needed flora, aided so cooperatively by Arkadas' young deputy, Jairo. The captain was forced to admit to himself that, despite his own initial misgivings about him, particularly his sudden chemistry with Fletcher, the man had been a godsend. His scientific expertise and field knowledge were precisely what Green and Reyes needed to conduct their work swiftly and efficiently. Just that morning, Green had given him some sample seeds as proof of their progress. *With any luck, we'll be gone before the month is out*, he thought.

Luck. He didn't trust it. It had betrayed them on the voyage here. And yet none of his fears about the return to Cygnus had yet materialized. Sure, the military seemed more formal, more vaguely menacing than he remembered from his first visit, but that might be no more than his own imagination. The intellectuals had been welcoming, and the crew were taking their scheduled turns on the surface, engaging in the usual pastimes of sailors in a foreign port – seeing the countryside, eating exotic food, relaxing, and socializing with the local women and men who always seemed to make themselves available.

"Captain."

Zoltan Szakonyi, the ship's surgeon, cadaverous and humorless as ever, was waiting in the shuttle bay, apparently for him.

"Doctor," Pearce answered. "What can I do for you?"

"Come with me to Surgery," Szakonyi said. "There's something you need to see." The captain frowned. The ship's surgeon was a spare, gray man, too old at a glance, yet he never showed fatigue or complaint. Pearce realized that despite their months together on the trip from Earth, he knew precious little about him. He occasionally included messages in the *Harvest*'s interstellar communications packages, directed at a grandchild, uninteresting though vaguely affectionate. Szakonyi messed with the officers, but rarely entered conversation, and always seemed preoccupied with his own thoughts. He was not, Pearce certainly knew, a frivolous creature. Whatever it was he wanted, it must be important. The physician made a gesture, and then followed behind Pearce.

Surgery was a tiny, cramped space, with a single DATA (Diagnostic and Treatment Alcove) and workstation. The rest of the cabin was given over to storage of medical equipment, surgical tools, and pharmaceuticals. Naturally, given the appetites of too many able jacks, the place was always locked. Szakonyi shut the door peremptorily, and began to speak without preamble.

"You have no doubt noticed the avidity with which our crew members respond to the Cygni."

Pearce had to smile. There was an old axiom in the service: "Past Pluto, all men are bachelors". He had never really subscribed to that personally; he loved Mary, and had seldom been tempted, even in some of the more notoriously licentious locales he had known. That said, he knew life belowdecks well enough that he looked the other way at most of their shore leave behaviors. Most of the crew were unmarried anyway, either too young, or too sullen to attract a spouse, or simply content with their unattached life. There was, even so, truth to the surgeon's words. Pearce had noticed, even on his first visit ten years before, that the natives here seemed unusually eager to please their guests. And the crew even more eager than usual to take advantage of that offered hospitality. He had ascribed it, with disinterest, to the remarkable handsomeness of the Cygni, and the remote isolation of the system. He shrugged.

"Past Pluto, Doctor."

"Yes, yes." The surgeon waved a spidery, dismissive hand. "I've been in space since before you were born, sir, and have seen no shortage of shore leaves, many during much longer cruises than this. I've treated every venereal discomfort we know of – Apraxian syphilis, star itch, scorpions." This did concern Pearce.

"Are the jacks complaining of some new ailment?" The last thing he needed was a – literal – rash of sickness among the crew. That would slow down progress. "I seem to recall from a decade ago that the Cygni were clean in that respect."

"No," Szakonyi responded. "I bring the matter up only to remind you of my breadth of experience in this arena. The Cygni appear to be relatively disease-free, though whether they remain so after our visit is an open question."

"What, then?"

"This." The surgeon powered up the wide vidpanel above his desk, tapped a few times at the keypad, and the monitor became a kinetic display of bizarre shapes, lurid green and pink against a dull gray background, swimming feverishly against one another like a maddened mob.

"Beg your pardon, doctor, but I'm a starman, not a scientist," Pearce said. "What the hell am I looking at?"

"You are looking, Captain, at a sample, magnified a hundred times, of the exhalation of a typical Cygni. A male, in this case, and young, but representative of the type. Women appear much the same, from our studies. Much of what you see closely resembles our own respiratory wastes – carbon dioxide, et cetera. As has been observed, the Cygni are remarkably similar to us in their physiology."

"But you've found something different." A chill was creeping up Pearce's spine, the beginnings of a vague, cold premonition.

"With the help of Dr. Reyes, yes. The little green circles, you see them? Those are, as far as my extensive experience goes, unique. They appear to be, for lack of a better term, pheromones."

"Phero-what?"

"Pheromones. A chemical agent, secreted and released by the endocrine system of the individual exhaling, mixing with their breath during respiration. These agents, upon entering the body of another individual, produce a curious reaction. I should say, rather, a range of reactions, from a calming of the nervous system, generating a sense of ease, of well-being, to a more visceral, more excited response, verging on sexual pleasure."

"Come, Doctor," Pearce said. "You want me to believe these people spit love potion?"

"Don't be absurd." Szakonyi seemed offended. "First of all, it's not saliva, it's gaseous. And it's nothing so trite as *love* potion. It's a complex chemical reaction, which I'm certain depends on a host of societal and biological factors. You've no doubt observed that the Cygni are a widely dispersed, highly tribal civilization. Dr. Reyes suspects, and I concur, that it likely emerged as an evolutionary advantage enhancing the mating prospects of certain Cygni, as well as a facilitation of breeding across tribal groups. There are comparable phenomena, she reports, in certain flora, including the…"

"Dr. Szakonyi," the captain interrupted, unwilling to endure a secondhand lecture from Dr. Reyes on plant biology, especially given his own ignorance on the subject and how often he'd been required to display that ignorance over the last few weeks. "If I understand you, and it's entirely possible that I don't, you're saying that there's something in what these Cygni exhale that makes others want to like them?"

"Or even love them," the surgeon replied, stiffly. "Or, more properly, react to them with sexual favorability. If our physiological systems are sufficiently similar to the Cygni that we can metabolize their food, I have to imagine we would have some susceptibility to this effect as well. Much more controlled study is needed, of course, before we can even begin to understand the chemistry involved. But I tell you about this so you will be aware that our responses to the Cygni - the crew's, even yours and mine - may be artificially softened by this quirk of biology. And if there are other attractions - friendship, say, or sexual desire - they may be strengthened and intensified by these agents. It could act as an intoxicant, compromise decision making, even blunt other loyalties and priorities." He raised both sparse white eyebrows in emphasis. The doctor was not a stupid man, and he was making a point. "Perhaps substantially."

Damn, thought Pearce. *Fletcher.*

Eleven

Grounded

Follow me, he had said. *Trust me.*

Christine Fletcher would have followed Jairo to the far reaches of the universe, so she followed him now. It should have bothered her, she knew, at least a little, that she was so infatuated, so quickly. She had known her share of lovers, of course, but never had she known such raw ignition of her passions. She had always held some part of herself apart, in reserve, but now Jairo compelled a complete surrender, giddy and terrifying. That should have upset her, but it didn't. She had never defined herself by her relationship with any man, and yet now the entirety of her world orbited the fiery star of him. In some irresistible way, he reminded her of her grandfather, utterly male, strong, and yet kind, too, with a depthless reservoir of love.

And it was not just him, but him and Cygnus.

You'll have to leave him, and Cygnus, too, said the voice inside her that spoke hard and ugly truths.

Not yet, she replied to herself, shoving the voice aside, burying it beneath layers of ecstasy and immediacy.

So she followed him, as she had when he showed her the oceans and woods of this world, the fields and bakeries and markets. Now he brought her into parts of Horfa she had not seen, that no Englishman had seen. These were older districts, with rough-hewn stone walls, some even unmortared, along narrow streets where no children played; places where age lay thick and heavy. If buildings could be made of dust and memory, it was these, aching with the effort of remaining upright, leaning on one another in companionable dotage.

"You are about to see something forbidden to any eyes not of Horfa," Jairo said, a cheery dismissal of a taboo that should, perhaps, have given him greater pause. It thrilled her and made her hesitate, but the warm hand in hers pulled her onward, inexorably, to a small open plaza of inlaid stones, a mosaic of milky white with coppery tendrils that formed an intricate pattern throughout.

"This is the Hearth," he said, his voice low and reverential. "And there," he pointed to a stone-and-beam structure facing the plaza, topped by three black-and-red spires that reached skyward to the heavens, twisting and entangling until the eye could not pull them apart, "that is where we are going."

"A cathedral," Fletcher said in hushed English, unable to find the Cygni linguistic counterpart. It was a fraction as tall as most buildings on Earth, but it dwarfed its neighbors, seeming to stretch impossibly high, spires threatening to puncture slate-colored clouds gathering in the gloaming.

"Perhaps in your tongue, Christine. This is a *takat*, a Faithhouse. The *Takat*, in truth, the first and oldest in Horfa. Come. It will be better if we go in early, before the crowds of evening worshipers." He smiled, radiant in the half-light, and took from his pack two long robes of gray. "Put this on. We all wear them for the service. None will know you do not belong."

Fletcher took the robe, shrugging into it hurriedly, glancing about the deserted plaza. Jairo reached out and lifted the cowl of the robe, tucking in her hair as he did so.

"Why gray?" she asked, as Jairo donned a similar garment.

"Because in the *takat*, there are no blue soldiers, no brown scholars. In the eyes of the Faith, we are all the same." He indicated the massive black iron doors in the stone face of the Faithhouse. "Those won't open for another hour or so, but I know another way in." He held out his hand again, and in his eyes was the same message. *Follow me. Trust me.* Again, Fletcher did.

She trailed behind Jairo as he rounded a corner of the *takat*, moving quickly down a blind alley where the base of one of the spires jutted out from the wall, almost into contact with the adjacent building. Jairo pulled her behind him, squeezing through the remaining space, coming to a set of stone stairs cut into the wall, so cleverly hidden behind the tower that they would escape all but the most determined investigation. They descended these, finding at the bottom a small wooden door. Fishing in his pockets, he produced a small black key with a red stone set into its head.

"How...?" asked Fletcher, and for the first time, she felt the tiniest twinge of uncertainty.

"Very few know of this door," he admitted. "But I'm an intellectual. It's my business to know things others don't. And as for the key, well, let's say it has always been of benefit to my caste to keep an eye on the clergy." With a soft click the key unlocked the door, which creaked ever so slightly as it swung inward. Jairo slipped into the impenetrable darkness and the odor of stale antiquity beyond. Curiosity overwhelmed her indecision, and Fletcher plunged after.

When the door closed behind them, there was no light inside, not the scarcest hint of the dim twilight world outside. Then Jairo was there, his mouth on hers, his hands on her body, moving under her robe, and the suddenness of it made her almost cry out. When they finally broke, she was out of breath.

"You didn't bring me all the way here to take advantage of me," she whispered, while she ached to continue.

"No," he replied, formless and near, still holding her, heat radiating from him. "But it will be quite some time before we can emerge from this basement and safely merge with the crowds. Can you think of a better way to spend the time, knowing that any night might be our last together?"

"In that case," Fletcher whispered, groping for the front of his robe and yanking it open, pulling him toward her in a fierce embrace.

That was the last time.

After, they readjusted their vestments as best they could in the blackness. Fletcher felt Jairo's finger laid tenderly across her lips. She nodded her understanding, and he moved away, leaving her suddenly and completely alone. Being alone had never held any terror for her, nor had the dark, but at that moment, she felt his absence like an amputation, and the weight of it, of all the days to come when she would be without him, fell on her.

You'll have to leave him.

Not yet.

Light spilled into the room then, a thin spike of gray, turning the blackness into murky gloom. It was a basement, the outlines of stacked tables, bookshelves, and other such artifacts coming into half-focus around the walls. She could see Jairo, too, his hooded form huddled by the door. He beckoned, once, swiftly, and she hurried to join him as he stepped into the hallway beyond. It was empty, a bare corridor of thick stone, chilly and damp despite the heat of the summer evening above. In the space of a few dozen steps, it ended in a circular stairwell which they swiftly ascended. After a few moments, Jairo turned and leaned in close to her.

"You are not prepared for what you are about to experience," he said plainly. "And I will not spoil it for you. Keep your hood up and your face hidden. And no matter what happens, do not be afraid. I am with you."

These words from the man she knew she had come to love above all in the galaxy chilled her blood and set her mind racing with excitement. Most likely it was mere religious pageantry, meaningful to the Horfans and unlikely to move her, but it should still prove a fascinating cultural observance. And they were together.

The curving stairway ended, debauching into a much larger and wider hall, paneled with wood. Every inch was carved in minute detail, gilt throughout, with scrolling stonework similar in color and style to the plaza outside. Fletcher tried to examine it more closely, but Jairo was walking rapidly, and she hastened to catch up. Ahead, she could see more hooded figures, in swirling clusters, and she had no desire to lose contact with him in the gathering mob. Collectively, the Horfan mass streamed through a wide arch. Beyond was a huge hall, wider and deeper than any interior space Fletcher had yet seen on Cygnus, stretching high above to disappear into a distant unknown ceiling. *It truly was a cathedral,* she realized, or its analogue. Hundreds of robed natives clustered, standing, in a gray mass of humanity.

Humanity? thought Fletcher, and then, *why not?* There were those on Earth less human than the Cygni.

A muteness fell over the throng then, a hush of expectation. A high dais ran across the front of the long sanctuary, and there, three figures materialized from behind a massive woven tapestry. They were all young women. Young, or perhaps not so much young as of an indeterminate age, and beautiful, wearing hoodless robes of red trimmed with black. All had brown hair, or at least so it seemed at first, but as the light flickered along the rows of guttering torches in wall sconces that flecked the nave with gold, Fletcher's eyes played tricks on her, casting the tresses of the priestesses in black, then red, then shimmering silver.

Fletcher began to whisper a question to Jairo, but he made a tiny shake of negation and she fell quiet. Music began, slow, insistent, thrusting, emanating from unseen musicians. The priestesses were moving in time with the glacial harmony, creating something less than dance but more than pantomime, in deliberate, exaggerated, almost sensual movement. Slowly, methodically, the volume built, pounding in an inexorable rhythm, vibrating the base of Fletcher's skull and reaching out to her at some level below her civilized consciousness, beneath her aware self; some level more visceral, more primal, more savage.

Then another woman came onto the stage, taller and perfect. Looming like a vague, slender giantess, she raised long arms draped in jagged red. The lesser dancers melted away behind velvet black curtains as the music reached a holy crescendo followed by absolute silence. The audience's breathing came in regular, modulated cadence as if they were not many individuals but one communal creature, poised in avid anticipation. The head priestess spoke, and as she did, her words were rhythmic, archaic, and difficult for Fletcher to follow. At the same time, they felt as familiar as the blandishments of a hundred other faiths, words of pronouncement and prescription, their literal import less gravid than their effect on the gathered faithful. Fletcher had never been a pious woman, though the Ochoas were nominally Catholic, but she was not immune to the charisma of the priestess. It acted like a physical force upon the worshippers as she wove together ancient stories with guidance for modern life. Fletcher began to feel warm, then drowsy, as the words washed over her like lapping poetic waves, until the congregation shouted in responsorial unison, repeating the mantra "Horfa is chosen" two, three, then four times. It was then, in the midst of such fervor, that Fletcher felt the raw soul of the Horfan people unvarnished before her, with such beauty and power that tears came to her eyes and it was all she could do to keep from falling to the floor or embracing Jairo then and for the rest of her life.

Eventually the services ended and they departed along with the other parishioners, her heart swollen with love for this place, these people, and this person. Still in their dull robes, she pulled him into a shrouded alley and stared at him with incredulity.

"Why did you show me that?" she asked.

"It is the heart of who we are as a people," he replied with a stormy flash of gray in his pale blue eyes. "And I would have you know our heart. My heart. Because custom demands that I shouldn't, and I don't want any custom or taboo between us; no secrets or regulations. Limitations are for lesser loves than ours, Christine." He kissed her, and she responded, there in the shadows of those ancient walls, fiercely and long, and as they broke their breath mingled in the cool dusk air.

"Your scientists have almost finished their work," he said huskily. She nodded in response, unable to speak. "You will be leaving soon?"

"The…the ship will, yes."

"And will you be on it?" His gaze was searching, powerful, and she had to look away, down, anywhere but into those eyes of melting ice.

"I have no choice, Jairo. Desertion is the worst crime there is in the Royal Navy, short of mutiny. Captain Pearce couldn't allow it." A bold and sudden idea seized her then, and she blurted it out. "You could come with us! As a cultural and scientific ambassador from…" her voice trailed off as she saw his shaking head.

"I can't, my love. I can't leave my work here, my obligations, any more than you can yours. You know I am slated to succeed Arkadas in leadership of my caste when he retires in a few years. I would leave the task to someone else, but I fear how weak the intellectual influence would be under less prepared leadership. And this is something I have long desired and worked toward."

Fletcher sighed, a sigh that became a laugh that became a choked sob.

"I don't know if I'll be able to leave," she said, softly, gathering his gray robe in her fists and pressing her face against his chest.

"But you must, as you say. Just as I must not." He put a hand under her chin and forced her face up, gently, and smiled at her. "Do not cry that you are leaving. I would cry if you had never come. And I meant every word I said about lesser loves. This is not the end for us, Christine Fletcher. We will see each other again, I know it."

She stepped away from him then, pushing her knuckles into her eyes, taking a long, slow swallow of the clean night air. Her mind was full of the vastness of space between here and Earth, of time and distance, and it threatened to swallow her whole. She battled back against the yawning chasm of despair before her, pushing it back one more time.

"You have been so generous and helpful," she said, desperate to change the subject. "And have asked so little for yourselves in return."

"We're a generous people," Jairo said. "Of what you've asked for, we have plenty to give. And it has certainly been the pleasantest month I have ever known."

"Even so." Fletcher pulled free of him again. "We've gotten what we came for. I would feel bad if all you got in return were technological advances you likely would have made for yourselves in a few decades. I wish there were something more tangible we could do."

"If you're going to insist," responded Jairo, "there is one thing I will admit to being curious about."

****

It seemed wrong to Pearce that Jane Baker, the greatest star-mariner Earth ever produced, had come to rest here. A spreading *pilapus* tree, looking very like an elm, shaded the simple and lonely stone marker. It was quiet here, nestled alongside the sandy beaches of a vast ocean. It was all very pleasant, and all very wrong.

"I always imagined you at St. James," Pearce murmured, aware that he was speaking only to rocks, trees, wind, and himself. "A statue in Trafalgar, alongside Nelson's column, or maybe at the Admiralty gates." He smiled, and let the fantasy play out, picturing in his mind how some sculptor would try to depict the great Captain Baker, try to make her look all stern and proper, maybe a hand shading her eyes in some nonsensical, fanciful nautical pose, or else seated primly and erect in the captain's chair. *No*, he thought. The immortal Jane Baker should be on her feet, leaning over her helmsman's shoulder, adjusting the *Drake*'s trim, her plain face aglow with focus, joy and genius. The galaxy would never see the like again, in flesh or marble.

"If you had to be lost on duty, it should have been out there, with a deck under your feet."

He sighed, knowing that such a thing would have meant the deaths of other star-mariners, perhaps even his own. He had not been an intimate of Captain Baker's; he wasn't one of her three-voyage veterans like Captain Clark or Commandant Martinez, or the scores of ables who had flocked to her roster whenever she slipped moorings. She had been a walking deity to him, a god made bone and blood, the woman who landed on a comet to make repairs and came away whole, the woman who had mapped endless parsecs of the galaxy, the woman who had tackled space scurvy and relegated it to history. *The woman who fell at Cygnus.* And now she lay here, under a strange sun, under strange dirt.

It was wrong. *But,* he thought, *what isn't these days*? He sat stiffly in the grass, still very much aware of the slightly stronger gravity of Cygnus. It made breathing a bit more difficult, moving a bit more tiring, and he had never adjusted the way some had, like Christine Fletcher. The thought of her made him a little sad and more than a little angry. Something was very amiss with that woman. It had begun as soon as the *Harvest* was under way, and had only gotten worse during their stay on Cygnus, as she spent more time in the company of Jairo.

A huge shadow fell across Pearce. Squinting, he looked up. Orpheus Crutchfield loomed overhead, blotting out the sun and much of the sky. Even in the heat of the day, the sergeant wore his full uniform. Every buckle and button was fastened, every strap in place. *If ever there was a spit-and-polish officer, it's this one,* thought Pearce. Two of the machrines flanked him, like mechanical henchmen.

"Yes, Sergeant?"

"Sorry to disturb you, Captain. It's Luther-45."

"Yes?"

"He's gone, sir. Missing." The sergeant, Pearce noticed, was trembling, ever so slightly, either with anger or concern, or both. Pearce stood, a little too quickly, and nearly stumbled.

"Damned gravity. No, I'm all right, man. What the hell do you mean, missing?"

"Just that, sir," Crutchfield said. "Luther didn't return from his scheduled duty this afternoon, and I can't locate him on the tracker."

"What duty was that?"

"He was assigned to Lieutenant Fletcher, sir. In the city."

"I see. Well, there must be some plausible explanation." Pearce tapped a stud on his communication wristlink. "Fletcher, please respond."

A few moments passed, as Pearce ground his teeth, his jaw working side to side in noiseless agitation. He disliked being made to wait by a subordinate, especially one in whom his trust and confidence had been so severely frayed. Eventually, there came a brief burst of static, and Fletcher's voice, somewhat out of breath.

"Fletcher."

Pearce ignored the omitted "sir" and the increasing throbbing in his head.

"Running, Lieutenant?"

"What?" she responded. "No, nothing like that. Just…just stepped away from my bracelet for a moment." There was a rustle in the background, muffled voices. *What the hell was going on*? Background racket from Horfa, perhaps?

"While on duty?" Silence was the only response, and Pearce plowed forward. "Fletcher, is Luther-45 with you?" Again, she only replied after a long pause.

"Not exactly." This time she added, belatedly, "sir."

Not exactly?

"Fletcher…" another crackle of interference hummed across their connection, and Pearce spat out a string of vulgarities, damning this alien world and its odd magnetic fields, damning his own luck at ever having been stupid enough to go into space in the first place. Finally the noise subsided. "Fletcher, you will report to me at once. Five minutes ago, do you hear?" He cut his signal before she could respond. He stood stock still, vibrating with impatience. Nearby, Crutchfield was almost as edgy. The robots, true to their emotionless programming, betrayed no trace of unease.

Breaking the heavy silence, Pearce's wristlink chirped with an incoming message. *If it's her with some excuse,* he thought, activating it savagely.

"What!" he bellowed.

"Sir." It was the calm, twanging voice of Pott, with the clarity of broadcast that only the Harvest's transmitter boosters could achieve. "Sorry to bother you, but are Lamb and Briggs there? Their shore leave expired fifteen minutes ago and we've been waiting for their signal for the shuttle. I didn't know if perhaps they were having some trouble reaching us. When I try their frequencies, I get nothing."

"No," Pearce replied evenly, regaining his temper. He glanced at Crutchfield, who shook his head. "No sign of them here, Pott. Hold on."

He knew it was useless before he did it, but like a man joining a crowd at a locked door, he had to try it himself. As he expected, transmitting to their numbers returned nothing but the low hum of a deactivated unit. *What now?* He switched back over to the *Harvest* frequency. "Nothing."

"Sir, I'll send a shuttle to search for them."

"Belay that," Pearce ordered. "An aerial search probably wouldn't do much good. But have Mister Hall prep a shuttle and stand by." From the corner of his eye, he saw a lone figure approaching along the broad causeway linking the point to the mainland. He could tell from her gait, slow enough to irritate him further, that it was Fletcher. "Pott, stand by. I'll handle matters here."

"Yes, Captain." There was a hint of reluctance in his first officer's tone, but Pearce ignored it and terminated the connection. He fixed his gaze on Christine Fletcher, watching intently and simmering as she sauntered closer. *I gave her five minutes, and she takes near twenty.*

"Fletcher," he greeted her as she arrived, endeavoring to keep his voice flat as he gathered the shreds of his composure together.

"Captain." Fletcher seemed relaxed, either unaware or disinterested that her commander was seething.

"I will ignore your tardiness, but I insist that you explain your earlier comment. Where is Luther-45? He was assigned to you."

"He was. I gave him to Jairo."

"You gave…!" Crutchfield stepped forward, the words escaping his throat in a canine yelp. Pearce held up a hand, and the sergeant stopped, his eyes wide with confusion.

"Lieutenant Fletcher, I must have misheard you," Pearce growled.

"Not at all, sir." She smiled, and it took every last ounce of Pearce's will not to surrender to fury. "Jairo was curious about Luther, so I made a gift of him. It seemed a fair exchange, given how much help they've been, and how much we've collected. You did order me to engage in cultural exchange, and to nurture our relationship with the Cygni, after all. I didn't think it would be a problem."

"You didn't think it would be a problem," Pearce repeated through clenched teeth, ignoring Crutchfield's slow-burning horror off to his periphery. "You've been in our briefings. You know our regulations about making inappropriate technology available to other societies. You didn't think it would be a problem? You didn't think I would mind? You didn't think it would upset me? No, Fletcher, you simply didn't *think*." In an incandescent moment, his tenuous grip on his temper failed, and he roared unintelligibly. "I was a damned fool to bring you. To insist on having you on this voyage! You've been deliberately defiant!

Insubordinate! All but bloody mutinous!" Fletcher had taken a step backward, but he closed the distance between them, his purpled face scant inches from hers. *That face*, he thought through his wrath, *that beautiful face*, and then it suddenly all made sense to him.

"Jairo," he spat, his voice suddenly and dangerously low, "is manipulating you, Lieutenant, and doing a splendid job of it, I should say."

"What are you on about, Bill?" she asked, unsettled, forgetting herself.

"Captain!" he snarled, "or sir, damn you! It's these Cygni; they breathe some bewitching fog, some miasma that makes others like them, even *love* them." He said this last with a sarcastic timbre. "I've seen the two of you together. Unofficerly, schoolgirl conduct. He is using you, Fletcher, and you're too damn infatuated to even notice."

She slapped him, and the alien world seemed to stop rotating on its fat axis.

"Damn you, Bill Pearce," she hissed, and everything between them was irreparably broken. He touched his cheek, gingerly, disbelieving.

"Sergeant Crutchfield." The words did not catch in his throat, as he was afraid they might. Sadness and anger comingled and filled him like a cold liquid. "You will take Lieutenant Fletcher into custody, please." Pearce stared at her, his eyes boring holes into her, his rage and misery a living, writhing dance within his gut. The massive officer spoke a quiet command, and one of the machrines, Victor-11, stepped forward in mute obedience. He enclosed Fletcher's hands in his, and a blue-tinged immobilizer field emitted from his wrists. She did not resist, did not even look at the robot, never taking her eyes off the captain. Pearce finally tore his own gaze free, and signaled Pott, in orbit high above.

"Lieutenant Pott, please have Mister Hall report to the surface with Ambrose-226." That would leave no machrines on board the *Harvest*, which made Pearce uncomfortable, but he saw no other way. "I have arrested Lieutenant Fletcher for gross insubordination, striking a superior officer, and..." he was about to say *treason*, but at long last words failed him. "...and theft of the ship's property," he finished. "She is to be confined to quarters with no access to any ship's network, and no contact with any other crew members." There was silence on the other end. "John?"

"Aye, aye, sir," the lieutenant replied at last. "Right away."

"And Pott...find Green and Reyes. I want the final shipments of samples brought on board now. All other shore leaves are hereby terminated. All personnel are to report to the ship within the hour. Pearce out."

He ended the transmission and turned to Crutchfield.

"When Hall arrives with the shuttle, remit custody of the prisoner to him with one of the machrines. Probably Victor, but I leave that to you. They can escort her back to the ship." He glanced sidelong at the woman he had thought was his friend, the woman he had thought so vital to their success. Feeling the anger rising within himself again, Pearce shoved it back down. He didn't have time to lose his temper again, not right now. He stabbed a thick finger in her direction. "I'll deal with you when I get back to the ship." Christine Fletcher said nothing, her silence full of seething and hurt.

"Where are you going, sir?" Crutchfield asked.

"After you transfer her to Mister Hall, you take the two other machrines, and you find Lamb and Briggs." During the exchange with Fletcher, Pearce had begun to suspect a connection between his missing crewmen's absences and the abduction of Luther with Fletcher's complicity, unwitting or otherwise. It could, of course, simply be a matter of desertion, and the timing a mere coincidence, but Pearce wasn't about to bet his ship, the future of humanity, and his son's life on it.

"Where are you going, sir?" repeated Crutchfield.

"I'm going to find Luther and bring him back."

"Alone? Is that wise, captain?"

"Wise or not, that's what I'm doing." He looked one last time at Fletcher, allowed himself the shortest instant to feel grief at the final dissolution of their long friendship, and then dismissed it from his mind. "It's time Venn Arkadas and I had a talk."

Twelve

Paradise Lost

Figuring out where to go had been a simple matter. The machrines were more than just guards and training partners; they were ever-watchful sentinels and dutifully reported to their sergeant, whichever Cygni Briggs and Lamb had been seen with most frequently. Sergeant Orpheus Crutchfield, like soldiers before him for millennia, had nurtured a kind of professional rapport with the mid-ranks of the indigenous military. With their cooperation – and a little too much of the intoxicating Horfan beverage, *edan* – the identities of the native collaborators were readily established.

"The Burned Hills," they told him. "They'll head for the Burned Hills."

So Crutchfield headed there, too, following their directions, eager for the moment when they drew near enough to make use of the machrines' tracking capabilities. The "painting" of crew members as friendly was more than a tactical advantage, it was also a useful method for keeping track of wayward crew. *It would only be a matter of time, really.* He would have enjoyed the assignment if it hadn't been so damned hot.

Crutchfield had been on exploration or garrison duty on a score of worlds, but he had never experienced this kind of sticky, roasting heat. He had been slick with sweat ever since venturing forth from Horfa, through the surrounding countryside, and into the vast wilds beyond the farthest settlements. The farmhouses and cultivated fields, with their odor of herd manure and growing things, gave way to untended chaparral, russet grasses, and the insistent chirp of some kind of red-winged birds that circled overhead by the dozens. Crutchfield had been mildly interested at first, having only the vaguest understanding of birds, but now the damn things were an annoyance.

Worse than the birds, almost than the heat, was the openness.

Despite his wide and varied experiences in the service, Crutchfield had remained, at heart, a child of the close spaces, narrow hallways, and windowless rooms he grew up in, in the subterranean apartment complexes honeycombing what was once the northern deserts of Africa. His parents had worked in the copper and bauxite mines, kilometers below the surface, in the dirty and dangerous labor of extracting vital minerals for the ever-hungry apparatus of empire. He could vividly remember the first time he saw the sky, venturing to Cairo for a school field trip. He had been seven years old and terrified. Older kids at school had told him that people sometimes fell off, up into the sky, if they didn't hold on to things while on the surface. Eventually he learned better and paid back his tormentors, but he never forgot the terror of that first glimpse of the heavens.

Where he really wanted to be was with Captain Pearce, retrieving (the word rescuing came to mind, but he dismissed it) Luther-45 from wherever it was he had been spirited off to. He had no paternal romanticism that the machrines were his children, but they were certainly his responsibility, and he took that seriously. Trained extensively in combat but also in the maintenance, programming, and management of his robotic squad, Crutchfield was the very model of a modern soldier-technician. Captain Pearce had ordered him to hunt down and apprehend these deserters, and so he would. He was a martial creature, the habit of deeply ingrained obedience, and yet he felt an even more pronounced sense of filial devotion to the old man. *A right proper commander, not one of your mollycoddlers or gladhanders*. He had served under those sorts of permissive officers before, the ones who were always courting the love of their jacks, only ever earning a soft kind of pitying derision. *The crew might not love this captain*, Crutchfield thought, *but they respect him, and even fear him just enough*.

Discipline, the god of gods in the service, demanded the return of the starmen. If desertion were not properly punished, the *Harvest* – any ship, really – would lose crewmen at every port of call. But it wasn't that he didn't sympathize with Peggy Briggs and Saul Lamb. Crutchfield was a big man – enormous really, ogrish, gargantuan – in a world engineered for maximum efficiency where the taking up of space was concerned. This was especially true in his chosen starfaring profession. He had to admit there was something almost intoxicating about the freedom to move about without the fear of knocking his head or elbow on some bulkhead. And like the furtive crewmen, he was a born commoner, from the lower echelons of common, and this open world promised a kind of liberty and comfort not to be found on board His Majesty's ships or back on Earth. But Crutchfield had been around long enough to know that such promises were illusions, cruel in their beauty and short-lived.

The intoxication of Cygnus was mitigated, and forcefully, by the heat. There was more sky above than Crutchfield had ever seen. It formed an unbroken dome of cerulean with only the wispiest hint of clouds, which did nothing to block the baleful gaze of the huge and reddish native sun. He was beginning to wonder if the heat would affect the machrines, and glanced back at them in concern. Despite the white glare gleaming from their plexisteel skins, they showed no outward signs of distress.

"Sergeant," intoned Ambrose-226, with that disembodied, eerily human voice that these artificial things used, each unique and each taking no small amount of getting used to, "are you all right? You appear to be leaking."

"It's perspiration, Ambrose," Crutchfield growled, though he knew that in another time, in another context, it would be funny. The machrine's fussy, high-pitched voice was masculine, but only just. "Access your file on human heat regulation and secretion of wastes. I'm fine. Your status?"

"Internal gauges show temperatures in excess of thirty-eight degrees Celsius, but well within operational parameters, sir."

With a grunt, Crutchfield continued to climb. The baking fields had given way to baking hills and stony scrambles leading inexorably upward. It all formed an oven with no cover, no trees, no shade. The sergeant drove himself forward with the pleasing thought of catching the deserters and dragging them back in irons. Each outcropping of rock yielded to another, the stone hot to the touch, and the sergeant unflaggingly crested each with increasing appreciation for the name Burning Hills.

"Two hundred meters, ahead and to your right, sir."

Ogden-92 had a lower voice than Ambrose, more grating and less cultured. The Ambrose model was newer, resulting in more human tones and mannerisms. Still, there was something about the Ogden models, a certain gritty toughness, which Crutchfield had always liked. And for some reason, though the programming and software was identical across the models, the Ogdens always seemed to be superior trackers. If he didn't know better, the sergeant would say the thing relished the task. Crutchfield stopped, crouching behind a ledge of gray boulders and gesturing to the two robots to get low, as well. It was blessedly cooler in the shadow cast by the rocks, and he paused, wiping the sweat from his eyes before creeping to the edge, coiled and taut, silent despite his bulk, his lips curling back from his teeth in a grimace of anticipation.

From his protected vantage point, Crutchfield could see across a broad, pebbled plain to a grove of dark green trees. There was movement there, and voices. With the patience born of years in the service, he waited, watched and counted. As he had on many a mission before this, he gave thanks for the stolid machrines behind him, neither moving nor speaking, asking no stupid questions, waiting with their own kind of inanimate patience for their orders. Six, he thought after ten minutes.

There were the two ables, Briggs and Lamb, and four natives – three women and a man, as best as he could tell. He had known there were Cygni with the deserters, but it scarcely changed the calculus of the operation. He beckoned to the robots and they approached soundlessly, within arm's reach.

"Unpaint Briggs and Lamb," he whispered. "Ulster Protocols." *Apprehend targets. All force short of lethal approved.*

Crutchfield turned again to observe the fugitives. He didn't see the sharp blue of Cygni military uniforms, and he would have been shocked if he had. Civilians. That didn't guarantee that they would be unarmed, but the likelihood of facing a trained, hardened resistance was much less. *Good.* He wanted to get this done, to get out of these scorched hills and back to the ship, so that he could find his missing machrine. In rapid succession, he made three hand signals. Ogden and Ambrose disappeared, swiftly and soundlessly. Crutchfield toggled the safety on his hand laser, and the indicator light shifted from red to green. *Green means go,* he thought. Once upon a time, it was something his instructor had shouted during drills, but short of the alliteration, he still had no idea what the hell it meant. Slowly, he emerged from behind the ledge, running silently, at almost full speed, despite being bent nearly double, making less noise than a breeze. Nonetheless, he expected to be seen at any moment. The bright red of his uniform was one of the longest traditions in the marine service, intended to convey utter confidence and irresistible strength, but he knew that was one thing in a large-force maneuver and yet another in a small team dependent on concealment.

Somehow, his luck and skill held, and Crutchfield reached the edge of the copse undetected. The rocky scrabble had given way to yellow grasses midway through his sprint. This, in turn, had given way to green. He heard running water now, less than thirty meters ahead, in the heart of the grove. *Some kind of spring must bubble up through the ground here,* he thought, giving life to the trees, the bushes, the huge orange flowers with petals like dinner plates. He waited, crouching in the midst of a dense thicket of greenery. The vegetation brought relief from the heat and unrelenting openness of the hillsides. From his vantage point he could see Briggs, seated against the base of a wide tree, a silver-haired native male reclining against her in casual intimacy. Lamb was moving about the small clearing, rigging up what looked like rough tents, while the three Cygni women busied themselves preparing a cold meal. *Just a temporary stop,* Crutchfield thought, wondering where they planned to go next. It hardly mattered.

Crutchfield emerged from the bushes, his sidearm drawn and trained on Briggs.

"Not one move," he said, his voice low and commanding. She didn't move, not at all, still as a mountain except for her eyes. Those eyes, the human, feminine part of her, glittered. The Cygni male with his head in her lap started, but she calmed him with a murmured word. He was a small, mousy sort, still handsome in the manner of his people, but short, and oddly delicate. He was nestled under the crook of Briggs' arm, her fingers tangled in his hair. *Is she his lover or his mother?*

Lamb had taken three quick steps forward at the first sound. He was shirtless, his muscled, scarred torso glistening with sweat while his meaty fingers clutched a thick wooden club. His eyes were wild, like an animal, and Crutchfield prepared himself to shoot his crewmate.

"Leave it, Lamb," Briggs said archly. "You idiot. You think he's here alone? There's at least one 'rine, maybe two, in these woods, and if you swing that stupid twig they'll burn you quick." She called over her shoulder, to the women, who had melted into the brush; her gaze never left Crutchfield. "Don't worry, girls, he won't hurt you. It's just us he wants. Just us." Pale faces peeked out from the trees, furtive and uncertain.

Lamb dropped his club and it struck the ground with a sullen thunk. He spat.

"Damn that Pearce to Hell," he growled. There was no malice or violence in his voice, only misery. "He could have left without us." He looked at the sergeant. "Figured if we got up here, got far enough, it might be more bother than not to come looking for us."

"Idiot," murmured Briggs again. She resumed stroking the native man's hair.

"The King takes desertion seriously, and the Captain is the King himself to lads like us," Crutchfield said, his weapon still centered on Briggs. He knew Luther and Ambrose had Lamb covered, and could handle him. It was Briggs he didn't trust.

"The Devil take the King, too," Lamb replied, again in that flat, lifeless tone.

"Watch that," Crutchfield warned.

"Or what? We're dead already, whether you kill us now or he kills us later." A thought seemed to come to him suddenly. "You could say you couldn't find us, you know. Or better yet, come with us."

"Are you really that stupid?" Briggs asked cuttingly. "If they came looking after your useless ass, they'd sure as hell come after two machrines. And Orpheus is a good King's man, right?" She laughed, a sound Crutchfield had never heard from her before. It was a disquietingly beautiful, melodious sound.

"Why?" he asked, before he could stop himself. "What were you thinking, Briggs?" She shrugged.

"Worth a try." Her eyes assumed a faraway look. "You ever been to the Glasgow yeast pits, Orpheus?" He said nothing, which she apparently interpreted as negation. "Lamb was a yeastie, before he ran off to space. What were you, Lamb, seventeen? Fifteen years later, and still the stink of it on him. Some things never wash off. Almost as bad as my childhood home." She said these last two words with a slow, biting sarcasm, as if neither home nor childhood had ever truly existed for her. "The pits stink, but at least they're dry. The Alberta algae flats, now, they stink and they're wet. And cold. And they go on forever. Nineteen thousand square kilometers of green scum, all alive and breeding and in your hair and between your toes. My old man, even his eyeballs and teeth were green. Algae and yeast. Belowdecks is no kind of life, but compared to that..." She shook her shaved head and laughed again. "Made this Eden. What's another touch of the Cat compared to a grab at paradise?"

Crutchfield had never heard Briggs string ten words together before, much less hear her talk about herself at such length, and with such intimacy. It was almost enough to make him feel bad for her. Almost.

"Everyone's got a cross to bear," he said. "Time to come back to the ship."

"No!"

To Crutchfield's surprise and horror, the diminutive Cygni sprang up from Briggs' lap, seized Lamb's club from the ground, and threw himself at the sergeant. Before any of the mortals could react, there was a flash and a beam. The native fell. One of the Cygni women screamed. From the edge of the clearing Ambrose-226 materialized, his hand in the air, the emitters of his narrow-field microwave projector still evident on his metal forearm.

The Ulster Protocols, recalled Crutchfield, staring at the machrine, *make no provision for the safety of bystanders.* He knew, without having to check, that the man was dead.

Silence, smoke-thick, hung in the air for a prolonged moment. Briggs was the first to break the tableau, unfolding onto her feet, her bare arms cords of sinew and tensed muscle, the tattooed anchors on her neck showing a deeper inky black against the reddening skin.

"Go to Hell," she whispered at Ambrose, the words coming from some deep, enraged part of her. She knelt in the dirt beside the Cygni's crumpled, inert form, and cradled his head. The machrine's weapon had left no mark, no indication that any damage had been done at all, but the

Cygni's internal temperature was likely still in excess of eighty degrees Celsius. Minutes before, it would have been above a hundred, his blood rising to a swift boil, his organs cooked inside his skin. "Timma wouldn't have hurt you." Briggs continued, agony in her quiet voice. "He was weak and gentle." Poison in her eyes, she looked up at Crutchfield. Overcoming his initial shock, Lamb made to move forward and found himself suddenly and securely in the grasp of Ogden-92, who had silently slipped into the clearing. He began to struggle, but then grunted as the robot tightened its inhuman grip on the starman's upper arms.

"He'll break both your arms," Crutchfield said. It wasn't the first time he'd seen a man cut down, and probably wouldn't be the last. He didn't have time or attention to spare, at the moment, for sympathy or remorse. The bystander had complicated this operation, and that had to be remedied. "This isn't one of your stupid roulette games now. Stand down, or be put down."

"I ain't going back," Lamb roared suddenly, thin spiderwebs of saliva flecking the black whiskers on his cheeks. His chest surged forward, muscles straining, but Ogden's hold was immovable. Lamb's arms remained static until a sickening crack filled the clearing. The flesh gave way, and he bellowed in pain as jagged white bone jutted through the skin of his bicep.

"Or maybe he'll just break one," Crutchfield said with a sigh. "The hard way, then. End it."

The tip of the index finger on Ogden's left hand swiveled aside, a short syringe emerging into the vacated space. The machrine inserted the needle into Lamb's side with precision, and the writhing crewman abruptly crumpled into a heap. Ambrose approached Briggs, who never shifted her gaze from Crutchfield and never let go of the Cygni male, not even when the tranquilizing injection paralyzed her muscles and drove her silently to the ground.

"The Cygni females?" inquired Ambrose-226. Nearby, Ogden deftly reset and temporarily braced Lamb's fractured arm, a procedure during which the man was fortunate to remain insensate. Crutchfield glanced around the clearing, but there was no sign of the three women. They appeared to have melted away during the confrontation.

"We don't need them," the sergeant said, finding himself suddenly and immensely tired. "Just keep an eye out in case they come back with friends. Keep these two sedated." He touched his wristlink wearily. "*Harvest*."

"This is *Harvest*, Pott here. Report, sergeant."

"Briggs and Lamb in custody. One native casualty, three fled. Standing by for shuttle extraction."

"Stand by. Shuttle to your location in forty minutes. *Harvest* out."

Crutchfield sat heavily on a nearby rock, wiping the sweat from his face. The Cygni male – *Timma*, Briggs had called him – lay in her unconscious embrace, and it looked for all the world that the two were lovers in a peaceful shared sleep. Crutchfield felt as though he were intruding on something both profoundly intimate and deeply disturbing. *The sooner we get off this damned planet*, he thought, *the better*.

****

It did not take long for Pearce to find Venn Arkadas. The intellectual leader was home, and waiting for him.

"I knew you would come," the Cygni said, "once you discovered what became of your robot."

"You know, then?" Pearce asked.

"Know?" Arkadas' face eased into a placid smile. "William, it was my idea."

Pearce stood in the dooryard of Arkadas' handsome house, shaded by a row of charming little trees, flanked by low plots of blooming flowers his wife had planted, and nowhere the slightest hint that a yawning chasm had just opened in the ground, threatening to swallow him whole.

"Your…"

"Come in, please," Arkadas beseeched. "I will admit I am surprised to find you alone, however. I half suspected you would come in force."

"Your idea?" repeated Pearce, numbly, before regaining some measure of his senses. "No, damn your white head, I don't want to come in! I came here to see if you knew what was going on, if you knew who stole my machrine!"

"I can appreciate your irritation, but please, keep your voice down." He glanced anxiously over his shoulder at the interior hallway. "My wife has no idea about any of this, and I would prefer not to involve her." Arkadas stepped outside, closing the door behind him. He looked at Pearce, not unkindly, and sighed. "Will you let me tell you everything?"

"I'll let you give me my property back!" Pearce spat. "And then we can discuss whether or not my ship will rain fire and death on your city."

"If you meant one word of that, I would be afraid," Arkadas replied in calm tones that Pearce found increasingly infuriating. It was all he could do not to rip the silver head off this man he had thought a friend. First Fletcher's betrayal, now this...it was almost more than he could stand. He had not labored so long, sacrificed Rowland and el-Barzin, come back to this birthplace of nightmares, to see it all slip away now. Rage, and more than a little shame at being so easily and thoroughly duped, began to build, until a sudden and blinding realization struck.

"You planned all this," he said with the swift dawning of understanding. "You set up Jairo to suborn Christine Fletcher from the moment we arrived." Then, rapidly on the heels of the last, another thought occurred to him. "My crewmen! Briggs and Lamb!"

"They are in no danger," Arkadas replied. "At least, not from me. Some of our people are with them now, some distance from here. That particular wrinkle was General Leyndar's idea, one of his rare good ones, I'll admit, as a way to divert and divide your forces. I do have to tell you that it took very little encouragement for them to be convinced to desert."

I should never have come back here, Pearce thought. *Or we should have come with an armada, and simply taken what we needed.* Now he was ensnared in this web of intrigue and lies, and the one man he had hoped to trust on this planet was the chief architect of his woes.

"Come with me now," said Arkadas gently. "I have something to show you." He held up a hand, warding off Pearce's question before it could be spoken. "Yes! Yes, then I will take you to see Luther-45."

"If this is a trap," Pearce hissed, "know that in the event I do not return soon, I have left specific orders for my officers to follow. They are not orders your people will find pleasant."

"Well, maybe you have and maybe you haven't. Follow me. I know you are angry, and hurt, but I believe there is still a way for us both to profit from this."

With a weary exhale, Pearce nodded. There wasn't much else he could do. At the moment, Arkadas held all the cards. He followed as the tall Cygni moved down the path to the main road, and then walked with swift dignity to the Law-House, past the threshold, and into the library where they had first met weeks ago. That was when a swift and smooth achievement of their goals had still seemed possible. Arkadas strode to the broad fireplace, depressed a cleverly disguised stone button, and the entire hearth slid aside on floor casters, revealing a gaping entryway.

Down the rabbit-hole, Pearce thought, remembering Mary's comment not so very long before at Spring Grove.

"You must understand," Arkadas was saying as they made their way down a wide, curving stairwell, "just how much unrest you left in your wake ten years ago. When you came, when Jane Baker came, that initial contact with beings from beyond the stars shook us to our core. We are isolated here, far even from our closest neighbors. Our identity is tied to our city. We are Horfans, and have been for the thousand years our histories record, dating back before permanent buildings were here, when the name *Horfa* referred more to a tribe than a place. The Faith..." Here he hesitated, clearly uncomfortable talking about a subject that was wrapped in a great many taboos, but he glanced at Pearce, cleared his throat, and continued with difficulty. "The Faith bears the central tenet that we are a chosen people, that Horfans are the inheritors of all the bounty of the land and the sea, that all things will come to us in our need. That we are, and always have been, the pinnacle of all that is."

"And then we came," Pearce murmured. They had stopped in the stairwell. Arkadas, tall and elegant as ever, though visibly agitated now, remained one step higher.

"You came," he repeated. "You came from the sky in an airship, a...spaceship, like nothing we had ever seen. You brought your tools and your weapons, your technology, so vastly superior to our own, and many of us, perhaps all of us, wondered that such creatures could exist. Our society, always at tenuous peace amongst the castes, was riven with disunity. We intellectuals argued that there was so much we could learn from you, that this was an opportunity like no other for a great leap forward in our knowledge and wisdom. There was no such enthusiasm from the High Priestess. The Faith was threatened by your presence, by your very existence. It jeopardized the position of the Cygni in general and the Horfans, in particular, as the preeminent beings in our universe. They were," he said, his eyes wide and so very blue in the semi-darkness, "afraid, my friend. Afraid for the culture we have built over the centuries, afraid for their role in it, and, I truly believe, afraid for the hearts and souls of our people."

"So," Pearce said, his voice low, "the intellectuals and the priestesses stood in opposition to one another."

"Yes," Arkadas replied. "And it fell to the leadership of the military caste to make their choice and thereby determine our policy." He blew out a long breath and shook his head. "That debate was long, I have been told, and heated. I was not there, of course, not yet senior enough to sit on those councils, but the tale of that Council session has been told and retold over the years. The three leaders of that time will probably still be written of in histories many centuries from now, remembered for their stewardship in that pivotal time. My predecessor, Pag Branit, at the end of his illustrious career, his eyes on the future of our people. High Priestess Kaitsma, the only one of the three still in power, her eyes on the past. And General Tavar."

"Yes?" prodded Pearce, after a prolonged silence. He was anxious to get to the bottom of these stairs, to find what it was Arkadas had hidden all these years, to retrieve Luther, to try to extricate himself from all of these mysteries and to complete his mission. They had been on Cygnus too long, he knew, his crew getting too accustomed to the idleness, to the verdure, to the companionship of the natives. There would be more desertions soon. But he was finally getting the truth now, or some version of it, at least.

"General Tavar was the most powerful of the three," Arkadas said. "He was a brilliant tactician, and had been responsible for the glorious victory over the invading Etela forces from the south many years before. He was – and remains, five years after his death – a hero. A legend, really. So while Branit and Kaitsma debated, Tavar weighed the options. Would he partner with The Faith, declare you Englishmen from beyond to be marauding enemies and try to repulse you, in order to prop up our eroding sense of superiority? Or throw in with the thinkers and extract what knowledge we could from you during your stay?" He sighed. "You must understand, we knew nothing of you. You could have been the vanguard of a conquering armada, or raiders, or enslavers. We were terrified. It would have been the easiest thing in the world, and probably the most politically expedient for an old man at the end of his days, to agree with Kaitsma and succumb to fear and demagoguery. But Tavar, ah, Tavar, he was too shrewd for that." Arkadas smiled at Pearce. "He knew there was no way to defeat you militarily, not overtly. His plan, or so the story goes, was to welcome you, at least initially. To take your Captain Baker's overtures at face value and learn what we could from you. To welcome you, to draw you in, to lull you into security."

"And then to spring the trap." Pearce had bitter tang in his mouth and a churning in his stomach. "Damn you, Arkadas. I lived with your family. We ate together. I played with your children. I thought you were my friend."

"I was!" he protested. "I tell you, I knew nothing of this ten years ago!"

"And now?" Pearce mounted the higher step, his nose coming within inches of the Cygni's.

"I am still." Arkadas was whispering, and Pearce could see the slightest glimmer in the man's eyes, the hint of tears. "I want no strife between us, judar. But I am a leader of my people now, and theirs is the welfare I must put first. You spoke of my children. Their future, and that of their children and grandchildren, is more to me than any friendship. It is that I seek to secure. You do not understand us." His voice cracked.

"You do not understand General Leyndar. He is no Tavar, no tactician, no hero. He is a brute, and he hates you."

"Hates me?"

"His brother died that night, William. Right next to him. And even if it weren't for that, for that personal vendetta, he isn't a forgiving man. His dreams are of power and revenge. He will kill you, all of you, given the chance. But for all that, he is a creature of duty and has his own kind of honor. He will deny himself his dreams for the welfare of his people. At least," Arkadas spread his hands, "that is my read of the man. I have been wrong before."

As they continued their descent, the stairs began to widen and the quality of the light to change. Most of the stairwell had been suffused with flickering lamplight, making each step dance with shadow beneath their feet. Pearce had grown accustomed to such illumination during evenings at Arkadas' home and elsewhere on Cygnus; there was a kind of rustic romance to it, and it reminded him of the fire in the hearth at Minister Banks' house so many evenings and parsecs ago. But the deeper they went, the more smooth and unchanging the glow became, spilling upward from some unknown source below. At last, they reached the bottom. The stairs ended, without doorway or other barrier, opening into a huge room that Pearce knew he would never forget for the rest of his days, however many might remain.

It was wide and deep, the size of a cricket pitch, though the ceiling was low, no more than three meters above. All of it was blindingly white and sterile, like a hospital. *Or a laboratory*, thought Pearce. For an instant, his attention was drawn to the recessed panels at regular intervals overhead. These were the origin of the clear, even lighting, and he was struck by the incongruence of it, but then what was in the room, the realization of what it had been so clearly built to house and to study, drove all other thoughts from his mind.

"My God," he murmured. "Alexander."

The remains of the robot – even in this condition of obvious inhumanity, Pearce could not help but think of them as remains – were spread, dissected and sprawling, across the square meters of the white tile floor in the approximate pattern of an absurdly distended, spread-eagled man. The jumble and layout resembled the fossil fragments of some ancient beast, laid out for articulation. Wires ran alongside painstakingly deconstructed servos, gears, and circuits, all bracketed in ghoulish silhouette by segments of the plastisteel exoskeleton. Here and there the casings showed scrapes and dents, and Pearce knew those were where Cygni blows had fallen a decade before. He stood alongside Arkadas, hands hanging loosely at his sides in astonishment, just above what had once been the head of the machine. Near Pearce's foot was the rounded dome of the skullcap, crumpled and misshapen. Just below, farther apart than they should have been, and darker than they should have been, too, were the translucent optic covers, one cracked almost precisely in half.

Pearce wanted, absurdly, to apologize to Alexander-457. Staring at the desecrated mechanical innards of the robot, his mind kept replaying the thing's…what? Death? *Why would you apologize to a machine?* he thought. Would you apologize to a desk computing unit, disassembled for recycling when broken or worn out? And yet, a computer had never given up its existence, sacrificed itself for him. Those forever darkened optics glared at him unblinking, reproachful, abandoned, and violated.

"You see before you," Arkadas whispered, his voice low, as though they were in a place of worship instead of illicit science, "the salvation of my people."

"I see before me," Pearce growled, his hands balling into fists, "the theft and vandalism of His Majesty's property." Arkadas smiled, a bit indulgently.

"Come now. Theft? You abandoned this piece of equipment in your haste to flee, remember?"

"I remember. And I remember why we had to flee that night. Have you forgotten?"

"I haven't," Arkadas replied softly. "I told you before about the shrewdness of General Tavar. Part of his signal brilliance was his mastery of timing. When he felt the time was right, he swung the military's support behind Priestess Kaitsma, and together they drove you from Horfa."

"Why?" demanded Pearce. "Surely we had demonstrated during our stay that we were neither bloodthirsty conquerors nor plundering raiders. We exchanged knowledge, shared our technology with you…" He trailed off, his eyes returning to the meticulously preserved ruins of Alexander-457.

"Yes," said Arkadas. "You descended in your marvelous vessel – merely a rowboat compared to your interstellar vehicle, we later came to understand – and paraded about with your automatons and your advanced weapons. And then you so generously doled out your vast technology in nice, digestible chunks, so appropriate to what you considered to be our stage of development. Not unlike your performance upon your recent return to Horfa, my friend. Farming techniques. Steam power. Discoveries and advancements we would have achieved within decades without your help." He fixed Pearce with his unwavering blue stare. "And you say I lied to you ten years ago. Who lied in the Council chambers, Commander? Well, if you want what you came for, we demand fair exchange."

"Arkadas, where is Luther-45?"

"You know," the Cygni replied, one corner of his mouth twitching into a near-smile, "it took us the better part of two years just to take this one apart. It was clearly non-operative, but we had no idea what manner of energy powered the thing, or what kind of damage might occur – to us or the robot – if we proceeded too swiftly. We understand electricity, of course, and have for some years now. But generating it reliably, capturing it and taming it for our own purposes has always eluded us. Ah, but what your Alexander taught us! We learn swiftly, *judar*, and with time and effort and caution we deduced a great deal from what you see before you." Arkadas gestured upwards at the lighting panels. "It is, of course, an ongoing process, and one limited by the defunct nature of this machine. What we needed was a working example." He was pacing now, just a little, his hands clasped behind his thin back. "Would you ever come back? I, and many of my caste, thought it unlikely, but General Tavar, in one of his final letters, surmised that you were too great an empire to overlook what happened for long, and that in time you would return to chastise us." Arms outstretched, he almost laughed. "All we wanted was another robot to study. More of your technology to penetrate and mimic. Perhaps The Faith is correct. All comes to those in need."

"Where is Luther?" repeated Pearce, grinding his teeth. They had been played for fools from the moment the *Harvest* arrived. *No*, he realized, *long before that. From when the Drake came.* He thought of Captain Jane Baker, cold in that grave at Friendship Point – how that name rankled – and that stone monument. *Visitor and benefactor indeed.*

"Oh, he is here. Or rather, it is here. I've noticed you use the terms interchangeably, which I can appreciate. It is an object, a thing, but it replicates sentience well enough that it can be difficult to remember that it is not a living creature."

"I am running out of patience," Pearce snarled. "Men and women died that day, ours and yours, and you speak as though it was all worthwhile so you can greedily devour whatever knowledge you can steal from us. Jane Baker was a great officer and a great woman, and she is dead because of you."

"Not me. Tavar. Or, more accurately, because of Tavar's tactical genius mixed with her refusal to treat us as an adult society."

"Enough! You must know that there are laws and regulations that prohibit us from introducing inappropriately advanced technology into a society that is not ready for it. You will not blame Captain Baker, or me, for adhering to those rules." Now Arkadas actually did laugh.

"Appropriate by whose evaluation? Yours?"

"Yes," said Pearce, through a clenched jaw. *This is taking too long.* "We are centuries ahead of your people, Arkadas. The Kingdom earned every advance, through the mistakes and trials of our scientists, through our own intellectual labors, every step built upon others in a meaningful process, our leaders forced to deal with the moral consequences of each advance in its own sequence."

"You lie again," Arkadas said simply. "You once told me yourself that your United Kingdom of Earth comprised hundreds of disparate tribal nations, united through commercial and military means. I will not believe that you never absorbed the innovations of another culture, one that may have been more highly developed than your own in one area or another. Discovery is never linear. And," he added, with a tinge of accusation in his voice, "I have watched some of your crewmen, and how they treat our citizens. You are not as advanced a civilization as you would like to believe."

"Give me Luther."

"No."

Pearce sighed heavily and drew his laser sidearm, pointing it squarely at the middle of Arkadas' chest.

"I don't want to hurt you. I don't want to hurt anyone. But I will have that robot back." The Cygni seemed unconcerned with the weapon aimed at him.

"You told me upstairs that your Lieutenant acted without authority when she agreed to give us the machine."

"That's right."

"Would your authority be sufficient?"

"I would be in violation of a score of Admiralty regulations, but if anyone had the authority, it would be me. But it doesn't matter, I would never agree."

"Never?" Arkadas asked. He raised his voice ever so slightly, and said, "Now, please."

Eight doors opened in the walls of the wide room, and eight Cygni military personnel emerged. One of them was General Leyndar, with his perpetual scowl. Each was armed, not with a kerabin, but with the strange weapons Pearce had noticed earlier. He suspected he was confronted with another technological advance cribbed from the study of Alexander-457.

"They will shoot you, Commander. We will kill all of you, if need be, or drive you off again. We have done it before, and we are more formidable now than we were then. We have no true desire to hurt you," he added, with a sideways glance at Leyndar, "at least, most of us do not. What I told you before was true. Alexander-457 was – is – the salvation of the people of Horfa. With his acquisition, we have come to common terms, finally. The military, the intellectuals, even the priestesses. We know now that we are not alone, and we know that if we are to fulfill our destiny as a chosen people, we must grow and learn and develop our technology to ensure we will never again be at the mercy of those stronger than us."

Pearce said nothing. He looked at each of the eight weapons, all trained on him. He looked at General Leyndar's face, at his scar, at the desire for vengeance in his gray eyes. He looked at Arkadas, so in control, so brilliant, so suffused with righteousness. And he looked again at the scattered machrine on the floor, at the tiny labels attached to each piece, and tried to shut out the memory of ten years before, of the nightmares since. He closed his eyes, and in his imagination, the lifeless figure prone on the floor was no longer Alexander, but his own son, James, arms and legs outstretched in the same pose. And he thought of the tens of billions of others who would die, too, if he failed.

He did not hear the soft click as another door opened, but he saw the eyes of the soldiers flicker toward a far corner of the subterranean chamber, and he felt the air change, becoming suddenly warmer and somehow thicker, harder to breathe. Reluctantly, he turned his attention away from the guns pointing in his direction, and saw her.

The woman walking across the tiled floor was inordinately beautiful, though through the gauzy haze that clung to her, Pearce could not have described her features in any detail. Her flowing robes were red and black, clinging first here, then there, hinting at a chaste and yet seductive form beneath. As she came closer and closer, it was like the moment he first met Mary, the moment he fell in love with her, the first time they made love, all added together and multiplied by infinity and stretched out for eternity.

"My friend," Arkadas said, quietly, "permit me introduce the third elder of our councils. This is Kaitsma, the High Priestess of The Faith."

"Captain," she said, a soft thunderclap in his ear, "I know you will help us."

She touched him then, lightly, a hand on his cheek with the merest hint of dry, smooth fire, and his knees nearly buckled beneath him. His heart hammering in his chest, his pulse sprinting at the nearness of her, a corner of his mind wondered, *is this how Fletcher felt?*

"I must have those plants and seeds," Pearce murmured huskily, searching out each word through the fog in his brain. "If we get what we need, you can have Luther." It was wrong and he knew it, wrong in any interpretation of Navy regulations. He did not have the authority to unilaterally interfere with the technological development of an alien society. Neither, though, did he have the authority to condemn all of human life to starvation and death through a slavish devotion to orders. What use, what possible use, to preserve Cygni society at the cost of the entire Kingdom? *If this is the only way, then so be it.* "Hell, I'll recommend to the Science Minister a full-scale exchange of technology between the Kingdom and Cygnus. But I must have those plants and seeds. Tell them to power down their weapons."

"Of course," Arkadas replied graciously, stepping nimbly forward and taking the gun from Pearce's suddenly flaccid fingers. "We haven't gotten those things to work right yet anyway." He nodded, and the soldiers returned their weapons to their holsters. Even Leyndar did so with demonstrated reluctance, though he then strode forward, glowering, until he was very close to Pearce.

"Were it up to me," the Cygni general said, gravel in his voice, "I would kill you where you stand."

"Go ahead," Pearce spat back. "And when word reaches my ship, they'll…"

"They'll do what?" the general interrupted. "Turn tail and run away, like you did ten years ago? You're a spineless people. To think we were afraid you had come to conquer us. Bah. Maybe we should come and conquer you."

"See you in four hundred years, when you develop space flight," said Pearce, returning Leyndar's unblinking gaze.

"This is not helping," interjected Kaitsma. "General, Captain, please." Her smiling face, coming more clearly into focus, had a calming effect on both men, but it seemed to Pearce that she was not nearly so young, nor so warm, as she had appeared moments before. "We are to be friends again, our two peoples."

Pearce felt weary, hundreds, thousands of years weary, and impossibly distant from anything he loved. He had wanted to go back into space so badly, had wanted that elusive captain's commission as desperately as a drowning man fighting for air. Now, in this too-modern basement, surrounded by strangers and strangeness, he wanted nothing more than to finish this business and go home to Mary and James.

"Take the machrine," he said, his voice sounding thin and reedy in his own ears. He looked at Arkadas, and the Cygni had the grace to not appear smug. "Promise me we will leave with what we need."

"All that and more, *judar*."

Thirteen

Fruitless

It was dusk when Pearce returned to Friendship Point and the waiting shuttle. He had heard the reports from Pott and Crutchfield. The deserters were aboard and in custody, as was Christine Fletcher. He had recalled Dr. Reyes and Sir Green from their field work, instructing them to collect whatever specimens they had, in whatever condition they existed, and prepare for departure. There was to be no more exploration, no more botanizing in the countryside, no more languid nursing of seedlings in the sprawling farms outside Horfa.

It was time to leave.

He stood in the gathering darkness on that tiny spit of land where Baker had died, where Fletcher had slapped his face, where the bookends of his adult life had been forged, and he wondered if any of it could have been any different. Venn Arkadas stood alongside him, his sole escort, the man who had saved his life ten years ago and yet was the architect of his troubles now.

"Do not look so sad," the Cygni scholar/bureaucrat/schemer said, shadows falling across his aging but still-handsome face. "The holds of your ship are full of the plants you sought. Your mission will be a success, William. So the price was somewhat higher than you anticipated. What of it? You've been a trader long enough to know that negotiations are always part of the deal."

Pearce stared at the sky, watching pinpricks of light grow among the rising stars, draw closer and then show themselves to be the running lights of the *Harvest*'s shuttle. He sighed. *Perhaps he's right*, he thought. And if he was wrong, it hardly mattered. Let Banks and Exeter and others sort out the morality of it. Even his own promotion in the service mattered little to him at this point, as long as they delivered on their promise to help James. The two men stood in silence, watching the small craft approach. As it drew near, Arkadas put a hand on Pearce's arm.

"This is for you," he said, and he took from inside his robes a large package wrapped in brown paper. "Don't open it now, but when you are alone, in your cabin."

"What is it?" Pearce asked wearily. He took it listlessly, not caring what it contained.

"A gift. These are *tervis* berries. Very rare, and very precious. I am giving them to you as a symbol of our friendship, *judar*. A gesture of thanks. A hope that we will meet again someday, and we will recognize one another as the savior of our peoples."

The shuttle had landed. Charles Hall emerged as the door opened, electrostatic engines still active.

"Thank you." Pearce was gruff. "But I am telling you the truth when I say I'm never coming back to this damn planet ever again. Goodbye, Arkadas." Without a look back, he strode to the small craft, package under his arm.

****

It was a wordless flight back to the *Harvest*, Kepler-22B shrinking behind them. Pearce had nothing to say and Hall had the good sense to say nothing. As the shuttle docked alongside its sister and the doors of the cavernous bay closed, Pearce felt a wave of relief crash over him. He was back on his ship, in a place where the world made sense. *I will never set foot on Cygnus again*, he vowed. The only planet he would ever see or walk upon again would be his own.

He was greeted by John Pott and Orpheus Crutchfield as he disembarked.

"Captain," Pott said. "As per your orders, everyone is aboard, and the ship is ready for departure."

"Thank you, Lieutenant. Well done."

"Not everyone!" growled Crutchfield.

"That will do, Sergeant. I know your feelings toward your machrines, but Luther is staying behind on my orders." He thrust out his chin, almost daring the massive red-jacketed officer to gainsay him. *I've already got three crew members locked up*, he thought. *What's one more?* But Crutchfield deflated in front of him.

"Aye aye, sir," he said meekly.

"I congratulate you on your apprehension of the deserters," Pearce continued. "Once we have left orbit, we will see to their punishment. You will assemble the crew, and both Briggs and Lamb will taste the Cat twice in succession."

"Good God," swore Pott, not quite under his breath, while Crutchfield stood stock still, silent and aghast.

"You disagree?" roared Pearce. "By the letter of the King's regulations, I am within my rights to have them lobotomized and sent back to the damned algae pits. I may yet. You have your orders!"

"Yes, sir," they said in unison, and scurried away. Pearce turned to see Hall hanging back, near the shuttle.

"Come on then, Mister Hall. Step lively, now. Drop that package in my cabin and report to the Quarterdeck. Make preparations for our departure from orbit. We're getting the hell out of here."

Pearce moved down the corridor, intent on leaving the Cygnus system, but also aware that there was one conversation he had to have first. Alone, he went to the section of the vessel housing the officers' quarters, and directly to Fletcher's cabin. Without preface, he entered.

It was dark inside, and quiet. He had never been in these quarters before, and now he was struck by just how much distance had arisen between the two of them since the *Harvest* left Spithead months before. *Did I really misjudge her so badly?* Or had something changed her? The lights were on the lowest setting, casting the entire snug cabin in gray shadow. Dimly, he was just able to make out a seated figure on the rumpled bed.

"Christine," he began, determined to keep his temper under control. He was still angry, but his experience in the hidden Cygni lab had shaken some of his certitude. She did not respond. He cleared his throat, loudly. What was he expecting? Contrition? "We are leaving," he continued. "We are going home."

"Home." The word dripped like venom from her lips.

"Yes, home, damn you. Our home. Earth, not this fantasy land!" But he broke off, raising both hands in a gesture of forbearance. "I do not want to keep you locked in here the entire voyage. Cygnus is behind us, now."

"Behind you, perhaps," she said coldly. She had risen from her bed and moved into the half-light that spilled in from the corridor. Her eyes were red-rimmed, fuming and sad. "The best part of me is still there."

"What you felt for Jairo," Pearce started haltingly, seeking common ground. He fumbled for words, trying to express how he had felt when the priestess Kaitsma had come near, how his head and heart and lungs had all seemed to liquefy. "I know…"

"You don't know shit," Fletcher snapped, her voice full of invective. "You shut your mouth about him, Bill, you shut your lying mouth. If you came here to belittle me, to belittle what we had…"

"I came here to effect what reconciliation we can! We have been a long time in space together, you and me." More than ever, he ached to tell her their entire purpose, to make her understand just how important their mission was, but just as he had weeks before in his cabin, he held back. It was then he noticed she was laughing at him.

"Why are you being so damn reasonable now?" she asked. "Where was my old friend Bill Pearce, this Bill Pearce, not the raging ass of a man he became down on the surface?" He began to say something then, shrugging off his building irritation at her insults, but she waved his words away unspoken, and her eyes narrowed.

"I'll rot in this room until the end of time before I lift a finger to help you. So go ahead, drag us all back to Earth and parade your stupid plants before the King and get your promotion. Drum me out of your ridiculous Navy, too, as soon as you can. I was a fool to follow you, to trust you." She was trembling now, tears spilling down her red cheeks. "I've lost everything, and it'll all your fault. Get out." This last was no more than a whisper, but it had the ringing finality of a scream.

There is no reconciliation here, Pearce thought. *No understanding or accord to be reached.* He turned to go, all of the rage in his heart turned only to leaden sorrow at the stupendous waste of it all, at the loss of his old crewmate, partner, and friend.

"My log will reflect your insubordination, Lieutenant Fletcher," he said over his shoulder, a tart formality back in his tone. "If you're lucky, discharge is the best you can hope for. More likely, your future includes a sentence at Newgate Gaol." He tried, without much success, to keep the snarl out of his voice. "Ten or twelve years in a cell, most like. And you can forget about any wild dreams of a return to Cygnus. You'll never leave Earth again, not on so much as a cargo tug."

Without further commentary, without a backward glance, he let the door close behind him, and tried not to hear the sobs coming from the other side as he left.

****

Much later, Pearce lay on the bed in his cabin, his eyes screwed shut, trying to ward off the monstrous headache that had been building for hours. The *Harvest* had broken orbit seamlessly some time before – he meant to include a glowing word in his log for midshipman Charlie Hall, whose navigation skills were good and getting better – and finally, they were headed home. The weeks in orbit around Cygnus had enriched the gravity engines and they were making swift progress already. While Sir Eustace had grumbled about the truncation of their expedition, Dr. Reyes had, in her characteristically terse way, assured him their collected specimens were more than sufficient for their needs. Through the starbursts of his pain, Pearce's mind turned back to the kids, Hall and Worth.

I shouldn't call them that, he thought wearily. Even though both were very recent graduates of Greenwich, they had proven themselves on the outbound voyage. According to regulations, and practical considerations, the ship required two lieutenants. With Fletcher incarcerated in her quarters for the foreseeable future, Pott was the only one, and despite the man's competence, he could not do a job designed for two. Pearce was within his rights, indeed his duty, to grant one of the mids a commission as acting-lieutenant. But which one? *Later.* He pushed it out of his mind as the door chime sounded.

"Enter." It was Dr. Szakonyi, thin and pinched as ever, but deeply welcome. "Thank you, Doctor," Pearce said, gratefully accepting the bright red pills and swallowing them.

"That should help a great deal," Szakonyi murmured, "though I would further recommend some rest." Pearce nodded.

"I suppose I can't stay awake for two months, can I?" He rubbed his eyes with the backs of his hands. "Lamb's arm?"

"Attended to, Captain. He will be sore for some time, but he will heal."

"Good. Good. Oh, Doctor – there was one other thing I wanted to ask you about." Szakonyi raised an inquiring eyebrow.

"Yes?"

Pearce rummaged underneath his bed and found the package Arkadas had given him. He untied the string and tore open the paper. Within was a handsome woven basket, full of fat purplish-blue berries.

"These were a gift from Venn Arkadas," he said. He took one and handed it to the doctor. "Would you be so good as to run an analysis on them? He said they were rare, and I know I've never seen them before, on this trip or my earlier visit. I'm sure they're fine, but just to be safe…"

"Of course." Szakonyi took the proffered fruit in the small paper cup he had used to bring the captain's medicine. "And now, Captain, get some sleep, before I make that a medical order. Lieutenant Pott has things under control for now."

Pearce yawned and stretched out his arms. He suddenly felt endlessly weary, even as the sharp edge of his headache waned. With benign suspicion, he eyed his ship's surgeon.

"Just something to help you sleep," he said, and for the first time Pearce could remember, Szakonyi smiled. He wasn't sure if the doctor left or if he fell asleep first.

He did not dream.

****

The *Harvest* carved its path through the stars for some days after that, the routine of shipboard life reasserting its control over the minutes and hours of officers, crewmen, and one prisoner alike. Briggs and Lamb were punished, and though Pearce had begun to regret his order of two lashings apiece, he kept his word. He knew that to do otherwise would weaken him. Starship captains relied on the appearance, if not the reality, of infallibility. While the order was carried out, and after, he heard the grumbling of the crew and noticed their stares, but he ignored them. It was a pitiless exhibition, forcing both offenders first to their knees and then to the deck. Lamb, strong as he was, his broken arm still in a splint, screamed on the eighteenth lash with such anguish that Pearce was sure the man's lungs would rupture. But it was done, and he was determined to cultivate a happier ship for the remainder of the voyage home.

Szakonyi had analyzed the berries and found them not just harmless, but also a mild stimulant to the body's immune system and the pleasure centers of the brain.

"A rare gift," he had said, upon delivering the news to the captain.

There was an ample supply in the basket Arkadas had provided, so Pearce ordered a small allowance doled out to the crew along with their rum ration. In addition to their curative and intoxicating effects, they were remarkably tasty, with a sweet flavor not unlike ripe watermelon. They swiftly became popular amongst the crew.

A rare gift indeed, Pearce thought as he sat in his command chair on the Quarterdeck, watching the stars glide past the viewscreen, the parsecs smoothly and slowly devoured by the *Harvest*'s deep space engines. The first days following their sudden exodus from Cygnus had seen a sullen, brooding ship, resentful over the cessation of the idyllic shore leaves, the grotesque reprimand of Lamb and Briggs, and the fall from grace of Christine Fletcher. It had the feeling of an ion engine running dirty, pulsing, an explosion in waiting. The *tervis* berries had been the perfect tonic for his people, easing some of the lingering tension. And the cargo, the precious cargo they had come for, was safe aboard. The vast holds of the Harvest had become a virtual jungle of sprouts, seedlings, and mature plants, floating serenely in their hydroponic vats, blithely and blissfully unaware of the human frailty surrounding them.

Pearce's musings were interrupted by a chirp on his arm console.

"Go ahead."

"Captain." Szakonyi. "You'd best meet me in your quarters."

"Doctor?" Before a response could come, Pearce stood, and tapped Hall on the shoulder. "Your ship, Mister Hall. Steady as she goes."

"Yes, sir."

Pearce rode the lift down the Harvest's command fin, wondering what the doctor could possibly want. He made his way swiftly to the upper deck and the officers' quarters, and there he found Szakonyi waiting in the corridor, alongside a door that had clearly been forced open.

"What's all this?" he asked the waiting surgeon.

"What it looks like, I believe," came the reply. "Someone's been in your cabin, Captain."

Pearce brushed aside his mounting feelings of violation and studied the door mechanism.

"How could someone have done this without setting off the alarm?" Szakonyi shrugged.

"I'm a doctor, not a burglar. I merely noticed this on my way from the Surgery to the Quarterdeck and thought I should report it."

"Of course." Pearce ran a hand through his thinning hair. "Quite right. Is anything missing?"

"I did not search," Szakonyi replied. "I thought it best to leave that to you."

Pearce entered his chambers, trailed by the doctor. He didn't see anything amiss at first glance, no drawers left open or items out of place. Then, with sudden apprehension, he checked under his bed and found nothing.

"The berries," he said. "They're missing." He stood up, feeling the familiar building of anger in his throat. He let it build. "Thank you, Doctor." Tapping his wall unit, he sounded an all-ship communication. He coughed once, gathered himself, and then spoke.

"All personnel report to the shuttle bay," he snarled. With the cargo holds full of plants, it was the only area of the ship large enough to accommodate the entire crew. "Five minutes, please."

"Captain, is it worth it?" asked Szakonyi, his hands spread in a conciliatory pose. "They are only berries."

"The berries are the least of it!" Pearce roared. "Someone broke into my cabin, damn them! You think this is about berries? This is about my authority! Proper shipboard behavior! No, we'll get to the bottom of this." And he stormed out, the doctor trailing behind. They reached the shuttle bay quickly, and there Pearce waited, pacing, while the crew assembled. They were minus Hall, a few others responsible for piloting the ship, and of course Fletcher, still ensconced in her cabin. When they had arrived, he stared at them for long minutes, glowering, silent. Then he spoke.

"I do not doubt the lot of you are fine starmen," he began, a tremor in his voice the only hint that his control was wavering. "I have seen your conduct on board ship and ashore, in crisis and quiet, and most of you do the service proud." He looked at each of them in turn as he talked, looking for furtiveness, for guilt, for shifting eyes or shuffling feet. "We have had our troubles, our mistakes, but in the best traditions of the Fleet, once fair punishment is given and received, we are back on square footing and no grudges are held." Still, no telltale signs. Frustrated, his emotions getting the best of him, Pearce exploded.

"We have a liar and a thief among us," he bellowed. "Those of you who have served long know there is no Jonah aboard worse than a scoundrel who would steal a shipmate's property." He drove one fist into an open palm as he spoke, punctuating his words with the slapping of knuckles on flesh. Waiting, breathing heavily, he forced himself into a smile he meant to be reassuring. In reality, it was anything but. "If the perpetrator comes forward to me, if the stolen property is returned, I am prepared to be lenient. Indeed, if any of you knows anything…" he broke off that line unspoken, knowing none of these ables would rat on their mate. And he was fairly sure it was an able. *What officer would conduct himself so abysmally?*

"I see," the captain said after a lengthy, gravid pause. "Whomever the thief may be is also a coward. Very well. Sergeant Crutchfield?" The towering officer stepped forward crisply. "The rum ration is hereby stopped." A wave of whispered remarks swept the room, but Pearce rose his voice above it. "Until further notice! If the guilty party comes forward and the property is returned, I will consider reinstituting the privilege." He glowered at them all, savage justice on his face. "If, by this time tomorrow, we are no closer to a conclusion to this sorry business, I will order a random crew member subjected to the Cat every twelve hours." At this there was a chorus of gasps.

"He's inhuman, he is," called a voice from behind him. Pearce spun around, but not in time to identify the speaker.

"Who said that?" No one moved. "Do not blame me," he said, his voice calm again, his control returning. "Blame the criminal in your midst. Perhaps in light of these measures, some of you will be motivated to uncover the thief. That is all. Dismissed."

The crew melted away like spring snow, many shaking their heads in disbelief and exasperation, with the exception of John Pott.

"Sir," he said, low and submissive, "I am not questioning your orders or your authority. However…"

"However what, Lieutenant?" Pearce snapped. "You have some gentler means of addressing the matter? Something more effective? I am happy to hear it!"

"The Cat, sir. You know it works best when used sparingly."

"And I have used it sparingly! Good God, I have been nothing but indulgent with this rabble!" Pearce pressed his knuckles to his temples. "We'll talk no more about it. You have duties, Mister Pott. I suggest you be about them."

****

Pearce was not surprised when Eustace Green appeared at the doorway of his star cabin not long after his accusatory, and probably futile, speech. With a sigh of fatigue and resignation, he turned his attention away from the report he was working on to the elderly gardener.

"Yes, Sir Green? Come to criticize shipboard discipline?"

Green stepped into the office, the door sliding shut behind him.

"Tell them," he said. He glanced around the cabin, anywhere but at Pearce's eyes as he spoke, but his voice was level and firm.

"I'm not sure I understand," Pearce replied, and it was true, he didn't. "Tell who what?"

"The crew." Green crossed the small room in two steps and sat in the chair before the desk. Pearce ignored this breach of protocol, as he had when Green had entered uninvited. The usual courtesies extended to the captain of a naval vessel were clearly not observed by knights and friends of the King. "Tell them our true purpose."

"I will not." Pearce responded stonily. "I was ordered not to do so in the strongest language by Lords Banks and Exeter. I believe you and Dr. Reyes are under similar constraints, though somewhat more voluntarily, but I am an officer of the King, and my orders carry the force of law." Green nodded at this.

"Nevertheless, Captain, I am afraid that if you do not impress upon the crew the absolutely vital nature of our errand, we may be courting disaster."

"How so?" Green had said "we", but Pearce had heard the distinctly implied "you".

"They are unhappy. Yes, your floggings are part of it, to be sure. They understood when offenders like Lamb and Briggs were punished, but to subject random crewmen to the lash…"

"I am not interested in your opinions of my management of my crew," responded Pearce icily. "We have had this conversation before. If there is nothing else?"

"There is," Green said, ignoring Pearce's hint that the discussion was at an end. "Think about it from their perspective. You have shown them paradise and taken it away. And for what? So that I can bring a prize back for the King to coo over for an hour and then forget forever after? Are we on a greengrocer's mission, a florist's?" He shook his head. "They need a larger reason, a more compelling mission. They need to understand. Or I fear the grumbling will only get worse."

"Sailors grumble," said Pearce dismissively, though in the back of his head he could hear one of Captain Baker's famous adages – "when crews grumble, officers crumble". She had always had a special relationship with the belowdecks, something Pearce had hoped to achieve with Fletcher as an intermediary. *And look how that turned out.* "In the end, they will obey, Sir Green."

"Will they?" he asked, and there was a certain timbre to his words. For the first time, Pearce began to feel a hint of resolve in this man whom the King had knighted and befriended, something deeper and more resolute than the elderly gentleman among his flowers. "Two of your crew tried to desert on Cygnus. Another, your first officer, disobeyed you as well."

"Regulations," Pearce grunted, trying to get back to comfortable ground, "are clear on these matters. I am bound by Admiralty Law."

"Ah." Green held up one long finger. "Laws and regulations you violated by leaving that machrine behind."

"Necessary to accomplish our mission."

"I am telling you that this might be necessary, too, Captain."

"Sailors will grumble," Pearce repeated, though somewhat lamely. Green stood.

"John Banks and the Star Lord felt you were the best man for this job," the noble gardener said. "I believe they were correct to think so. We are very close to success, and all the rewards that come with it, for the Kingdom as well as ourselves. If you allow your pride and your stubbornness to ruin our chances, our failure will be on your head alone."

And he left the captain there, alone with his thoughts.

****

When Dr. Zoltan Szakonyi showed up in her chambers, Christine Fletcher had no idea what the hell he wanted, but she doubted it was anything she cared about. What she wanted, no one could bring her.

"How are you, Lieutenant?" he asked, solicitous.

"Here to psychoanalyze me, Doctor?" Fletcher asked in scornful response. She was drunk and had been so for most of her imprisonment, even though it didn't really help.

"Quite to the contrary," Szakonyi said quietly. "I believe you to be one of this ship's saner inhabitants. No, I am here to offer you a way out." His smile, a thin curve on his wrinkled face, was a cryptic thing.

"Of this cabin?" She was puzzled, both by his words and his smile. If it hadn't been for Peckover, the perpetually humorless boatswain, Szakonyi would have been the sourest creature aboard. *Then again*, thought Fletcher, *maybe I am*. Her world had descended into perpetual night, with no prospect of any morning. Surrounded by billions of suns, and yet dawn would never come for her again. "Or of this situation?"

"Both."

"The only thing I want," Fletcher said with a throaty growl, "is light-years behind us, and I will never have it again."

"Don't be so sure. Never is a long time, and the universe is full of possibilities."

With a wry smile of her own, Fletcher got up from her chair and walked to the nutritional unit that was a perk of her rank, a perk she would hold onto until they could reach Earth and a court-martial would strip her of that, her freedom, and her dignity. *A perk that makes this a convenient enough prison*, she thought. She punched in the code for a serving of rum.

"Self-prescribed," she said. "Sit down if you like, Doctor. My officer's ration is more than enough for both of us." She turned her attention back to the machine as it beeped at her, pleasantly but resolutely. Her cup, under the dispenser, was still empty. "What the hell? Have they cut me off?" She didn't think she'd exceeded her ration, but with the use she'd been making of it lately, it was entirely possible.

"Not just you," Szakonyi said, easing into the seat she had offered. "Everyone."

"What? Even Bill's not that crazy."

"Oh, he might be. At least, once sufficiently provoked. You see, his cabin was broken into, and someone stole his tervis berries. He has stopped everyone's rum. What's more, he has ordered random whippings of the crew until the perpetrator is revealed."

"You're joking."

"I wish I were."

"Why are you telling me this?" Fletcher asked. "It's awful, but someone will talk him out of it. Pott, or you. Maybe even himself, once he comes to his senses."

"You know him better than anyone. Does he ever countermand his own orders, especially in matters of discipline?" She shook her head, and the doctor continued. "Lieutenant Pott may try, but he won't be any more successful than I would be."

"Who took them?"

"I have no idea. But I would be shocked if anyone were to own up to it now, given the captain's current blood thirst. We are in for a rough time, I'm afraid."

"Don't tell me your troubles," Fletcher retorted. "It won't do any good. I'd have to care, and then I'd have to be able to help."

"You are." Szakonyi leaned across her tiny table, his eyes aglow behind his thick white beard. "It may be that our troubles have a common solution. I believe the crew is ready to follow someone else."

Fletcher stared at this old man who she did not really know. *It's a trap*, her gut told her. Pearce was setting her up for even bigger trouble. She rejected the thought. He might have become an enormous ass, but entrapment wasn't the man's style.

"You're talking mutiny. You're the damn doctor; why don't you just declare him unfit?"

"Please. Crutchfield would never arrest the captain. And I'm fairly certain Pott would be even less supportive. No, a more radical surgery is needed."

"You're talking mutiny," she repeated. It was crazy. There was no worse crime in the Fleet. *You're already a criminal, Christine. What did it matter if the fires of Hell were a thousand degrees hot or a million?* She could think of no worse crime than what had been done to her. Everything she loved, her very life, taken away over a stupid robot. "I don't want to hurt anyone."

"No one needs to be hurt. The crew will follow you, Christine Fletcher. And I'm sure many of them want to go back to Cygnus as much as you do."

The word was a thunderclap in her ears. Cygnus. Jairo.

"The captain...the other officers..."

"We have two shuttles," Szakonyi said simply. He rose abruptly. "You may be able to save all of us, and yourself along with us." With a hiss of the door he was gone, and Fletcher was left with a sudden silence – and a decision – weightier than any she had ever known.

****

In the corridor, Szakonyi allowed himself a brief smile at his own cunning as he walked to Surgery. He had a coded report to compose for Djimonsu. And some excellent *tervis* berries to enjoy.

Fourteen

Seizure

The Quarterdeck was a quiet place during the middle watches, an ancient term that was still sometimes used in the modern Navy for the small hours of the morning. The ship's boatswain, Thomas Peckover, handled the helm of the *Harvest* under the supervision of the Officer of the Watch, who tonight was Hope Worth. She didn't mind the silence, or the middle watch; in truth she liked both. She had never been a boisterous person or felt at home in crowds, and the relative solitude was welcome.

A gentle chime sounded, the ship's bell, announcing the time as two hours past midnight. Glancing at the *Harvest*'s position on the stellar chart monitor, Worth saw no reason to make any adjustments. Her trim was just right and she was sailing fair. With a nod at Peckover, Worth murmured the expected "steady as she goes", and settled into the command chair for another hour of welcome tedium.

If nothing else, it gave her time to think about Charlie.

While the *Harvest* slept, her belly full of greenery bound for Kew, Worth allowed her mind to linger on her shipmate. Shipmate? *Hardly*, she thought, as a ghost of a smile crossed her face. *Lover?* That seemed a melodramatic descriptor, but when she thought of Cygnus and their time spent together there, she was hard-pressed to think of anything more apt. She was not an experienced romantic – her shy awkwardness had contributed mightily to that – and lacked the worldliness that might have allowed her to grasp a better word. They had been together as much as their duties allowed during the weeks ashore and since, and it had rapidly become very difficult for her to imagine a universe without him in it.

You're in love with him, Hope Worth. So why not call yourselves lovers?

What did that mean, anyway? Was there any kind of future for them? They were homeward bound from what was, despite some hiccups, a successful mission. There would be rewards for all involved, including advancement on the promotions list. It wasn't all that unusual for midshipmen returning from a deep space voyage to sit for their Lieutenant's exam fairly quickly. If they both were to do so, and passed, the chances of them being posted together on a future assignment were remote. As she thought of that, of working a ship somewhere millions of miles from him, a weight pressed down on her chest. She might very well love him, but she was determined to make a career and a name for herself, to live up to both her father's expectations, and more importantly, her own. *How, then, to satisfy both demands of her heart?*

This was the conundrum occupying Hope Worth's mind when the door to the Quarterdeck hissed open and three men, armed with pulse-rifles, burst in. Saul Lamb came first, swarthy and cocksure. With him were the quiet Korean able, Xing Xiang, and Yancy Waugh, the boatswain's mate. Waugh was utterly unremarkable in every way – average height, average build, forgettable face. In all the weeks on board, Worth couldn't remember three words the man had strung together.

"What's this, Mister Lamb?" asked Worth, bewildered. "Are we under some kind of attack? Are..." She never completed her second question. Lamb slammed the butt of his weapon into her stomach, driving the wind from her lungs and doubling her over. Black and yellow starbursts of pain exploded in her eyes, and she fell to her knees. There was a lot of shouting and cursing, and a loud crack. Thick fingers grasped Worth by the hair and forced her to her feet. The Quarterdeck had become a watery blur, but she could make out a still form on the floor near Peckover's station. Waugh was there, standing over the body.

"He dead?" Lamb jerked his chin in the direction of Peckover as he asked, and Waugh prodded the boatswain, his immediate superior, with the muzzle of his rifle.

"Looks like it."

"Hell," spat Lamb. "We wasn't supposed to kill no one. Why'd you kill him for, Yancy?"

"Because he was a pain in the ass."

"Well, it's your ass now. Wasn't supposed to be no killing."

Lamb bent Worth's arm, painfully, and she stumbled forward. Xiang grabbed her other arm, and she was held firm between the two as they frog-marched her toward the door. Turning to look over his shoulder, Lamb shouted to Waugh.

"Unsteady as she goes, Yancy." He chuckled, and along with Xiang, pushed Worth into the lift. She opened her mouth and began to ask a question, but Lamb seized her by the throat, slammed her into the wall, and leaned in so close that their noses nearly touched. Dark face mottled with red, the crewman squeezed so tight that Worth could scarcely breathe.

"Don't bother, little girl. No one to hear you." *I don't care what he said before*, Worth thought. *He's going to kill me.* To her surprise, she wasn't afraid. She was angry. *Promotion. Charlie.* To have that future snatched away from her, so pointlessly, was more than she could bear. In a sudden burst, she drew her legs up in front of her, jammed her feet into Lamb's chest, and pushed as violently as she could. The hands came free from her neck, tearing deep gouges in the soft flesh, as both of them fell heavily to the floor. Worth gratefully sucked in a few ragged breaths. Xiang was laughing nearby.

"Shut up, Xing," growled Lamb as he pushed himself back up. "Not bad. But that was your last shot." Raising his pulse rifle over his head, Lamb brought the butt of it down swiftly toward Worth's face. There was a loud sound, a brief rush of pain, and then oblivion.

When Worth returned to consciousness, the floor she was lying on was cold, and she had the sensation of being in open space. *Where the hell am I?* Struggling to open her eyes, she became aware of a stabbing in her head, like a bolt of lightning every few seconds. *I'm hurt.* As she tried to rub her face with her hands, she discovered that they were bound at the wrists behind her back with some sort of strap. Images, blurry at first, began to penetrate the shroud of pain, well enough that she could perceive her location.

The shuttle dock.

Other than the main cargo bay, it was the largest interior space on the *Harvest*. The launches themselves were nearby, perched serenely in their usual spots, casting multitudes of shadows in the harsh overhead light of the dock. The rest of the huge room was mostly empty and featureless, except for the large reinforced window to the control room. And across from that, there was nothing. *The door is open*, Worth realized. Usually the dock was entirely enclosed by the outer hull, including the massive exterior door, but now the blackness of space was visible. As her vision cleared, she was able to see the vague crackle of static that told her that the thin energy field was in place, keeping the livable atmosphere inside the bay and the vacuum of space outside.

She wasn't alone. She was able to see Lieutenant Pott, propped against the bulkhead a few meters away, slumped and dazed but alive. Zoltan Szakonyi, the surgeon, was there, too, as were Sir Eustace Green, the gardener, and Heywood Musgrave, the gunner. All looked unharmed, though all were tied in the same way that she was. Watching over them were Lamb, Taryn Hadley, Xing Xiang, and Tom Churchill.

Worth's mind tried to assess the situation, even as white bursts of agony exploded in her brain from the effort. That had been some crack to her skull earlier. She probably had a concussion, or worse. *What was going on? Where was the captain? Where was Fletcher? What about Crutchfield and the machrines?*

The next thing she saw turned her soul to ice.

Charlie.

Two more people had come into the dock through the main access door. One was Peggy Briggs and the other was Charlie Hall. Briggs was pushing him in front of her, twisting his arm at an awkward angle, so that he cried out, which made the ables laugh. Briggs was in her duty uniform, but Hall had clearly been sleeping, and was dressed in no more than a long white shirt and a pair of gray shorts. His feet were bare, and his sandy hair was sticking out in all directions. The barest hint of a beard shaded his lip and jaw.

"Another one rounded up," Briggs said, a cruel smile on her lips. "More to come." Seeing Hall manhandled, in obvious pain, was more than Worth could bear.

"Let him go!" she shouted, trying to scramble to her feet, to go to him, but Lamb casually knocked her down again with his rifle. Worth's head struck the flooring, and her ears began to ring. Even so, she could clearly hear their mocking laughter.

"We've got a few minutes," Lamb was saying above her. "This bitch has been teasing me for weeks. Time to finish what we started back in the galley. Easy, girl," he rasped, as Worth felt herself hauled roughly up. He easily enfolded both her wrists with one of his thick hands. His other arm he wrapped around her slender waist. To Briggs he said, "I won't be long."

"All the same to me," Briggs replied.

"Hope!" Charlie tried to come to her aid, but Briggs cracked him in the leg with her rifle, and he collapsed heavily to the deck.

"No," Hall croaked. Pushing to his knees, he tried to crawl. Peggy Briggs put a foot on his back, pushing him back down.

"I'd watch my own ass if I were you," she said. One more time Hall struggled to rise, until he felt the cold tip of a pulse rifle press behind his left ear.

"Down boy," Briggs muttered, as Xiang chuckled nearby. "This is just the beginning."

Worth struggled, but Lamb held her firm with one hand. With the other, he began to grope at her, but paused as another pair arrived. It was Mathias Quintal, and before him, arms held tight in his grip, was a shorter man in a long white nightshirt, missing several of the buttons from the front, barelegged, with what looked like a sack over his head.

Worth knew at once that it was the captain. He wore an officer's jacket over the nightshirt -- his commander's jacket, navy blue with the yellow braid of his rank, some absurd joke at his expense. A heartbeat behind them limped the massive Isaac Pratt, half-carrying, half-dragging the huge, still form of Orpheus Crutchfield. Pratt's nose was clearly broken, the lower half of his face a scarlet mess, and he was panting.

"Fought like a damned demon," he muttered thickly, spitting a gob of red phlegm mixed with a broken tooth. "Not his first alley scrap." He dumped the sergeant heavily to the deck.

"Dead?" Lamb asked.

"Naw. Close enough, though. I almost had to kill him so we could get to Pearce. He got wind of this somehow, and went right to the captain's cabin to protect him. Brave idiot. If he'd activated the machrines first, who the hell knows what would have happened."

For the first time, a word percolated through Worth's mind, through the pain and the fear.

Mutiny.

The crewmen were seizing the ship.

Quintal tore the bag off Pearce's head, and the captain blinked in the sudden brightness. There was, Worth saw, no terror on his face, only a preternatural calm as the man drank in the sight of his captured officers and his rebelling crew. His shoulders were not slumped, his jaw, unshaven, was set and did not quiver. The only kinetic thing about him was a blazing wrath in his eyes, fierce and defiant. Despite having obviously been roused from slumber, standing there shorn of every badge of office except the mocking jacket, he looked like some ancient god out of myth, and while Worth had long admired the captain, she felt something closer to worship now, at the end of all things.

"Gonna be fun to do this in front of the old man," growled Lamb, panting, and he resumed his pawing at her.

"Lamb, stand down," Pearce said in the same even and measured voice he might have used to order the helm to change course, and Quintal punched him in the mouth. Somehow, the captain didn't go down, but just staggered. "Where is Fletcher?" he asked thickly.

"Here," said a voice from behind him.

It was Christine Fletcher, and she was neither bound nor escorted. She walked forward, in her full duty uniform, a laser pistol pointed at Dr. Adina Reyes. The xenobotanist looked, for the first time Worth could remember, unkempt and scared, her usually pale features even whiter, those shrewd eyes darting about in wide terror, edging closer to panic. Fletcher pushed Reyes toward the other prisoners and marched forward, pointing a laser pistol at the chest of William Pearce.

"Enough," Fletcher said to Quintal, and then, louder, to Lamb. "Stop! I don't want them harmed!"

For the first time, Lamb seemed to notice her. He laughed.

"Harm? You're the one holding the gun. No harm here. Just good times. Ain't that right, Hope?" Worth struggled harder, though to no better effect.

"No harm? Peckover's dead. Ask Yancy about harm."

Fletcher moved away from the captain and toward Lamb and Worth. She was wild-eyed, her hair unbound and spilling crazily about her face and shoulders.

"I said enough!"

Lamb did not listen. There were a couple of shouts of encouragement from Quintal and Churchill, a sob of impotent rage from Hall. Without another word, Fletcher aimed her sidearm and shot Lamb in the head.

The silence that followed was sudden and all-encompassing. The body of able starman Saul Lamb, minus the upper two-thirds of his head, slumped into a heap on the deck. Stunned, Hope Worth scrambled away from the smoking ruin, toward the spot where Hall lay under the boot and rifle of Peggy Briggs. No one made any motion to stop her, and even Briggs took a step backward, as the two young lovers reunited in a battered embrace.

We're already dead, she thought. *And this is Hell.*

****

Christine Fletcher had been in Hell for weeks.

The deck swam around her, and she fought to keep her balance. *What am I doing?* She couldn't answer, any more than she could put a stop to the events she had set in motion. She was at war against herself, split in half down the middle, bone and muscle and soul splintering asunder. She wanted to scream, to rage, to give free rein to the agony she felt, but instead she turned away from the ruin that had been Saul Lamb, pointing her weapon back at her captain, her friend, her prisoner. She had already made her choice.

"Fletcher, stop this madness." A trickle of blood seeped from the corner of Pearce's mouth, a streak of red on the white-and-black of his new stubble. Fletcher could not remember seeing him unshaven before. "Stop it now," the captain said, in a bizarrely calm voice. "If you all stand down and return to your stations, there will be no charges. We will all return home and forget this whole affair."

"It is too late for that," Fletcher replied angrily, and some of her was genuinely sad, the parts not consumed by fury and pain. "It is too late for reasonable, Bill! Where was reasonable on Cygnus?" She was shouting now, one hand pressing against her eyes, trying desperately and ineffectually to wake up from the nightmare of these last weeks. "I am in Hell!" she spat, her inner torment boiling out of her.

"You don't need to be…" Pearce began, and he was so sane, so in control, that Fletcher hated him for it.

"Shut up," she cried. "You shut your mouth!" She grasped one lapel of his jacket and shoved the barrel of her weapon into his neck.

"Kill him," urged Briggs. "Kill the lot of them, Fletcher, the way you did Saul."

"No," she said, slow and quiet. "No, I'm done with killing." She threw the pistol to the deck, where it clattered echoingly until Hadley swiftly scooped it up, and she released her grip on the captain.

"What then?" asked Churchill, trembling, though with excitement or anxiety, Fletcher couldn't tell. "We can't take them back to Cygnus with us."

"Quiet!" hissed Quintal, the suave tenor gone from his voice. "Damned fool, you'll have the whole Fleet turning up out there looking for us." Fletcher raised a hand, and Quintal subsided. She balled her fingers into fists and then loosed them, once, twice, breathing.

"No," she repeated. "No, we won't kill them, but we won't take them with us, either."

"What then?" Briggs asked the question, but any of them could have done so, even Pearce, still erect and still defiant.

"The shuttle," Fletcher said, glancing at the nearer of the two small craft. "We'll put them on the shuttle."

"No!" Churchill shouted. "They'll follow us!"

"I doubt it very much," Fletcher said. She smiled. "Hadley, board this shuttle and disable its NavWork system, its main propulsion system, its weapons array, and the nutrition dispensers." Hadley hustled to comply.

"Might as well kill us," muttered Pott, barely audible.

"It's murder," Pearce put plainly. "Mutiny and murder, Fletcher."

"If the universe kills you, Bill Pearce, so be it. I guess you aren't the navigator you always claimed to be."

"Not just us, damn you!" Pearce bellowed. Inside him a battle raged between the confidentiality of his orders and the end, not just of all his hopes, but those of Banks and Exeter and the future of humanity. The struggle was brief and one sided, and his devotion to the letter of his duty capitulated. *I should have taken Green's advice sooner.*

"You don't understand! The plants we gathered, they're not for a garden for the King! They're to save us all. The food supply back home is…" he groped for the right words to convey the situation in a way they would understand and would compel them to reconsider. "…it's going bad. We need these plants, these seeds, to save everyone!"

A slow, singular, sarcastic applause filled the shuttle bay. Xiang was clapping, that crooked smile wider than ever.

"Nice story," he said. "Bullshit, of course."

"No!" croaked Green, trying to rise. "It's true, every word!"

"And?" Briggs yelled. "So what if it is? What has humanity ever done for us that we should save it?"

"You have your duty." Pearce's voice was low, but it echoed in the bay. "You are starmen in His Royal Navy."

"Not anymore," Fletcher said, and Pearce knew it was over.

Then Hadley emerged from the launch with a fistful of wires and control chips.

"Done," she said.

"And so are we. The shuttle, now," Fletcher said, and there was no animus in her words, only a feverish severity, echoed by the leers and laughter of the mutineers arrayed about the shuttle bay. Pearce, his eyes blazing with impotent fire, nodded once, sharply.

"You're mutinous scoundrels, all of you," he cursed, the twin embers of his eyes focused on Fletcher. A tiny, sad part of her screamed out silently for some reconciliation, some other way, but it was too late, much too late. Pearce beckoned to the officers. "Into the launch."

Frozen in a tableau of hesitation and history, no one moved; each side unwilling to be the first to make those ultimate steps that would cement this unknowable future. Fletcher did not waver, even as her mind flirted with those parts of herself she had walled off, thoughts of her home in St. Kitts, which she would never see again, and of her grandfather. Papi! her heart cried, but it was pale, pathetic stuff next to her towering passion for Jairo, and the thought that she would soon return to him. She knew the shame her grandfather would feel when he learned of her actions here tonight, how it would seem to justify all of his worst assumptions about her worst nature.

He may never hear of it, she thought with a ragged surge of hope. Put to naked space in a steel coffin with no navigation systems, little propulsion, and less food, Pearce and his companions would most likely be swallowed up by the universe. Maybe, thought Fletcher with stray morbid grief, her Papi would be dead as well before any word reached Earth, and so would die without knowing what his granddaughter had become.

There was a sudden movement at the edge of her vision, and she turned her head just enough to see Hope Worth walking toward the shuttle and Bill Pearce, staggering just a bit, her eyes bright with tears. Fletcher had liked the girl, had seen some of the iron emerging in her, and was saddened to condemn her life to a likely end before it had truly begun. But that dismay was a tiny ripple in the tempest of her despair, and faded as swiftly and scarcely noticed as it had come. The girl made it across the deck, all eyes on her, and reached the captain in the tiny portal of the shuttle.

"Well done, Mister Worth," Pearce said, and the growl in his voice conveyed shame on the other officers that this young woman, still so recently at Greenwich, had been first to master herself. She paused a heartbeat before passing Pearce into the guts of the shuttle, looking back over her shoulder, her eyes searching. Fletcher knew what – or rather, who – the girl was seeking out. A moment later Charlie Hall came, slowly, responding to the summons in Worth's eyes, and the two of them disappeared together into the shuttle.

"Come now," the captain said, raising his voice. "Better we few against the stars than to stay here with these damned pirates."

"You heard the man," roared Quintal, and, giving a wide berth to the motionless corpse of Saul Lamb, he strode to where the captured officers lay strewn against the bulkhead. "The sooner we get them off the ship, the better." He seized Dr. Reyes by the elbow, and she briefly recoiled, but allowed herself to be led to the shuttle hatch, her eyes still unfocused. Pearce opened his mouth as if he were going to protest the rough handling of his civilian passenger, but then seemingly thought better of it and snapped his mouth shut, taking Reyes by the hand gently, and steering her inside the shuttle.

The rest followed: Pott under his own power, though shakily. Sir Green, his face a vague mask of disbelief, guided by a grim Musgrave. Early in the voyage, Fletcher had joked with the gunner about the Harvest's armament over cups of grog in the officer's mess. *A toad with fingernails*, Musgrave had said, and they had laughed. *No one is laughing now.* Fletcher felt she might never laugh again.

"Up, you," Pratt said, nudging Crutchfield with the toe of his boot. The sergeant groaned. Szakonyi moved to the man's side, crouching next to him on the deck.

"Three of his ribs are broken," the doctor declared. "Probably a fractured skull as well. He should probably come to the Surgery with me."

"No."

It was Crutchfield himself who spoke, though the word was barely audible. He forced himself to his hands and knees, gasping with the pain and effort, and then slowly, excruciatingly, to his feet. With one hand he seized the doctor's shoulder, steadying himself. He looked awful. Blood streaked across the entire front of his duty uniform, red on red, spattering the white trim, his face twisted in a contortion of agony, but he shuffled forward, leaning on the doctor, who seemed about to crumble under the big man's weight. Pearce himself descended the two steps from the hatchway to help bring Crutchfield aboard. There was a whispered exchange between the two, and Pearce winced briefly, then nodded.

"The machrines," he said.

"No," replied Fletcher, stonily. With those robots, Pearce and his adherents could retake the ship, and she wasn't about to go back in figurative irons. "I'm not a fool, and I don't trust you." She heard Pearce sigh, and saw him mouth a silent apology as Pott and Hall emerged, taking the sergeant under the armpits, and easing him into one of the eight seats on the shuttle.

"He may not survive," Szakonyi said, and Pearce almost smiled.

"He will, Doctor. We all will. You have my promise as an Englishman and a sailor." And the captain offered his hand.

"You're full," the doctor said, wryly.

"Never in life," Pearce replied. "I'll not leave a soul here with this rabble." But Szakonyi shook his head.

"I'm too old, and would only be a burden to you. No, sir, I'll stay here, and do what I can to protect them from themselves."

Sly old bastard, thought Fletcher. He was hedging his bets, throwing in with the mutiny he had inspired while covering himself in case Pearce somehow made it back to civilization. She hardly cared. None of them in that shuttle bay were ever going to see Earth again.

Pearce's mouth grew hard, then, his jaw working sideways. She knew it was eating at him inside, losing his ship, losing his command, losing control.

"Very well, Doctor. I'd wish you luck, but it's a fool's errand. I'll be sure to tell the Admiralty you had no part in this crime." His eyes left Szakonyi, and swept the bay, hard, fierce, alight. "As for the rest of you villains, I'll see every one of you swing," he vowed, the last words any of the mutineers heard from the deposed captain of the *Harvest* before he stepped back and the hatch closed with a harsh clang.

It's done, thought Fletcher, as the electrostatic engines of the shuttle whirred to life. As the tiny craft lifted off the deck and began to slowly reverse out of the bay, her mind drifted back to that day in Basseterre when Bill Pearce had come to her grandfather's house, and they had talked for hours of adventure, promotion, and friendship. The shuttle pierced the energy membrane at the mouth of the bay, slid seamlessly through it and out into the void beyond. Fletcher watched, unable to turn away, heedless of the shouts and cries of triumph from her

co-conspirators, as it diminished in the distance, until it disappeared among the other specks of white.
They're gone.
Christine Fletcher turned her back on them, and faced the future she had chosen.

****

They all sat, except for William Pearce, who stood absolutely still, one hand on midshipman Charles Hall's shoulder as he piloted the small launch. Watching the hijacked HMSS *Harvest* grow ever smaller in the forward view screen, his other hand unconsciously balled itself into a tight fist that pressed so hard against his own mouth that his teeth cut into his knuckles. In the turmoil, he wasn't even aware of the pain or the metallic taste of blood. *Any minute now,* his brain shrieked silently, *any minute now I'll wake up and be in my cabin, or home on Earth with Mary, or out somewhere on the Britannia before all this mess began.* But of course he didn't, because this was true, this was real.

"What the hell is that?" Pott asked. He was seated in the second forward chair, alongside Hall, and he was pointing at a bizarre trail of jetsam emerging from the Harvest's underside.

"The seedlings," Pearce growled, his voice little more than a hoarse whisper. "They're jettisoning the plants." One last show of defiance….or a crew out of control? It hardly mattered. It was thousands of kilometers away, going on millions, and it was the end of everything.

Only if you let it be.

Pearce touched the breast pocket of his jacket. Within, he could feel the model of the HMSS *Drake* his son had sent with him, a touchstone he had taken to carrying with him as a constant reminder of the importance of this mission, now in such utter shambles. Alongside the toy there was one other thing, something he had forgotten about since the day on Cygnus when Sir Eustace Green had given it to him. It was a tiny packet of seeds, a sampling of the corn, wheat, and rice species that they had come so far to acquire.

Would it be enough? Pearce let his gaze sweep the tiny compartment of the shuttle, from Charles Hall and John Pott up front, dazed and aching but gamely manning the controls, to the battered man-mountain of Orpheus Crutchfield, being tended to by the resourceful and dependable Hope Worth, despite her own injuries. Heywood Musgrave, lost in his own thoughts, and Dr. Adina Reyes, still stunned and pallid, sat silent and still. At the last, his eyes found Sir Green. He withdrew the small packet and showed it to the gardener.

"Is it enough?" Pearce asked.

"We'll never know," he replied, weary, old, defeated. "We'll never get back to Earth."

"There'll be none of that!" Pearce covered the distance from prow to stern in three steps, thrusting the packet into Green's trembling hands. "I will get us safely home. That is up to me. That," he pointed at the seed packet, "is up to you."

Without another word, he turned back to the viewscreen. The *Harvest* was gone, lost. Pearce touched the bulge of the *Drake* again, and thought of another promise he had made.

I'm coming, James, he thought, *even if I have to cross the universe in an open rowboat.*

I'm coming.

Epilogue

Whitehall Tower
2188 AD

"Months, now, with no word."

Banks spoke in a hoarse whisper, scarcely loud enough for the ponderous Star Lord to hear as he stood close at his elbow, listening intently while trying to appear not to be. They were in a shallow corner of the Privy Council Chamber, engaged in the usual pre-session minuet of political chatter, salacious gossip, and last-minute lobbying, not the most private of meeting places. The Duke's face was a mask of worry and age, his beard now more white than black. *We're getting old*, Banks thought inanely. *Though soon that may be the least of our problems.* Exeter frowned.

"None at all. If I had any, you would know." The message had been so joyously received by them both, a seeming age before: *Cargo aboard, homeward bound.* It had been slightly more complicated than that, Pearce's report inferring some discipline issues and his own violation of some regulations, but both Banks and Exeter had been prepared to forgive almost anything in exchange for success, and it seemed at hand. Then, nothing.

"They should have been back by now, regardless." Banks looked over Exeter's shoulder, at the end of the Council table, where the Chancellor of the Exchequer sat in his usual spot, with his usual attitude of prim control. If anything, he seemed more smug than ever. He happened to catch Banks' gaze and smiled broadly, with a slight nod. Banks returned the cordial greeting. "I want to choke that little bastard. He's had some role in this. I know it."

"Things happen in space," Exeter whispered, trying to achieve a confidence Banks knew he didn't feel. "It's a big universe, Minister, and not without perils. They could have been delayed by stellar storms, forced to change their route, suffered communications equipment failures, or any number of things, not all of them sinister."

"No." His gut was a tight knot. The *Harvest*'s tardiness and silence were personal. Eustace was with them, sharing their danger, but it was more than that. Their errand was so vital that failure was virtually unthinkable. "No, something's wrong." He turned and faced the First Lord of the Admiralty fully. "It's time we start to consider our next move." Exeter laughed, choked, reddened. A few glances came his way from the other ministers and dignitaries gathering in the chamber, but he waved them off in feigned good humor.

"What the hell do you propose, John?"

"A rescue mission."

"You're serious, aren't you?" Exeter shook his head. "You would have me send my ships to the edges of the galaxy looking for that tiny pinprick of steel? John, we don't know where to look."

"Look with more than your eyes, damn you! You have tracking technology to search for their signal!"

"Lower your voice," the Duke hissed warningly. Their conversation was beginning to attract closer scrutiny, and many of their counterparts were making their way to their seats, signaling that the meeting was about to begin. Exeter leaned in close, his eyes narrowed. "Don't take me for a fool. If their signature was operational, we'd already know where they were."

"We have to find them," Banks said, more than an edge of despair in his voice. The Duke sighed, and put a thick hand on the Science Minister's shoulder.

"It may be that there's nothing out there to find. We may have to accept that the *Harvest* is lost."

Author's Note

Writing the first novel in a trilogy is like embarking on a marathon. After eight or ten miles, you feel like you've accomplished something until you look at how many miles remain ahead. Still, a good start is important, and I'm grateful to all of those who have lent a hand so far, knowingly or otherwise.

The Harvest series is a reimagining of the classic Mutiny on the Bounty trilogy as told by Charles Nordoff and James Hall back in 1932, set in the future rather than in the past. It's a story that has held my interest since my brother Al introduced me to it as a teenager. Those familiar with the work will surely be able to identify the parallels (and departures) I've fashioned here. That original text has been at my fingertips throughout the writing of this first volume, and the narrative similarities are intended as literary homage. Other sources of both inspiration and reference have included the journals of Captain James Cook, the Hornblower saga of C.S. Forester, Patrick O'Brien's Aubrey/Maturin series, and a truly excellent historical investigation into the true story the original mutiny by fellow New Hampshire native Caroline Alexander, titled The Bounty. Also useful, and enjoyable, has been Arthur Herman's To Rule the Waves: How the British Navy Shaped the Modern World.

Thanks of course go to those who have valiantly read all or some of this manuscript in its various stages of life, and whose critiques I have greatly appreciated, whether I followed their wise advice or not. These include my old friend Robert Burns, with his masterful feel for character development; my new friend Gabe Zentner, with his writer's attention to craft and his scientist's impatience with imprecision; Laura Morse Cucci, with her biologist's expertise; and Jennifer Cyr, with her usual unerring eye for things I've done wrong. Holly Scatamacchia and Jeanette Lackey, thank you for your editorial and proofing work. I am also honored and grateful that Christine St. Jean, my intrepid high school history teacher, took her red pen to my work once again. For your indefatigable editing, Kate Kokko, one of your despised sentence fragments.

Bill Coffin, your cover work, as always, is perfect.

I am also deeply indebted to Derrick Eisenhardt and the crew at Reliquary Press for their continued support and assistance. Without them, there's no book in your hands, or whatever you're using to read this.

Thanks also to all of you who bought or borrowed Minotaur, my first novel. No, you don't need to read it to enjoy Lost Harvest. The two are different universes. But you do need to read Minotaur to enjoy Minotaur.

Finally, my everlasting gratitude and love to my boys, Bobby and Xavier, who let me steal away to write once in a while, and to my wife Sarah. She's the real star of the family, and none of this would be possible without her.

Joe Pace
Summer 2015

About the Author

Joe Pace is a writer of science fiction, historical fiction, and short stories. He studied political science and history at the University of New Hampshire, and his writing reflects his ongoing academic and practical interest in both.

Joe has also served in elective office, taught American history, and worked in business banking. His assorted interests include comic books, pickup basketball, Greek mythology, and the occasional marathon.

As a storyteller, he seeks to weave classic science fiction with political intrigue full of memorable characters in the tradition of Isaac Asimov, Piers Anthony, George R.R. Martin, and Gene Roddenberry.

Joe was born and raised in seacoast New Hampshire and still considers it home, even as he wanders around the country with his wife, Sarah, and their two sons, Bobby and Xavier.

His first novel, *Minotaur*, was published by Reliquary Press in 2012.